Enlightened

Untwisted Book Four

Alice Raine

Published by Accent Press Ltd 2015

ISBN 9781783757688

Copyright © **Alice Raine** 2015

The true value of a human being can be found in the degree to which he has attained liberation from the self.

Albert Einstein

Important note to reader

This concluding instalment of the Untwisted series is written from the perspectives of all four main characters: Nicholas, Rebecca, Nathan, and Stella. To ensure the story reads smoothly for you, please make sure to read the chapter headings so you know whose perspective each section is written from.

Enjoy!

Alice x

Karen W – seeing as you helped name this book, it seems only right to dedicate it to you and your amazing friendship x x x

PROLOGUE – NICHOLAS

First week of September

'To have and to hold, for better or for worse, for richer, for poorer, in sickness and in health, to love and to cherish; from this day forward until death do us part.'

I read the paper again then narrowed my eyes as Rebecca pulled out a pencil and pad and tentatively pushed it across the coffee table towards me with an eager smile.

'Don't look like that, Nicholas!' she chastised me, with a giggle, but I immediately pushed the paper back towards her and shook my head.

'The vows are fine as they are, Rebecca, we don't need to write our own version,' I said firmly with a shake of my head.

Rebecca's soft, full lips pursed into a deliciously sexy pout that was usually enough to persuade me to change my mind about almost anything – a fact that she knew all too well and took advantage of frequently – but it wouldn't work on me today. Seeing my reluctance, the playful grin on Becky's face suddenly disappeared, and she started to fiddle nervously with a strand of her long blonde hair before tucking it behind her ear. 'Shit … is this all too much? Don't you want to be involved in the preparations?' she asked in a small voice, making me feel like a complete bastard as my chest compressed with guilt.

Knowing I needed to work fast to reassure my girl, I quickly stood up and stepped towards her with a smile. 'I do want to be involved, Rebecca, of course I do.' I moved closer and cupped her cheek looking down into her stunning green eyes. God, I loved those eyes. 'It's the day where I get to finally keep you for myself for the rest of my life, and tell the entire world about it at the same time. But all this girly stuff …' Scooping up a swatch of material samples for possible chair covers I wafted them in the air, failing to keep the grimace from my face, '… is just a bit much.' I knew those words probably made me sound like an inconsiderate bastard, and perhaps I was one, but I'd been so emotionally detached throughout my life that this was all a bit overwhelming.

I wanted to marry Rebecca more than I wanted to take my next breath, but to be honest I'd be perfectly happy if it were just her, me, and a registrar at the service. I didn't need the other embellishments that went with it. Lifting a hand to scratch at the back of my neck I licked my lips. 'Can we compromise? Share out the jobs?' I suggested hopefully as an idea sprung to my mind.

The concerned expression that rested on Rebecca's face a minute ago was replaced by an assessing look as she narrowed her eyes, pursed her lips, and nodded, 'I'm not going to be some Bridezilla, Nicholas.' Lifting a hand she placed it reassuringly on my chest and I felt the same thrilling spark I always did from her touch, 'I want you to enjoy this day as much as I do. What do you suggest?'

Seeing my opportunity I spoke quickly before she could change her mind. 'You do the flowers, room decorations, vows, outfits, meals, cake, that sort of thing, and I'll sort out the venue, music, entertainment, and cars.' As I said it I realised just how unequal my allocation was and saw Rebecca's eyebrows rise high in her forehead, so I quickly added, 'We'll help each other, of course, and I'll obviously get your consent before I book a venue or make any final decisions.' Although where the venue was concerned I did have a little secret up my sleeve that I'd need to share with her fairly soon.

Raising my hands, I cupped Becky's face with my palms, enjoying the warmth that flowed into me and soaking up her small sigh of pleasure. She was so small and fragile compared to me, but as I remembered just how strong she'd been since we'd been back together I felt my chest puff with pride. 'I'm not the most emotionally open of men, Becky, I know that ... but I'd feel comfortable sorting those things out and that way I'd still be involved.'

After chewing on the inside of her lip for a few seconds Rebecca finally nodded and swivelled her head so she could place a kiss on my palm. 'OK. But part of the deal is that you at least think about the vows while I'm out,' she said, reaching up to drop a swift kiss on my jaw. I tried to turn to capture her lips with mine but she stepped back with a cheeky smile. 'For me?' she asked, with a flutter of her eyelashes. 'Maybe you could ask your best man to help you? If you've chosen one yet,' she added, blowing me a kiss, licking her lips, then breezing from the lounge while deliberately swaying her delectable arse and humming happily to herself.

Shaking my head I smiled ruefully. That goddamn little minx was using every one of her seduction skills today, wasn't she? Watching her departure I flopped back down onto the sofa with a moan and adjusted my excitable groin within the suddenly tight confines of my trousers.

My head fell back onto the sofa cushions and I stared at the ceiling as I contemplated our conversation again. Rubbing a hand over my face I rolled my eyes. Bloody wedding. We'd left it all a bit last minute; there were less than seven months left until our proposed wedding date and we'd only started properly planning it two days ago. In just forty-eight hours I'd already had it up to my eyes with flowers, colour schemes, and guest lists. This girly shite just wasn't for me, I just wanted Rebecca. Officially. None of the other details mattered to me. A ring on her finger and piece of paper to tell the world that she was mine was literally all I cared about. Unfortunately for me, Rebecca had a few more specifics in mind for our big day. Grimacing, I looked at the notepad on the table again and let out a long, slow breath between my teeth. Now she wanted us to write our own vows as well? It wasn't happening, not in this lifetime. My suggestion of splitting the jobs had seemed to go down rather well, though, so perhaps that would make it all a bit easier.

There was one thing I didn't need to worry about – I had already decided on my best man. There really was no other choice for me; it had to be Nathan. I just hadn't asked him yet. To be honest I wasn't sure how thrilled he'd be, he'd never exactly been the most emotionally open of men either.

A grin split my lips as I imagined asking Nathan to help me write my wedding vows. I knew he was making a good go of things with his girlfriend, Stella, but I also knew that they still chose to live a percentage of their life as Dom and sub. I actually laughed out loud as I thought about what Nathan's version of wedding vows might be: 'To submit and service, for paddling or for flogging, for fucking and for spanking, in sickness and in health; from this day forward, until sexual exhaustion do us part.' Maybe I should write *those* vows and see what Becky made of them.

ONE – NATHAN

Two weeks later

Sitting back on one of my comfy dining room chairs I smiled to myself at how completely bizarre my life now was. Bizarre in that it was so fucking startlingly normal, and believe me, 'normal' was not a word I would ever have used to describe myself before I met Stella Marsden. Pig-headed, arrogant, sexually driven, and narcissistic perhaps, but *normal*? No way, and yet here I was sat having a nice 'normal' family gathering with Stella, my brother Nicholas, and his fiancée Rebecca. To top it all off, I was actually enjoying myself.

Who would have thought that a little blonde-haired beauty could walk in and wreak such havoc in my ordered life? I'd never felt this way about any woman I'd been with before, and believe me when I say I'd been with plenty in my time. For whatever inexplicable reasons, Stella was different. I wanted to protect her, spend time with her, and keep her by my side one minute, then pounce on her and fuck her senseless the next. For someone who had kept themselves as emotionally distant in life as I had – and wasn't that just the fucking understatement of the year – I now felt like a whirlwind of emotions was blowing through my life on a daily basis.

Christ, and the sex was just *incredible*. Shaking my head I blinked several times as a secret smile slipped to my lips; any time, any place, anywhere, Stella was up for it, and just as insatiably as me – if not more so – which with my raging libido was a goddamn heaven-sent miracle. With her stubborn streak there was no doubt that she kept me on my toes too, that was for sure. And as for me being in control? I might still act like the dominant male I once was, but with all the compromises we'd made recently my feelings and emotions were so churned up that I barely knew which way was up any more. All I knew for sure was that I was happy. Genuinely happy, possibly for the first time in my fucked-up life, and all because of this one woman. Apparently wonders would never cease.

Compromise. It had never been a word that featured much in my vocabulary, I didn't make concessions, I simply stated what I wanted and damn well got it. Well, at least that had been the case until Stella landed in my life over a year and a half ago and wreaked her own delicious version of chaos. My lips quirked as I remembered that night in the hot, sweaty, sex-saturated confines of Club Twist, the night I had met Stella Marsden for the first time. She had instantly blown me away with her natural beauty, shy, tentative replies, and endearing blushes. I'd immediately sensed that something about her was different from other women I'd been with, but unbeknownst to me that first meeting had signalled the start of a whole new chapter in my life; a life now full of compromises, but oddly satisfying ones.

I ran the word around my mind again with a smirk: *compromise.* The compromises I'd made were fairly simple – our lives when we were together were shared as equals; we would shop, cook, socialise, and relax together, but she would still assume her ready position at any given time if I gave her the signal. Stella didn't call me 'Sir' on a daily basis, but she still occasionally used the title when we were having sex. Regardless of titles, I still controlled all of our bedroom time. The collar I had given her, which showed she was mine, was a necklace instead of a formal collar, but as per my wishes it never left her neck. In simple terms – my needs were met and so were hers. Perhaps they should put that in dictionary under the word 'compromise'.

I suppose domination and submission meant different things to different people, and the happy balance we'd come to amazingly suited both of us down to the ground. After years of living my life as a strict 'no-emotions-involved' Dominant I had been terrified that I was going to fuck things up with Stella and push her too far, but she'd turned out to be a natural. Just as there was a part of me that needed to dominate and control, Stella obviously had a submissive tendency which moulded with mine to perfection. Much to my own surprise, here I was after a year and a half with the same woman and I'd never felt more content, satisfied, or happy in my life.

If you had told me a few years ago that having sex with only one person and no one else could be satisfying, I'd have laughed in your face and probably called you several insulting names, but it really was true, I hadn't been even slightly tempted to stray. To be honest, I'd almost go as far as to say that sex with Stella seemed to be getting better as time passed and we learnt each other's nuances in depth.

All in all my life was pretty fucking awesome at the moment. Stella really was amazing to put up with me and my shitty baggage, and I made a mental note to tell her later, when my brother had gone. Smiling, I let my gaze drift across to the sofas, where Stella and Rebecca were pouring over bridal magazines and deep in discussion about the size of the bouquet Rebecca should have at the wedding.

'A year ago you would have ribbed me no end for having that look on my face.' Nicholas' voice broke me from my thoughts and I turned to look across the table at my brother. Schooling my features into a bland expression I mentally kicked myself for getting caught fawning over

Stella, then frowned and pretended not to know what he was talking about. 'What look?' I asked cautiously, ninety-nine per cent sure that I'd been caught red handed in my wistful gazing at Stella.

Nicholas dipped his head to suppress his smirk, causing a chunk of his dark hair to fall over his forehead and almost cover his eyes, 'The lovesick puppy dog look,' he said with a grin, confirming my suspicion. 'Admit it, bro, you've got it as bad a as I have.'

Initially frowning at his use of the 'L' word – one I was pointedly avoiding thinking about – I then sighed and rubbed at my chin while glancing across at Stella one last time. As if she knew I was looking at her, Stella's gaze suddenly shifted and locked with mine as she flashed me a soft smile. My chest did that strange compression thing that it often did when she looked at me. It was an almost suffocatingly warm sensation that flooded my lungs, but was somehow pleasant too, and certainly a feeling I had never experienced before Stella.

As she gave me a tiny wink and returned to her conversation with Rebecca I shook my head slightly and looked back at my brother's expectant face. 'Perhaps,' I conceded gruffly. I might be making some small inroads on my ability to express my emotions to Stella, but discussing this with Nicholas was a whole different issue.

'Avoid it all you like, Nathan, but it's clear in your face. I think you'll be following me up the aisle before you know it,' Nicholas joked softly, but his words brought me up short. The pleasant warmth in my chest instantly evaporated as my blood suddenly felt like chilled ice in my veins, and my heart accelerated almost painfully. Flicking my gaze from my brother back to Stella my jaw clenched until my teeth squeaked. *No*. He had that wrong. There was no way I was marrying Stella, or anyone for that matter.

Chewing on the inside of my lip I acknowledged the

background rumble of my thoughts. The reason I would never marry Stella was simple – I could never be fully sure that I wasn't going to end up a bully like my father. I'd worshipped him as a kid, believed his beatings were for my benefit, and with every grain of my being I'd wanted to be just like him. It might be over a year since I'd last seen him – thankfully there'd been no sign of him since that awful day where he'd turned up at Nicholas's house – but seeing him so bitter and twisted was when I'd finally realised what a complete fuck-up he was. Since that day I'd been terrified that my boyhood wish would come true – that I would eventually become just like him. There was no way I'd risk trapping Stella with someone like that. Never. It was definitely better that I stay unmarried and besides, why did you need a piece of paper to be happy with someone? Stella and I were doing just fine without one.

Shifting uncomfortably in my seat I pointedly avoided my brother's gaze. I'd never told Nicholas about my lack of faith in myself or my objection to marriage, but both were hugely sensitive topics for me. If he wanted to marry Rebecca that was fine for him, but not for *me*. Completely unaware of my inner turmoil, Nicholas glanced over his shoulder at where the girls were cooing over some floral samples, then looked back at me.

'Stella looks hooked. I reckon she'll secretly be making a list of her own choices.'

Breathing suddenly became quite difficult, and I felt a sudden, powerful urge to be sick. Fuck, how could I have been so stupid? I hadn't even considered it … what if Stella *wanted* to get married? Christ, I was almost hyperventilating. I couldn't do it, I just couldn't. Would she leave me if I told her I never wanted to take it to that level? Panic made me increasingly fidgety in my seat and I found myself gripping the edge of the table with sweaty palms as I struggled to regain my usual composure. Trying one of my tested calm down routines I counted down from five to zero in my head. Once I was finished I swallowed, firmly pushed the thoughts of marriage from my mind to consider at a later date, and poured another glass of wine for myself and my brother. I'd found in the past that situations like this could be easily dealt with by using a firm dose of avoidance mixed with a good shot of alcohol, so there was no reason it shouldn't work just as well tonight.

At least an hour and nearly two bottles of very decent wine later, Nicholas and I were now sat on the balcony while the girls continued to look through bridal magazines inside. It was a beautiful September evening, so we had decided to make the most the seasonable weather and soak up the last warming rays of the day's sunshine. This was my favourite place in my apartment. London looked stunning and from up here, the view over Docklands and the glittering water of the Thames really couldn't get any better. An added bonus was that it was high enough to be quiet, because we were nicely separated from the chaos and noise of the city below.

'So I have a theory about you and Stella.' We'd been sat in companionable silence for quite a while so Nicholas' slurred statement took a few seconds to sink in. Perhaps my little brother had had enough wine for one day, and was about to make uncharacteristic speculations about my relationship with Stella.

Intrigued enough to indulge him I raised an eyebrow and sunk lower in my seat so I could stretch my long legs onto the footrest in front of me. 'Really? Do tell,' I asked in a sarcastic tone that my drunken sibling totally missed.

'Well, it started when I was trying to work out why Rebecca was sticking with me and not leaving, but I think the same theory could be true for you and Stella.' Taking a sip of wine he sat up straighter on the lounger. 'You still like to be dominant, don't you?'

Christ, was that really his start? It didn't exactly take a genius to work that out, so I rolled my eyes and sighed. 'Well done for noticing, Nicholas.' I replied dryly.

'Hear me out, brother,' he said, turning on his seat so he could stare at me with slightly unfocused eyes. 'What I meant was just like me, you like to dominate, but you've never kept a relationship going until you met Stella.' Once again he was stating the obvious facts, but deciding it was easier to stay quiet I simply looked at him so he could continue. 'So it got me thinking, why Rebecca? Why is she the one for me? And why Stella for you? And I've worked it out!' he stated proudly with a flap of his arms that resulted in him sloshing wine over the balcony. Suppressing my smirk at my brother's complete loss of his usual composure I gestured with a waft of my hand for him to continue.

'The women we've been with before were all experienced submissives, they wanted to submit to us and we wanted to dominate them, but really, where's the challenge in that? If they want to submit, it wasn't us that was making them, was it? But with Rebecca and Stella, they're independent career women, they're strong-willed, they know their own minds, and by the looks of it they are both just as stubborn as each other,' he said with a dry laugh. 'I think we've become so attached to them because of their independence, the challenge of dominating them excites us.' Blinking at my brother I couldn't help but nod my head. Just the thought of Stella willingly submitting to me had my cock twitching and a flush rising to my cheeks.

Nicholas gave a jerky shrug. 'It's certainly the case for me anyway, not that we do as much of that any more. We're pretty vanilla nowadays, but Rebecca keeps me in line and interested better than anyone else has ever managed. I'd place money on the fact that it's the same for you and Stella.'

Topping up his wine, which clearly wasn't necessary as

11

he'd had way too much already, Nicholas seemed intent on continuing his speculation. 'And the best bit is, I think it's the same for them; they're so used to being in charge during their everyday lives that being with us and giving up control for a while excites them. I think letting you overpower her is probably a huge turn-on for Stella.' Cutting him off with a sharp look I swiftly sat up and frowned at my brother's boundary pushing conversation.

'Enough talk about what turns Stella on,' I growled. 'That's not something you need to worry about, I have it in hand.' But as I dismissed his conversation I realised that even in his drunken state, my little brother had probably managed to hit the nail exactly on the head.

REBECCA

Stella's enthusiasm for my pile of bridal magazines made me grin. Since I'd started buying them a few months ago they'd been driving Nicholas mad, but Stella was just as keen to trawl through them as me, which was turning out to be fantastic fun.

'More fizz?' I asked, indicating to her almost empty glass as I topped mine up with the Cava we were drinking.

Lifting her glass in my direction she beamed at me. 'Yes please!' Her cheeks were a little pink, and I decided to ask my important question now before I got tipsy and forgot. 'Actually I have something we might be able to toast to,' I said speculatively. Putting the empty bottle down I turned to Stella with an expectant smile. 'I was really hoping you'd agree to be one of my bridesmaids?'

Stella's eyes flew wide open as she spluttered on her champagne and nodded furiously. 'Wow! Gosh, yes!' Putting her glass down she grinned at me. 'I'd be honoured, Rebecca! Thank you so much for asking me!' I couldn't help sharing Stella's excitement – we might only have known each other for the last year, but we'd grown incredibly close in that time and I now considered her to be one of my closest and most trusted friends.

'How funny, me a bridesmaid and Nathan a best man!' she said with a giggle. Nicholas had asked his brother a week ago. Nathan had apparently been slightly hesitant, but after an impassioned speech from Nicholas, finally agreed. 'At least we'll be colour co-ordinated!'

As I chinked my glass with Stella's and we grinned at each other, I had a sudden recollection about the night when I'd first met her, back in the earlier days of my relationship with Nicholas, which seemed like forever ago but was actually just over a year ago now. We'd probably been dating for about five months at that point, and his brother had invited us over for dinner. Having only met Nathan once before I'd been ridiculously nervous that night. All I'd had to go on was what Nicholas had told me – that his brother was an emotionally detached man who lived his life during the day purely for business and his nights as a sexual Dominant. Not exactly what I'd consider to be an ideal dinner companion. After Nicholas explained to me that Nathan had saved his life when he'd tried to commit suicide after his father's beatings, his obvious affection for his brother seemed rather justified, and so I'd grudgingly decided to try and accept him too.

Right from the start of our relationship Nicholas had liked to take the lead in the bedroom, but even in the beginning we didn't have a contract or safe words, so the idea that Nathan was a Dominant had freaked me out. After being introduced to Stella that night I'd quickly realised that she was Nathan's submissive, and I'll admit that I'd been pretty horrified by that fact. A smile slipped to my face now and I felt my cheeks flush as I remembered my rude behaviour that night. I'd been gunning for Nathan from the start of the evening, throwing foul looks his way and assuming that he was somehow forcing Stella into their relationship. My face crinkled into a rueful smile – I probably hadn't been the most well-mannered dinner guest that night.

Looking across at Stella's relaxed face as she looked through a brochure of wedding venues I smiled. Now that I knew Stella properly and we'd chatted about the set-up of her relationship with Nathan I understood more fully. I wasn't sure I could ever live the way she did with Nathan, but it was completely consensual so I would never judge her for her choices. To my surprise, Stella had told me that the start of their agreement had been rather impersonal, a contractual agreement for a no-strings relationship where he would dominate her in the bedroom and she would happily submit to him. The thing that had shocked me the most was when Stella had told me that *she* had been the one to seek it out. I still struggled to get my head around that, but knowing how independent and headstrong she was I could sort of imagine her doing something so brave – or perhaps reckless should be the word.

From what I'd gathered in our chats over the last few months, Stella and Nathan's relationship had changed significantly about a year ago after he'd asked my advice about 'mainstreaming'. Stella said they now had a relatively normal relationship and that although Nathan was still in charge in the bedroom, rules and safe words rarely came into their time together anymore.

Glancing across at Nicholas and Nathan as they sat on the balcony highlighted by the late evening sun I smiled; as brothers went they were a pretty stunning pair. My eye narrowed slightly as I looked at Nathan, his sharp gaze focused on Nicholas, his head tipped to the side as he listened intently to what his brother was saying. Having gotten to know about their past I knew that both of them still carried deep scars from their abusive father. I still found myself a little cautious around Nathan – there was just something intrinsically intimidating about him, but it was clear to see how he relaxed when Stella was around, and the little flashes of a softer side that I saw in his eyes when he looked at her were incredibly endearing.

My gaze shifted across to my man and I felt my heart give a little kick. Rather uncharacteristically, Nicholas actually looked a little tipsy tonight. His cheeks were redder than usual, his hair flopping wildly over his brow, and the sleeves of his shirt rolled up clumsily. I couldn't help but smile fondly at seeing him so relaxed. As dishevelled as he looked through the reflective window glimmer he was still so frigging attractive, and even sitting here, as far away as I was, I felt my body responding to his – a sensation I would never tire of. It was like we were linked on some carnal, chemical level.

Blinking the thoughts away, I shrugged slightly to refocus my mind and turned my attention back to my friend. Whatever the setup of the partnership between Nathan and Stella I was immensely glad to have her as a friend, and I was thrilled she'd just agreed to be my bridesmaid. Raising her champagne flute Stella caught my eye and beamed at me.

'Here's to some fun preparations and a fantastic wedding!' A toast I wholeheartedly agreed with.

TWO – NATHAN

A marginal heaviness at my temples indicated that I'd probably had a little too much wine this evening, but as well as drinking too much my mind had been more active than I'd have liked – no matter how hard I tried, I couldn't forget Nicholas' words about Stella perhaps wanting to get married one day, and even now, almost an hour after my brother had left, I kept playing his words through my mind over and over again.

Frowning, I leant forward and rested my hands on my knees as I stared at the unlit fireplace deep in thought. One thing kept going round and round inside my head; what if Stella's continued reluctance to move in with me had something to do with the fact that she somehow knew about my aversion to marriage? I'd asked her to live with me multiple times now, but she'd flat out rejected me every time. What if deep down she knew she wanted to get married someday, and was just waiting for the right time to tell me that we would be incompatible in the long run?

Christ, my heart was suddenly thudding. The thought that she might up and leave me was almost enough to tempt me to consider the idea of tying the knot. No matter how much I was adverse to the idea of marriage, I really wasn't sure I could function without Stella in my life any more. Images of my father suddenly flashed in my head; dark and foreboding, and I scowled at the sickeningly unwelcome thoughts. What was that old saying? "Like father like son?" Biting down hard on my lip I shook my head vigorously. No. I wouldn't ever tie Stella to me if there was even a remote chance that I'd one day end up like my old man.

Letting out a heavy sigh I sat back on the sofa. Perhaps I should discuss the subject of marriage with her? The mere thought of that conversation made my eyes narrow and my stomach twist with apprehension. A huge sigh left my chest, leaving me depressingly deflated. Maybe I could convince her that living together would be enough ... A scowl twisted my brow as an immediate problem sprang to mind – she wouldn't bloody well agree to live with me, would she? Which totally scuppered that plan. Running a hand through my hair in agitation I decided to avoid the hugely volatile subject of marriage and instead try one more time to find out why Stella was so reluctant to move in with me – perhaps the answers would shed light on some of my concerns.

With this in mind I had decided to go in search of Stella when the lights in the lounge suddenly went off, plunging me into complete darkness. What the fuck? Wondering if it was a power cut the sidelights suddenly popped to life, illuminating the room with a soft, mellow glow similar to candlelight. Blinking in the dim light I frowned and looked towards the light switches. The sight that met me caused every nerve ending in my body to erupt at once.

Holy fuck. Stella was standing by the entrance to the lounge, one hand on the switches and the other hand on her bare hip. She was wearing black lace, barely-there knickers, a black bodice I'd never seen before, and not much else except for a saucy smile on her lips. She looked utterly gorgeous and I instantly hardened at the sight. *Well, well.* My dull mood had rapidly evaporated, thoughts of talking departed my mind, and the remainder of the evening suddenly looked distinctly rosy.

Seeing as Stella made no move to come closer I grinned at her teasing little game, stood up, and began to prowl my way towards her. I knew Stella loved it when I stalked her like this and I watched in satisfaction as she licked her lower lip, excited desire clearly twinkling in her eyes. Pushing off the wall she gave me a seriously seductive 'come hither' look, turned away from me, and began sauntering her sexy arse in the direction of the bedroom. *Christ.* Her knickers were actually a thong, the thin material tucked up between her cheeks, leaving her beautiful bottom exposed to me. A growl escaped my throat as I sped up my steps and made a click of disapproval with my tongue that completely stopped Stella in her tracks – there was not a chance in hell I was letting her get as far as the bedroom. That seemed like fucking miles away, and after Stella's barely clothed arrival in the lounge I wanted her, right here, *right now*.

'Not so fast, Stella,' I barked, gripping her wrist and pulling her up against me. A gasp escaped her throat and her beautiful eyes widened at my sudden movements as a split second later I had her firmly pressed up against the wall and pinned by my body.

The heat from her skin felt like it was burning through my clothing. Fuck, I needed to get naked right this second to try and cool the flames licking at my skin. 'You are a little temptress, aren't you?' I growled before I crashed my lips onto hers in a frantic kiss, stealing the breath from her lungs as I smothered her with both my body and mouth. Finally I gave us both some breathing room and leant back slightly, panting against her neck, 'Not that I'm complaining, but what brought this on?' I sounded as breathless as I felt as I ran a finger across the lace of her very sexy corset. Damn, she'd strapped herself in so tight her nipples were practically spilling over the top.

'Rebecca asked me to be her bridesmaid today, I guess all the talk of romance got me horny ...' she panted. 'I want you, Nathan ... now,' I found myself ridiculously pleased that she said 'romance', and not 'all the talk of marriage'. Grunting my approval, I bent my head to kiss her again, but Stella pushed against my chest and met my eyes. 'Bedroom ...' she whispered, trying to lead me in that direction, but once again my impatience got the better of me, and instead of taking her to the bedroom I stooped down, hauled her over my shoulder, and carried her to the nearby sofa, responding to her shocked cries by giving her bottom a firm spank which echoed in the silent space.

I was like a man possessed, and in record time I had her panties off and myself naked. Within seconds I was sweeping the TV remote and a magazine from the sofa as our bodies crashed down onto the cool leather in a jumble of arms and legs. Keen to give Stella a little payback for her teasing I leant to the side and swiftly pulled the belt from my discarded trousers, then with a grin I took hold of both of Stella's hands in one of mine and used the belt to fasten them over her head. Tilting my head I eyed her response. 'That OK, sweetheart?' I murmured, a gesture I'd never have bothered with back in my old Dominant days.

Smiling shyly Stella shifted slightly below me, then nodded and bit her lip, 'I'm good.' She lifted her head as she tried to reach my lips so I wasted no time talking and swiftly kissed her on the lips hard, driving my tongue into her hot mouth and groaning as she immediately ran the velvety softness of her tongue against mine. Breaking my lips from hers I dipped my head, running a trail of wet, open-mouthed kisses down her jaw and neck before using my teeth to pull her already hard nipples from the tempting prison of the corset. Stella let out a sharp gasp as I tugged harshly at her with my teeth, but by God I was so turned on there was no way I could be gentle now. Besides, when I briefly lifted my head and caught her gaze, desire was clear in Stella's eyes and I couldn't help but smile. My girl liked a little pain mixed with her pleasure. She really couldn't be a better match for me.

With her hands bound Stella couldn't reach out for me like I knew she wanted to, but instead she writhed beneath me until she had her thighs apart, snaking one of her legs around my hips and drawing me sharply down against her so our groins collided, forcing the tip of my erection to push against her, a sensation that nearly made me delirious.

As my hands roamed over her body, gradually making their way towards her groin, soft panting moans escaped from Stella's lips, spiking my pleasure to almost feral levels. *She was mine. I was making her feel this way.* Running two fingers over the damp, quivering flesh at the apex of her thighs caused Stella to buck herself against my hand, coating my fingers with her arousal as I ground them against her nub. Oh God, she was so wet. Groaning, I kissed her again. She felt so damn good against me. Stella was so fucking sexy she almost drove me out of my mind. I could barely think straight now, let alone breathe, and as our joint pleasure escalated I couldn't hold back a second longer.

Shifting myself marginally to the side I reached down to position the head of my pulsing cock at Stella's quivering entrance. 'Yes,' she whispered, almost sounding victorious in her desperation. As I felt her shift impatiently below me I locked my eyes with hers and then thrust myself down hard and deep, causing us both to shudder as pleasure flooded our systems and my head fell to the crook of her neck.

'Fuck! So good!' I don't know who said it, but one of us cried out as our bodies joined. Perhaps we both did. I had no idea any more. Raising my head I gazed down into Stella's wide eyes and after we both regained our composure I began to thrust in long, steady strokes, causing Stella to clamp around me like a vice. *Christ.* She was so tight. Every time with Stella felt like a brand new experience, she was so fucking incredible.

Leaning her lips against my neck Stella pecked and licked below my ear as I continued to drive us both on with steady, regular thrusts. I was carefully holding myself in check so I didn't lose it too soon, but that control was disappearing by the second. 'Harder, Nathan ... please ...' she murmured against my skin, causing my cock to stiffen even further. Her words took me right back to our first time together on this very sofa; that night she'd begged me to fuck her harder and deeper too. And just as I'd obliged her then I did now, increasing the speed and power of my thrusts until Stella let out a strangled cry and came in pulsing bursts, triggering my own powerful orgasm that swept through me until I collapsed on top of her completely drained.

Several minutes later, when our breathing had returned to normal, I shifted my weight from Stella's pliant body, undid the belt around her wrists, and pulled her against me so she was snuggled into my chest. I rubbed her wrists and allowed myself to relax below her as I tried to sink further into my contented state, but infuriatingly I found that my bloody mind was still partially focusing on my earlier concerns about marriage and living together.

At the return of these depressing thoughts a long, deep breath left my lungs. I was always so in control of my life that having an issue I had no power over was leaving me floundering. It was so fucking annoying. Chewing on my lip a devious thought slipped into my mind – perhaps if I broached the subject while she was sated from our sex Stella might be more co-operative.

Turning my head I placed a kiss on her forehead, which caused her to snuggle in closer to me.

'We're so good together, Stella, and I'm not just talking about the sex ...' I hesitated briefly before diving right in, '... why won't you move in with me?' I tried to soften the blow by stroking my hand through her hair in a soothing motion, but I still felt a warm sigh blow across my chest.

22

Leaning up onto one elbow she looked me directly in the eyes, a small frown puckering her eyebrows, and I cringed. God, I really must sound like a frigging broken record, asking her the same damn question. That must be, what, twenty times I'd asked her in the last year?

'Fine, you really want to know why?' she asked, her voice soft but determined nonetheless, a description that summed her up perfectly. I swallowed hard and an uncomfortable feeling rose in my chest. Now it looked like she was going to relent I suddenly had my doubts – did I really want to know why she'd been so hesitant for so long? What if the answer was as awful as I'd imagined? What if she was desperate for marriage and planned to leave me to find someone better? Forcing my paranoid guesses away I nodded my head apprehensively.

Seeing my nod she didn't waste another second, seemingly keen to get it off her chest. 'The main thing is this apartment. I don't want to live here,' she said simply. Trying to process her words I blinked several times as relief rushed through me. She hadn't mentioned marriage, thank God, but my apartment? That wasn't what I'd expected her to say at all. Did she want me to move in with *her*? Was that what this was all about? 'But your place is only small, we'd never fit all our stuff there,' I replied, still somewhat perplexed by the turn this conversation had taken.

Shaking her head a small smile tilted the corner of her lips. 'That's not what I mean, Nathan.' She let out a long breath and seemed to be steeling herself to drop yet more bad news on me. 'Look, I know how much you love your apartment, you designed it; you're allowed to love it.' Leaning down she placed a brief, chaste peck on my chin, 'The thing is, I just don't like it.'

My eyebrows rose significantly at her words, and even though Stella was talking sense I couldn't help but feel my hackles rise and body tense. This place had every convenience possible, what the fuck was there not to like?

As if reading my mind Stella shook her head and smiled wryly, 'Don't get me wrong, it's a beautiful apartment, Nathan. Perfect really.' Lowering her eyes she seemed to be choosing her words carefully so I lay there and attempted to reign in my impatience. 'The thing is, if I moved in here it would never feel like "our" apartment to me, it would always be yours.' Denial was about to spring from my lips, but Stella halted me by placing a finger gently on them. 'I know it's stupid, but when I'm here I can't get the image of your previous women out of my head. They lived here with you, shared this space ...' Her hand wafted around as if to prove her point, '... and as stupid as it probably sounds, that's why I can't live with you. It's not about you, it's about this apartment and its history.'

Taking a moment to process her words I couldn't help a frown deepening my brow. It was true other women had shared this space with me, but I never gave them a second thought now – how strange that Stella would dwell on it. 'But you come here every week and you've never seemed bothered before,' I stated, fairly sure that I was right.

Shrugging, Stella lowered her eyes, 'Perhaps not outwardly, but there's a reason I always try and manoeuvre our time so that we're mostly in your bedroom.' Raising her gaze she looked directly into my eyes. 'You told me you'd never taken another woman in there before me, that's why I like it so much.'

Wow. That was news to me, and it hit me like a punch to the stomach. 'This is a little crazy, sweetheart, we've been together a long while now. Those women are in my past; they mean nothing to me.'

Sighing, Stella nodded as her fingers absently played over my bare chest, 'I know, and I also know that this is probably irrational of me, that's why I never told you before, but I can't help it, they always spring to my mind.'

24

Stella's eyes narrowed as a look of distaste settled on her features. 'For example, can you honestly tell me that I'm the only person you've had sex on this sofa with?' My loud swallow spoke a thousand words. No, she was not the only woman I'd fucked on this sofa. I winced, in fact I think I'd struggle to count the number on women who'd been below me on this leather ... not that I'd share that thought with Stella.

Seeing my wince Stella sighed, 'You see? I *hate* that thought,' she grimaced, pushing herself upright as if the sofa was suddenly repellent to her. Standing, she began pulling on my discarded shirt for cover, leaving my arms feeling achingly empty as I sat up. 'I'm sure I'm not the only woman who's pleasured you on the kitchen table either? Or against those windows?' Her voice was rising now, and although I did agree with her that it was a little irrational, it was clear that the thought upset her. 'It's too crowded here for me. I know that sounds stupid, Nathan, but that's the reason, OK? I could never live here full-time and be happy, and I know your apartment is beloved to you so I guess we're at an impasse.' She smiled weakly at me. 'Plus, you don't have a conservatory,' she added in a soft attempt at a joke, 'I've always wanted to live in a house with a conservatory.'

Even with her attempt at lightening the mood I found myself sat in stunned silence. Wow. This was a hell of a lot to take in. It certainly explained why Stella was always so keen on having sex in my bedroom though ... I'd never thought much beyond the fact that the bed was big and comfortable, but clearly Stella had chosen the location for a whole different reason. Running a hand through my hair I licked my lips, unsure what to say next. Christ, so I'd have to move out if I wanted to live with her? Leave the first building I'd ever designed, the apartment that was hugely symbolic to me as not only the start to my new life, but also a final end to my abusive childhood? I'd designed this apartment when I was still living at home with my parents, long before I'd even qualified as an architect. It had been my way of releasing some of the tension I held inside me, and I'd poured out my frustrations and longings to escape into planning where I would live when I eventually did leave. In that sense, this place had been my refuge over the years, even before it had even become a reality – but on the other hand Stella was fast becoming my rock. Shaking my head to try and clear my thoughts I realised I was going to need to do some serious thinking to sort this problem out.

Turning to the left I raised my head and my gaze locked with Stella's. I was expecting her to be annoyed at my hesitation, pissed off because my apartment meant so much to me, but to my surprise I saw a sympathetic smile on her face. Reaching her hand across she took mine and lifted it to her lips, kissing the palm. 'I know what you went through to build this place, Nathan, and I totally understand why it's so important to you. Let's not rush things, OK? Maybe given time I'll feel more at home here.'

Even now, when it should be me making her feel better, Stella was still trying to look out for me. Shaking my head I smiled weakly. Her compassion never failed to amaze me. Drawing in a deep breath I remained silent, not yet sure what to say, so instead I stood up, scooped Stella into my arms, and carried her towards the bedroom, her only real haven within my home.

Gazing down at her as I walked my eyes travelled over her features as she loosely draped an arm around my neck for support and rested her head on my shoulder. My chest tightened in that strange, war, way again. I cared for her so fucking much it hurt. Well, that was that question answered then … it looked like I'd be visiting some estate agents in the next few weeks.

THREE – NICHOLAS

Pushing through the doorway to Rebecca's bookshop I made my way inside, rubbing my hands together and glad to be out of the cold day. Just last week I'd been sat on the balcony of my brother's apartment enjoying the sunshine, but it seemed like the change to October had brought with it near-torrential rain and sudden temperature drops, making it feeling much more like the start of winter.

Weaving between the stacks of books that always seemed chaotic to me, but according to Rebecca were apparently completely ordered, I finally got to the counter and smiled at Louise, Rebecca's assistant.

'Hi, Nicholas, all set for this weekend?' she asked with a knowing grin. Louise was in on my surprise because I'd had to call her last week and check Rebecca's intended shifts at the shop. Luckily, she was off for the entire weekend so I could carry out my plan without disrupting the other staff member's shifts.

'Yes, everything's ready, is she out back?' I asked, tilting my head in the direction of the small office at the rear of the shop. As much I liked Louise – she was one of Becky's closest friends and also one of her bridesmaids-to-be – I wasn't exactly one for small talk, so I was keen to find Becky and head off.

'She is, go on through,' Louise said, turning her attention to a customer who had just entered the shop.

Making my way down the narrow corridor I had to dodge and negotiate several large piles of books and boxes, presumably new stock – *definitely* not in any sort of order – before I came to Rebecca's cosy office. When I say 'cosy', I'm being polite. In actuality her office is about the size of a broom closet, and that's being decidedly generous.

Poking my head in, I found Rebecca shoving her laptop into its bag before spinning to me with a huge grin on her face. As much as I might think of myself as a tough guy I just couldn't help the way I reacted to my girl when she looked at me like that, and as was now the norm, I found myself reflecting her grin like a giddy teenager as I felt my heart start to thump a little faster in my chest. 'All done?'

Shouldering her laptop bag and grabbing a holdall Rebecca nodded. 'Yep. I packed a weekend bag this morning like you told me to.' Stepping forwards she wrapped an arm around my neck and pulled my head down for a quick kiss which sent a fire racing from my lips straight to my groin before she leant back and levelled a narrowed glance at me. 'Are you going to tell me where we're going now?' I had no idea if Rebecca felt the same spark between us every time we touched, but for me, even after a year and a half, the thrilling effect hadn't faded. I hoped it never would.

Getting a grip on my runaway libido I tried to think with my brain and not my trousers as I smiled down at her. 'Just for a nice weekend away,' I replied vaguely, with a waggle of my eyebrows as I took the bag from her hand. 'Come on, let's head off and beat the rush hour.'

Just over four hours later we arrived at our destination, Langdale Chase, a beautiful and exclusive country house hotel on the shores of Lake Windermere. Rebecca might not have known my exact destination as I drove, but being born and bred in the Lake District she had realised we were heading for Cumbria as soon as I'd turned off the M6 at junction 36, and had been giddy with excitement ever

28

since.

As I slowly negotiated the gravel driveway towards the hotel Rebecca drew in a gasp. 'Nicholas, this place is beautiful,' she murmured softly as she gazed out of the window while I parked the car. 'I used to do a cycle route as a kid that took us past this hotel, but that's about as close as I've ever been to it.' Swivelling back around to me as I turned off the ignition I saw Rebecca frown, 'It's pretty exclusive here, Nicholas. I wish you'd picked somewhere a bit less pricy, that way I might not feel like such a freeloader.' Watching as she nervously chewed on a fingernail I smiled and reached across to tug her hand from her mouth, pulling it to my own lips and placing a kiss on the tip. Lowering her hand I stroked her knee reassuringly and gave it a squeeze until Rebecca took the hint and met my calm gaze.

'But this is my treat for you, Rebecca. I don't want you paying for anything; that would defeat the point of it being *my treat*,' I explained patiently, knowing that Rebecca was still a little uncomfortable with the amount of money that resided in my bank accounts. She had no reason to be, I knew she wasn't after me for my money. After all, I'd seen her own bank statements – Becky had plenty of cash coming in from her business, she wasn't as well-off as me perhaps, but none the less, she was more than comfortable.

'Hmmm.' She hummed a noncommittal noise in the back of her throat, but didn't sound convinced and I found myself sighing heavily and drawing my hand back into my own lap. Rebecca might be a business owner, and a good one at that, but she was *my* girl, mine to look after and mine to treat to a night in a nice hotel if I bloody well wanted to. Not that a casual treat was entirely my motive for this trip, but Rebecca would find that out soon enough. Enough was enough, I might be softening up, but she still needed to know that I could and would take care of her if I damn well wanted. Swinging the car door open I fixed her with a firm look and saw her slightly flinch as she registered it. 'Rebecca, stop overthinking everything. Just relax and enjoy yourself. For me?'

At my exasperated tone I saw Rebecca's eyes soften and she eventually smiled ruefully. 'I'm sorry, Nicholas.' Blinking several times, she exhaled a deep breath through her nose and then nodded towards the grand building. 'I didn't mean to be ungrateful, this place looks amazing. Thank you.'

I had in no way intended for this weekend to start off with tension, so as I rounded the car to Rebecca's side I calmed myself and rolled off my shoulders before opening her door and flashing my award-winning grin at her. 'Come on, my beautiful girl. Let's get inside.' Glancing down at her again I saw her cheeks were pink and I grinned – I loved the way Rebecca flushed when I complimented her; it seemed to make her entire being glow with happiness. Happiness that *I* had caused, which in turn did stupidly soppy things to my own insides.

Smiling shyly at me Rebecca took my extended hand and allowed me to assist her from the car as if I were a true bred gentleman and not some ex-loser fraud attempting to turn over a new leaf. Letting the warmth from Rebecca's palm soak into my skin, I absorbed the tingles with a smile, pushed thoughts of my less than salubrious past aside and focused on the present. Quite simply, it was this woman and her gentle ways who had changed me so radically, and I couldn't be more thankful for that fact.

Taking her hand we began crunching over the gravel towards the impressive building, her thumb caressing the back of my hand and me probably squeezing her digits just a bit too tightly because of my anticipation. This was it, I'd get to tell Rebecca my secret soon. God, I hoped she was pleased. But I suppose only time would tell. Mounting the steps together we entered the beautiful wood panelled entrance hall and I felt Rebecca's arm lag slightly as she paused to take in the impressive surroundings. After a brief glance around my eyes landed on the reception counter and as we approached I drew in a steadying breath, desperately hoping that the smiling girl there was the one I'd spoken to on the phone just as few hours earlier.

'Good afternoon, welcome to Langdale Chase.' She beamed at us both before raising her eyebrows expectantly as her fingers hovered over the keyboard, waiting to check us in.

'Good afternoon,' I reluctantly released the warmth of Rebecca's hand as I reached into my jacket pocket to retrieve my wallet. 'We have a room booked in the name of Mr Jackson. Nicholas Jackson,' I added. The girl's eyes flicked to mine briefly and I saw a spark of recognition there. Quite apparently she was the staff member I'd spoken to earlier, and from the small smile now playing on her lips it was apparent she remembered my request to delay our check-in. Thank goodness for that, part one of my plan was slipping into place.

As if on cue she clicked a few buttons on the computer keyboard and then frowned minutely. 'I do apologise, Mr Jackson, your room isn't quite ready yet,' she said with an apologetic smile. Persuading the hotel to tell us our room wasn't ready had actually taken quite some doing – apparently a fancy hotel like this didn't keep its paying guests waiting for their rooms, even if it was for a good reason, but after explaining my intentions the manager had warmly agreed and handed me over to the receptionist so I could explain what I needed her to do.

'It shouldn't be too long. Would you would like a drink in the lounge? On us, of course. Or perhaps you'd like to make the most of the lovely afternoon and have a stroll around the house and gardens?' The small smile and blink of her eyelashes would have looked completely innocent to most people, but seeing as I knew I wanted to take Rebecca around the house I couldn't help but smile back at the girl conspiratorially.

'That sounds like an excellent plan,' I agreed, managing to suppress my smile as I turned to Rebecca and retook a hold of her hand.

'Which would you rather? Drink, or wander?' I asked, fairly sure that I knew her well enough by now to guess that Rebecca was inquisitive and liked to explore new places.

'Let's walk. My legs could do with a stretch after all that time in the car,' Rebecca said, smiling at the receptionist and then stretching out her shoulders. Perfect, that was exactly what I'd hoped for.

Nodding, we set off around the extensive property. The grounds were very impressive, and as we walked we passed beautifully tended beds one minute, and then wilder, wooded areas the next, but the most awe-inspiring thing was the lakeside positioning of this beautiful building. Wandering down to the water's edge we had a great view over Lake Windermere and paused on a small jetty to watch the gentle breeze propel a small sail boat across the surface of the water. Rebecca glanced over her shoulder and then shuffled back a few steps so she was positioned in front of me with her back pressed up against my chest. Smiling to myself at her move I wrapped my arms around her and tugged her backwards even further so that not a scrap of space was between us and leant my head into the side of hers.

Once we had lingered in our own little world for a few minutes we set off again, this time back inside the building where we set about a brief exploration of the house. Wandering through a series of wood panelled rooms, all a beautiful dark oak that seemed to have mellowed over time to a gorgeous warm caramel colour, we eventually came to a room which I immediately recognised. Smiling to myself I felt my heartbeat accelerate in my chest from anticipation. This was it, the moment was nearly here. This room was a little smaller than others we had passed through, but beautifully decorated, with a stunning staircase wrapping its way around one wall before curving down to the centre of the room. Behind the staircase was a series of huge picture windows, giving masses of light to the space and allowing almost panoramic views over the stunning grounds beyond.

I felt a slight sweat break out on the back of my neck, I felt almost as nervous as the day I'd proposed. 'This place is like something out of a fairy tale,' Rebecca murmured softly as her gaze travelled up to the walkway and balconies that ran around the upper half of the room. As if in a daze she dropped my hand and made her way up the first few steps to gaze out of the window down towards the lake.

I simply couldn't wait any longer – it was as if a bubble had formed inside of me that had suddenly grown to such huge proportions that it was likely to burst at any second, and suddenly I found myself almost tripping as I charged up the stairs behind Rebecca and grabbed her hand. Seeing her look of surprise at my uncoordinated dash, I marginally reined myself in and paused to control my voice before asking the question I could no longer hold back. 'Shall I book it, then?' I asked, cocking my head to the side so I could fully absorb her reaction.

Looking at me in confusion Rebecca frowned, 'I thought we already had a room booked for tonight? The receptionist just said it wasn't ready yet.'

Allowing a smile to break on my lips I took hold of her other hand so that both were clasped in mine. 'For our wedding. Would you like to get married here, Rebecca?' I enquired softly, praying she said yes, because even with my significant bank balance the amount I'd paid as a deposit for this place would definitely be missed.

My pulse was pounding as I waited for her reply, but the reassuring touch of her hands was keeping me grounded. Just.

'I … I …' Rebecca tried to speak several times, her eyes darting around the room again until they rested on me and I saw the first flicker of excitement mix with her stunned confusion. 'What?' she whispered, her grip on my fingers strengthening significantly.

'I told a little fib, this isn't just a weekend away. I wanted to show you this place as a potential wedding venue. What are your thoughts?' I asked, my heart practically in my mouth by this point.

Blinking at me several times with wide eyes I began to panic at Rebecca's lack of response until suddenly she took me completely by surprise and hurled herself at me with an excited yelp. And I mean she literally threw her whole body up into my arms so she was clinging to me, legs wrapped around my waist, arms tight about my neck, and her face burrowed into my shoulder. Thank fuck that I was paying attention otherwise we might have both ended up falling down the bloody stairs, but as it was I caught her, adjusted my stance, and cradled her trembling body against mine as I lowered my lips to her hair and spoke near her ear. 'Is that a yes?' I asked as I inhaled her beautiful scent, 'You like it?'

Raising her face from my neck I saw tears welling in Rebecca's eyes, but just as I was about to go into full panic mode I watched the most stunning smile curve her lips. 'I love it, Nicholas, it's amazing. *You're* amazing.' Seconds later her lips found mine and as she kissed me senseless I tasted her sweet, soft flavour mixed with the salt of her tears.

As her tongue danced with mine Rebecca's hands slid up my neck, ran through my hair, and even clawed a little at the nape of my neck. By the time she had finished laying that stunning kiss on me I had such an enormous hard-on that I winced as she brushed against me while I lowered her back to her feet. Grinning wickedly she then leaned in and cupped me through my jeans, giving my cock a warm, firm squeeze that very nearly finished me off there and then. 'Rebecca,' I warned in a low growl as she continued to rub me, making me swell even more, but she ignored my warning, licking her lips and simply continuing with her teasing touch. Catching her wrist in a firm grip I halted her mischievous hand and gently pulled her to my side whilst I adjusted my groin and then flashed her a rueful smile.

Tipping her chin up I dropped one final firm kiss on her lips and then leant round to nuzzle her ear, now intent on some teasing of my own. 'Just wait until we get to our room, Rebecca, I'll make you pay for that little tease.' My soft endearment and affectionate nuzzling must have briefly disguised my dark intent, because it took a second or so until Rebecca gasped and leant back with wide eyes as she bit down on her lower lip expectantly. 'I'm going to get you so desperate for release that you'll beg me to let you come,' I added, my breath hot on her neck as I decided that I rather liked the idea of Rebecca begging and screaming my name in the elegant setting of this hotel.

Just to keep her on her toes I then completely changed tack and pulled back as if our lusty encounter had never occurred. 'This room can seat fifty for the ceremony, I know that's probably a little smaller than you were hoping for, but seeing as I have barely anyone I want to invite on my side it should help keep numbers down. Plus they have a larger room for the evening do so we can invite more to that.' I watched in amusement as Rebecca attempted to reconnect her scrambled brain and get over her arousal to focus back on wedding plans.

Swallowing several times she let out a shaky breath, smiled at me ruefully, and then nodded. 'Fifty is fine. I know you don't like the spotlight, so I was also thinking we'd keep it small.' Spinning on the spot she looked up at me with a tiny frown forming on her brows. 'This place is just perfect, I love it, Nicholas, but the chances of it being free in March are pretty slim,' she murmured, sounding dejected. 'That's less than six months away, I bet this place gets booked years in advance.'

'It's already ours,' I murmured, trying not to sound too smug and failing miserably.

This time her face flew up to mine so quickly I was surprised she hadn't hurt her neck. 'What?'

Rolling my lips I prepared for my confession. 'I actually made a reservation the week after I proposed.' Now it was my turn to look contrite. 'I didn't tell you then because I was worried you might think I was rushing things. I came to this place years ago to play at a wedding, they have a beautiful music room just along that corridor,' I added, indicating in a direction we hadn't explored yet. 'As soon as you agreed to marry me I thought of this place. I know how much you love the Lake District and seeing as most of your family are up this way it seemed perfect.'

Shaking her head I watched as more tears formed in Rebecca's eyes as she gazed up at me. 'I'm speechless,' she snuffled, swiping the back of her hand over her eyes again in a pointless gesture as more tears immediately seeped down her cheeks.

'I love you,' she mumbled shortly before burying her head in my jacket and slipping her arms around my waist. Cuddling her to me I ran a hand up and down Becky's spine as my eyebrows rose in surprise – I'd thought she would be upset that I'd booked it without consulting her first, but thankfully that didn't seem to be an issue at all.

'So what date do we have it? Saturday the twenty-ninth of March like we'd planned?' she asked, excitement now replacing her tears as she stepped away from me with drier eyes and started to lightly bounce on the balls of her feet.

Hoping she wasn't going to take my next statement as an over-the-top gesture I shrugged slightly awkwardly, 'I booked the whole weekend. Friday night to Monday morning.'

Rebecca ceased her bouncing and paused to gawk up at me with several long, slow blinks of her beautiful green eyes. 'What do you mean you booked the whole weekend?' Her voice was a mere whisper, as if she already knew the answer to her question but needed me to clarify it anyway.

Here it comes, I thought, bracing myself. 'I booked out the whole hotel for the entire weekend from the evening of the 28th to the morning of the 31st.' Taking the chance of her stunned silence I put on my most boyish face and raised my eyebrows. 'Please don't be mad. I just want everything to be perfect for you – for *us*,' I corrected quickly, 'and they don't cater for evening functions here unless the whole hotel is booked out privately.'

My beautiful girl was obviously stunned into silence because she just continued to stare at me as if I had suddenly grown two heads. Jumping into the lull in conversation I gently took hold of her shoulders and spun her around so she was facing into the room again. 'See the balconies that overlook the room?' I asked softly, and in response I felt a small nod of her head. 'Well, I was thinking that if your sister was up to the journey she'd be able to sit up there and watch the ceremony.' Feeling a small, sobbing shudder run through Rebecca's body I quickly persevered, 'I know that since the ... accident ... Joanne hates crowds, but I'm sure she'd also hate to miss your big day, if we got it set up so she was away from the other guests and was just sat quietly with your mum, or maybe her nurse, then she could still feel part of our big day. What do you think?'

Spinning in my embrace I once again found myself wrapped up in Becky as her arms slid around my shoulders and she tucked her sniffling face into the crook of my neck. 'You've thought of everything, Nicholas. I'm not

37

going to moan at you about how stupidly extravagant you've been, because it's all just perfect. Thank you. I love you so much.'

'Not as much as I love you,' I said with a smile, using our standard reply and making Becky flash a big watery smile in the process.

'Do you think we can check in to our room now? Because I must look totally hideous,' she joked, wiping at her reddened nose again. Admittedly she did look a little tear-stained, damp, and ruffled, but she was still my gorgeous girl, and so with a final squeeze I released her and led her back towards the reception.

REBECCA

I was still in a bit of a daze as we made our way back towards the main entrance. The beautiful paintings and exquisite art that had held my attention earlier were now just a blur beside me. Nicholas had booked this amazing place for our wedding ... I could hardly absorb it, talk about a bombshell! Not only that, but Nicholas' plans for how Joanne could be included were just so considerate – he knew how important my sister was to me, and for him to actually work out how she could be involved was incredibly touching.

When the reception hall finally came into view I saw to my horror that not only was the young receptionist waiting for our return, but that she had also been joined by two smartly suited men. Great, more spectators to witness my blotchy face and red nose. I shook my head with an amused roll of my eyes and straightened my back. There was very little I could do about it now, so making sure that I at least had a smile on my face I turned to them and found three expectant faces.

'You have yourselves a confirmed booking,' Nicholas said happily as he gave my hand a squeeze. Glancing up at him I saw uncharacteristic openness on his face as he shook hands with one of the two men. He was practically grinning, his eyes were crinkled at the corners with happiness in an expression that even *I* only saw on rare occasions, let alone anyone else. Seeing him so thrilled about our upcoming marriage I felt my heart fall just a little harder for my complex man.

'You must be Mr Jackson and Miss Langley,' the taller man said, stepping forwards to shake my hand as well. 'It's a pleasure to finally meet you in person. I'm Paul, the hotel manager, and this is James, he's our master of ceremonies and will be overseeing your big day.' James was younger than Paul, but had an air of command about him that would no doubt make him perfect for the job.

'I was thinking that while you are here you might want to meet with James or myself to discuss further arrangements? How about we get you checked in and then after you've rested and freshened up we could meet before dinner?'

'Sounds good,' I said with a nod. 'I got a bit emotional when Nicholas told me he had booked this place so I could do with sorting my face out,' I remarked with a grin. At least now they knew why I looked such a state. To our right the receptionist was busy laying out a sheet of paper and our room key with a sympathetic smile. 'Why is it us women cry when we're happy?' she remarked, 'I'll never understand it!' she added with a friendly, supportive grin.

Once we were checked in Paul insisted on seeing us to our room, but to my surprise after he picked up my weekend bag he headed out of the main door, and not up the staircase as I had expected. Flashing a confused glance at Nicholas I saw him suppressing a smile as he placed a hand on my lower back and guided me after Paul down the front steps in the direction of the lake. 'We're not staying in the main building,' Nicholas commented mysteriously.

Following a path through the beautiful gardens I realised that we were in fact headed to an elegant stone house sat at the water's edge. Leaning down close to my ear Nicholas finally filled me in, 'This is the Lake House, it has eight rooms, all with lake views.'

Wow. The surprises just kept coming, didn't they! 'I've just booked one room for this stay, but during our wedding weekend I thought that we could have the rooms on the top floor for just us, and that the rooms on the lower floor could be used for your parents, sister, and her nurse. That way Jo can have privacy if she needs it.'

As I continued to stare at the gently lapping water of the lake behind this stunning house I felt a trembling start in my lower lip and I had to work really hard not to burst into tears. *Again.* I was so overwhelmed by all the thought Nicholas had put into this that I hardly knew what to say, or how to express my immense happiness and gratitude. I hardly believed that all this had been arranged by a man who less than a year and a half ago had declared that he wasn't sure he was capable of sustaining a real relationship. Shaking my head at the enormous changes that I'd witnessed in Nicholas Jackson during our time together, I licked my lips and drew in a deep, fortifying breath that helped keep my tears at bay before I turned to him.

'You are an amazing man,' I whispered. My words were such an understatement for the gratitude I felt, but I was so lost for what else to say, so instead I slipped my arms around his neck and pulled his face down to mine for a kiss that might better express how much I appreciated his incredible gestures. Running my tongue along the seam of his lips, he immediately granted me access with a low growl before our tongues began twirling and rubbing across each other, exploring and arousing and quickly making things rather heated.

A polite cough behind us had me pulling away from Nicholas with an embarrassed flush as I realised that the hotel manager was still behind us and patiently waiting. *Oops.* Cringing I screwed up my face, knowing that I now had to turn around and face the man who had just witnessed me practically humping Nicholas on the pathway, and my blush deepened even further. My step away was hindered by Nicholas, as he kept a firm hold on my forearm and flashed me a warning glance that I didn't understand at all. It wasn't until I allowed him to guide me in front of him that I realised what his earlier expression had been about – he had a monster hard-on and needed me to stay in front of him to cover it.

Trying not to grin at his predicament I obediently placed myself before him and smiled apologetically to Paul, who I noticed had a fairly decent colour to his own cheeks as well. 'I'll show you in and leave you to … er … *unpack*,' he stuttered, sounding like he knew exactly what we would be up to the second the bedroom door closed behind him – and it certainly wouldn't involve any suitcases.

Once we were in and Paul had made a speedy exit I took a second to look around the room. Just like the setting and main building, the room was beautiful; a huge bed dominated the space, made up with soft cream linens and complete with a high-backed leather headrest. At the foot of the bed was an elegant roll top bath and spanning the opposite wall were floor to ceiling windows, revealing a private balcony and breath-taking views over the lake.

'Wow … Nicholas, this is just …' My words dried in my throat as I turned and saw a familiar look of lust burning in Nicholas' eyes as he stalked towards me. *Oh God*. Lust flooded my body as just one brief look at his expression had my knees weak and my heart rocketing in my chest. 'I believe I promised payback for your earlier teasing,' he murmured as my gaze fixed on his hands where he had begun slowly undoing his shirt. His words caused my gaze to flash to his and from just a second of his heated gaze I felt a low, heavy pulse start between my legs. I'd thought that with all the excitement of the hotel tour and talking to Paul that Nicholas might have forgotten his earlier words, but the dark, desire-filled look on his face left no doubt that he fully intended to fulfil his promise to 'make me beg.' I could hardly wait.

Licking my parched lips I found myself frozen to the

spot and holding my breath as he completed his journey across the room and arrived at my side. His eyes were heavy lidded and the small smile that tweaked the corner of his lips told me that he enjoyed teasing me just as much as I enjoyed the thrill it gave me when he was in control like this.

'I'm going to strip you now, Becky,' he informed me in a low voice as his hot breath fanned across my neck and sent tingles cascading along my skin. 'Then I'm going to lick you and arouse you until you can barely see straight, but I won't let you come until I'm ready. You'll be begging me, baby.' A groan escaped me, frustration mixed with arousal, because from experience I knew that delayed gratification was a game that Nicholas was very, *very* good at. Somehow his immense reserves of self-control meant that he could still look cool, calm, and collected after tormenting me for hours until I was sobbing and begging for release.

'Do you know what I'll do then, Becky?' he asked, his fingers making short work of the buttons down the front of my blouse. Leaning in to nip at my earlobe I gasped, and then felt his tongue soothe the small sting as I let out another soft moan of arousal.

I was fairly sure I knew what he had planned for me – hours of arousing torture with no release – so I hazarded a guess, 'You'll start all over again?' I murmured, my voice weak and thin already, and we'd barely even started. A warm chuckle broke across my collar bone as Nicholas slipped my blouse to the ground and trailed his fingers down my arms until I shivered from the unbearable desire building up in me. 'No, Becky, we have a meeting with James later so unfortunately we're a bit pushed for time.' Pausing, he licked a warm, moist path up my neck until I was dizzy and clinging to his shoulders for support. 'My intentions are simple, when you have begged me loud and long enough, I'm going to fuck you so hard that you'll scream my name until you're hoarse.'

'*Oh God.*' I *already* sounded hoarse, and that was just from him speaking to me. Nicholas didn't use dirty talk that often, although when he did I rather liked it. His filthy words today were almost enough to make me come on the spot – my stomach muscles were already clenching, my channel felt wet and frustratingly empty, and my clitoris was buzzing as if it had been electrified.

To an outsider, Nicholas' hunched shoulders and intense stare would probably make it appear that he was set on outright domination and tortuous teasing, but as he unclipped my bra and stepped around to look at my breasts I watched as his face softened and his lips parted in appreciation. 'Perfect,' he murmured, a small smile tweaking his lips and giving away his charade. Lifting a hand Nicholas slowly rubbed the pad of his thumb across one nipple and the next, causing them both to harden and ache for more of his delicious touch as I arched forwards shamelessly.

No matter how desperate I might have been earlier, his careful attentions made me relax, and over the next ten minutes as he stripped and pleasured me, I loosened and calmed as my body became attuned to his slower, more loving rhythm. When my wobbly legs could no longer support my weight, Nicholas scooped me up and carried me to the bed, laying me in the centre of the soft quilt and cushions before beginning his teasing kisses again. My lips curved into a broad smile as I watched the top of his head slowly making its way across my body, dropping licks and nips over my heated skin. Nicholas was clearly set on taking his time today and nothing I could say or do would change his mind – not that I minded in the least.

True to his earlier threat, Nicholas brought me to the edge of ecstasy so many times that I lost count as I writhed below his patient, skilful lips as he covered my body with heated touches until I was almost delirious. Finally, when I

44

really could take no more, I did exactly what he told me I would – I began to beg.

'Please, Nicholas ... *please*.' I heard, and felt, a hot satisfied chuckle break across my belly from his perfect lips, but he ignored my request and continued on his last trail until his mouth was hovering above my clit, his tongue darting occasional hot swipes across my quivering flesh until I was frantic below him. 'Please! Nicholas, I'm begging you!'

'Again. Louder. Say my name louder,' he urged me as he shifted himself above my body and began to suck hard on one of my painfully erect nipples.

'Nicholas!' I yelped, louder and definitely in a tone that was saturated with needy desperation.

'I love it when you shout my name, baby,' he murmured. If that really were true, then seconds later I must have made him *really* happy, because I positively screeched his name as Nicholas nudged the head of his cock against my entrance and then filled me with one long, hard thrust.

'Fuck! *Fuck!*' I wasn't prone to much swearing, but I was so lost to the moment that I honestly couldn't help myself this time.

'Eyes, Rebecca, let me see them, baby,' he ordered softly, as he thrust into me again, hitting my G-spot with such precision I saw stars. I was panting hard, barely lucid, and sweating profusely, but I managed to follow his request and give Nicholas the eye contact that he constantly craved. The blue pools that met my eyes were so filled with desire that his pupils seemed huge, but the joy in his expression when our gazes collided was enough to make me fall in love with him all over again.

Not breaking the treasured eye contact he began a hard, rocking motion against me, grinding himself against my clit before pulling his cock almost all the way out of my body, then thrusting in hard and fast and making me jerk

45

and writhe from the pleasure.

My hands slid down his sweat-slicked back and found the taut deliciousness of his bum, where I gripped the firm muscle and began to tug him against me on each of his downward thrusts. I could feel my climax rearing up on me with every clash of his hips against mine and I desperately tried to hold it off to extend this amazing experience.

With a slight shift of his hips Nicholas used his grip on my hip to pull my thighs open even further, causing his next thrust to be so deep that I was surprised it didn't hurt. It did quite the opposite, in fact, almost triggering an instantaneous climax as I clawed at his arse, no doubt leaving my mark there, and then struggled to speak. 'Oh God … Nicholas … I'm not going to last,' I warned him in a gurgled voice.

His forehead was slick with sweat, his hair matted and damp, but his eyes were still fixed to mine as Nicholas nodded his understanding, 'Me either. Come for me, my beautiful girl, take me over the edge with you,' he panted, dropping his head and capturing my mouth as his talented hips continued their relentless rhythm. His words, combined with his near perfect thrusts against my G-spot, were all it took to send me spiralling into a climax so strong that it verged on painful as my muscles repeatedly clamped around him almost viciously. An animalistic roar left his throat as Nicholas pulled out jerkily, before bucking his hips back inside me one last time and flooding my quivering channel with his hot release before collapsing on top of me.

Holy fuck. That had been truly phenomenal. As we both lay there panting and recovering my eyes flicked lazily around the room. I had no idea if this was the bed we would be staying in on our wedding night, but one thing was for sure – it would take a hell of a performance to improve upon the sensational sex we'd just shared.

FOUR – STELLA

'So, when you mentioned that Nicholas and Rebecca were away this weekend checking out a possible wedding venue, it made me think that I should start some enquiries about ideas for her hen do. I've left it a bit late actually,' I added nervously as I scrolled through my phone to find the list of possible restaurants and bars that I'd made to check out today.

'Remind me again why I have to help you with this?' Nathan enquired in a low tone as he fingered the grimy seat of the Underground train with an amusing look of distaste on his face. To my surprise I then watched as he pulled a small bottle of antiseptic hand gel from his pocket and proceeded to meticulously clean his fingers before gingerly placing them on his thighs. *Clean freak.* My eyebrows were almost bursting from my forehead at that action. Nathaniel Jackson was still an enigma to me in so many ways. He was also wearing his trademark suit even though it was Sunday, so he looked even more out of place amongst the casual weekend travellers. As odd as they were, I had to admit that I quite liked his quirks, so I merely shook my head and supressed the smile that wanted to break on my lips.

It had taken lots of persuasion over the last few months, but miraculously, even with his loathing of public transport, not to mention his clean hands fetish, I now had Nathan using public transport on quite a regular basis. Mr 'I only like to travel in my car' even knew how to work the ticket machines now. Wonders would never cease.

'Because you said you wanted to help, and because we're combining it with lunch and a few drinks,' I reminded him patiently. 'The idea for the hen do is that we'll be out for most of the day, possibly having afternoon tea somewhere at about two-ish to start the day, and then drinks and dancing. Maybe a meal, but that will depend on if we do afternoon tea or not. So I need to find a good bar, restaurant, and club that might be suitable, I thought we could visit a few of the contenders today and see what we think.'

Rolling his eyes with a small smile Nathan pretended to be hard done by, but I could tell that he was actually quite excited by the prospect of an afternoon spent bar hopping. Standing from his seat as the train pulled into Covent Garden station he flashed a wink at me and then held out his newly cleaned hand. Accepting his palm I smiled happily as his warmth re-invigorated me and we departed the train and made our way down the platform. The familiar whoosh and clanking of the train leaving the station sent a rush of air around my ankles and I leaned into Nathan a little as the train sped up. As we reached the end of the platform I groaned and pulled to a brief stop. Damn it. I'd forgotten the lack of escalators at this station and seeing as I don't do lifts because of my mild claustrophobia we would now have the joyous task of taking the stairs. All one hundred and ninety-three of them. My face twisted into a grimace.

Beginning my plod up the spiral staircase I quickly found myself puffing and slowing down much quicker than usual. Fitness guru Nathan wasn't struggling at all though – in fact he sped off at such a rate that I quickly fell behind and cursed his rapidly disappearing bum. Another twenty steps and I was definitely starting to sweat. What was wrong with me? It wasn't like I was particularly lazy or anything. This staircase just seemed endless today. Just when I started to wonder if there really was a top to the bloody thing I finally emerged into the sunlight to see Nathan leaning on a pillar, cool as a cucumber with his suit completely unruffled and a smirk on his handsome face.

'Looking good, Stella,' he quipped, causing me to narrow my eyes at him. No doubt I was red and sweaty, but my time with Nathan had obviously had some effect on him and his manners, because instead of just openly laughing at me he just smirked quietly to himself and found us a seat on a bench so I could recover. I had no idea what had caused my sudden bout of unfitness, but thankfully after just a few minutes I was feeling much better. My throat felt a bit sore, but I probably just needed a drink so we set off meandering amongst the cafés and side streets of Covent Garden.

Feeling Nathan's hand slip into mine and link our fingers made me grin so broadly that my lips hurt. He was regularly the one to initiate contact like this these days, and I loved it. I felt a little smug really, because life with Nathan was pretty amazing at the moment. Since the dreadful day just over a year ago where Nathan's father had reappeared and thrown both Nathan and his brother's lives into chaos we'd all come a long, long way. Nathan's father thankfully hadn't been seen or heard from since, Nicholas and Rebecca were deep in plans for their upcoming wedding, and the relationship between myself and Nathan was getting stronger every day. In fact, Nathan had developed in ways I'd never imagined possible; he was open, caring, protective, and making a genuine effort to be a 'regular' boyfriend for the first time in his life. He was doing a pretty good job of it too.

Two hours later we were sat in a very funky little bar and restaurant just off the main drag of Covent Garden piazza after a superb meal and some very colourful cocktails. Well, *I'd* been on the cocktails, Nathan had stuck to bottled beer. 'Wow … this place is amazing. So we'll definitely come here on the hen-do for drinks then, if not a meal,' I said cheerfully, as I gave my full belly an appreciative pat. 'Now I just need somewhere for later in the evening. Rebecca likes dancing, she said she's not very good at it but she enjoys it every now and then. I don't think she's too fussy about the type of music as long as it has a good beat.' I personally hated dancing – well, my uncoordinated feet did anyway, but I'd be more than happy to humiliate myself on the dance floor if the occasion was my best friend's hen-do.

'Any suggestions?' I asked Nathan, hoping he'd be sensible enough not to suggest Club Twist. It might be his standard club of choice, but it wouldn't exactly be the ideal venue for Rebecca's hen do. Seeing how long it had taken to convince her that my relationship with Nathan wasn't the sordid coupling that she had first imagined, she'd no doubt *hate* it in there. All the PVC, leather, and naked flesh would totally freak her out, and I couldn't help but grin as I imagined her reaction if she ever did venture in there. I didn't mind it so much, and now that it was common knowledge on the circuit that I was with Nathan he occasionally suggested a visit every now and then. No one would dare come near me when we did venture in, that was for sure, now word of Nathan's possessiveness over his sub had spread – the guys there always gave me a very wide berth.

Considering my question for a few moments Nathan raised a hand and rubbed at his chin. His action immediately drew my gaze to his jaw. It was lightly stubbled today because he'd skipped his shave in favour of accompanying me. *Hmm.* I loved the way he sometimes used his stubble to tease me by rubbing it across my skin. As I sat there watching him ponder I had the most ridiculous urge to lean over and run my tongue up his jaw bone just to feel how prickly it would be, but thankfully I was distracted from public embarrassment as Nathan chose that exact second to click his fingers as an idea struck him. 'Got it. I think I might actually know the perfect place. There's a very sought after club behind Oxford Street called Project that I happen to have connections with. Have you heard of it?'

Had I heard of it? The question should really be who *hadn't* heard of it. My eyebrows rose as I turned to him in surprise. Project was a very swanky, *very* popular destination amongst London's rich and famous – it was constantly featuring in the entertainment pages of newspapers and magazines and infamous for its strict member's only policy. 'You can get us into Project?' I asked in a slightly disbelieving tone.

Looking rather smug Nathan took my hand again and rubbed his thumb across the knuckles as I stifled a sudden yawn. Gosh, this afternoon had been very successful, but clearly from my exhaustion, organising a hen do was tiring work. 'I can, yes. My company did the refurbishments, so I know the owner.' Wow. Drinks at a fantastic cocktail bar followed by a night of dancing at Project? As far as planning an awesome hen-do went that surely had to be a winner on all fronts. Plus there was the idea of starting the day off with an early afternoon tea somewhere that I was also toying with, so surely I couldn't really go wrong now.

'Now that's sorted let's get one final drink in here and then head home.' Nathan said, signalling the waiter for a refill of his beer and my Cosmopolitan. Crikey, with this much afternoon drinking it was no wonder I was suddenly feeling a bit warm and sleepy. As I tried to fight off another yawn Nathan tapped something out on his phone and then checked his watch with a small nod. 'Tired?' he asked with a frown, apparently having seen my attempt at a hidden yawn despite being on his phone.

Nodding, I smiled back, 'A little. Two cocktails with lunch will do that though.' I joked as the waiter arrived with my third drink on a tray, much to my delight.

The waiter left us in peace and over the next few minutes I gradually felt Nathan begin to tense up beside me. Taking a sip of my drink I turned to him and saw him observing me over the rim of his bottle with narrowed eyes. Shifting slightly on his seat at being caught he rolled off his shoulders and proceeded to fiddle with a beer mat on the table. Talk about tell-tale signs of discomfort! Nathan was usually so calm and poised that with him shifting and fiddling constantly like this it was screamingly obvious that something was on his mind.

'What's up?' I asked, reconnecting our hand hold and finding his fingers stiff within my grasp, which instantly made me feel nervy.

'Nothing,' he murmured, still avoiding eye contact and still barely returning my grip, which only added to my anxiousness. Giving his hand a firm squeeze until it surely must have been verging on painful I finally got a reaction when Nathan huffed out a breath and looked up at me. 'OK, OK ...' Pulling in a deep breath through his nose Nathan blinked several times as he stared at me, his heavy lidded gaze travelling all around my face until it settled on my eyes again.

'I'm a little uncomfortable with the idea of you going out clubbing with a group of girls,' he suddenly confessed, his face an almost impassive mask that was impossible to read. Was he being serious? I really had no idea, so frowning I tilted my head and said the first thing that sprung to my mind.

'Don't you trust me?'

This time Nathan's exhalation wasn't smooth or controlled. Instead he huffed out a breath, puffing his cheeks as he did so, and lowering his brows into a frown that matched my own. 'I trust *you,* Stella. I just don't trust all the pricks who will be trying it on with you all fucking night.' His growing agitation was clear, but I wasn't really sure how to deal with it because what he was saying was just ridiculous.

'You're not my keeper, Nathan. As it is I hardly ever go out without you. Besides, even if every man in the club tried it on with me they wouldn't have any luck because it's you that I'm committed to,' I told him simply, meaning every single word. He might have his oddities, but Nathan was it for me. No man had ever made me feel the way he did, and the fact they we were a perfect match in the bedroom too just added to our amazing compatibility. I couldn't believe he would doubt me like this.

I watched as Nathan remained in his dark place, his frown deepening as his mind obviously dwelled on unrealistic images, no doubt containing me surrounded by packs of rabid men with their hands all over my body. 'If you were my sub I'd simply tell you not to go,' he muttered petulantly, but his words shocked me into almost dropping my drink.

A horrible chill descended upon me, instantly cooling the hot flush that I'd been experiencing earlier. 'Is that what you want?' I asked in a ghost of a whisper, 'To order me around? To go back to how your life used to be?' My trembling hand managed to place my drink down before gripping the table to steady myself. He'd made such progress lately, surely he couldn't want it to go back to the days of non-emotional sexual encounters where I was simply his sub and nothing more?

Blinking several times Nathan seemed to wake from whatever trance he was in, cocked his head, and studied me intently before shocking me completely by breaking out into a wide smile that complete lit up his lovely face. 'What? No, of course not.' His smile turned into a full, mega-watt Nathan grin, one that not many people beyond me ever got to see, 'It would just make dealing you and your stubborn, difficult ways easier sometimes, that's all.' He smirked as he took another sip of his beer and placed the empty bottle on the table.

He was kidding with me – or at least I thought he was – but the sudden change in his demeanour was still concerning me. 'Wanting to go to my friend's hen do makes me difficult and stubborn?' I asked with a disbelieving laugh, hoping that my earlier concerns had just been misplaced.

Raising his eyebrows he shook his head, but I could tell from the twinkle in his eye that Nathan was definitely teasing me, which made my shoulders relax. 'No, but wanting to go to your friend's hen do in a club full of randy arseholes and no doubt dance and shake your body in front of them? *That* makes you difficult and stubborn to deal with,' he concluded with a firm nod.

Rolling my eyes at him I shook my head and couldn't help but giggle. As I sipped on my cocktail I watched as Nathan chewed on the inside of his lower lip and even though he was playing around with me I suspected that my night out with the girls really was causing him concern, which on the one hand was rather sweet, but on the other was also way too possessive and probably needed to be addressed.

On the table Nathan's phone chimed with an incoming message which broke me from my pondering and halted any thoughts I'd been having about continuing the conversation. Glancing at his phone he pocketed it and then spoke, 'Drink up, our car has arrived.' My forehead creased at his words. Car? We'd come by train, so I looked up at him in confusion hoping for an explanation.

Shrugging, he gazed at me intently, his big blues immediately sucking me into his spell. 'You said you were tired, so I sent a quick text and requested a company car pick us up,' Nathan explained, lifting his chin in the direction of the curb outside the bar where a very long, sleek black Mercedes was idling on some double yellow lines. After my initial shock died away I grinned at Nathan and once he had dumped some cash on the table I allowed him to help me to my feet.

Perhaps I'm a touch cynical, but part of me suspected that this incredibly sweet gesture by Nathan was actually his cunning way of avoiding public transport, but for once I decided not to question his actions – after all, I *was* feeling tired and this certainly beat the walk back to the crowded station. Not to mention the masses of steps back down to the platform …

With his hand possessively on the base of my spine Nathan led me from the bar and across the pavement to the waiting car. As soon as we approached it an impeccably dressed driver, complete with peaked cap, got out and nodded his greeting to Nathan. 'Good afternoon, Mr Jackson.'

Replying with a swift, 'Hello, Ryan,' and a handshake, Nathan allowed him to open the back door for me with a polite smile and a dip of his head. Sliding into the cool interior of the car I looked around in appreciation. This had to be the fanciest car I'd ever been in. It was complete with two sets of seats facing each other and a small side table that surely must have contained a mini bar. Wow. Breathing in I got a nose full of the luxurious smell of leather from the seats mixed with a faint hint of Nathan's lovely aftershave and quickly decided that as a treat I rather likèd this car.

'How come I've never been in one of your company cars before?' I murmured, turning to Nathan as he slid in beside me, somehow appearing graceful in even the simplest of movements. The corners of his mouth twitched into a near-smile as he shrugged.

'This isn't any old company car.' Nathan said smugly, flicking me with a smirk. 'It's a Mercedes Pullman limousine,' he informed me, not that that really meant a great deal to me. 'It's only used for special events, but it was the only car available today. And as for why you've never been in here before?' he shrugged, 'You don't seem interested when I try and flaunt my wealth so I gave up trying to impress you with money a long time ago.' Oh. Well that was true – Nathan's money was a nice extra I suppose, but his cash certainly wasn't the reason I was with him. 'Plus you seem to have some bloody obsession with public transport,' he muttered with a baffled shake of his head looking genuinely mystified.

'After that lunch I doubt we'll need a proper dinner tonight, but we'll stop off and grab some snacks just in case we get hungry again.' Leaning forward he spoke to the driver, 'Home please, Ryan, but could you stop off on the way at River Deli and get us two of their sandwich tasting plates? I have some calls to make, so no interruptions please,' Nathan said, leaning back and pressing a button that raised the privacy glass and effectively closed us in our own little bubble.

Leaning forwards I touched his arm gingerly, well aware that I was about to bring up one of his sore points again. 'Actually, Nathan, can we stop in at my place on the way too? I need to grab some clothes for work tomorrow,' I murmured softly, before sitting back and bracing myself for the anticipated rant.

Watching his body tense Nathan's expression darkened as he narrowed his eyes and made a growling noise in the back of his throat, 'If you lived with me you wouldn't need to keep bringing a bloody overnight bag with you,' he mumbled petulantly, before taking several deep breaths and muttering a countdown from five to zero under his breath. Staying silent I patiently let him do his counting thing. This was a foible of his that I was well used to now. Initially when I'd caught him counting under his breath I'd thought it was my imagination, but when we had started to spend more time together I had noticed the habit a lot more frequently. A few months ago I'd finally plucked up the courage to ask him about it, and Nathan had begrudgingly informed me that he used the countdowns in combination with deep breaths to calm himself when he was feeling particularly highly strung, stressed, or angry.

My forehead creased as an unpleasant thought suddenly came to my mind. 'Did you do your countdowns before you met me?' My voice sounded small in the quiet interior of the car, but truthfully I was a little concerned what answer I might get. Given how frequently he did them whilst I was around I couldn't help but think that perhaps my presence in his life had disrupted his usual order.

'Yes, why?' he asked cautiously, turning to me.

Chewing on my lower lip I shrugged slightly, suddenly feeling self-conscious. 'I was just wondering if I stress you out,' I murmured, feeling stupidly needy as I spoke.

Turning to me Nathan's blue gaze stuck on mine intently and I watched enthralled as he blinked several times, 'You do stress me out,' he agreed in a low tone. 'And before you ask, yes, I do use my countdowns more often since I met you.' Oh God, he'd just confirmed my fears – I was bad for him. My stomach plummeted as a sickening sensation settled in my chest, but his gaze was holding me captive and no matter how much I wanted to drop my eyes, I found that I couldn't.

It felt like we stared at each other in silence for at least ten minutes, but in reality it was probably just a few seconds. The movement of his upper lip tweaking caught my eye and I glanced at his mouth to see it flickering in that way that meant he was supressing a smile. 'Don't panic, baby. I'm winding you up. Yes, I stress out over you, but not *because* of you. I worry on a daily basis about your safety, your happiness, and your health, but I wouldn't have it any other way.' Clearing his throat Nathan suddenly looked embarrassed, not an expression I'd seen from him very often. 'You've enlightened my life, Stella. Given me purpose. I'll take all the stress in the world if it means I get to keep you by my side.' Crikey. I was utterly gobsmacked. What a declaration. He might not have ever said the 'L' word to me out loud, but if that wasn't a statement of love I didn't know what was. Licking my lips I watched as Nathan raised a hand and scratched self-consciously at the back of his neck.

His sudden outpouring of emotion was so uncharacteristic that I barely knew how to respond. Not wanting to ruin the moment by attempting to compete somehow, or respond by listing everything I loved about him, I simply leant forwards in my seat and placed my lips softly against his. 'I love you, Nathan,' I murmured against his lips, causing a contented humming noise to rise up his throat as his hand found my hair and slipped through the long strands, pulling me closer to his exploring tongue.

Heat shot through me from his contact, but then before we'd barely even got started Nathan broke the kiss and leant his forehead on mine, still looking a little sheepish and apparently embarrassed by his outpouring, so I tried to lighten the mood. 'In addition to worrying you, I'm pretty sure I also piss you off sometimes,' I murmured through a smile as I leant back in my seat.

Raising an eyebrow Nathan pressed a button to lower the partition. 'Yes,' he agreed sagely, 'sometimes you do.' Then turning to speak to Ryan Nathan asked him to bypass my house after getting the sandwiches before he sat back in his seat. 'Like your stubbornness about moving in with me,' he stated in a mock accusatory tone as he raised the privacy screen and once again isolated us in our own little bubble.

'I explained my reasons,' I murmured, but then thinking that my words might sound like a threat about his apartment I quickly added, 'I'm sure I'll get used to your place in time.' I wasn't sure of that at all – it had already been over a year and I still disliked it, and to be honest I think I'll always associate it with his previous lifestyle, but if it calmed the moment for now then I was happy to tell a small untruth.

Sensing the tension leave his frame as Nathan sat back I intrinsically found myself relaxing too. Puffing out the last of my anxiousness I lowered my gaze to fiddle with the seatbelt as I realised that I hadn't belted myself in. I wasn't focussing on Nathan, but paused in my task when he spoke again, this time in a far lower tone that echoed around the interior of the car and once again made the air seem thick, but this time with sexual tension.

'Don't bother with the belt, Stella.' Flicking my eyes up I watched with rapt attention as Nathan slid across the car so he was sat on the bench seat opposite me. Running a hand down his suit he smoothed the flawless material before raising his dark eyes to mine, spreading his legs and adjusting himself so that his erection visibly tented his trousers. My throat suddenly felt as parched as the Sahara desert. Blimey, where had that come from? Had pissing him off caused *that* reaction? Because that was certainly an impressive bulge I could spy – not to mention the dark, lusty expression on his face which made the overall look quite a tempting package.

'Come here.' Two words and a heated gaze was all it took to get me completely fired up. Just those few syllables uttered in his low, domineering tone had my heart racing, cheeks flushing, and my knickers soaked – the way my body reacted so instantaneously to this man would never cease to amaze me. Letting out a slow breath I tried to calm my hammering heart and rationally consider the sensibility of his intentions.

'Here?' I whispered, simultaneously shocked and hugely aroused by the idea of doing it in Nathan's company car. Still, surely it was only normal to be shocked when someone proposes car sex? 'But ... but I thought you said you had calls to make?' I stuttered stupidly. Watching my reaction I saw Nathan's face alter as a frustrated expression clouded his eyes, making his lustful look fall away as he let out a sigh. 'I do,' he said, pulling out his phone and dialling a number without so much as giving me another glance.

Disappointment crashed over me as I slipped back in my seat and cursed myself. What the hell was I thinking distracting him? I should have kept my stupid mouth shut and just let him continue with his illicit sexual plans. Digging my fingernails into my palms I tried to distract my body from its huge excitement but it was no good, my groin hummed with unspent arousal and as I inwardly chastised myself I tried to get comfortable by parting my legs to ease the pressure of the throbbing.

In my bag my phone began to ring and I huffed out a grumbly breath of irritation. In my highly strung state I didn't particularly feel like talking to anyone, but seeing as Nathan was making calls I may as well answer it – and on the positive side at least it might distract me. Digging around in my bag I retrieved my phone and pulled it out only to see Nathan's number flashing on screen. Looking across to him in confusion I was met with a completely blank expression; he merely raised his eyebrows and jerked his chin towards my phone to indicate I should answer it.

Confused but still hugely turned on I didn't even bother to argue the stupidity of the situation. Instead I pressed the accept button and lifted my phone to my ear whilst looking him directly in the eyes. 'I said, come over here, Stella,' he stated darkly, his eyes flashing with the challenge I had accidentally presented. 'Don't make me ask you again.' Nathan clicked off his phone with a flick of his wrist, slipped it back in his jacket pocket, and sat back expectantly with his hands resting on his spread thighs, all the while burning holes in me with his heated stare.

The car suddenly felt very warm. Really, *really* frigging warm, and I instinctively ran a finger around the collar of my shirt to loosen it even though it wasn't particularly tight. Gulping in some air I swallowed, sat up straighter, and attempted to mimic some of his calm disposition with a flippant comment – 'No seat belts, Mr Jackson, that's a little dangerous isn't it?' – but my pretend composure was ruined when I fumbled my bag and ended up dropping my phone on the floor of the car. Bending to pick it up with a curse I suddenly found myself being gripped around the waist and hoisted up so I was splayed facedown across Nathan's lap where he landed two short, hard spanks on my upturned bottom. A yelp of surprise escaped me, both from my sudden position and the slight sting in my bum, but there was no time for more thoughts or words because he then manhandled me upright so I was sat astride his lap facing him with my mouth just inches from his. 'Watch that sarcasm, Miss Marsden,' he murmured, his blue eyes twinkling with obvious excitement. Then, with a growling sound emanating low in his throat, Nathan's lips found mine before proceeding to almost kiss the life out of me.

Oh God, as he kissed me his stubble was doing its thing again, scratching against my soft chin and turning me on beyond all belief. A few moments later Nathan lifted his mouth and left me feeling dazed, overheated, and decidedly needy. Looking down at my undoubtedly flushed face he gave me one of his trademark sexy, sly smiles while somehow still managing to look calm and sure of himself. 'Concerned about not being locked in, are you? It's just as well I went shopping a few weeks ago then. I got something especially for you,' he added cryptically, shifting me off his lap and then opening a small compartment in the middle of the seat.

Taking a second to collect myself I smoothed my hair and made a vague attempt to see the contents of the compartment, but was in too much of an aroused and fidgety state to do so subtly, and failed when Nathan blocked my view with a low chuckle. Drawing out the suspense he paused, his hand hovering above the small cupboard, as he turned to me with a wicked glimmer in his

61

blue eyes. Closing the lid without removing anything from inside, he lowered his hand to his flawless suit and slowly popped the button open before leaning forwards and slipping off his jacket. My gaze was locked on his every move. Even with his shirt still on his toned chest was obvious as it caused the material to stretch across the flat planes of his pecs. Calmly folding up the expensive material Nathan placed in on the opposite seat and then began to unbutton and roll up his shirt sleeves into neatly folded chunks just below his elbows.

'Kneel on the seat facing the headrest,' he suddenly instructed me briskly while he continued to arrange his left sleeve to his perfect satisfaction.

I was about to argue, but he obviously saw my hesitation and shook his head slowly, his eyes darkening to a dangerous blue-black hue that silenced me immediately. Swallowing loudly I stared at him in rapt fascination as I recognised the look growing on his face as a sign of his Dominant self making an appearance. 'Usually I like your challenges, you know that, Stella, but we don't have time today to play your *"I'll do it in the end, but I'll argue first"* games. Now, do as I say.'

He was right, I would no doubt do it in the end, so feeling deservedly chastised I swallowed hard as I felt my submissive side pushing to the surface, ridiculously excited by the prospect of it getting an airing. Reacting to his authoritative tone I lowered my gaze and meekly mumbled a reply of 'Yes, Sir,' before turning myself and positioning my body as instructed. I was now knelt on the rear seat holding the headrest and facing out the back window as we trundled through London past busy throngs of unaware commuters. I heard the sound of Nathan opening the compartment again followed by some unidentifiable rustling, before he came to sit next to me and ran a soft finger down my cheek that had me leaning into his touch and closing my eyes in pleasure.

'So perfect in your submission,' he murmured appreciatively. Reaching up Nathan removed one of my hands from the seat and secured a brown leather cuff around the wrist before deftly reaching across and closing an identical cuff around the other arm. Gasping I looked at my wrists and saw that the leather cuffs were actually a pair of handcuffs. The two ends were attached with a silver chain which was also coincidentally wrapped around the car headrest, effectively holding me in place. 'Nice, aren't they?' Nathan murmured, idly stroking his fingers around the soft leather and occasionally brushing over my fluttering pulse point. 'They're softer than the handcuffs I have at home, more sensuous. Do they feel OK? You're comfortable?'

Since we'd been making a proper go at a relationship Nathan had reduced the kink factor quite a bit, but our relationship was still fiery in bed and I often called him 'Sir' in the bedroom just because it felt right to me, but in general we used toys and accessories a lot less. Looking at my bound wrists I felt a thrill run through me and realised now just how much I'd missed it. Licking my dry lips I tried to answer him, but no words came out. God I was so turned on that I literally couldn't speak, so instead I nodded.

At my nod Nathan flicked my skirt up onto my back and landed a hard stinging slap to my bottom which had me yelping loudly and digging my nails into the headrest. 'You know my rule on nodding, Stella,' he reminded me firmly. Rubbing my bottom where he'd spanked me I found myself pushing it back into his palm, silently begging for more. I heard a soft contented sigh slip from his lips. 'You look beautiful like this, Stella, wrapped in leather and begging for my touch, but you know that I'm going to need you to answer me verbally.'

In my aroused state I'd completely forgotten his dislike of nodding. Clearing my throat I tried again, desperate not to disappoint him. 'Yes ... yes, Sir, I'm green. I'm good.' Green, wow, I hadn't used the safe word colours for ages. We'd used them when we'd first got together as Dominant and submissive – green meaning happy and safe, yellow indicating a slight discomfort and need to discuss what was happening, and red meaning stop immediately, but they hadn't passed my lips for months. Obviously Nathan's sudden return to his Dominant ways had flicked me right back into my submissive zone and from the feel of the copious dampness between my thighs I was clearly loving every second of it.

'Green?' Nathan repeated softly, apparently thinking the same as me about how our current situation had temporally reverted us right back to the Dom/sub balance from the start of our relationship. Turning my head I looked him directly in the eyes, the flickering lust there no doubt reflecting my own, 'Yes, Sir,' I panted, knowing how much my use of his title would arouse him further .

Rubbing his hand repeatedly over my heated bottom until I moaned wantonly Nathan then chuckled. 'Well, Stella, I have to say the afternoon is certainly looking up,' he murmured before leaning across to tangle one hand in my hair and tug my mouth hard into his lips for a searing kiss. As his lips continued to shake my senses and send my arousal spiralling higher I clung to the head rest and allowed Nathan to do his thing as the hand on my bottom slipped further under my skirt and worked my knickers down until they fell around my knees.

Detaching his lips from mine with a growl Nathan swiftly moved himself onto the floor of the limousine, freed his erection from his trousers, and after a cursory stroke to ensure I was wet enough he rammed inside me in one hard thrust that threw me forwards into the seat. Greedily I quickly righted myself and pushed back against him to increase our contact by forcing him deeper within me, groaning and gyrating against him, which just seemed to further inflame him as he reached around and found my clit with his fingers. Nathan wasn't playing soft and gentle today, his movements were hard, fast, and demanding which suited me just fine and for every thrust he gave me, I pressed back into him to ensure it was as deep as he could possibly go. With each stroke Nathan pulled himself out to the tip and then rammed back in to the hilt, hitting my G-spot and flicking my clit with his thumb as he continued to grunt and groan like a wild animal. Before long I felt the bursting pleasure of an orgasm break over me as I cried out sharply in pleasure and bit down on Nathan's forearm to try and stifle my screams. Briefly my thoughts flew to the driver upfront as I tried to muffle my noises, but then Nathan let out an animalistic roar as he came that was so loud I almost laughed. If the driver hadn't heard me, there was certainly a large chance he'd heard that. Oh well, hopefully the privacy divider was soundproof – failing that I could only hope the driver was discreet.

Collapsing his head into my back and panting fiercely, Nathan's heated breath warmed me through my T-shirt, then after placing a kiss on the back on my neck he carefully allowed his softening cock to slip from me. Using a handkerchief to gently clean me he then undid the handcuffs, turned me in my seat, and took a minute to plug me into the seat belt. 'Belted in … safety first,' he murmured with a dirty smirk, dropping a kiss on the side of my mouth before sitting himself beside me and fastening his own seat belt, taking my hand in his.

Still panting, I leant my head back and closed my eyes contentedly whilst a large, satisfied grin spread across my face. Nathan's thumb was rubbing soothing circles on the back of my hand and soon the tiredness from my earlier drinks, not to mention the exhausting orgasm, began to overwhelm me and as the car rocked and swayed its way through London I felt my eyes growing heavier and heavier.

I must have fallen completely asleep because the next time I was aware of anything I realised my head was nuzzled into Nathan's shoulder at a sharp angle. As I tried to sit up my neck groaned its protest and I grimaced slightly as I straightened the crick out and rubbed at the sore spot. Prying my eyes open I pulled in a deep breath as I tried to wake up properly and felt Nathan's body shake below me as he chuckled. 'Morning, sleepyhead. Or should that be afternoon? Wear you out, did I?' His voice was low and full of male self-satisfaction.

'Mm-hmm ...' I agreed sleepily. Rubbing my hands over my face I blinked my heavy eyes several times until finally I could focus properly on the handsome, smiling face before me. How did Nathan always look so impeccable? It wasn't so long ago that we'd shagged rampantly in the back of this very car and I no doubt looked creased, flushed, and thoroughly well-fucked while he just looked totally together and radiant.

Gradually I acknowledged that the car was no longer moving. 'Are we home?' I asked hopefully, I had no idea why, but even after that nap I still felt exhausted. A proper snooze in Nathan's huge double bed would no doubt sort me out though.

'Not yet, sweetheart.' Leaning across me, Nathan began to unclip my seat belt and then in next to no time he'd dragged me across the small gap between us and settled me on his lap. Humming my appreciation of this new positioning I snuggled even closer and buried my head in Nathan's chest and his intoxicating spicy scent. 'We've stopped at the deli whilst Ryan grabs us some food for later, then we'll pop by yours to get your clothes, but we'll be home in no time.' Pausing thoughtfully a small smile pulled at the corner of his mouth, 'I like that you call my place "home",' he added, 'Maybe that means you're finally coming around to the idea of moving in with me.' God, not that subject *again*, I thought, with a roll of my eyes, but thankfully it was hidden by his chest so Nathan didn't see.

As I settled happily into place Nathan's head lowered and he nuzzled his face into my hair breathing deeply. Curious about what he was doing I didn't move, or say anything to disturb the moment, and was quite amazed when he simply seemed to take a second or two to inhale me and then cuddle me closer. The simplicity of his romantic gesture very nearly had me saying 'yes' to moving in with him there and then, but as he dropped several kisses on my temple and pulled me tighter into his chest, my eyes grew heavy again and I contented myself with surrounding my senses with his reassuring scent and strong muscles as I drifted back to sleep.

The next time I woke up my nose informed me that I was still in Nathan's lap, because my first conscious breath was filled with his spicy deliciousness. Taking vague stock of my position I noticed my legs were curled up to my tummy, my head rested on his chest, and one of his arms was circled protectively around my back. Given that I was now horizontal it was probably a fair bet to say we were no longer in the car. Opening my heavy eyes I blinked in confusion as I blearily took in my surroundings. I was right, we weren't in the car anymore, but as my blurry vision marginally cleared I realised we weren't at Nathan's apartment as planned either. We were in my flat, on my bed, and he was holding me with one hand whilst also simultaneously checking his emails on my laptop.

It crossed my mind how funny he looked sat on my messy bed still dressed in his expensive suit, but then seeing me rouse myself from sleep Nathan glanced down and smiled, 'Hey, sweetheart.' Closing the laptop he pushed it away, shifted himself to the side of me, and placed a thumb under my chin to tilt my face upwards and meet his gaze. Looking into my eyes I saw concern reflected in his blue depths. 'How are you feeling?' Frowning at his odd comment and worried tone I tried to sit up only to discover that my entire body felt like it was stuck to him with a thick layer of sweat on my skin. *Ugh*, my T-shirt was soaked through. As I shifted myself again my head chose that moment to spin like a merry-go-round and then a heavy thumping settled in my temples as it became clear that I also had aching limbs and a sore throat. *Ugh*. Talk about a symptom overload.

'Ugh … I feel awful, what …' The pain in my throat quickly stopped me from speaking any more as I clutched my neck with a clammy palm and swallowed with a wince. God that hurt. I felt like I'd eaten glass shards for breakfast.

Feeling Nathan nod against the top of my head he gently shifted my leaden body across onto the cooler sheets on the other side of the bed and leant over, placing a hand on my forehead to check my temperature. My head was swimming and my vision wasn't exactly great, but I kept my eyes open so I could watch my man fuss over me.

'I thought you were just tired in the car so I left you to sleep, but by the time we got back to your flat I saw you had broken out in a fever. I carried you inside and you've barely stirred from your sleep for the last three hours.'

Three hours? I blinked sticky eyelids as I wondered where the heck this had come from. It felt like just minutes ago that I'd been enjoying the sunshine of Covent Garden and having risky liaisons in the back of a car. I really was becoming rather shameless. My self-analysis was brought to an abrupt halt as a painful shudder ran up my entire body, causing me to groan and roll up into a ball as yet more sweat popped out on my already burning face.

'Try and lay still, I think you're coming down with something, baby,' Nathan murmured as he pulled the sheets further up to cover me.

If I didn't feel half delirious I'd probably have been

thrilled by the attention I was getting, but I could barely even focus now; Nathan's gorgeous but troubled face began to blur and spin in front of my eyes and I suddenly felt like the bed was on fire. 'Too hot,' I gurgled, desperately trying to dislodge the sheet he'd just tucked around me so I could pull off my soaked T-shirt, but Nathan stopped me by gently pushing me back onto the bed. 'I'll get a cool flannel and a change of clothes, hang on, Stella, I'll be right back.' But before Nathan had even had the chance to leave my side I felt my weary eyelids pulling closed as a fitful sleep once again claimed me.

FIVE – NATHAN

Fucking stupid cupboards. How the hell could Stella need so many different storage units in one small bathroom? According to her *I* was a clean freak, and even *I* didn't have this many cabinets. For fuck's sake, if she lived with me this would all have been so much easier; it had taken me an age to find anything remotely resembling a flannel to help cool her down, and then a further two minutes to get the sodding water cold enough. Returning from the bathroom as fast as I could my eyes went immediately to the bed and I saw that Stella had fallen asleep again. Sighing my relief I rolled my shoulders as I approached her sleeping form. It was a good thing really, as much as I selfishly wanted her awake to reassure me she was all right, thrashing around deliriously wasn't going to do her any good at all. Using the flannel I'd eventually found I dipped it into the cool water and wiped at her face, only to see sweat beads instantly pop up to replace the ones I'd wiped away.

Frowning, I chewed nervously on the inside of my lower lip as I noticed a strange strangling feeling tightening around my chest, one I'd only ever felt for my brother until Stella had come along – overpowering possessive concern. It was different from the overwhelmingly hot sensation I got in my chest when I looked at her on a day to day basis; that feeling was pleasant. This was almost sickening. I hated seeing Stella sick like this, *hated it.* I knew it was most likely just a flu bug, but it scared the shit out of me to see her so ill.

Gritting my teeth I did a countdown to help calm myself and felt a half smile curve my mouth as I thought about her worry in the car earlier – bless her for thinking she was the cause of all my countdowns. She knew me better than anyone, but if Stella thought she was the sole reason for them then she clearly didn't know the full extent of my fucked-up-ness.

Nothing else mattered to me at this moment; not work, not eating, not the state of my crumpled clothing, nothing. All I could think about was taking care of her, protecting her, and keeping her safe. Blinking, I wondered exactly when I'd gone from considering women as mere playthings to how I felt now – it was a total juxtaposition to my life a little over a year ago. I wasn't a selfish arsehole anymore, in fact I'd go as far as to say that I'd willingly change positions with Stella and take her suffering myself if it meant that she was all right. I took a second to briefly marvel at how much I'd changed since meeting Stella and shook my head in astonishment. The words I'd said to her in the car were God's honest truth – she really had brought a shining light into my once dark life.

Stella bought my pondering to a halt as she began thrashing around in bed, gurgling noises coming from her throat and her arms flailing until I was so stressed with worry that I had to gently hold her down so she didn't injure herself. As I leant over her and she calmed I noticed just how rampant my heartbeat was and I shook my head ruefully – this girl could get me worked up even when she was unconscious, that was for sure.

Just then my phone began to ring on the bedside table and I frowned at the inconvenient timing, grabbing it on a curse and almost slamming it into the side of my head as I answered. 'What?' My voice was practically a growl, but with Stella sick and in need of a change of clothes I wasn't exactly in the mood for small talk.

'Um ... hello? Nathan, is that you? Is Stella there please?' My frown deepened when I heard a female voice on the line and I yanked the phone away to look at it in confusion. Seeing the pink phone cover I immediately realised that I'd answered Stella's phone by mistake and then glanced at the screen to see Rebecca's name flashing.

Wincing slightly at how abrupt I'd been I put the phone back to my ear and no doubt sounded just as sheepish as I felt. 'Oh ... Rebecca, hi. Yes, it's me. Stella's sleeping at the moment, she's come down with something,' I explained. I didn't bother to apologise for my earlier rudeness, there was no point; Rebecca knew me well enough by now to know that I was usually pretty blunt with everyone. Everyone except Stella, that was.

'Oh no! What is it?' she asked, concern obvious in her voice. I was keen to get off the phone so I could continue with my task of caring for Stella, but Rebecca sounded so genuinely worried that I forced a deep breath into my lungs and tried to lower my aggravation level.

Placing my palm on her damp forehead again I frowned at the heat. 'Some sort of flu I think, she's got a bad fever and the last time she was awake it sounded like she had a pretty sore throat too.' A sudden sharp pain erupted in my mouth and I raised my hand to touch at my lower lip before pulling it away and seeing a smear of blood on the pad of thumb. Fuck. I'd been nervously chewing on it so hard that I'd obviously broken through the skin. Licking the blood away I tried to focus on ending the call so I could do something proactive rather than just standing here staring helplessly at Stella.

'I need to go, Rebecca, but when Stella's feeling better I'll tell her you called,' I said in my nicest, politest tone hoping it might make her disengage quicker.

'It's OK, I was only phoning to tell her about the hotel Nicholas has booked for the wedding. I can catch up with her another time. Do you need anything? Should we come over?'

Sitting back down on the bed I ran my fingertips over Stella's sleeping face. She was clearly out of it at the moment, but even with her fever and sickness her head lolled sideways into my touch and I felt an affectionate smile tug my lips at the tiny gesture. The only thing I *needed* at the moment was for Stella to get better, but apart from that there was little that Rebecca or Nicholas to do – it was just a case of Stella sweating it out. As stupid as it was, even though I was on the phone I found my head shaking with my reply as I decided now was the time to end the call so I could care for her. 'No, we're fine, I'll look after her. Thank you for the offer though, Rebecca. I'll keep you updated.'

'OK, Nathan, you know where we are if you need us. Goodbye.' As rude as it was, I didn't even return her goodbye, instead simply hanging up and immediately returning to the job of wiping Stella's brow. Frowning, I once again noticed the dark sweat patches on her T-shirt and decided I really needed to get her out of her wet clothing.

Pushing my hair from my face I pursed my lips thoughtfully. These last few hours had really brought it home to me just how important this woman was to me, because as impossible as it seemed, I could barely consider the thought of leaving her side for even the briefest of moments. Shaking my head I smiled. My brother would love to see me like this – I'd never hear the end of it. As reluctant as I was to leave her, I eventually dragged myself to the drawers in Stella's room and dug around until I discovered clean bed sheets and a large T-shirt which would have to do as replacement pyjamas for now.

The job of shifting Stella so I could change the bed turned out to be much trickier than I'd first expected. Stella didn't have an armchair or sofa in her room that I could temporarily move her to, and there was no fucking

74

way I was laying her on the floor, so I'd had to try and change the sheets with her still in the bed. With much manoeuvring of Stella's limp, damp body the clean sheets were finally on and I was halfway through peeling Stella's sodden T-shirt off when I heard the front door to her flat slam shut.

'Stella? You home? The door was unlocked so I'm guessing you are, sweetie ...' Scowling at the loud noise I realised it was Stella's housemate Kenny out in the hall making the racket, but luckily his banging hadn't woken Stella. Ignoring his calls, I concentrated on my task of pulling her arms through the sleeves to release her body from the sweat-soaked garment, and had just succeeded in getting it over her head when the bedroom door suddenly burst open. Acting on pure impulse I spat out a curse and launched myself at the bed to cover Stella's exposed body, my forearm wrapping around her breasts and my other hand supporting her lolling head. The fact that Kenny was gay was totally irrelevant to me; nobody, *nobody at all*, was seeing my Stella naked.

Flashing a glare at the door I saw Kenny frozen to the spot and wide eyed, 'Oops, sorry to interrupt ...' he said with a blush fast rising under his goatee and up into his cheeks. Quite apparently he thought he'd disturbed something sexual, but as he began to hurriedly spin away he must have seen Stella's deathly pale complexion because he paused, frowned, and turned curious eyes on me.

'Haven't you heard of fucking knocking?' I growled as I finally succeeded in dragging the sheet up over Stella's bare chest and throwing her soaked T-shirt to the floor.

'Sorry ... I didn't know you'd be here,' As he began taking a few steps closer I once again felt a warning growl rising in my throat and my fists actually tightened by my sides. I literally had no control over these reactions. Fuck, it really was crazy how bloody protective I felt over this woman. Talk about primal instincts flooding to the surface.

Hearing my warning Kenny stopped dead and flashed me another nervous glance from a safe distance away. Sensible lad. 'Uh … she looks awful, what's the matter with her?'

Shrugging helplessly I turned back to Stella and chewed on my sore lower lip before bending to gently brush some stray hairs from her sweaty brow. 'A bad flu I guess, it just came on suddenly about three hours ago, I've called my doctor and he's on his way.'

'Do you need any help?' Kenny asked carefully. His tone was respectful, but he was giving a pointed glance to the clean T-shirt in my hand that I had been about to dress Stella in. Feeling my eyebrows lower and furrow, my jaw tensed at the idea of him seeing her undressed and I found myself adamantly shaking my head. 'No. I'll take care of her,' I muttered in a low tone turning to face him fully and probably sending a death glare his way if his shaky backward step was anything to go by.

Tugging nervously on his goatee Kenny seemed to be considering making a run for it when he suddenly straightened his back and looked me straight in the eye with more courage than I'd ever thought he possessed. 'I love her just as much as you, Nathan,' he said quietly and in response my entire body seemed to tense unpleasantly as the image of punching him sprang to my mind, 'just in a different way,' he added quickly.

Forcing myself to acknowledge his words I pushed a breath from my lungs in an attempt at calming myself down. I hadn't even had the balls to sit down and really work out if I was capable of real love yet, let alone vocalise any such emotion to Stella. I was pretty sure I did love her – that must be what these overwhelming feelings of care, protection, affection, and desire inside me meant, but I was actually quite jealous of how Kenny could just stand there and say it like it was the easiest thing on earth.

Sucking in a deep breath I glanced at Stella again and felt my heart melt and a smile tug my lips. Being with her *was* the easiest thing on earth. Talk about an enlightening few hours – I felt like I'd been on a voyage of self-discovery and finally emerged into the clarity of daylight. Except it was Stella that was my blinding light.

I let my gaze wander over her again before nodding decisively; once she was better I'd sort myself and my tangled feelings out and then talk to her, but for now it was obvious that I was getting worked up and predatory for no reason. Kenny was right, he was Stella's best friend and definitely not a threat to my relationship with her in any way, shape, or form.

Ramming my hands into my trouser pockets I dipped my head.

'Sorry.' My apology was difficult for me to say, feeling like sawdust in my throat and came out quietly, possibly too quiet for him to hear. 'I'm just worried about her. Is there any chance you have some soup in the flat for her when she wakes up? She's sweating so much that she's bound to be dehydrated.'

Looking pleased to have a job to do Kenny grinned at me and visibly perked up. 'We haven't, but I've got lots of fresh veggies in the fridge and I'm a whizz in the kitchen, I'll make a homemade broth, it won't take too long.' Springing into action Kenny swung away with purpose and left the room so I could turn my attention back to Stella.

The next few hours felt like torture. I hated seeing Stella sick with me being helpless to do anything, but at least on the positive side her fever seemed to be reducing slightly. She came in and out of consciousness several times, always drowsy and confused, but she did at least manage to eat a little of the soup that Kenny prepared, and occasionally murmured things to me that were sometimes lucid, and sometimes utter nonsense.

At about seven o'clock Kenny knocked on the bedroom door before poking his head around. 'If you need to leave I can look after her, Nathan.'

Shaking my head firmly I looked between him and Stella. 'No. I'll take care of her,' I stated, my cool tone leaving no room for discussion. *My* girl, *my* responsibility.

'What about work?' Kenny questioned cautiously, mirroring my own thoughts. I had no intention of leaving Stella while she was sick, but I did have a couple of important deals happening next week which I needed to contribute to. Unfortunately it was work that I couldn't do from Stella's laptop because I needed the programs on my home computer and access to my office network.

I absently stroked my fingers across the palm of Stella's hand and felt a small smile tug at the corner of my mouth from just how much I cared for this woman. Loved. How much I *loved* this woman. There – I'd finally admitted it, if only in my head. Turning to Kenny I saw he'd watched my affectionate moment and was smiling goofily at me as if I were starring in some crappy rom-com. Glaring at him he soon wiped the smile from his face and disappeared after telling me he would be in his room if I needed him.

Turning back to Stella I sighed as I considered my options. 'This would be so much easier if we lived together,' I said out loud, my voice causing her to shift and blink a few times still half asleep. 'Move in with me, baby,' I murmured softly, the thoughts from my head just spilling out before I could stop them.

Thrashing her arms slightly, her eyelids fluttered briefly. 'Nope,' she murmured thickly, and I rolled my eyes. She was still bloody stubborn even when delirious, ill, and half asleep. Watching every tiny movement of her face in fascination I immediately noticed when a crease appeared between her eyebrows as a small frown took shape. 'Other women,' she mumbled on an expelled breath.

Shifting myself closer to her I frowned. Other women? What on earth did she mean? Our conversation about my previous subs came back to me and my frown became a full-on grimace. She must be referring to her dislike of my apartment and the fact that she associated it with them – my 'other women'. I sighed heavily. At least I hoped that's what she meant, I certainly wasn't seeing any other women and I had absolutely no intention of it either. Stella was it for me. Surely she knew that? Didn't she? 'There are no other women, Stella,' I softly reassured her, stroking her clammy face again. 'Only you, baby. Just you.' Not even sure if she was conscious at the moment or not, I left it at that and dropped a kiss onto her brow.

When my phone rang a few minutes later – and it definitely was *my* phone this time – I was still distracted by my concerns about Stella's health and her possible misunderstanding of my commitment to her, but when I saw my brother's name I tried to push my worries away for now and took the call.

'Nicholas, hi.' Good, my voice sounded normal and gave away no clue that I'd just spent the majority of the last four hours fretting and acting like a pathetic baby all because Stella was ill with the flu.

'Hello, brother. Rebecca mentioned that Stella was unwell. How is she now?'

Looking at her sleeping peacefully I felt a little happier than I had a few hours ago and found myself nodding even though he wouldn't be able to see it. 'A little better, I think. She's more peaceful now, but still has a fever.'

'There's a horrible flu bug going around, it sounds like she might have that.' There was a pause on the end of the line, but somehow I just knew he had something else to say to me. 'Rebecca also mentioned that you sounded a little … tense. Everything OK now?'

Keeping the phone to my ear I tipped my head back and

felt my nostrils flare as I drew in a long, deep breath to maintain my composure. I knew Nicholas was just checking up on me because he cared, but in my aggravated state it just riled me and made me think he lacked confidence in my ability to control my anger. I grimaced as I begrudgingly realised that I often did. My free hand came up and scrubbed across my face to try and rub away the tension of the last few hours before raking it through my hair and finally coming to rest on my neck as I continued to stare at the ceiling. 'I'm fine.' Regardless of my previous deep breathing I still sounded terse, so with a huge amount of effort I performed a silent countdown and forced myself to relax.

'My apologies, Nicholas. Seeing Stella so sick has been quite trying. I'm sure she'll be better soon though, plus the doctor is coming soon.'

'Quite trying' – talk about an understatement. The last few hours had been hideous. Not to mention a complete eye-opener with regards to acknowledging the depth and gravity of my feelings for Stella. Shaking my head I sat on the edge of the bed. I loved my brother, but I wasn't going to have *that* conversation with him. Clearing my throat to ease my discomfort I changed the subject, 'I heard from Rebecca that you have the wedding venue confirmed. Congratulations.'

I heard a soft chuckle down the line. 'Thanks, brother. Yes, we've just arrived home now. Rebecca loved the hotel so it all worked out really well. We'll have to meet up soon and I'll tell you all about it.'

'Sounds good,' I agreed, not entirely happy with the idea of getting too soppy discussing wedding venues.

'Actually, thinking about it, Rebecca is going to be away for a conference soon, maybe you and I could get together then? I'll just need to confirm the dates with her,' Nicholas suggested.

'Sounds good, we could meet for a meal or drinks.

Perhaps that Italian place you love so much?' I suggested, thinking that being out and about would limit the possibilities for too much wedding talk.

'Perfect, I'll drop you a text with a date. Well, I'll let you get back to Stella. Call me if you need anything, Nathan.' With that my brother hung up, leaving me to fuss over Stella some more. After checking her temperature again and finding that it was still too high I called my personal doctor again and arranged – demanded – for him to bring forwards her appointment and meet me at my apartment in an hour. Then I placed a call to my driver before finally packing some of Stella's clothes into a case. Stella might not want to move in with me, but this situation left me little choice. If I moved her temporarily to my apartment I could continue to care for her *and* access my computer to do the work I needed, thus solving both my issues in one go.

As I anticipated, Kenny wasn't too keen on my plan, but after I gave him Stella's key to my apartment and told him he could come over at any point to check on her he gave in and offered to shift her case for me. With Kenny's assistance, I bundled Stella into a blanket, scooped her limp body up into my arms, and carried her down to the car where Ryan was waiting for us.

I was mid-way through trying to untangle Stella's arms from around my neck so I could fasten her in when her little hands clutched at my neck and she murmured against my cheek, 'Nathan ... don't let me go.' My heart constricted at just how much her words meant to me. I was never letting her go, and I dropped a long, possessive kiss on the top of her head as I climbed into the car and settled Stella in my lap. 'Never,' I murmured. If Stella wanted me to hold her, then fuck it, I would – seatbelt rules would have to be broken this time.

SIX – STELLA

Hmm ... I was so comfortable. My bed was cosy and warm and just utterly lovely. Rolling over I sunk deeper into the mattress before it occurred to me just how very deep and squishy the bed was. Too squishy. My bed had a firm mattress, but this was positively sumptuous. Stretching out, my feet hit against something firm and cool, causing me to frown as I reluctantly began to peel my eyes open.

Books, shelves, and some very fancy framed certificates filled my bleary view. OK, so from that view I knew this definitely wasn't my bedroom, and from the confusing images before me it wasn't Nathan's bed either – although the covers did seem to hold a hint of his lovely aftershave scent. Where the heck was I? Feeling distinctly unnerved I shoved the thick duvet away and began to push myself upright. Coming to my senses properly I realised that I could hear voices behind me and I swivelled round to see Nathan sat at his desk with a bank of monitors in front of him. I was in his office? Utterly confused I blinked several times as I gazed around and realised I was swaddled up in amongst a mountain of duvets and pillows on the sofa in Nathan's home office. What the heck? Why was I in a makeshift bed at Nathan's place?

Just then several voices came from the screens on his desk, drawing my eyes back to him as I realised that Nathan must be on some sort of video conference call. Thank goodness the monitors were facing away from me,

imagine the sight the businessmen would get otherwise –
me popping up behind him tucked into bed! Regardless of
the call he was on, I saw Nathan catch sight of my
movement and turn his eyes to me. A small smile curved
his lips and his eyes darkened and glimmered a silent
'hello' at me as our gazes met, sending a thrill rushing
through my newly awakened body.

'Gentlemen, just give me one moment please,' Nathan
murmured to the screens, his eyes still on mine, before he
pressed a couple of keys on his computer and stood up.
Walking directly to me Nathan crouched down beside me
and smiled so sweetly that my heart squeezed tight in my
chest. 'Hey, sweetheart,' he murmured as he leant
forwards and placed a kiss on my forehead. 'God, it's good
to see you awake and looking better.'

His lips felt cool against my heated skin, but so good,
and unconsciously I found myself leaning into his touch,
which brought a chuckle from Nathan's lips and caused
him to pull me into a warm embrace. 'Why am I in your
office?' I asked, as I snuggled closer to his firm chest and
Nathan's lovely unique scent that I so adored.

'You've been ill.' Smoothing some hair from my face
with gentle fingers he leaned back to gaze down at me
with his crystal blues. 'Let me just wrap up this call and
you can have my undivided attention.' Placing another kiss
on my head Nathan stood up and towered over me. He
didn't move away immediately, instead choosing to stand
there with his legs spread and hand in his pockets as he
simply stared down at me for a second or two, before
finally blinking and retaking his place at the desk. Clicking
a few buttons I saw the screens flash to life as Nathan got
back to work. Sitting up, I rubbed my hands over my face,
ran my fingers through my tangled hair to smooth it, and
then sifted through my mind trying to recollect any
memories of being ill. As my sleep fogged brain began to
clear I recalled the car ride home from London with

Nathan and then waking up in my flat feeling hot, achy, and very tired, but apart from that not else much came to me apart from glimpses of memories about soup and strange conversations which for all I knew might well have been dreams.

In the few minutes it took Nathan to finish his call I took the opportunity to discreetly watch him in action. I'd never really seen him conducting his business, certainly not for this length of time anyway. It was fascinating to see his work demeanour fall into place as he fluidly took control of the meeting; finalising some key issues, delegating a number of tasks, and then smoothly drawing it to a conclusion. He really was the ultimate professional. As he closed off all the monitors and turned his heated stare onto me I shuddered as unexpected lust rushed through my body and I swiftly revised my thought – forget ultimate professional, he was the ultimate temptation. With the way my body was suddenly thrumming it was clear that illness or not, his commanding business demeanour was a huge turn-on for me. Mind you, seeing as I loved him when he was in full domination mode it was hardly surprising that seeing him commanding other people turned me on too. When Nathan pierced me with a look as loaded as the one currently aimed at me I could barely maintain normal breathing, let alone any other human functions, and I hastily licked my dry lips in anticipation.

With my eyes glued to his, Nathan stood and used a finger to loosen the navy silk tie around his neck, then popped open the top button of his shirt and began to walk towards me, his intent becoming clearer with every stalked step he took. Unfortunately my treacherous stomach had other ideas and let out a loud growl that caused Nathan to stop mid-step and shake his head as if trying to clear a fog from his brain.

'Christ, what am I thinking?' he muttered with a sardonic grin. 'I was fully intent on ravishing you just minutes after you've woken up from a serious illness.' Clicking his tongue he made the final two steps to me. 'What you really need is food and a shower.'

With no warning Nathan bent and scooped me up into his arms and then kicking the duvet aside he made his way towards the kitchen. I still felt a bit dodgy, but with him in close quarters like this I couldn't help but push my luck. 'And then ravishing?' I asked hopefully, as I looped my arms around his neck and held on for the journey. There was no point telling him I was capable of walking, I'd long since learnt that when Nathan had set his mind to something nothing would sway him off course.

Chuckling, Nathan grinned down at me. 'We'll see how you're feeling, but yes, if you really are as well recovered as you look then there will definitely be some ravishing going on later. It's been a while and I'm only human, after all.' My eyebrows rose at his comment; he might only be human, but he had enough sex drive for five men.

Pausing by the kitchen Nathan looked down at me thoughtfully. 'Food first or shower?' Eyeing the fruit bowl my stomach growled again and I grinned at him as one of my hands rubbed across the beautifully taut muscles of his chest.

'Banana, shower, and then proper food,' I said, removing my hand from his chest and holding it out in the direction of the three ripe bananas on the kitchen surface.

'Deal,' Nathan agreed, walking me closer so I could pluck one off. Carrying me to his master bathroom he gently placed me on the sink unit and whilst he set about turning on the shower and setting the temperature I promptly ate my fruit, glad to feel some nourishment hit my empty stomach.

Turning to me and eyeing the empty banana skin in my hand Nathan raised a blond eyebrow. 'That was quick, did you inhale it?' he joked dryly. Grinning he walked to me and deposited the banana skin in the bin for me. 'Do you want me to get you another?'

Shaking my head I smiled, happy to be feeling so well again. 'I'm fine, one was enough to hold my hunger at bay.'

Any remnants of hunger I might have been feeling were well and truly forgotten as Nathan peeled off his shirt to reveal his beautifully toned chest and its sprinkling of blond hair. Sighing happily it soon became apparent that Nathan was intent on joining me in the shower as he also undid his belt and zip and let his trousers fall to his ankles. Crikey, now *that* was a sight for sore eyes. Not that I was complaining in the slightest. 'I still feel pretty exhausted, but I have to say my memories are blurry. I remember bits and pieces, but nothing solid since we were out together in your company car. How long was I sick?' I asked, curious as to how much of my life I'd lost to the shadowy mess in my brain.

Jerking his chin Nathan indicated for me to raise my arms, which I did without question, allowing him to peel off my T-shirt and leave me sat there in just a pair of black cotton knickers. 'Two days, but you'll probably take a few more days to fully recover,' he murmured, a frown creasing his brow as his eyes flicked to mine, full of concern. 'You were in and out of sleep the whole time.' Running a hand through his hair he let out a sharp breath, 'Fuck. It was horrible, Stella, your fever was so high, I felt so fucking helpless.' he whispered, his uncharacteristic anxiety obvious.

'Hey, I'm OK now,' I assured him, reaching out and touching Nathan's shoulder to bring him back to the present. 'Actually, considering you've just told me that I've been out of it for more than twenty-four hours I have to say I feel pretty great.' OK so that was perhaps a bit of an exaggeration, I was still achy and tired, but at least I was properly awake and thinking clearer. Reacting to my touch Nathan took my hand in his and kissed the knuckles one by one, making me grin like a lovesick teenager. 'Thank you for looking after me,' I told him.

Apparently not comfortable with my praise Nathan merely shrugged, and grunting a reply he stepped out of his boxers to reveal his gloriously naked body in all its entirety. Swallowing hard and loud I felt my stomach tighten and my pulse accelerate as the final parts of him were revealed. I might have been struggling with a few side-effects of my illness, but the sight of Nathan's naked body ignited something inside of me and I suddenly knew that this shower wouldn't just involve a quick wash. 'I could do with brushing my teeth,' I mumbled, horrified by the thought of my stale 'illness breath'. As if reading my mind Nathan loaded a toothbrush with paste and handed it to me with a faint nod of his head as a smile finally returned to his lips.

As predicted the shower lasted longer than it should have done. Nathan insisted on pampering me completely, washing every inch of my body with care, cleaning under my fingernails, and gently shampooing my limp hair. Once I was clean his washing gradually turned into massaging, which then turned to a lazy lovemaking session. I was sleepy again and uncoordinated from my flu, but as usual Nathan was more than happy to take the lead and gently pushed me against the tiled wall of the cubicle, supporting my weight and gallantly exerting far more energy than me as he reacquainted our bodies.

Once we were finally clean and dry I opened the wardrobe where I kept a few spare items of clothing, hoping to find a snuggly jumper that I could pull on to curl up on the sofa in, or something suitable of Nathan's that I could borrow. Before I even got as far as looking for a jumper I came to a halt. Holding the handle to the cupboard I blinked several times and frowned. The cupboard was full, its rail literally crammed with hangers containing *my* clothes. There wasn't a trace of Nathan's stuff in here, it was all mine. Turning silently I found Nathan watching me cautiously, his jaw sawing back and forth as he frantically chewed on the inside of his lower lip. 'You moved me in *again*?' I asked, gob-smacked and unable to believe that Nathan had tried to do this two frigging times now.

Finally giving his lip a rest Nathan shrugged guiltily, his expression remarkably similar to a disgruntled child. 'You were sick and I needed to work so I brought you here. I didn't know how long you'd be ill for so I packed up a few of your things.'

My eyebrows shot up and I swung back to look at the rail. 'A *few* of my things?' I spun back to look at him. 'Nathan, this is practically every item of clothing that I own!'

Apparently tiring of my completely valid argument Nathan pulled on his T-shirt with a grunt and circled the bed so that he was stood just two feet away from me. From the look on Nathan's face you would have thought it was *me* that had done something wrong, and I was once again reminded of just how domineering he could be.

'Move in with me, Stella,' he demanded suddenly, his tone low and gritty and causing me to swallow hard. Now it was my turn to bite my lip. Here we go again. I was way too tired and achy to be discussing this now. I'd already told him of my objections, what else could I say? I was starting to feel like a broken record and becoming more and more uncomfortable saying no all the time in case he took it as a rejection of him, and not his apartment.

'You know how I feel about you, Nathan, but like I said the other day, I'm just not ready to live here,' I said, my irrational hatred of the idea of living here in the apartment he had shared with his previous women pushing to the surface again and making my stomach twist. Ugh, every time I allowed myself to consider it I felt positively sick.

'If we moved somewhere new would you move in then? Or just find another reason not to?' he enquired sharply, not sounding like he believed me for a minute. Interesting, my ears had certainly perked up at that, it sounded like he was genuinely considering moving, which thrilled me no end, but seeing my shocked expression at his tone Nathan seemed to force his face to soften. 'If it's just the location bothering you then that's fine ...' he paused, taking another cautious step closer, '... but when you were sick you said something about *"other women"*.' His voice had lowered and he reached over to tip my chin upwards with his thumb so I was forced to meet his steely gaze.

God, what else had I reeled off in my sleep? My childhood love of pickled onions? How much I loved his sexy, wide-legged stance perhaps? I hated that I sometimes spoke in my sleep. How embarrassing. Not noticing my awkwardness Nathan tilted his head and studied me intently. 'You do know you're the only one for me, Stella, don't you?' Perhaps sensing my ever growing reliance on him, or just needing the contact himself, Nathan closed the last space between us and enveloped me in his huge, strong arms. 'There are no other women, not now, not ever again. Just you.' His words were so lovely that I very nearly cried, especially seeing as they were coming from Nathan, Mr Non-Emotional himself. Instead of crying I somehow managed to swallow down my tears and lean up to place a kiss on his warm lips. 'I love you,' I murmured, hoping it would be enough for now.

He made a contented humming noise in the back of his throat as he returned my chaste kiss, but his lips soon parted and he briefly deepened our kiss, running his tongue along my lower lip and darting it in to flick across my eager tongue. 'But you still won't move in with me here, will you?' he said, apparently intent on trying his luck one last time.

Nathan may have made it out as a joke, but I knew him well enough now to catch the note of hurt that seeped into his tone, presumably from the idea of leaving his beloved apartment, and I frowned, hating the fact that it was me causing him hurt. Perhaps if we did a bit of redecorating and made it "our" apartment as opposed to just "his", then I'd get used to the space? It was probably worth a try. I wanted to reassure him, especially as he'd just been so open and honest with me, so I didn't give Nathan my stock answer of 'no', instead I kissed him again and then leant in close to his ear. 'Let's see how we go in the next few weeks, OK? Maybe I could try …'

If I'd ever had any doubts about Nathan's feelings towards me they would have been cleared up that very second, because upon hearing my words he leant back and gazed down at me with a huge grin on his lips. Wow, that smile was incredible, and the happiness in Nathan's eyes was un-mistakable, he was clearly overjoyed. Well, that settled it then, I either needed to get over my jealousy and move in here, or somehow have to break the news that I still wanted him to move out of his beloved apartment.

SEVEN - REBECCA

Tiptoeing along the corridor towards the kitchen I fiddled with my hair nervously as my mind ticked over my options. I needed to approach this subject with the upmost care and delicacy. It wasn't one of those things I could carelessly toss out into the air, otherwise Nicholas would freak out and lock himself in his piano room for the remainder of the day – or perhaps even the entire weekend if I was unlucky.

The wedding flowers. This was one of my allocated tasks for the wedding, and today was my first appointment with some florists to see bouquet samples and possible table arrangements. The quotes I'd had were astronomical, and even though Nicholas and I weren't hard up for cash this was one of those times that I wished I was creative so I could do my own displays and save us some money – perhaps add it to the charity donation we were making as part of the wedding – but unfortunately, that wasn't the case, I was terrible at anything artsy. I'd hoped that Stella and her spectacular flair for interior design might have been able to create some fantastic floral work, but regardless of her recent illness, apparently her style skills didn't quite transfer into the actual making of things, so it looked like I'd be calling in a pro.

Now we'd picked the venue for the wedding I knew I either needed a florist in the Lake District, or one who was willing make the trip north. The three florists I'd arranged to see were from various parts of the country, but willing to travel within the UK for an additional fee if I liked their selections. Today's outing had all been arranged weeks ago – Stella was supposed to be accompanying me and we were going to make it into a lovely girly day out, but after her flu last week she was still really run down and had called and cancelled, apologising profusely, and saying that she simply didn't have enough energy for a shopping spree. Louise, my second bridesmaid, was working in the bookshop today so I was officially partnerless. I didn't fancy making decisions like this on my own, so that left only one option: Nicholas.

I was sure I could persuade Nicholas to come and look at a couple of bouquets if I engaged my best coercive skills, but unfortunately today's meetings wouldn't just be a quick trip to a florist – no, my appointments were in Earls Court.

Or more specifically, the National Wedding Show at Earls Court Exhibition Centre.

Pausing on the threshold to the kitchen I closed my eyes and grimaced. With over three hundred stalls ranging from florists and bridal boutiques to photographers and cake makers it was going to be stuffed full of cooing brides, over excited mothers-in-law, and soppy romantic music. Basically, it was Nicholas' worst nightmare come true. My poor, emotionally deprived man would hate it, I just knew it. If I'd felt comfortable making the decision on my own I wouldn't even bother to ask him, but this was a big deal and I wanted – *needed* – a second opinion.

Taking a deep breath for courage I entered the kitchen and immediately forgot my worry as I felt my lips tug into a smile at the sight before me. Nicholas, my usually immaculate and well-presented gentleman, was stood at the kitchen counter in a pair of loose pyjama bottoms and a crumpled, dark grey T-shirt with stylistic piano keys printed across the shoulders. I loved this particular T-shirt on him. It was tight across his muscles in all the right

94

places, and from memory, had the same colourful logo across the chest too. The most incongruous things though, were his unshaven stubbly jaw and his dark hair, which was in absolute disarray on his head flopping all over the place and looking so unbelievably sexy that I found myself biting down on my lower lip and squeezing my thighs together. Blimey. Nicholas looking rough and ready, what a sight to start the day.

His legs were spread, his broad shoulders slightly dipped as he studied a newspaper on the counter intently, and I was suddenly filled with the overwhelming temptation to forget the stupid flowers and drag him onto to the kitchen floor to have my wicked way with his delicious body. Heaving out a breath I forced the lust to the back of my mind and instead approached behind him and slid my arms around his waist so they were linked on his flat belly. Pushing onto my tip toes I rested my chin on his shoulder and placed a kiss on his neck. Hmmm, he smelled just as good as he looked; warm and sleepy with a hint of his aftershave still remaining from the night before.

'Morning, sweetheart,' he murmured. 'You slept in.' Swivelling in my arms Nicholas turned so I was met with a close up of his tousled gorgeousness and a contented sigh slipped from my lips. Lifting his arms he rested one lightly on my shoulder and used the other to grip my bum and pull me firmly against him so our hips were melded together and our faces just inches apart before dropping a soft, lovely kiss on my lips.

'Hi,' I replied, my eyebrows raising as I felt the stirrings of his groin hardening against my tummy. He was always so horny in the mornings, but at that thought I had to grin because actually given half a chance Nicholas could get horny pretty much any time of the day. Shifting slightly so I could glance down between us I blushed as I saw a glimpse of hard, pink skin poking from the slit in his pyjamas. He clearly wasn't wearing any boxers, a fact which suddenly made me feel shy – a ridiculous reaction given how long we'd been together. Shy, but also quite lusty. Perhaps my kitchen floor sex plan would become a reality after all.

'I was thinking we could have a lazy day in bed today. I could do with a break after all the concerts and wedding plans recently and I've got nothing in my diary at all. What about you?' *Bugger*. Talk about ruining my horniness. It was like he'd thrown a bucket of ice water over me. Well, it was now or never, I might as well just get it out there I suppose.

'Um … I do have some things I need to do today.' Looking up at him hopefully I found myself twiddling with my hair – my little tell, as he called it – and I just knew that he'd be internally trying to work out why I was anxious. 'Actually, I was hoping you might help me out.'

Both of his hands now rested on my waist, gently massaging me as he slowly circled his hips to rub his erection against me, all the while giving me a considering look. Talk about distracting. 'Of course … what do you need my help with?' Nicholas has often said I was transparent to him, and I was almost certain from his slightly narrowed eyes and marginal tension in his shoulders that he knew he wasn't going to like my answer.

As his arousal became harder against me I genuinely struggled to remember what the heck I needed his help with, and had to forcibly focus my mind. Wedding. Flowers. *Not* sex. 'Stella was supposed to be helping me pick out a wedding bouquet today, but she's still not on top form after her flu. I don't want to do it on my own, so I was hoping you might help me?'

Beneath my hands I felt his muscles relax, 'Is that all? Of course I'll come with you.'

That was the easy part out of the way – now to drop the real bombshell. 'Great! Thank you, Nicholas,' I gushed, before biting my lower lip and taking a deep breath, 'The thing is, it's not just a florist shop we need to go to ... I arranged to meet with several florists today because there's an event they will all be at together.' The tension in his muscles returned, this time accompanied with a much deeper eyebrow lowering. The only good thing was that he stayed quiet so I could get it all out in one go. 'It's at Earls Court Exhibition Centre.' Clearing my throat I chucked the last nugget of information at him. 'This weekend is the National Wedding Show ... that's where my appointments are.'

I could literally feel his arousal ebbing away as my words sunk in. Poor man. In general Nicholas was opening up to me far more regularly, but I still struggled to really read him because as much as he was beginning to let his guard down, he still kept quite a good deal hidden. Right now though, his emotion was blindingly obvious; he didn't want to go to the event – *at all* – but he was torn because he felt like he should accompany me.

'I'm not sure, Becky ...' he started hesitantly, 'It'll be crowded, hot, and full of overly hormonal woman fighting for the best deals, won't it?'

'No! It'll be nothing like that!' I replied cheerily, brushing off his concern, even though I suspected that it would be *exactly* like that. 'There's a bar ... with free champagne,' I blurted in desperation, although given how rich Nicholas was, the pull of free champagne was probably dimmed slightly by the fact that he could buy as many bottles as he liked without even marginally denting his finances.

He clicked his tongue in annoyance and shook his head in apparent exasperation, 'Exchanging a lazy day of sex with being squashed in a hot, busy room whilst we're hassled to death.' Exhaling a long breath Nicholas stared at me for several more seconds before finally nodding curtly once. 'Let me go and change and we'll leave,' he mumbled petulantly as he slid from my arms, 'It's just as well I love you,' he muttered, dropping a kiss on my forehead as he lumbered from the room with far less grace than usual, leaving me giggling in his wake at his continued struggle to be a 'normal' boyfriend. Bless him.

Thank God the traffic hadn't been busy today. We'd made it to Earls Court and managed to find the parking space that I'd pre-reserved when I booked the tickets, all within half an hour of leaving Nicholas' house. Nicholas hadn't complained again about accompanying me, but he had been rather quiet during the drive and if we'd ended up stuck in traffic as well that might just have topped off his brooding mood and caused him to turn for home.

Following the signs pointing us from the car park up to the front steps of the building and into the main hall we stepped through the doors and were immediately met by a cacophony of sounds and sights, and as Nicholas had predicted, it was totally rammed with people.

Crap. Even to me, the supposed blushing bride, this place looked like a nightmare. God only knows what Nicholas was thinking. I got a pretty good idea about a second later when his hand found mine by my side and took hold with such a tight, panicked grip that I almost winced before turning my head to look up at him. The urge to laugh was almost impossible to hide; Nicholas looked like a deer well and truly stuck in the headlights. His face was pale, eyes wide, and a sheen of sweat was actually forming on his brow. I knew he hated crowds, he'd told me previously that the only way he survived his concerts was to lose himself in his piano music, and now I was going to make him traipse around his own personal version of hell. Oops. I suppose the fact that he was even willing to do this showed how much he cared for me.

'We'll be as quick as we can,' I promised. Stella and I had planned to spend the morning checking out bridesmaids' dresses, then grab some lunch and free champers, before going to my florist appointments and looking around at the flower arrangements and table decorations. But there was no way I could do even half of that now. Firstly we were far later arriving than I'd originally planned – my accidental lie in was the cause of that – but in addition to the lack of time, the very thought of making Nicholas look at bridesmaid dresses as well as flowers was nearly enough to make me laugh hysterically. The free champagne might not be a bad place to start though, it was gone lunch time, after all, and it could work to loosen him up a bit.

Checking my map I saw the bar was to our right, as was the first florist I needed to see, so I tugged my reluctant man through the throngs of people and after depositing a full glass of sparkling wine in his hand I watched in amusement as Nicholas downed it in one and then looked at me with a raised eyebrow.

'You know I have a plan to get you back for this hell,' he said with a smirk. 'Next weekend I'm going to take you to a ballroom dancing event, and I'm going to make you dance every single dance I know.' His mouth tweaked with one of his half smiles and I laughed at his statement. Nicholas knew how much I hated formal dancing. I could wing it on the dance floor of a club for a while and enjoy myself, but actual choreographed dancing that involved skill, timing, and rhythm? I was disastrous. *Worse* than disastrous. I tried ballet as a child and was told that as well as having two left feet, my co-ordination was akin to that of a newly born foal, as in, completely absent.

However, the idea of Nicholas being able to dance was rather appealing, and not one we'd ever discussed before. 'You can dance?' I asked curiously, swapping his empty glass with my full one, which he immediately took to his lips, although thankfully with a more refined sip this time. It had never crossed my mind that Nicholas might be able to dance, it seemed quite a soft thing for a tough, closed-off guy like him to know.

'I can,' he stated, slipping an arm around my waist and pulling me in closer where he started to slightly sway his hips in demonstration. Now that I thought about it, his hips were clearly skilled in other rhythmic and naughty activities, so dancing would probably come pretty easily to him. 'I learnt at school. Nathan and I did as many after-school clubs as we could to avoid the house.' Which I took to mean, to avoid being around his abusive bastard of a father. 'During certain terms the only clubs available were dance ones, so I did lots of classical dancing and even some salsa for a while.' *Ho-ly* shit. The idea of Nicholas salsa dancing almost blew my mind; hips gyrating, torso slick with sweat as he moved to the hot, sensual beat of the Latin music … what a thought. It was enough to make my groin wet and throat suddenly dry, and I snatched back my glass to have a sip and moisten my parched mouth.

'Maybe I'll teach you one day,' he murmured, lowering his lips into my hair and still lightly swaying his hips against mine, 'After all, I seem to have failed to teach you how to play the piano with any great skill, so I may as well try something else.' His dig at my piano skills bounced right off me because he was right, I was still dreadful no matter how much practice I did.

'You didn't exactly give me much time to learn though, Nicholas, did you?' I responded in a pointed tone, keen to tease him back and distract my mind from my raging arousal. 'You would drag me off to the bedroom almost as soon as I arrived for my lessons. It's no wonder I'm still crap.' Grinding his hips firmly against mine he flashed me a welcome smile, and I was relieved that our banter was relaxing him, even if it was getting me turned on almost to the point of no return.

'I suspect the same thing might occur if I were to attempt to teach you to dance,' he said breathily against my ear as he performed another rub with those devilish hips that had me moaning whilst he merely leant back and grinned down at me. 'Except I doubt we'd make it as far the bedroom.' With the way he was making my arousal soar by just swaying against me I doubted we'd even make it to any proper dancing, but still, it was quite a tempting thought, especially when he leant in close to my ear and added his final remark, 'I'd probably end up fucking you right there on the dance floor.' Nicholas didn't curse that often, and although he often gave commands when we were in the bedroom they weren't dirty talk as such, so his statement literally made me shudder with arousal as images of him losing control and taking me on the dance floor leapt to my mind.

A wave of dizziness swept my body and I ended up clutching at his arms to steady myself before I gave in to the temptation to beg Nicholas to take me right there in the packed exhibition centre. Raising the glass with the remainder of my champagne Nicholas finished it off in one swift swig, and then looking completely unaffected by the last five minutes of hip grinding, pulse raising teasing he gave me a calm smile and offered me his elbow. 'Let's go and look at these flowers, shall we?'

Blinking several times in disbelief at his ability to change so erratically from one second to the next, I eventually steadied myself enough to slide my hand through the crook of his arm and nod, but I have to say I felt far from steady as we made our way through the crowds to meet the first florist. My dizziness certainly had nothing to do with the minimal champagne I'd had though, but it might have had a little to do with my man and his talented hips.

By the time we were at the third florist stand in a particularly busy section of the hall it was well over two hours later. The florist – a lovely lady called Julie – was telling us the details of how the bouquet could be taped and trimmed when Nicholas suddenly stood up, his chair almost toppling backwards with his haste. Flashing me a desperate glance he began to dig in his jacket pocket, removed his silent phone, and then blinked twice at me as if trying to pass some secret message to me which I completely failed to understand. 'I have to take this call,' he blurted. So he had to take a call, did he? The call from his phone which *wasn't* ringing? With that he spun on his heels and was gone through the crowd quicker than a flash.

Watching his rapidly disappearing figure I turned back to Julie with a relaxed smile. Nicholas' departure didn't overly worry me, to be honest, given the cloying environment we were in I was amazed he'd lasted this long. Three overly enthusiastic florists vying for his money was more than I'd ever thought he'd deal with. 'Sorry about that, Julie, he's very busy with work at the moment.'

The florist smiled politely, and then continued to write up a quote for me. 'No problem, Rebecca. Good-looking fella, isn't he? Lucky you! That's what I say.' With that she folded up the quote and some sample photographs, gave me a wink, and slid them into an envelope. I had a good feeling about Julie, her prices were competitive with the other florists' and her arrangements were beautiful, but the biggest point in her favour was her relaxed, down-to-earth manner.

Once I had finished with Julie I gathered up my handbag and the various freebies I'd been given earlier and set off in search of Nicholas. As much as I hadn't been surprised by his sudden departure from the wedding fair, I was slightly worried it might have freaked him out and that he might be in need of calming down.

The cold air of the December day almost took my breath away as I burst from the stuffy hall to the steps outside the centre. Initially as I looked around the people milling about the pavement outside I couldn't see Nicholas and felt panic rising in my chest. What if the wedding fair had panicked him more than I'd thought? Scanning the crowd again I was just about the reach for my mobile phone when I felt a hand at my wrist.

Turning with the pull of the grip I found Nicholas leaning on the wall beside the numerous sets of double doors, still with a slightly pained expression on his pale face. For a second or two we just stood there staring at each other; his eyes locked on mine as he blinked slowly and me holding my breath whilst I waited for him to say something. His grip was looser now, but his hand was still on my wrist, and suddenly he used this link to guide me forwards into his arms where he pulled me tight against him and immediately buried his head in my hair.

After seemingly inhaling my scent for a second or two Nicholas burrowed his face deeper and kissed the skin of my neck by my ear. 'I'm sorry, Becky,' he whispered, his voice was hoarse and strained, the warm breath making my skin tingle. 'I let you down. I tried to stay. I wanted to, I know that stuff is important to you ... but it was so crowded, I had to get out.'

Leaning back so that he was forced to look at me I smiled reassuringly. 'Actually, given the event and the fact that you were practically the only man in there I think lasting over two hours is pretty good going.' Glancing at my watch I grinned. 'Nearly three hours actually.'

Watching as his eyebrows rose I maintained my calm smile and felt his arms begin to relax around me. It seems he had been expecting me to angry with him, but how could I when he'd tried so hard for me?

'I know you want a nice bouquet and for the tables to look good, but in all honesty, the only thing I need on our wedding day is you,' he murmured. Given his occasional reluctance with emotions that was quite a statement. 'Seeing as I deserted you in there my opinion might not count, but I really liked Julie.'

103

Nodding I smiled broadly, 'Me too. She's based just north of Birmingham and she's willing to travel so I guess that's the florist chosen!' Taking his hand an idea suddenly occurred to me and I felt excitement settle in my belly. 'Kensington isn't far from here, is it?' I asked as Nicholas turned us in the direction of the car park.

Looking down at me as he wrapped a possessive arm around my shoulders Nicholas shook his head, 'Just north of here, probably five minutes in the car. Why?'

'I have a reward for you for being so good and coming with me today. Will you let me drive your car?'

Now Nicholas looked completely confused as he continued to walk but stared down at me with furrowed brows. 'You're insured on it, but why do you want to drive?'

'You can drive now, but I'll drive us home later. Take us to Kensington High Street, you'll need to find somewhere to park near the Tube station.' I instructed him, smirking at his baffled expression as I dished out my instructions.

Just over fifteen minutes later we were standing on the pavement outside Piano, a very funky bar on Kensington High Street famed for its live piano music. Granted we were a little early, it had just gone five o'clock and the bar had literally just opened its doors, but that was actually perfect because the place was deserted and a little calm would do us both good after the hectic environment of the wedding fair. I knew from my internet search that the live music didn't start until seven and so my plan was to try and get Nicholas a slot at the piano beforehand. Regardless of how much of a bad day he'd had, Nicholas could always turn to his music to relax him, and after the stress of the wedding fair I was hoping that this distraction might soothe his earlier tension.

Pushing open the door we stepped into the plush interior and made our way towards the bar. 'I found this place on the internet a while ago and kept meaning to bring you here. I thought you might like it,' I murmured as Nicholas looked intently at the large grand piano across the room with the stirrings of a smile beginning to twitch on his lips. 'Seeing as we were just around the corner this seemed like a good reward for coming with me today. Am I forgiven for dragging you to the wedding fair?'

Turning back to me I could see an excited twinkle in Nicholas' eyes as he slid his hands around my waist and pulled my hips firmly against his until the heat from his body almost seemed to be burn through my jeans. 'You have no reason to need forgiveness. It's my wedding too, I want to support you with the plans. I'm sorry I freaked out,' he murmured as he dropped a brief kiss on my lips, making the skin tingle. 'However, you will be especially in my good books if you get me a few minutes playing that piano,' he added cheekily, throwing another glance at the huge instrument in the corner.

Straightening my spine confidently, I nodded. 'Leave it to me,' I said before wandering over to a man sat at the end of the bar with a large smile on his face. The man turned out to be the owner, Les, a lively fellow who clearly loved his music, and after instantly recognising Nicholas gave him a sturdy handshake and quickly ushered him towards the piano with great enthusiasm.

'I saw you play at Wigmore Hall about two years ago, Mr Jackson, you were bloody fantastic,' Les said with a hearty nod.

Nicholas settled himself on the stool looking far more animated. 'I remember that gig; it was a concert raising money for the local hospital. Intimate venue, but great acoustics. I'll have to set up another concert at the Hall now you've reminded me of it.'

Leaving the two men to talk piano I slipped away to the lone barman and ordered myself a bottle of chilled water. Just to try and perfect this experience for Nicholas I got him a double shot of his favourite single malt whisky – the reason I had asked if I could drive him home – and after paying my tab I crossed the bar, placed the drink on a table beside Nicholas, and propped myself on a stool by a high table to listen.

'This is no ordinary piano, Becky,' Nicholas informed me in an impressed whisper, looking like a kid in a sweet shop. 'It's a Collard and Collard. *Amazing*,' he murmured in awe. 'This must be over a hundred years old,' he added with a respectful stroke of the lid.

'Actually, it's one hundred and sixty years old,' Les informed us proudly as he stepped away from the piano and joined me at the table.

I had to stifle a grin at Nicholas' enthusiasm; pianos were beautiful, even I could see that, but they were clearly precious to Nicholas because he looked almost on the verge of orgasm from just touching the keys. Smiling contentedly I sipped my water and let Nicholas wow Les with some of his music while enthusing about what a fantastic instrument it was. First we'd found our florist, and now my idea of a treat for Nicholas was going down rather well, it seemed today had been resurrected into a good day after all.

EIGHT – STELLA

'It's great to see you looking so much better, Stella, and I can't tell you how pleased I am that you're well enough to come shopping this weekend,' Rebecca said as she sifted through a rail of bridesmaid's dresses of all imaginable shapes, colours, and sizes. 'Taking Nicholas to that wedding fair last weekend was an absolute nightmare!'

The thought of slightly socially awkward Nicholas Jackson surrounded by frantic women in a wedding fair made me grin so much that my cheeks hurt, and I paused in my dress perusal to look across at Rebecca in amusement. 'I'm still amazed he actually went with you. What did you have to promise him? A blow job a day for a month?'

Spluttering out a laugh Rebecca flushed bright red and shook her head, 'No!' To be honest, I doubted Nicholas would need extra action in that department, from the chats Rebecca and I had shared about their sex life I knew it was very healthy and *very* regular. 'He just said he'd do it for me,' she said with a shrug, which was really rather sweet. 'He lasted longer than I'd expected too. But it wasn't as fun as it could have been if me and you had gone together.'

'Yeah, I'm sorry. I'm gutted I missed it too. Still, look on the positive side, I bet this shop is a much calmer buying environment than the wedding fair was?'

Nodding her head Rebecca gave me a knowing look, 'God, yes. It was absolutely rammed. I'm surprised Nicholas even ventured through the doors, to be honest.'

'I doubt Nathan would have,' I pondered out loud, which for some reason made Rebecca completely stop her search and turn to me as she cocked her head curiously.

'Do you think you and Nathan might get married one day?'

That was the question I just knew Rebecca had been dying to ask me for months, but my responding head shake was immediate and definite. 'No chance.'

Frowning slightly, Rebecca moved closer, out of earshot of the assistant who was helpfully waiting to carry our choices to the fitting rooms and no doubt enjoying listening in to our gossip. 'That sounds like a very sure answer. Why not?'

I couldn't really describe it out loud, especially not given our surroundings and possible audience, but for some reason marriage to Nathan just wasn't that big a deal to me. I had his necklace after all – his collar that claimed me as his – which was an ultimate show of commitment from him. I very much doubted he'd ever want marriage, but as long as he wanted *me*, I didn't really mind.

'You know Nathan, he's not exactly the marrying kind.' I said instead, trying to keep it brief. As one of my best friends Rebecca knew a lot about my relationship with Nathan; she knew that there was still a Dom/sub side to our lives, but I didn't think she'd like or agree with the collar around my neck, so I hadn't told her the significance of my necklace. When she'd commented that I always wore the same one I'd simply brushed her off with the excuse that Nathan had given it to me and it was one of my favourites. Which in essence *was* the truth, so I wasn't technically lying to her.

'And you're OK with that?' she asked, sounding more curious than pitying.

Nodding, I smiled reassuringly, 'I am. More than OK. What we have together suits both of us pretty perfectly.'

Watching me thoughtfully Rebecca continued to chew

on her lip before eventually smiling too. 'Well, that's all that matters then.'

Just as I was about to tell her that I was now seriously considering moving in with Nathan, we were interrupted by the door to the shop banging open loudly and Louise bursting in from the frosty day outside. 'Don't panic! The cavalry has arrived!' she announced, practically launching her handbag onto a chair and ripping her winter coat off with a flamboyant tug at the belt.

For a second the shop assistant looked a little taken aback, but ever the professional she quickly hung up Louise's coat and set about pouring some more champagne.

'If anybody knows their Prada from their Primark it's me! Not that I could afford Prada, obviously. But still, the knowledge is there!' Smiling broadly, Louise gave us both a hug and then accepted the glass of champagne from the shop assistant with a yelp of joy. 'Oh! Fizz, how lovely! So, what have I missed?'

'Not much, we only just got here five minutes ago,' Rebecca said as she turned back to the rail full of dresses.

'Is your dress here so we can see it?' Louise asked keenly, which was something I'd been dying to know too.

'Oh yes! Is it? I can't believe you bought it without us!' I joked playfully.

Smiling shyly, Rebecca shook her head. 'I know, sorry, girls, but when Mum came down the other weekend and we saw it here I instantly knew it was the one. It's off having the length altered at the moment, so it's not here, but you should be able to see it at the next fitting.'

'I can't wait that long!' Louise moaned with a mock pained expression.

Grinning, Rebecca rolled her eyes at Louise's dramatic outburst. 'It's quite classical in style, fairly simple, so any design of bridesmaid dress should match. Basically as far as today goes, it's a blank canvas, I want dresses that you will both feel comfortable in, something long and straight-ish perhaps, and if possible a colour that I can tie in with the table decorations and flowers.'

Sipping on her champagne Louise nodded. 'Got it. Any colour preference yet?'

'Well, I'm having cornflowers in my bouquet, so blue would be OK. We also picked roses, Stephanotis, freesias, and Lisianthus, but they're all white, and obviously we're not having white bridesmaid dresses!' Rebecca said with a grin. 'Anything that goes with those colours ... I suppose silver? Or perhaps we could do the powdery, light coloured dresses that are all the rage, you could both have different if you like, powder blue, yellow, or pink?'

'Please not that washed out pale pink!' Louise pleaded dramatically. 'It was all the rage in the eighties and it should have bloody well been left there!' My eyebrows rose in curiosity at her tone and Rebecca rolled her eyes prompting Louise to explain. 'When I was a kid I was bridesmaid three times in three months for various aunties and uncles, and all three dresses were hideous, huge, and *that* colour, so I now have a photo album full of me looking like a marshmallow fairy and an understandable dislike of the colour.'

Visions of Louise dressed up in a huge pink dress sprung to my mind, followed by several choice jokes, but before I could select which one to crack, Rebecca laughed and then spoke again. 'OK, no pale pink then. Start having a look through, see if anything takes your fancy, girls.'

The next ten minutes were spent mostly in silence, with an occasional 'What do you think of this?', and then Rebecca finally turned and announced it was time for Louise and I to do some trying on. 'Let me just get this last one ...' Louise mumbled. She was half-buried in a rack of dresses and obviously fumbling around for something right at the back.

'Oof!' Finally she came stumbling free holding the most hideous dress I've ever seen, and believe me, as the child of a wannabe hippy I had seen some *really* hideous dresses on my mother over the years. 'Ta-da!' she exclaimed with obvious pride as Rebecca and I simply stood there staring at her as if she had gone completely nuts.

'But ... I mean ... it's ... it's ... *cerise pink*,' Rebecca finally stuttered in total astonishment. The meringue bottom to the dress was pretty spectacular too, and definitely worthy of comment, but I guessed Rebecca was opting to deal with one thing at a time.

'It's just perfect!' Louise sighed happily. Nodding solemnly she stroked the dress lovingly and sighed again. 'We said no pale pink. Well, this might be pink, but it certainly isn't pale.'

She had that right, the *thing* in her hands was practically fluorescent. I thought I'd gotten to know Louise and her tastes fairly well in the recent weeks of helping with the wedding preparations, but apparently there were certain nuances to her style that I had missed. Her taste for neon clothing being one of them.

'I ... um ...' Rebecca was floundering for words, but to be honest, so was I. Blinking several times Rebecca turned desperate eyes on me. 'Stella, what do you think?'

Backing up I raised my hands defensively and shook my head rapidly. 'Oh no, no, no, you're not turning this on me! It's your wedding, you decide!'

Thankfully, before Rebecca had the chance to say anything else, Louise dissolved into a fit of giggles, doubling over and laughing so hard that tears were soon streaming down her reddened face. 'I'm kidding!' she panted between wheezy laughs. 'But oh my God, it was worth it ... your faces are priceless!' Feeling a grin slip to my lips I joined with Louise's laughter, massively relieved that I wouldn't have to wear the cerise fluff mountain after all.

'Thank God for that!' Rebecca said on a near-hysterical giggle. Louise was still laughing and wiping tears away from her eyes and in the background the poor shop assistant was looking slightly put out. Perhaps the dress was one of her favourites. Or perhaps she was rapidly beginning to understand that her peaceful morning was quickly disintegrating into giggly, crazy chaos.

Once we'd agreed on our favourites the immeasurably patient shop assistant sorted out the gowns for us to try on, and after topping up our champagne – maybe she was hoping the alcohol would numb us into calmness – she ushered us through to the changing rooms and then left us to it.

'Which one first?' I asked Rebecca expectantly, secretly hoping she'd say the gorgeous midnight blue one. It was slinky, stylish, and utterly gorgeous. Definitely my stand out favourite from the bunch.

'Hmmm.' Rubbing her chin Rebecca assessed the selected gowns again. 'I know Nicholas mentioned that he wouldn't mind a silvery grey colour theme to the wedding, so let's start with the silver one that you spotted, Lou.'

I hid my slight disappointment with a smile. I suppose the silver dress *was* beautiful too, so I grabbed one in my size and stepped into a large cubicle. Looking around my eyes widened – there was a sofa and a side table in here with me, adorned with a stunning vase of flowers. Wow. I suppose the changing areas here needed to be big because they catered for brides as well as bridesmaids, but this was pure luxury.

Assessing the design of the dress I decided that sliding into it from the bottom was the easiest option, and miraculously I managed to get my arms and head up through the underskirt and two layers of thin silk without any mishaps. Judging from the giggles and grunts coming from the cubicle next door, Louise wasn't having quite as much luck. Stepping out into the main changing area Rebecca looked over me and raised her eyebrows in pleasant surprise. 'Ooooh! I like it!' she said, almost skipping around me to check out the back view.

'How you doing, Lou-Lou?' Rebecca asked, circling me again with a growing look of pleasure on her face. 'It looks great on Stella, we just need you to match and we might have found our dress on the first try!'

There were several more huffing noises from behind the curtain to Louise's cubicle. 'Well, girlies.' *Grunt.* 'If it's a show stopper you want.' *Grunt.* 'Then this is the dress.' With a whoosh the curtain to Louise's stall whipped back and Rebecca and I were met with the sight of her standing there, hands on hips, bright red in the face, hair all over the place, and most obviously, with her bra clad boobs on full view squashed up outside the top of the dress. I looked at her cleavage again to check that what I was seeing was correct, but it definitely was. Her boobs were *outside* the dress.

'What can I say?' Louise said with a shrug as she blew some wayward hair from her face, 'My tits are clearly too boobylicious for this dress.'

Simultaneously Rebecca and I burst into laughter until we were clutching at our sides and clinging to each other for support. 'Wanna know the best thing?' Louise said over our giggles, 'I'm stuck tight like a frigging sardine so we might have to buy this bloody thing anyway.'

By this point Rebecca had a hand shoved between her legs and was practically hopping around the room, 'Stop! Stop! I'm gonna wet myself laughing!' she cried desperately as a knock on the changing room door instantly silenced us all.

'All right in there?' The voice of the shop assistant calling through the wood was tinged with disapproval, making us all grin and slap hands over our mouths and stare at it like three naughty schoolgirls about to be caught out smoking a cigarette behind the bike sheds at school.

'Everything OK, ladies?' the assistant called again. Rebecca was frozen by the wall, still with one hand over her mouth and the other clutched at her crotch, Louise was standing there stuck in her dress and clutching her boobs like they were going to fall off, and I was clamping my lips together to stop myself laughing and digging my hands into my hair, because quite frankly I didn't know what else to do with them. Waving her hands like an out of control windmill, Louise frantically indicated for me to go and help her. I dashed over and began desperately tugging at the dress to try and free her more than abundant cleavage, while Rebecca flashed us a comical expression and cleared her throat. 'Everything's fine, thanks!' she called, her voice high-pitched and slightly manic, which only set Louise and I off sniggering again.

After a five-minute team effort of tugging and coaxing the material over Louise's curves we finally had the bloody dress off of her and back on the hanger only looking marginally out of shape. Puffing out a breath I leant back on the wall. 'That was more exhausting than a run!' I quipped. At least I wouldn't need to go on the treadmill later.

'Well, that's one design out.' Rebecca said, giving the dress another amused glance. 'Let's try the blue one, it has a zip and it's a little roomier up top.' She lifted down the dress that had been my favourite from the start. Taking the hanger from her I almost pranced back into my cubicle in my eagerness to try the fabulous dress on.

The dress slid on like a glove and I stepped out to let Rebecca do it up for me before turning to the full length mirror on the wall.

'Oh!' It wasn't just my voice, expressing a happy exclamation, Rebecca and I had spoken almost in unison as we stared at the beautiful dress now clinging to my body. It was strapless, hugging my torso tight and then

114

falling to the floor in looser folds. It had to be said that the colour looked pretty amazing against my blonde hair too. We were joined then by Louise, who had a similar look of wonderment on her face as I quickly helped her with the zip before swivelling her towards the mirror.

The three of us stood there gazing at the reflection of the beautiful gowns. All it needed was Rebecca to be in her dress and the scene would be set. Hearing a sniff by my left ear I turned to Rebecca and saw her eyes welling up. 'These are the ones, girls,' she murmured happily. 'I know Nicholas wanted a silver theme, but I think he'll be just as happy with navy blue. Let's get the woman to properly size you up.'

NINE – REBECCA

Today called for my extra special new shoes. They needed to be comfy, while also utterly fabulous to look at, and they needed to match a black outfit – luckily this pair ticked all those boxes. The reason for my all singing, all dancing new shoes? Today was my hen-do, and I was so excited I'd barely managed to eat my breakfast. Nicholas had also hardly touched his toast this morning, but his loss of appetite was because he was in a bit of a sulk about the prospect of me being out all day and night without him, something I found rather over the top, but had so far refrained from commenting on.

Admittedly it was perhaps a little early to be having my hen-do because we still had nearly four months until the wedding next March, but after initially setting the hen do for the end of February I'd had a phone call last month that had changed all my plans and forced me to drastically shift my hen-do forwards. One of my oldest and closest friends Fiona – best buddies since our days at nursery – was heading off to Indonesia after Christmas and was going to be away for a full year working in an orphanage. She's a doctor, a very well-respected paediatrician at Great Ormond Street, and had been practically begging for the sabbatical needed for her trip, so when her hospital had finally agreed to the placement she couldn't turn it down or try to rearrange just for little ol' me.

We'd both been so disappointed when she'd told me that she was going to miss the wedding that we'd spent an entire evening in a cocktail bar drowning our sorrows and crying our eyes out, but when I'd told Stella the following day she thought for a few seconds, then simply suggested moving the hen-do forwards so at least Fiona could be involved in that. As soon as she'd said the words I couldn't believe I hadn't thought of it myself. There had been no reason not to – there wasn't a chance I was changing my mind about the wedding, so really it didn't matter when I had the hen-do.

After Stella had spent so long changing the arrangements so Fiona could be accommodated, I'd then spent the last few weeks thinking that my chief organiser herself wouldn't be able to come. The flu Stella had suffered – a 'super flu' according to her doctor – had really run her down for nearly three full weeks in the end, and as the date for the hen-do crept closer and closer I'd started to really panic. Luckily Nathan had picked up some antibiotics from the pharmacy, which had perked Stella up within a few days. Last weekend's dress shopping trip had been her first real excursion out of the house since her illness, and after no adverse side effects from the exertion she had announced herself recovered. Nathan had been a wreck during her illness, poor guy. He might not vocalise his emotions much, but it had been clear for anyone to see how worried he'd been about Stella.

So now here we were, the day of my hen-do, just after two p.m. on the first Saturday in December and we'd been picked up in a flashy long limo that comfortably seated all six of us – me, Stella, Fiona, Louise, and two of my other closest friends. As well as being roomy, the car had its own very well stocked mini-bar and sound system pumping out some brilliant music, and we were on our way to the first surprise stop of the day. I had no clue about Stella's plans for me, but I didn't care; I was surrounded by friends, we were all in fabulous moods, and that was all that mattered.

Stella had us all chinking our glasses together as she

raised a toast to "a fabulous friend, fabulous day, and fabulous wedding" which had me blushing with embarrassment, and then our limo set off. The driver didn't rush to the destination though, instead opting to take us on a route around Hyde Park and Regents Park whilst we sang along to classics by Wham!, Take That, and Mika and drank two glasses of deliciously fruity Pimm's. Once we had drunk the jug dry and were well and truly in the swing of things we finally pulled up outside The Ritz where Stella informed me that we had an afternoon tea date in the Palm Court. Afternoon tea in The Ritz – how exciting, and what a great start to the proceedings!

Thank God I had dressed up, because this room, not to mention the hotel lobby that we'd just walked through, were *incredible*. And I mean jaw-droppingly opulent. The salon was in the centre of the hotel and dripping with elegant style, history, and of course the occasional gilded statue. As its name suggested it also had large palm trees dotted around its perimeter which were somehow greener and healthier than any I'd ever seen on an actual beach.

The food and drink we consumed far exceeded any image of 'afternoon tea' I'd ever had before; caraway bread sandwiches with the most sumptuous fillings, freshly baked scones dripping with cream and jam, and the most mind-boggling array of teas I'd ever seen – I'd literally never heard of half of them. Not that we were drinking tea for most of the meal; chilled champagne arrived shortly after we did, and with me and my five closest friends all in rather high spirits it certainly didn't go to waste.

By the time we emerged from the arched doorways of The Ritz it was gone six o'clock in the evening and we were all well on the way to being rather tipsy. Magically our limousine was waiting for us by the curb and we all piled in to head back to Stella's house to change for an evening of dancing and merriment. That's literally all I'd been told, I didn't know venues or details, I'd merely been given a card that said to pack a change of clothes for dancing in. So I had – my favourite little black dress and the same plum coloured high heels I had on already. I got them in the Coast sale last month and I totally loved them; they were amazingly both comfortable and beautiful, and definitely my new favourites.

As it turned out, we'd ended up at Nathan's swanky Docklands apartment to change, much to the excitement of my old schoolfriends who ran around exploring like over excited children let loose at Disney World, and exclaimed they'd never seen such a beautiful home. Nathan was out, apparently entertaining Nicholas for the evening, which was just as well because after well and truly giving his apartment the once over we changed and then made rather good use of his balcony and mini bar.

We'd had a drink at a great little cocktail bar in Covent Garden – best Cosmo *ever* – and now it was half past ten and we were making our way into a nightclub called Project just behind Oxford Street. I'd heard of the place, it was a swanky, members-only club making all the headlines for its exclusivity and celebrity members, but I never dreamed in a million years that I'd ever be going inside it. 'How the hell did you manage to get us in here? I thought it was members only?' I whispered to Stella as the bouncers checked our ID and waved us inside without even a blink of concern.

Turning to me Stella gave a casual shrug, 'Nathan sorted it,' she said in way of explanation. Which immediately made sense; Nathan was probably even richer and more influential in London circles than Nicholas, so if anyone was going to blag entrance tickets to a swanky nightclub, he'd be the guy to manage it.

I might listen to Wham! on occasions as a guilty treat, but that doesn't mean I couldn't shake it on the dance floor like the best of them back in my student days, and as we made our way further inside, the heavy, hot air and thumping beat of 'Animals' by Martin Garrix surrounded me and I felt almost like I was stepping back in time. Let me correct myself – the deep pulsing beat of the music and its addictive rhythm was like stepping back in time, but the club itself couldn't have been more modern. Project London was certainly no student dive bar, there were no sticky floors or seedy lighting, no, everything around us reeked of glamour, wealth, and high class style. Neon lights of purple and red lit the large space, a bar ran the length of one wall, and the remainder of the floor was given over to either dance space or ultra-sleek leather booths.

Seeing beautiful dresses and chic three-piece suits everywhere I was just thinking that the calibre of the guests matched the classy surroundings when Louise grabbed my arm and shook me so violently that I staggered forwards several steps. 'Holy shit! Isn't that the woman out of that Tarantino film?'' she shrieked in my ear. Thankfully the music was loud enough to cover her outburst, but she was bloody well right, out on the dance floor swaying and rolling her leather-clad body like it was made of water was a genuine A-list celeb. Not that I could actually remember her name, but still!

Quite simply, I was having the best day ever. Apart from the day Nicholas had proposed, of course, that had been totally unexpected and had made for a pretty amazing day too. The music tonight was out of this world, I was tipsy and carefree, and I was surrounded by my five closest friends in the world as we giggled and lost ourselves in the beat. With my clumsy tendencies I wasn't the best dancer by any means, but when I let my inhibitions down like I had tonight I could really enjoy myself. Even Stella was dancing with gusto, and I knew she usually hated it. I couldn't help grinning with happiness, it had to be said that as hen dos go, Stella had done a pretty amazing job.

Half way through the following track I noticed that Stella's attention had become distracted by something over my shoulder as a frown settled on her brows. Wondering why she had suddenly stopped dancing and looked so pissed off I turned and followed her gaze to a low balcony area just a few steps above the main dancefloor. It was difficult to make out because of the dim lighting, but as the strobes swung across the floor I saw Nicholas and Nathan leaning on the railing, staring at us with matching frowns on their faces like a pair of moody gargoyles.

What the heck? What were Nicholas and Nathan doing here? I spun back to Stella in confusion. 'What are they doing here?' I watched as Stella shook her head and downed the rest of her cocktail.

'I have no idea, but this is just like Nathan to do something so bloody overprotective. Sorry, Becks, when I asked him to get us tickets I never thought he'd turn up here too,' she said apologetically.

'Well, they know this is supposed to be a girl's night so let's just leave them to their brooding,' I declared boldly, grabbing Stella and Fiona's hands and leading our group a little further away from our unplanned audience.

'Who do you think is worse?' Stella asked with a nod of her head towards the balcony where our pair of domineering men stood. Briefly turning my head again I saw both Nathan and Nicholas watching us intently and completely ignoring the music.

Now that I'd had more than my fill of alcohol I actually found this all quite amusingly sweet. 'I think they are probably just as bad as each other, although I have to say Nathan's got the Jackson death stare down to a fine art. I swear to God if any man comes near you he's going to fry him on the spot.' We both started giggling, but as the DJ switched the track to a remixed version of The Prodigy our hands were grabbed by the rest of the girls and we got swept along with a high-energy dance which had the dance floor full within seconds.

Needing a break I left Stella and the girls dancing and grabbed a bottle of water from the bar. After downing the whole thing in one very unladylike display I scanned the club and sought out Nicholas' indiscreet hiding place. Finally my eyes landed on him and I saw he was still in almost the same position as last time, and once again his eyes were on me and his face was decidedly unimpressed. I decided in my drunken state that it would be a good idea to go and see him and find out what he was playing at, but really if I'm honest, my tipsiness was making me quite horny and I also quite fancied sneaking a quick make out session in the dark confines of the club.

Sauntering up the four steps to where Nicholas was leaning I tried to look haughty and disapproving, and was immensely glad that my drunkenness didn't cause me to visibly stagger. 'Fancy yourself as an honorary hen, do you?' I murmured. It was dark, but even without direct light I saw Nicholas' cheeks flush with embarrassment at being so obviously caught out.

Sliding an arm around my waist he shrugged mildly and then tugged me against him firmly so our hips were now squashed together. Deciding to wind him up a little more I pretended to be annoyed with his presence and kept my eyebrow raised questioningly. It took all my restraint not to reciprocate his touch, but I left my hands dangling by my sides and my facial expression as blank as I could. Looking slightly panicked by my cold shoulder he chewed on his lip and then spoke quickly. 'It was Nathan's idea really. He mentioned where you were going and then when we were out for drinks we found ourselves in the neighbourhood.' He gave another shrug and took a sip of his beer while watching me carefully over the rim of his bottle. I could tell Nicholas was trying to decide if I was angry with him or not, but to be honest, I was so tipsy that

123

I didn't really mind him being here. In fact, with his hips still pressing against mine and the first stirrings of an erection making themselves felt against my stomach my earlier pretence at anger was rapidly fading and a cuddle was starting to sound quite tempting.

Just as I was about to make good on my idea Nathan swore loudly behind me, causing Nicholas and I to briefly break apart as we spun to look at him. My eyebrows nearly flew to my scalp as I watched as Nathan literally vaulted over the railing to the dance floor below before storming across the space and making a beeline for Stella and my friends. Crikey, talk about athletic. People were scattered by his progress through the crowd until he stopped beside Stella and glared at a man now quivering next to her.

Nathan's growl was so loud I heard it from all the way over here, 'Get your fucking hands off her.'

Once he had dispatched with the unwanted groper I watched Nathan bristling with anger until Stella pulled him into an embrace and started dancing with him, probably to distract him from wanting to go after the guy and punch him.

'I think my brother is a little over-protective,' Nicholas observed beside me as he resumed our closer position by sliding his arm around my waist again, but I only just managed to hold in a full blown laugh – talk about pot calling kettle black! 'Must be a family trait.' I muttered with a smirk, but luckily Nicholas didn't hear my sarcasm over the music.

TEN - STELLA

I couldn't frigging believe it when I saw Nathan leap from the balcony like some enraged version of Superman and begin his charge in my direction, but I did at least know the cause of his over-the-top and unnecessary hurdling. About two seconds ago a fairly attractive guy with a cute, shy smile had shimmied his way into our group and made the fatal mistake of putting a hand on my shoulder as he leaned in to speak to me. I was quite prepared to politely decline his tentative approach, but no, that wouldn't be enough for Nathan, would it? He clearly felt the need to charge in like a bull in a china shop and make a massive scene. Taking a deep breath I prepared for impact, and then a second later winced as Nathan arrived at my side, leaned into the guys face, and yelled so loudly that we both leant back to avoid the fallout. 'Get your fucking hands off her!' The poor guy had only been trying his luck, and he'd actually been very sweet about it, but now he was practically shaking in his boots as he stuttered an apology and began to back away.

Bristling with anger, Nathan took a step to follow the man and was no doubt set on continuing his rant, but I quickly intervened, grabbing him and pulling him back by sliding both my arms around his neck. 'Stella,' he growled in warning, trying to pry me off him so he could carry on his hunt, but there was no way I was letting him pound out his jealousy on a relatively innocent man. Tangling one hand in his hair I tugged on it until he winced and relented, allowing me to lower his head towards mine.

'Why would you want to follow him when I'm right here?' As I said my last four words I lowered my spare hand to his groin and cupped him through his trousers, giving him a squeeze. A *hard* squeeze.

Even above the music I heard the hiss that escaped his lips as his eyes widened. 'Christ, Stella, easy, woman,' he stuttered on a choked gasp and seemed to instantly forget all ideas of chasing after the man, clutching at my shoulders instead. Grinning up at him I felt him hardening in my grasp almost immediately and was quite content to play, but he gripped my wrist and gave me a warning look accompanied by a dirty smirk. 'Time and place, Stella, time and place. Save it for later, baby.'

I nearly laughed out loud at his remark, because it always seemed fine for Nathan to attack *me* in public when he felt like it; my orgasms in Club Twist, London backstreets, and the back of his car were evidence of that.

Deciding not to push it I reluctantly released Nathan's twitching groin and slipped my arms around his neck for a dance instead. 'If you take your brother and head home now, then I'm happy to ignore the fact that you came here during Rebecca's hen-do when you know you shouldn't have,' I murmured mildly, wanting him to know that regardless of what had just occurred, he had stepped over some serious boundaries tonight.

Making a dismissive noise in his throat Nathan jerked his head back and looked at me as if I was crazy. 'You expect me to leave after that fucker just tried it on with you?' Giving him an even firmer look I began to pull my hands from around his neck. Nathan held onto my waist to stop me moving further away, but I'd had enough of his overbearing behaviour for one night and twisted from his loose grip. Raising my chin I nodded definitely, 'Yes I do, Nathan, if you'd given me a few more seconds before you'd done your raging Hulk impression you would have seen me knocking back his advances.' Crossing my arms I drew in a deep breath before stating one final truth. 'If our relationship stands any chance of surviving then I need to know that you trust me, Nathan. *Me*. I would never have let anything happen with that guy, and if you had any faith in my commitment to you you'd know that.' I was close to shouting volume now and I could see Fiona and Louise watching from the sidelines and looking like they were debating whether to join in and help me, but I flashed them a quick reassuring glance then looked back to Nathan. 'What's it to be, Nathan?' I asked, amazing myself with how calm and authoritative I sounded.

Nathan looked so torn that in any other circumstances I might have felt sorry for him, but not tonight. Finally he threw his hands up in exasperation and ran them through his hair. 'Fine. *Fine*. I'll take Nicholas home.' Using his thumb he tilted my chin up and stared deep into my eyes, clearly not happy leaving me. 'I do trust you, Stella, more than you know,' he suddenly muttered softly, then without any warning he crushed his lips to mine in a kiss so possessive I almost felt branded from the searing intensity of it as I sagged against him and surrendered my mouth along with the last of my anger. 'Come home to my house when you're done with the girls then,' Nathan demanded against my lips, making me giggle at his continued desperation to be the one in charge.

In reality I knew the only reason he wanted me to go to his house was so he could feel like he'd won a small victory and claimed his prize – me. Not that I minded really, and if I hadn't promised Rebecca that I'd get her home safely then I probably would have caved in to his demand. 'I can't, Nathan, I promised Rebecca I'd stay fairly sober and make sure she gets home tonight. It'll be late by the time we leave, and your apartment is another half an hour from Nicholas' house so I'd have to get a taxi on my own, which I don't want to do. I'll take them up on their offer to stay over, and I'll head to yours tomorrow after breakfast.'

Watching carefully, I saw Nathan's entire body tense again as his earlier irritation resurfaced – even his legs seemed to straighten out a little more and his hands definitely formed into fists at his sides. 'You're spending the night at my brother's house?' he demanded on nothing short of a low snarl.

Rolling my eyes at my man and his stupid possessiveness I shook my head, 'Nathan, I'm spending the night at my best friend's house. Yes, she happens to be marrying your brother, and yes, they live together, but that does not give you cause for any more stupid jealousy. I'll be in the spare room for God's sake.'

Seeing Nathan still struggling with how to deal with this information I tried to reign in my annoyance and remember that his unnecessary jealousy was really just insecurity because of his inexperience with real relationships. 'Seeing as you're out with Nicholas you could head home with him and stay over too, I'm sure he wouldn't mind,' I suggested. 'That way I'd see you when I get in. You could have the bed all warmed up and ready for me.'

I'd added my last remark suggestively in the hope that it might loosen him up, but Nathan looked far too stressed out by all this to lighten up and instead turned to me, chewing frantically on his lower lip. 'I'm a fully grown man, Stella, I don't do fucking sleepovers,' he huffed petulantly. Raising my eyebrows I smirked at him, my troubled man might not do sleepovers, but quite apparently he did do full-blown toddler temper tantrums.

In the end it took me another ten minutes to actually get both of the Jackson brothers out of the club before I returned to Rebecca with a rueful smile as we resumed our dancing. Leaning over she was grinning from ear to ear. 'I fully expected Nathan to go into caveman mode and drag

128

you away over his shoulder,' she joked, but to be honest, I had kind of been expecting the same thing and was still slightly shocked that Nathan *had* left. Grabbing my hand with relish, Rebecca twirled herself under my arm and dragged me back to the group of girls so we could carry on celebrating in style.

When we finally got back to her Primrose Hill home later that night – technically the following morning – I made Rebecca drink a full pint of water and then gently pushed her through the door to her bedroom before retreating to the spare room. To my surprise, as I stripped off and crawled into bed I found Nathan's warmth under the covers waiting for me. So apparently he wasn't too grown up for sleepovers after all. I'd honestly believed that he was too stubborn to give in and sleep here tonight, but I was so glad he'd changed his mind. Thinking he was asleep I snuggled up to his back carefully, loving the scent of him on the pillow and his warm skin touching mine, but he moved, rolling over and feeling about to find me. 'About time,' he muttered thickly. Finding its target his arm snaked around my stomach and I couldn't help but grin as he tugged me against him so we were spooning.

Nuzzling in my hair Nathan let out a long contented breath. 'I have hated every single fucking second of my evening since I left you in that bloody meat market.' I was expecting him to lecture me or have a moan about the events of the night, but to my surprise Nathan just cuddled me closer and fell silent as he almost immediately began to fall back asleep. Pondering my complex man for a few more seconds I gave up trying to work him out and instead let my dance weary body follow him into slumber.

The following morning I woke up feeling surprisingly good – there was no hangover in sight whatsoever, so apparently there were some benefits to being the designated sensible person then. The guest bed in Rebecca and Nicholas' spare room was incredibly comfortable, and with the curtains filtering the early morning sunshine I could have easily stayed here for longer, but the warm sheets quickly lost their appeal when I discovered Nathan was no longer in bed with me. Dragging myself to the bathroom I grabbed a quick shower, pulled on last night's discarded clothes, and then went in search of him.

I was a little wary of finding Nathan, especially after his sleepy comments on my arrival in bed last night, and was desperately hoping he wasn't going to make a scene in front of Nicholas and Rebecca this morning. Finding him alone in the kitchen was actually quite a relief, until I took stock of the tenseness of his shoulders and my stomach plummeted. He stood leaning back against one of the kitchen counters, his legs spread and arms crossed over his chest looking so sexy and broody that I felt my heart give a kick in my chest. 'Good morning,' I murmured softly.

Instead of a reply I was greeted by silence and a pair of intense, heavy lidded blue eyes watching my every move. Hmmm … it looked like someone had definitely gotten out of bed on the wrong side this morning.

'I'd like to go home,' were his first words, but they were laced with petulance, and not anger as I had expected. A smile curled my lips; instead of being stroppy about last night he felt put out because his routine was off, and judging from his awkward stance, he didn't like it one little bit. 'Let's go,' he said, handing me a travel mug full to the brim of steaming coffee. I accepted the mug, but placed my other hand on his forearm to halt his movement.

'Can we say good morning properly first?' I murmured softly, and he immediately paused and looked down at me intently. I slid my hand up his arm and into the hair at the nape of his neck, which was damp, presumably from a shower. After running his gaze across my face a tiny flicker of a smile twitched on his lips before he leant down and placed his soft warm lips on mine in a brief but lovely kiss, and then leant back a fraction. 'Good morning, beautiful.' His endearment was so quiet that I barely heard it, but it was there, and my heart beat just a little quicker because of it as I instinctively leaned into his body.

'You're still not forgiven for last night. I wonder how I'll get you to make it up to me ...' he added, as he leant back and gently smoothed some hair from my face. Crikey, my heart was pounding now; the contradictory clash of his soft actions but firm words had fully awoken both my sleepy body and my thundering arousal.

'Rebecca said to say thank you for last night, and that she'll call you later.' Nathan said as he guided my stunned body towards the door with a firm hand on my lower back, but I felt too shocked to speak. How could he lace his previous words with a delicious threat of kinky naughtiness and then seconds later be conversing like nothing had happened? Mild amusement replaced my shock and I shook my head at how changeable he could be. I literally couldn't keep up with him when he was like this so I may as well just go along and enjoy the ride.

'They've gone out this morning, some appointment in Herefordshire with a group of musicians Nicholas knows. Turns out my brother is being very finicky about who will be playing at the wedding,' Nathan said with a small snort of dry laughter.

Nicholas wasn't the only one with his finicky ways, I thought with a smile as I allowed Nathan to guide me from the house and help me into his car. What with his hand-washing, suit adjusting, and general possessiveness Nathan could certainly give his brother a run for his money in the obsessive control department. Sipping my coffee as he drove I began to feel more alert from the caffeine and rather aroused at the thought that Nathan might have some sort of punishment planned for me today. Apart from the liaison in the back of his company car a few weeks ago it had been ages since he'd really let his Dominant side out. Imagining all the things he might do to me, all the things I *wanted* him to do to me, was enough to keep me quiet for the entire journey home.

Arriving at his apartment Nathan headed to the lounge and paused by the dining table before turning to me, widening his stance, and then slowly and deliberately pushing his hands into the pockets of his suit trousers as he looked at me from under lowered brows. Such a normal stance, but God Nathan looked sexy when he stood like that. Like me, Nathan was still dressed in last night's clothes, despite the showers we'd both taken at Nicholas', which meant he was suited and booted in a charcoal three-piece, and looking completely delectable.

'So, Stella. About last night. As much as I enjoyed dancing with you, I did not take any pleasure whatsoever in seeing you surrounded by a pack of men as you flaunted yourself on the dance floor.'

Flaunted myself? Pah! Hardly. I danced in a group with the women I was out with and paid no attention to any men. I was just about to huffily state as much, but as I studied Nathan's expression very closely I suddenly realised that he was playing with me when I saw the corners of his eyes crease with just the tiniest hint of a smile. Ah, OK, so Nathan wasn't really irritated, he was merely intent of setting up a scene, was he? Well that was just fine by me, especially as I was now completely recovered from my flu and feeling back on top form. Although truth be told, knowing Nathan like I did, he probably was carrying around a touch of lingering frustration about last night as well, bless him.

'Whatever shall I do with you?' he murmured salaciously as he cocked his head to the side and kept me pinned with his bright blue stare. At his domineering stance and words I felt my legs become a little rubbery, so lowered myself to lean on the edge of the dining table for support as I chewed expectantly on my lip, choosing the stay silent for now.

Leaning across the table Nathan tutted in apparent irritation and used his thumb to roughly dislodge my lower lip from between my teeth. 'You're really pushing my buttons, Stella; first last night and now chewing on your lip again.' Leaning back he ran his hands through his hair and genuinely looked like he was at his wits ends. It was at times like this when I loved him the most, when he tried to maintain his calm, strong front but failed and exposed a little of his vulnerability. I knew my lip biting bothered him, he hated it when I 'hurt' myself, but it wasn't exactly a conscious choice, just a habit that I was mostly unaware of doing. Poor guy, clearly my lip biting combined with the stress of seeing me out last night with the occasional bit of interest from the opposite sex was tipping him over the edge.

Looking at me with pleading eyes he exhaled a short, sharp breath and then seemed to gather himself. 'I've told you numerous times, don't damage yourself – this lip is *mine*. No biting it. Clear?'

Hearing Nathan's truly domineering tone for the first time in weeks sent an instant shiver of fear laced lust shooting straight to my core and delicious tingles sprang to the skin of my arms. As ridiculous as it sounds, after our 'handcuff car scenario' the other week I had realised that I'd missed this side of him, *really*, missed it, if I was being honest. Submission was obviously something inbuilt within my personality, or at least a certain degree of it anyway, because no matter how much I loved the responsibility of my job, my independence, and the equality of the relationship I now had with Nathan, I still occasionally yearned for the good old days when he used to so effortlessly take control of me and have his wicked way with me.

A small sigh escaped my lips as my mind suddenly ran wild with visions of all our passionate times together. The sensation of his total power over me was just exquisite, the biggest turn on I'd ever experienced in my life, and although I'm sure some women would hate it, I loved how powerless I felt when Nathan truly dominated me. Although perhaps "powerless" is the wrong word. It was the lack of responsibility I loved; I didn't need to worry or think about anything when we were in a scene, it was like emptying my mind of all thoughts and just existing in the moment. I sound like some Zen yoga buff, but it was true – it helped that I knew I was completely safe with him, one murmur of the safe word and I had no doubt that Nathan would cease immediately.

My thoughts had me craving that adrenaline rush again, *right now*, regardless of the fact that it was barely ten o'clock in the morning, and so with a deep breath for bravery I made sure I had his full attention before I slowly licked my lips, nodded to show that I'd heard him, and then teasingly took my lower lip in between my teeth again. Gently grazing my teeth back and forth on the soft flesh I watched as Nathan's eyes initially widened in surprise at my deliberate infringement of his rules, but then his pupils darkened and narrowed as his spine straightened from my challenge.

'Stella?' Nathan's voice practically rumbled across the small distance between us as I continued to toy with my lip, but I didn't answer him, just continued to look at him provocatively, no doubt with a devious twinkle in my eye.

'So be it,' he murmured. Standing slightly straighter I watched Nathan adjust his posture until it was utterly perfect; his broad shoulders squared and upright and his legs splayed as he pointed to his right and raised an eyebrow at me. This was my signal to submit to him, and I'd never been happier to see it, or keener to oblige in all my life. Sliding from the table I immediately took up my position at his side, linked my hands, and averted my gaze. My heart was hammering so loudly in my chest that I was sure he would be able to hear it and laugh at me for being foolish enough to start all this in the first place with my act of defiance.

'Don't move a muscle,' he told me in a low tone as he stalked around me once and then came to stand behind me. His lips lowered next to my neck, tracing a pattern up and down so closely that I could feel his breath fanning across my skin, but never once did his teasing mouth make contact with me. Once again circling me like his intended prey – which I suppose I was – he came to stand just before me and placed both his hands on my wrists in the lightest of touches before running just one fingertip up each arm, across my collar bones, and up my neck until they reached my mouth. His thumbs grazed across my lips several times and instinctively I bit on my lip to hold in the moan that wanted to escape. 'This lip is going to get you into trouble, Stella,' Nathan smirked, sounding rather pleased with himself as his thumb released my lip and briefly pushed inside my mouth where I couldn't resist gently sucking on it. Just as quickly as it started Nathan moved away and removed all contact with me and a groan escaped my lips as I swayed on my feet, my head now light and dizzy from the adrenaline and lust coursing through my system.

'Stay right where you are,' he murmured, thrusting his hands into his trouser pockets, then seeing my shiver of anticipation, he chuckled darkly, 'That's right, Stella, I'm nowhere near done with you yet.' Such teasing words! He strode in the direction of his office, leaving me panting and wondering what he was doing.

Just as he had requested I didn't move an inch – unless you counted the heaving of my chest from the ragged breaths escaping past my lips – but thankfully no more than a minute or two later I watched him stride back towards me purposefully with a single sheet of paper and fountain pen in his hand. It didn't escape my notice that he had dispensed of his shoes and socks and was now barefoot, his gorgeous feet making hardly a sound on the wooden floor as he approached me. Placing the paper down he began to roll up his shirt sleeves, taking his time to fold them perfectly until they sat just below his elbows. I wondered if he knew just how sexy he looked; still in his smart shirt and trousers, but barefooted and his strong, corded forearms rippling as he moved. It was such a tempting sight that I felt myself biting my lower lip again, only to realise what I was doing and then stifle a nervous giggle as I released it from between my teeth.

Ignoring me completely he slid onto one of the seats by the dining table, removed the lid from his pen with a flourish, and began to write something. I was too far away to see what he was writing, but I was starting to squirm a little on the spot, which he obviously noticed, because he finally sighed and then looked up briefly, 'Undress, then resume your position.' With that he went back to his notes.

Slightly taken back by his cold briskness I stood unmoving for a few seconds staring at him, almost feeling affronted by his treatment of me. Was this really how he had been with me at the start of our relationship? I thought back, and realised that yes, Nathan had been incredibly intimidating and blunt then, while also sexy as hell, and clearly from this display still had it in him just below the surface.

'Now, Stella,' he reminded me in a firm, barked order, not even lifting his eyes from the paper. But this time I saw that his words were accompanied by just the briefest curl of his upper lip, as if he was sharing my shock and finding it amusing. Well, I suppose I had been the one to deliberately taunt him in the first place, clearly he was just getting his own back now. Luckily, just that tiny glimpse of the Nathan I now knew, loved, and trusted reassured me and I immediately began to peel my clothes off, fold them neatly, and place them on a chair.

Just as I was about to remove my high heels I heard the shift of Nathan's chair on the wooden floor and glanced up to find him replacing the cap of his fountain pen and watching me intently with a lusty glint in his eye. 'The heels can stay,' he murmured, standing from his seat and pointing to where he wished me to stand. Pushing my foot back into my four inch high heel I stood as tall and confident as I could, and then approached him with what I hoped was a seductive gait until I was stood before him wearing nothing but my necklace, high heels, and a heated blush.

When I reached his side I heard a low growl of approval rumble from Nathan's chest. Then saw him pick up the piece of paper and wave it briefly, before stepping away from me and bending to place it on a low coffee table on the other side of the dining room. Then he walked back to me, placed a hand on my lower back which seemed to scorch my skin from his touch, and guided me to the coffee table.

'I want you to read this in your head and memorise the lines word for word for posterity,' he told me in a soft tone. Wondering why he hadn't just handed the sheet to me I bent to pick it up but almost immediately felt his warm hand settle on my lower back, keeping me bent over at a right angle. 'Uh-uh, Stella, no picking it up.' Then, after giving my lower back a gentle tap he spoke again, 'Hands here please.'

I complied immediately, the weeks and weeks of training we'd done together at the start of our relationship were still so ingrained in me that to be honest I found it hard not to comply with his requests. Lifting my arms up and behind me I felt one of his hands circle both of my wrists and gently rub as he held them at the base of my spine. 'Are you learning your lines?' he reminded me again, which made me remember why I was bent over the coffee table in the first place.

Flicking my eyes to the sheet of paper I began to read. Even Nathan's handwriting was somehow sensual in its curved formation, the glossy flow of the real ink from his pen somehow added to the overall eroticism of the scene. As soon as I began digesting the contents however, I very nearly laughed out loud.

I shall no longer bite the lower lip of my mouth and cause myself damage. I will never flaunt myself in front of other men because I belong to you, Nathan. My body and lips are yours, and as such, you, Sir, are to be the only one permitted to touch me or bite my lip in future.

Scoffing quietly I rolled my eyes, glad that Control Freak Jackson was behind me and couldn't see. But fine, if that was how he wanted to play this little scene I would go along with it. I was just beginning my second read through of the ridiculous verse when I heard the metallic sound of Nathan's belt buckle being undone. Talk about a distraction. Now all I could concentrate on was whether he was going to take me here, or perhaps bend me over the sofa to have his wicked way with me. All lusty thoughts evaporated from my mind a second later however, when I felt his palm gently caress my bottom, shortly followed by the sharp pulling noise of his belt being removed from his trouser loops. My mind was working at warp speed, was he about to punish me with his belt? Beat me with it? Hell no. I was brave enough to admit that I enjoyed a spanking from Nathan, and the paddle and flogger we'd used had been fun too, it heightened my arousal no end to mix a little dash of pain in with my pleasure, but a belt? I had never, ever thought that that could be pleasurable and I felt panic completely swamping my arousal.

Trying to stand up I was stopped by a firm pressure

138

from Nathan's hand on my spine, and before I realised it a safe word had popped from my lips, 'Yellow!' I blurted. I'd barely ever safe worded with Nathan in the past, he seemed to intuitively know my boundaries, but if he planned on using a belt on me I needed to voice my concerns. As soon as the word had popped from my mouth Nathan's hand was gone from my spine, both of his warm palms landing on my shoulders and pulling me up into the safety of his arms.

Releasing a breath into his chest I realised I was trembling all over and desperately tried to get a grip of myself. 'Talk to me, Stella,' he encouraged, one hand running up and down my back reassuringly as his other arm encased me against the warmth of his solid body.

'I don't like the idea of you ...' But I faltered, what word should I say? Beating? Hitting? Spanking? The first two sounded too excessive, but surely a spanking inferred a hand and skin on skin contact? Pausing briefly I kept it simple, 'I don't like the idea of being punished with your belt, Sir.' Suddenly the arms around me tightened to the point where I was struggling to breathe, and I heard a similar ragged breath escape from Nathan's throat.

Moving me so he could look in my eyes I saw a tortured expression on his beautiful face and immediately my chest coiled with concern, 'Never,' he whispered emphatically, dropping a fierce kiss on my lips. 'I would *never* use a belt on you that way.' Closing his eyes for a second he tipped his head back and then shook it as if he was gathering himself, before his eyes opened and I was almost knocked down by the clarity of his crystal blue gaze. 'You may recall me mentioning that the belt was my father's ... weapon of choice, shall we say.' Shit! Of course! How could I have been so stupid? Wincing, I looked up to see the same tortured expression on his face as his mouth thinned into a tight, bitter grimace. 'Whenever he punished Nicholas or me it would be with one of his many, many belts. On some occasions a cane.'

'I'm so sorry, Nathan, that had totally slipped my mind … I didn't mean to bring back bad memories.' I felt so awful, how had I not remembered this major detail about his life? Exhaling five long breaths through his nose Nathan seemed to be somehow trying to close a door on his past before he finally looked down at me again and smiled softly.

'It's fine, Stella. I was simply going to bind your hands with it, but if you are not comfortable we can stop.' Right at that moment the only thing I wanted to do was take away the look of vulnerability that I had seen in Nathan's expression minutes earlier, so I shook my head, pushed away from him, and resumed my position bent over the coffee table with my arms behind my back.

'Use the belt, Sir. Tie me up,' I offered softly, my eyes floating back to his silly note and hoping we could return to the fun of our earlier scene.

After a few seconds passed where he was apparently considering my offer I felt Nathan shift behind me again. Instead of immediately going for the belt he instead spent several minutes relaxing me by gently rubbing his hands across my skin, massaging my shoulders, back, buttocks, and arms until I was humming my pleasure and wiggling my hips provocatively. He'd obviously sensed my need to have my arousal rekindled, and perhaps his own, and boy had he done the trick. I was now thrumming with need again and could feel sticky wetness gathering between my thighs.

Finally I felt his hands moving to my arms and the texture of leather on my skin as he fastened the belt around my wrists in one loop and pulled it tight. My core clenched at the feeling of being restrained by him, and I let out a soft moan as my eyes fluttered shut. 'Let's not forget our original purpose, Stella. Keep reading,' he reminded me as he pulled the long, loose end of the belt and draped it down between my buttocks so it swung gently back and forth against my quivering skin. How he expected me to read in this situation I have no idea, but I did my best to stay focused on his words and he continued to gently touch me and soothe my skin with his palms.

My face flushed as Nathan suddenly crouched behind me on his haunches so his face was just inches away from my damp opening. 'Hmmmm,' he hummed appreciatively, 'I can smell your arousal, Stella.' To be honest I was so horny now that I wasn't really surprised, but it was still quite embarrassing for him to point it out. Taking hold of the loose end of the belt Nathan began rubbing the leather more firmly against my sensitive skin so it ran repeatedly back and forth across my slit, winding up my arousal to almost breaking point.

'You should see this, Stella, you're making my belt so fucking wet as the leather soaks up your juices.' At his dirty words I groaned, half from embarrassment and half from the scorching arousal now thumping in my groin. 'In fact, I have a very important committee meeting this week and I'm going to wear this very belt and think of you.' Christ. If I were any more turned on right now I'd be glowing like a Christmas tree.

'Enough of this,' Nathan stated suddenly, as he stood and retrieved the piece of paper from the coffee table. He made a show of folding it crisply in half, lining up the corners so the paper was neat, and then folding it again before tucking it in his pocket. Using gentle hands on my hips he turned us slightly so that we were now sideways on with the floor to ceiling windows that overlooked Docklands. The sun was at just the right angle that it was bouncing of the tint in the glass and making the window like one giant mirror. 'Watch,' he murmured, and as my gaze caught sight of our reflection I swallowed loudly at how raw and overtly sexual it looked; me, naked, tied up with a belt and bent over at Nathan's mercy as he stood behind me with a possessive hand on my lower spine and his shirt now unbuttoned and revealing his beautiful chest. He was clearly in his element, this was what he excelled at, and I was immensely glad that this side of him was getting an airing today.

Catching my gaze in the reflection Nathan smiled wickedly, picked up the loose end of the belt in his left hand, and wrapped it slowly and teasingly around his wrist until I felt my arms being gently tugged back towards him. I was now at his mercy, his to control. I was his, full stop.

'Let's see how you've done at your little memory task,' he murmured, still holding my gaze in the reflection. 'What did you learn, Stella?' All thoughts had left my mind apart from how incredibly hot we looked stood like this, so good in fact that I was almost tempted to ask him to photograph us, but blinking back to my role I licked my lips and tried to remember the words he had written for me.

'Um ...' I began, but before I could even properly begin, I watched as Nathan held the belt firmly with his left hand while pulling back his right hand and delivering a resounding slap to my right buttock. A yelp of surprise left my lips as my body rocked forwards from the shockwave, but Nathan's grip on the belt meant that I didn't fall over, merely bobbed in the air slightly.

'Wrong. I definitely did not write the word 'um' anywhere on that piece of paper. Try again,' he told me in clipped tones, but when I once again looked at our reflection I could see a tiny smile curving his mouth. Nathan was loving this.

My mind was fuzzy with desire for this man and the crazy things he did to me, so it took a moment for me to focus enough to recall the words I'd read. 'I shall no longer bite my lip.'

'Wrong again,' he said in an almost sing-song voice as he landed another slap to my opposite buttock.

'Ow! It did say that!' I yelped defensively, only to be rewarded by a further two hard spanks and a low, wicked chuckle from Nathan.

'Not quite, Stella, you missed out several words and I told you I wanted an exact recall of the sentence from the paper. In case you hadn't figured it out yet, I shall spank you for any incorrect words or retorts that slip from that beautiful mouth of yours, even if it is 'ow'.' Again I heard a satisfied bark of laughter and couldn't help but smile, this was so incredibly arousing.

Running my mind over and over I still had no frigging idea what words I'd left out, and knowing I couldn't leave it too long I made another attempt. 'I shall no longer bite my bottom lip?' I tried, wincing and tensing myself in anticipation of his delicious punishment.

'Close, but no cigar,' Nathan muttered, before letting go with a string of six faster, lighter slaps which he peppered on both cheeks in various locations so I could feel my entire bottom heating up. I was panting now. Desperate for this to continue, but also desperate for him to bury himself inside of me and ease my raging arousal.

Suddenly, like a bolt of inspiration from the blue I could picture his smooth elegant writing in my mind's eye and nearly giggled in excitement, 'I shall no longer bite the lower lip of my mouth and cause myself damage,' I stated, fairly certain I was finally correct.

Nathan's hand rubbed soothing patterns across my hot behind as a silence fell between us, 'Correct. Next line,' he murmured. It was something to do with my dancing last night and his supposed ownership of me, but he'd written it in such flowery wording that I knew without a doubt I would never remember it correctly.

'I won't flaunt my body because I belong to you, Sir. I'm yours. And so are my lips.'

I heard an appreciative humming noise from the back of his throat. 'Correct sentiment, but wrong wording I'm afraid, Miss Marsden,' he told me quietly, shortly before another tirade of blows flicked against my skin, some soft and almost teasing, whilst others were hard and stinging and sparking my curled desire to spread across my whole body. I lost track of time as the pain of his spanks mixed and swirled with pleasure and desire and I was left panting and groggy with arousal, thankful that he was affectively holding me up with the belt at my wrists. I have no idea how many times his hand contacted with my skin, it felt like fifty, although it probably wasn't anywhere near that number. All I knew was he was mixing in backhanded blows with his normal palmed ones and that he definitely swapped hands at one point. He ended with a cupping slap where he gripped my right buttock firmly in his hand and by squeezing it roughly managed to manoeuvre me several steps to the side so I was leant over the back of the sofa. Reaching around he picked up one of the cushions, placed it under me, and then bent me forwards again where I relaxed my leaden body weight onto the soft leather below me, grateful of its support.

I felt utterly boneless. 'Thank you, Sir.' I wasn't entirely sure whether I was thanking him for the relaxing position or the spanking, because both had been exactly what I had needed. Leaning in close to my ear Nathan flicked the hair away and placed several breathy, open mouthed kisses there. 'Good girl, so sweet in your submission.' His exertion was obvious from the way he panted into my neck for a minute as he recovered himself, before raising his head slightly. 'Now, Stella, I suggest you hold on for the ride,' he advised me, shortly before gripping my hips and impaling me on his throbbing cock in one harsh thrust.

I didn't even know he'd taken off his trousers, but a quick glance into the window showed me that actually, he hadn't, he'd merely unzipped his trousers and freed his cock in his desperation to claim me. He was so much less controlled than normal, still half-dressed and with veins bulging in his neck, and the fact that I was the reason he was that wild with desire made me clench around him and almost come on the spot.

Nathan's strokes were almost as furious as his spanking had been; fast and frenzied, as if he were merely using me as an orifice to gain his own satisfaction, but after an initial minute or so of sweaty, pounding thrusts he seemed to calm himself somewhat, his pace slowing and allowing me to briefly catch my breath. One hand stayed gripped on my hip to assist his steady thrusts, but his other hand began to trail across my skin, gently floating over my reddened bottom before finally reaching around me to cup one of my swinging breasts, where he tugged and tweaked my hardened nipple.

Now he had slowed his movements I could feel each and every touch of his skin against my hot bottom, every time he withdrew and then thrust back in again, forcing his stomach on my behind. The tingling sensations in my arse spread to my clit, racking up my arousal to nearly unbearable levels. 'Please, Nathan ... Sir, please ...' I begged, desperate for release and sure that I would explode if I didn't get it right this minute.

The hand on my breast moved to my mouth as he ran a thumb along my lower lip, 'Who does this belong to?' he demanded in a thick gravelly voice.

'You, Sir!' I cried, almost sobbing now with the need to come.

'And you won't be biting it anymore, will you?' His thumb continued to caress my lip and I very nearly bit down on his digit in my frustration. 'No! I promise!'

'Good girl,' he praised me, before lowering his hand between us and finally making contact with my much neglected clitoris. One swirl of his thumb very nearly undid me, but I held off for as long as I could, loving the sensation he was creating in my groin and desperate to make it just as good for him as it was for me. As soon as he increased the tempo of his hips again though, he began to circle my nub with more force and that was it, I was a goner, my climax rearing up to claim me in wave after wave of near blinding pleasure that had me clutching the sofa, screaming out his name, and finally collapsing forwards as huge, ragged sobs escaped my chest and hot tears streamed down my cheeks.

Sex with Nathan was always amazing, but Christ, sex *like that* that with Nathan was just mind-blowing.

ELEVEN – NICHOLAS

Picking up the pencil I began to jot a few names on the notepad in front of me, then chucked the paper onto the side table and swapped it for a wad of blank music sheets. Adjusting myself on my piano stool I opened the lid, but frustratingly I immediately found that my mind was too full to concentrate on writing music. Sighing in annoyance I twisted myself towards the window and stared at the garden outside hoping for inspiration, but the usually colourful garden lacked it stimulus. Most of the trees were just gnarled empty branches, having lost their leaves as winter took its grip upon them. Running a hand through my hair I smiled ruefully at how quickly the weeks seemed to be passing recently. It felt like just last week that I'd proposed to Rebecca, whereas in reality it was now over a year and nearly Christmas, which meant there was just under four months until the wedding. Christ, arranging a wedding was turning out to be far more complex than I'd believed possible and I couldn't believe how much we still had to do in preparation.

No wonder my mind was too full to compose the song that I had planned to start today. Turning back to my piano I placed my hand on the keys and closed my eyes, hoping that the familiar feel of the ivory might inspire me. I always referred to them as 'ivories', but technically the keys to my Steinway were elephant friendly and made from high-quality plastic and not elephant tusk, but regardless of material, the feel of them below my fingers was always infinitely reassuring.

The reason I was sat here was simple – I'd decided that instead of doing a long groom's speech at the wedding, which I would not enjoy presenting *at all*, that I would keep the speaking to a minimum. I didn't want to let Rebecca down with a short and stilted speech, and so I'd spent days pondering what to do, until last week when I'd been playing my piano and inspiration had hit – I'd simply do what I did best; express myself via the medium of music. My plan for today was to start writing a song which somehow expressed everything I felt for Rebecca and how she had changed my life. It was a big ask to get that much emotion into one song, but I was going to give it my best shot.

I had barely gotten anywhere at all with the music when I saw the blonde top of Rebecca's head pop around the door to my music room. Stopping my playing I turned to her and couldn't help the goofy smile that I felt curling my lips. She was just gorgeous. Perfect.

'Am I interrupting?' she asked, stepping inside and pausing on the threshold.

Holding my arms open wide I shook my head as my heart did its usual little jump at the sight of her, 'I like interruptions from you.' Grinning, Rebecca practically skipped across the room and into my arms, her enthusiasm making my spirit soar. As she reached me her little hands slid around my neck and linked behind my head as she climbed up and knelt on the piano stool with a knee on either side of me.

Lowering herself so she was straddled across my lap she stilled and smiled at me sweetly, her green eyes twinkling with reflections of the sunlight behind me. 'Hi,' she said quietly. Her face was just centimetres away from mine, her soft lips tempting me to lean in and kiss them.

'Hi, yourself,' I replied, before giving in to my urge and joining our lips. A second or so of chaste lips closed kissing was all we could manage before our mouths opened, hotly inviting the other to explore and tease. After several minutes of deep, breath-taking kissing I broke our lips to suck in some air and stared into her eyes. The masculine part of me couldn't help but smirk as I noted the blush heating Becky's cheeks. It was entirely possible that it was from the kiss, but the more likely cause was her embarrassment from feeling my erection below her, which was now attempting to force its way out of my jeans. I could hardly blame my body though, I had a beautiful woman straddling my lap and kissing me, I'd have to be a monk not to get a hard-on.

Shaking her head in amusement Rebecca rolled her eyes at me and shifted herself back to marginally reduce the pressure on my groin. Not that it would help, so long as she was sitting across my lap like this I would be solid as a rock. Clearing my throat in the hopes that it might help clear my lust filled head as well, I tried to distract myself from the tempting warmth of Becky's thighs. 'So, how's that guest list coming along?' I asked her, knowing that it was the task she'd been working on this morning.

Tilting her head to the side she licked her slightly swollen lips, further hardening my groin, and then nodded slowly, 'Pretty good. That's what I was coming up here to ask you about actually. Have you finished the list of people you'd like to invite?'

Keeping a firm hold upon Becky with one hand I twisted to my left and grabbed the pad of paper I'd written my list on earlier. As I handed it to her I prepared myself, already knowing full well what her response would be. First her eyes glanced down at the paper, then a small pucker appeared between her eyebrows as she scanned it, and finally she raised confused eyes to meet mine.

'There's only six names on here, Nicholas,' she said quietly, just like I'd anticipated.

'I know. I wrote it. You already know that I don't have

any relatives that I'm in touch with,' I said with a shrug, trying to push down the sickly feelings that thoughts of my parents always brought with them. 'The people on that list are the only ones in my life of any importance.'

I could see her mind working in overdrive. She sucked her lower lip in between her teeth as she thought and her right hand came up to twirl a length of shiny hair before finally tucking it behind her ear. Rebecca's tell-tale sign of anxiousness. 'Nathan and Stella are on here, but they don't count because they both have roles in the wedding party.'

Shrugging, I drew in a deep breath to try and help me deal with the pity that was no doubt about to come my way. Shifting my hands from her waist to her bottom I gave it a squeeze as I spoke. 'Well, I guess my list is just four then. Isla, Anthony, Mr Burrett, and his wife,' I said, going for a casual tone and hoping it might deflect any further questions from Rebecca. Of course Isla and Anthony from my jazz days were on there, after touring the country with them and playing gigs far and wide they were my most trusted and long term friends. Mr Burrett was the easiest guest to pick; he had been in my life nearly ten years now and was probably my closest confidant and sounding post for ideas, someone I could speak to about most topics and a man who had proven his loyalty to me again and again. Of course there were other people I *could* invite; my solicitor Peter was quite a close acquaintance, and there were numerous other musicians I was in touch with, but no one who had really cemented a place in my life over the years. Although granted that was probably down to my temperamental nature, and not their faults.

It hadn't bothered me that I had a very small circle of people that I trusted in my life, but when I'd scribbled down my guest list earlier even I thought six names was pretty pathetic. The fact that my list was so minimal was clearly making Rebecca think too deeply about things, probably my pitiful childhood – definitely something I didn't want to get into discussions about again – so I slid my hands up her back and around to her lower ribs, where I gave a small tickle which instantly made her laugh and squirm in my lap. 'That's my list, baby, don't overthink it. You are the only person I really need to be there.'

Rebecca wriggling on my lap might have been distracting *her* from the issue in hand, but her curvy bottom rubbing repeatedly across my crotch certainly wasn't helping the state of my poor tortured groin. 'Fine, OK ...' she gasped in between giggles until I finally relented. 'You'll have to give me more to go on that just "Mr Burrett and Wife" though. I know he's James, but what's her first name?'

Chuckling at my own lazy list writing I smiled, 'Maggie, but if it's for the place cards I guess you should use Margaret.'

Rebecca leaned across and plucked up my pencil to amend the list and I winced as her movement caused things to become almost unbearably tight down below. Suddenly dropping all humour from my face I put on my most serious expression and focused a solemn stare on my girl. 'Now that's cleared up we have a very serious matter to address, Rebecca.' I murmured my words in a low, authoritative tone which never seemed to fail in getting Becky simultaneously nervy and aroused at the same time – such a great combination.

Licking her lower lip she blinked at me several times, apparently trying to work out what on earth was going on. 'What's is it?' she asked, her voice small and curious.

'Well, it seems that whilst your positioning across my lap is rather satisfactory, your abundant levels of clothing most certainly are not.' It took a second for Becky to realise that I was playing with her, and as soon as she did the smile that I loved so much surged across her face as she leaned in to kiss me, laughing against my lips. 'You scared me for a second there, Nicholas, I thought there was something wrong with the wedding plans.'

Leaning back I took hold of the hem of her T-shirt and jerked my chin up to indicate that she needed to raise her arms. We were so attuned to each other that she followed my silent command immediately, and I swept the cotton from her body before tossing it aside and fixing my eyes on her beautiful lace-enclosed breasts. 'There's nothing wrong with the wedding plans, everything's going perfectly. There is, however, an issue with the wedding tackle that needs to be addressed.'

I gave an upwards thrust of my hips to support my point, which caused my rampant erection to rub her right between the legs as she let out a lusty moan which could have rivalled most porn stars. OK so my line had been a bit cheesy, but it worked, Becky fell against me, laughing for a few seconds, her warm breasts heaving against my chest and forcing me to use the last thread of my self-control as I cradled her body against mine. Leaning back she then began to undo my shirt buttons with nimble fingers until we were both topless and our chests were pressed together as she united our lips in hot, searching kiss.

Raising herself so she was fully kneeling on the stool Rebecca unzipped her jeans and then began to work on my belt and zip while still leaning down and kissing me frantically. Her lips and tongue were everywhere, and she seemed reluctant to break the contact between our mouths so that we could stand and actually remove our trousers. Finally, when I had almost reached breaking point, I groaned, gripped her by the hips, and shifted her so she was sat on the keys of my piano. It made quite a racket, uncoordinated notes ringing out in the quiet of the room, only accompanied by our ragged breathing and aroused moans.

This was almost a blasphemous action for me – my piano was pretty much priceless, custom-built especially for me – and as such I never ever placed anything on the keys except for my fingers, but right now I was almost out of my mind with lust and it had to be said that Rebecca looked pretty fucking amazing leaning on it half naked, her jeans undone and her eyes filled with desperate lust. Licking my lips hungrily I felt my cock give an almighty twitch and I closed the gap between us with just one thing on my mind – getting my woman naked, *right now.*

Peeling off her jeans and knickers, then following suit with my trousers, I took a second to grab a breath and ran my hands up the smooth length of her legs, coming to rest on her waist as I moved in for another hungry kiss. As my tongue explored Rebecca's willing mouth I reached behind her to unclip her bra and as she once again shifted and hit several more notes I couldn't help but tug her firmly against me with one hand while the other quickly closed the piano lid. Rolling my eyes at myself I stepped back and distracted my brain by peeling off her bra off and immediately dipping my head to take one hardened nipple into my mouth. Desire burned though me now, her skin tasted so good, sweet and lightly floral, a combination I just couldn't seem to get enough off.

Arching against me Rebecca was almost curved over my supporting arm, her spine resting on my palm and her shoulders leaning against the lid of the piano with her hair cascading over the shiny black surface. God, this was like every single one of my erotic fantasies come to life in one go. Taking my free hand I trailed my fingers from her belly button up the centre of her body all the way to her throat. On the return journey my hand wandered across to her breasts, rubbing the heel of my hand roughly across her tight nipples tweaking and rolling them until she was mewling and writhing in my arms. She was so responsive, so perfect. *Mine.*

'Nicholas …' One breathy gasp of my name was all it took to catapult me into ridding me of my boxers and retaking my seat on the piano stool, pulling Rebecca with me. Placing her hands on my shoulders to steady herself Rebecca resumed her kneeling position so she was straddled across my thighs with her hot, wet opening hovering just above the desperate tip of my cock.

Wide, lust-filled green eyes locked on mine as she bit her lower lip and began to lower herself onto me inch by inch, letting her legs splay wider as she did so. Rebecca's eyes didn't leave mine once, not even when she made the final adjustment that had me fully embedded inside her to the root. Christ, I was so deep like this. It felt fucking incredible. Just when I thought this really couldn't get any better Rebecca tentatively began to slowly circle her hips, her cheeks flushing as she started to move. Being this deep inside of her I knew that this had to be a pretty intense experience for Rebecca too, so as much as I wanted to thrust upwards into her, I didn't. In fact I didn't move at all, instead I carefully watched her eyes to make sure she was OK and not in any discomfort. Tension seemed to flicker around her eyes for a few seconds, but gradually as I felt Rebecca relaxing around me I saw her face also loosening up before she suddenly began to move more regularly.

Swivelling her hips, and lifting herself up and down on my heated cock, she began to mix in all the right movements to send me skyrocketing towards my climax as my balls tightened and my cock started to throb almost painfully inside her tight heat. Gritting my teeth I held off from the peak I so desperately wanted, determined that I would wait for her. Lowering a hand between our bodies I used my thumb to find her clitoris and began to rub firm circles over the swollen nub, matching the time of her movements. Throwing her head back on a loud moan Rebecca quickly reinstated our eye contact, her pupils dilated and a little unfocused. 'I'm close, Nicholas!' she gasped, moving in earnest now as our sweaty hips clashed together.

Lifting herself almost to the tip of me Rebecca then surprised the hell out of me as she dropped herself down onto my cock so hard and fast that there was no way I could hold off anymore and my climax roared up and shot from me, filling her channel and seeming to spark Rebecca's own orgasm as she yelled out my name and dug her nails into my shoulders so hard I felt the skin pop beneath her grip.

Christ, well, that was the guest list sorted *and* my family jewels taken care of, all within the hour. How very efficient of us.

TWELVE – NATHAN

I was sat on my favourite sofa – favourite because this was where my rather splendid spanking liaison with Stella had occurred just two weeks ago – reading the business section of the *Sunday Times* when I heard a key slip into the front door. The sound of metal sliding together as the lock opened briefly transported me back to the early days of my relationship with Stella when she had been just my submissive. I say 'just my submissive', but if I'm honest with myself I'd known right from the start that my feelings for Stella went beyond the realms of purely physical. Awaiting her arrival back then had become almost an obsessive craving for me, over the course of our first few months together I'd literally spent hours sitting in exactly his spot and staring at the door waiting for it to open. With these thoughts on my mind I was almost grinning by the time the door finally swung open tonight.

Dumping down a heavy selection of shopping bags Stella wiggled her fingers in apparent relief and then smiled across at me. 'So, seeing as I've just been dragged around Westfield shopping centre by Nicholas to buy winter clothes for Rebecca's surprise Christmas trip away, can I assume you're not spending the holidays with your brother as planned?'

What? Her words ruined my good mood and certainly grabbed my full attention. Throwing down my newspaper I sprang up and crossed the room to her as I felt tension seeming to radiate from every pore of my body. Stopping just before her I splayed my legs and crossed my arms over my chest defensively as I glared at her. 'You went shopping with my brother?' I demanded, but in response Stella simply rolled her eyes at me before heading to the sink to get a drink of water. 'As endearing as your jealousy used to be, it's starting to wear a bit thin now, Nathan,' she told me in a soft voice, giving me a firm, patient look that immediately made me feel thoroughly chastised. I fucking hated how jealous I could feel over Stella, it was like an ugly monster lurking deep within me that would rear up from nowhere at any moment and stamp on any logical reasoning. Scratching at the back of my neck I grimaced, knowing that it was still a new emotion for me and probably stemmed from my lack of experience with any other real relationships in my life. Taking in a deep, calming breath I tried to tamp down my irrational annoyance. This was Stella and my brother we were talking about for God's sakes, the two people I trusted most in the entire world.

Like with most things, Stella was good at reading me, and instead of losing her temper at my outburst she simply stayed quiet and let me work through my unease. Hopefully one day I'd manage to act like a normal human being around her, instead of an irrational lunatic. Why the fuck she was still with me was a mystery to me. Placing a hand on my arm Stella effectively interrupted my troubled thoughts and brought me back to the present with her warming touch. 'Trust, remember?' she said softly, instantly reminding me of the conversation we'd had a few weeks ago when I'd so gracelessly gate-crashed Rebecca's hen-do.

Taking a deep breath I did a calming countdown and then nodded before tentatively closing the gap between us and leaning down to place my lips on hers. 'Sorry,' I muttered, which was miraculously a word that I was now able to say without grimacing.

158

'I wasn't shopping *with* your brother, I was shopping and bumped *into* your brother. Very different things, Nathan,' Stella told me, and I remembered now that she'd said she was going shopping for my Christmas present. A little shiver of excitement ran through me at the thought of giving and receiving gifts with Stella this year. We used to get presents at Christmas when I was younger but my parents, my father in particular, had always seemed grudging about it. In fact I clearly remember one year when Nicholas had excitedly run down on Christmas morning and asked if Santa had been during the night, only for my father to toss a gift at him and tell him smugly that Santa wasn't real and the presents were bought with *his* hard-earned cash. I'll never forget the crestfallen look on Nicholas's face as he realised Father Christmas wasn't real. I think a little bit of my brother's innocence died that day. It wasn't long after that my father started regularly beating Nicholas too.

Swallowing down my bitter memories of the past my eyes flicked to the pile of shopping by the door. As tempting as it was to inspect the bags to see what Stella might have purchased I refrained and turned my eyes back to her.

'So what did Nicholas say then?' I asked, already knowing the general gist of it – my brother had phoned me just a few hours ago from the shopping centre to check if I minded him spending Christmas with Rebecca this year.

'He was very excited,' Stella said with a laugh. 'Practically bursting with energy, actually. Basically he said that he'd just booked a holiday for Rebecca's Christmas present and was glad he'd run into me because he needed help picking out some clothing for her, but no matter how much I interrogated him he wouldn't tell me where they were going,' she added on a pout. 'They must be going somewhere cold though, because he purchased practically an entire new wardrobe of warm clothes for her.'

'Iceland,' I said, recalling Nicholas' excited tone. It was somewhere he'd always wanted to go and I saw Stella's eyebrows rise in appreciation.

'Wow. Fancy,' she murmured.

'It's a surprise though, so don't mention anything to Rebecca,' I added, remembering Nicholas' warning to me.

'Of course I won't. So, what are your Christmas plans now then?' she asked curiously, stepping into my arms for a cuddle and slipping her hands round so they rested on the small of my back. I smiled at how enjoyable I now found this simple act. Hugging, cuddling, or snuggling had never been part of my life before Stella, but the contentment that I found when she was wrapped in my arms was one of the purest I'd ever experienced.

Sighing happily I lowered my head and nuzzled into her hair, loving the smell of her shampoo. 'I was going to spend it with Nicholas, but obviously that's changed now.' As my mind ticked over things an idea came to me. Seeing as Nicholas was going on holiday for Christmas we could too. Pulling back I looked down at Stella. 'Would you like to spend Christmas in a hotel with me? Chester perhaps? Or abroad if you like, New York is beautiful in December. What do you think?'

It was only two weeks before Christmas and I was well aware that most 'normal' people tended to plan their Christmases quite a way in advance, so Stella might well already have plans. I watched as she fidgeted briefly in my arms and felt my stomach drop as I realised I was right.

'Um … actually I didn't think we were spending Christmas together and my brother is home on leave from the Royal Navy so I … I um… I kind of told my mum I'd be home with them on Christmas day,' she said tentatively, apparently concerned about hurting my feelings.

Not wanting Stella to see that I was a little upset about the prospect of spending Christmas on my own I

160

straightened back and tried to remove the frown that had briefly settled on my brow. 'I see. Of course,' I murmured with a nod. I think my voice was convincing, but annoyingly I found my compulsive habits flooding to the surface as I stepped back, dropped my eyes to avoid her gaze, and began to fiddle with my shirt cuff.

Closing the distance I had just put between us Stella reached up and tipped my chin up so I was forced to meet her smiling gaze. 'I know it's a long shot, but how would you feel about joining me and my family for Christmas this year?' she asked in a hopeful tone as a smile tugged at the corners of her mouth.

Staring at her in surprise I blinked several times as I ran her words though my mind. Attend a regular family Christmas? *Me?* Christ, it had certainly been a while since *that* had happened. In fact, I wasn't even sure that the Christmas' I'd experienced with my parents had been 'regular' in any way, shape, or form. Pulling Stella back into my arms as she once again relaxed against my chest I pondered her request for a minute, before a slow smile spread on my lips. A family Christmas with the Marsdens? Well, I suppose there was always a first time for everything.

THIRTEEN – STELLA

Kicking off his shoes – his favourite black and white brogues – Kenny grinned like a kid in a sweet shop as he sunk back into one of the plush armchairs in Nathan's home cinema room. 'Oh God, Stella I'd forgotten how good these chairs were,' he remarked with an appreciative groan as he reclined the seat, stretched out his legs, and wiggled his toes within some seriously bright stripy socks.

Turning to me a sudden twinkle crept into my friend's eyes and he pursed his lips as a wicked grin began to curve his mouth. 'I bet you and Nathan have got down and dirty in at least one of these chairs, haven't you?' he asked with a suggestive bounce of his eyebrows.

'Kenny!' I yelped, as a blush of mortification – and guilt – swept up my cheeks. We had, on several occasions, but that was hardly the point.

'I thought so,' he said smugly, crossing his legs at the ankles and linking his hands behind his head.

I flopped down in the chair next to him so I could avoid looking him directly in the eye. 'I didn't confirm or deny it, Kenny,' I replied with a small smile. Really it didn't matter if Kenny knew a few juicy details of my relationship with Nathan, he was one of my best friends after all. Besides, it actually made quite a refreshing change for *me* to be the one with stories to tell, usually it was Kenny unable to contain his glee at his latest conquest or escapade.

'Your blush said it all, babes,' Kenny said smugly. Raising a hand to his goatee he began to twist the stands between his forefinger and thumb as he watched me. 'Besides, I know how you met Nathan, remember? It stands to reason that a guy who is a kinkster in the sack would probably be adventurous with his locations too. Adds a bit of variety, keeps things spicy.' Finally allowing my smile to broaden I rolled my head back on the head rest and giggled.

'Well, he certainly does that,' I confirmed with a nod as my cheeks heated even more. We'd definitely christened every room in this apartment. In fact, we'd probably shagged on, or against, every single inch of flat surface within Nathan's apartment in our time together.

Clearing my throat to disrupt my wandering thoughts and try to swerve the subject away from my sex life, I rolled my head to the side on the comfy sofa back so I could look across at Kenny. 'So, it's only two days to Christmas, my mum's shopping for the vegetables today so she wants to know if you're eating with us or not.' When I last spoke to him, Kenny hadn't made any certain plans yet, apparently it all depended on whether two of his buddies were flying in from the states or not. I tried not to be offended that I was his back-up plan, but in reality I knew that a sedate family meal with me and my parents wouldn't exactly be that exciting for a single guy like Kenny.

'Nathan's still going?' he asked carefully, fully aware of my concern that Nathan was going to panic and pull out of at any moment.

'He is,' I nodded. Nathan actually seemed to be getting quite excited about our Christmas plans. Just yesterday I'd found him in his walk-in wardrobe sorting out which shirt and tie he was going to wear. His advance preparations had been very sweet really, although I'd quickly told him that Marsden family meals were relaxed affairs, even at Christmas, so he didn't need to wear a suit.

'Simon will be there too,' I reminded Kenny, mindful

of the slight crush he had on my brother. Simon was also aware of this fact, and took every opportunity to tease poor Kenny by mercilessly flirting with him even though Simon was straight as a plank.

'What if your brother invites some of his Navy friends for drinks in the afternoon like he did last year?' Kenny asked, as he held his hands up to picture the image in front of him. 'I can see it now ... you, surrounded by handsome, suave officers from the Royal Navy ... Nathan exploding like a pressure kettle and going all caveman and dragging you off into the sunset,' he said on a chuckle. Frowning, I realised that his vision was actually a very likely possibility if one of Simon's friends even so much as breathed too closely to me. Wincing, I made a mental note to check with Simon and beg him not to wind up Nathan.

'Well, if it's definitely OK with your mum, then count me in!' Kenny said enthusiastically.

'Really?' I asked, surprised, but Kenny turned to me with the broadest grin on his face, 'Are you kidding me? Miss out on seeing uptight, brooding Nathaniel Jackson meet your parents for the first time? Not a chance!' Rolling my eyes at Kenny's statement I started to find myself feeling quite defensive of Nathan.

Picking up the remote control for the fifty-inch television Kenny tossed it in the air so it spun before landing safely back in his palm. 'So, has your fella updated his DVD collection yet? Last time I was over I requested *Pirates of The Caribbean*. Ahhh ... Johnny Depp in widescreen, now that would make my night! Has anyone ever told you that I look a bit like him?' he asked, making me roll my eyes. Kenny himself had mentioned it, a few *million* times before.

I heard Kenny's voice as he continued speaking, but couldn't comprehend his words because my mind was still dwelling on his earlier statements about Nathan. He wasn't that bad. Was he? OK so Nathan could still be a little uptight emotionally, and often looked quite intense and scary, not to mention that conversationally he could be difficult sometimes, but … *oh God*. Wincing with worry I found myself partaking in some illegal lip biting – Kenny was right … this could be an absolute nightmare Christmas.

FOURTEEN - STELLA

Slade burst forth from the car speakers proclaiming a Merry Christmas, and fun for everyone, but I felt more nervy than merry, and was definitely *not* having fun. It was Christmas morning, the sun was shining, and Nathan was pulling his Audi into my parents' quiet residential street in St Albans. As unbelievable as it might have seemed, Nathan was actually here with me for Christmas Day, I should be thrilled by this, but my nerves were on high alert because of three things; firstly, this would be the first time my parents would meet Nathan, which seeing as I was in love with him was a pretty frigging big event and was obviously causing me some anxiety. Secondly, for the entire hour of our journey Nathan had been remarkably quiet and tense, making me worry that he didn't actually want to be here at all. And on top of all of that, Kenny's joking words about Nathan being socially awkward had been swimming round and round my mind, driving me bonkers and making me sure with increasing certainty that this whole day was going to be a massive, disastrous flop.

'It's this one on the right, the one with the blue front door,' I said quietly as Nathan stopped the car outside my childhood house and turned off the ignition. The silence in the enclosed car was stifling, so I reached for the door handle to escape when I was stopped from opening it by Nathan's hand as it landed on my knee and gave a firm squeeze.

'Stella, wait.'

Turning to him I felt dread rising in my chest. This was where he'd say he'd changed his mind and would insist on leaving and basically ruin my entire day. But to my surprise he didn't. Nope, to my utter shock, Nathan drew in a deep breath and then confessed two words that I never thought I'd hear cross his lips. 'I'm nervous.'

He spoke in a voice so quiet I barely heard him. As bizarre as this sounds, his words made much of my earlier anxiety leave my body in an instant rush, because prior to my earlier beliefs, Nathan had been quiet because *he'd* been anxious too. Well I never.

Seeing my usually confident and composed man looking so lost I found myself struck speechless for a few seconds, before I placed my hand over his supportively and tried to will my tongue to say something remotely useful. 'There's no need, Nathan. It's just my parents, they're really nice. They'll love you,' I assured him, faking some needed confidence, but knowing my words were true as long as he was on his best behaviour. If he went all primal on any of Simon's friends ... well ... my folks might not be quite as keen on him then.

His right hand came up and ran through his hair, leaving it spiky and far from its usual neat style, so with a smile I used my free hand to lean over and smooth it down for him again, which earned me a cute, thankful smile. 'I ... I haven't had a family Christmas since my parents went to prison,' he confessed in a low tone. 'It's always just been me and Nicholas.' Chewing on his lower lip I watched as his eyes darted around the car before settling on me again, 'I'm not sure I've ever had a proper family Christmas, really. Mum would always get a tree because Nicholas would get really excited about decorating it, but then after we'd spent all afternoon dressing the tree Dad would get home and change all the decorations around to how *he* wanted them. It was fucking pointless.' He sounded so unsure that my heart just about broke for him.

Shaking his head, I saw Nathan's lip curl with distaste. 'I only carried on doing it each year because Nicholas enjoyed it.' Sucking in a huge breath, Nathan released it through his lips and sat back in his seat, staring blindly out of the windscreen. 'My mum always said she'd cooked the Christmas dinner, but I'd see the Tesco's containers in the bin afterward, so she obviously lied.' Another huge sigh escaped his lips, 'So much about them was bullshit. I struggle now to know what was real.' Lifting a hand he ran it across his face as if trying to remove the tainted memories from his mind.

'So,' he said decisively, as if internally deciding that he'd had enough reminiscing for one day. 'Is there anything I need to know about today?'

'Like what?' I asked, confused about his odd question. It was Christmas Day; we would eat, drink, and get merry, what else was there to know?

'Any festive traditions I need to adhere to? Routines? House rules?' It was a fairly simple question, but his addition of the word 'rules' once again made me think of the boy he used to be, disciplined to within an inch of his life, confused, craving love but finding nothing but punishments and rules everywhere he looked. It made me feel sick to my stomach, and I wished for about the hundredth time that I'd punched his father that day I'd met him.

Thinking hard, I shrugged. 'Nothing major, we open our presents after lunch and when we eat two people get to snap the wishbone from the turkey. The person with the biggest half makes a wish, but I think that's fairly standard. Oh, and my mum likes to watch the Queen's speech at three. That's about it.' I shook my head and smiled, 'No house rules either,' I added, immediately feeling Nathan tense next to me.

'None?' His question was reed-thin, his face completely pale and absorbed by my answer as I shook my head. God, this was horrible, this conversation had been a real eye opener. I'd known Nicholas had it bad when they were growing up, but from what he'd said today it sounds like Nathan's childhood had just been one long string of rules, strictness, and being made to feel inadequate. Licking my lips I tried to stay strong for him, but it was no wonder my fella was a bit obsessive and set in his ways.

I suddenly felt so damn melancholy and it was Christmas Day for goodness sakes! Trying to rid myself of the sudden gloom that had descended around us I gave myself a small shake and took a deep breath. 'You ready?' I asked with a smile that I hoped was convincing. Nodding his head Nathan went to get out of the car but first paused to look at me. 'Can I just have a minute in the car alone?' he asked, and I immediately knew he wanted to do one of his calming countdowns before facing the Marsden clan in all their glory. This really was a big deal for him, and the fact that he was willing to go through it for me just made my heart swell with love for him even further.

Leaning across the car I placed a soft kiss on his lips. It had meant to be a reassuring, chaste kiss, but Nathan suddenly ran a hand into my hair, gripped hard, and pressed his tongue into my mouth in an almost desperate act which made tingles rush to the back of my neck. Where had that come from? Pulling back I blinked several times as I struggled to focus on anything other than the chills of desire coursing through my system.

'Of course,' I finally stuttered, before sliding out of the car on wobbly legs.

When Nathan appeared from the car a minute or so later he was like a different man – still a little nervy perhaps, but his earlier sadness was gone, or certainly well hidden at least. Grabbing my hand he winked at me and nodded, but I think I was just gawking up at him because of that wink. Crikey, that been quite something.

'All set.' He waggled a posh bottle of champagne at me, slid his fingers into mine, and we set off up my parents' driveway to the front door and its elaborate holly wreath. Ringing the doorbell I heard a commotion of voices behind the door, which was slightly odd because we only had a small family – Mum, Dad, me, and Simon – and I was fairly sure my brother had said he wouldn't be arriving until about two o'clock.

'Hi, love! Merry Christm … oh!' My mum's words faded away as her smiling face settled on Nathan at my side and her eyebrows rose. I'm not sure if I was verging on hysteria after the tension and confessions in the car, but Mum's reaction to Nathan made me want to double over and belly laugh. Her expression now could only be described as 'slack jawed astonishment,' as she stood on the doorstep clinging onto the frame for dear life. Her eyes were already as wide as saucers, but they expanded even further when she noticed the furious grip Nathan had on my hand and the bottle of real champagne he was offering her.

Bless her, stunned didn't even go halfway to describing the look on Mum's face as she clearly struggled to take in the handsome man by my side. Suddenly behind her appeared Kenny, grinning from ear to ear and poking his head over her shoulder with a wiggle his eyebrows. 'Merry Christmas, folks!' he said in a fake booming tone, obviously attempting his best imitation of Santa Claus. Ah, so that explained the excited voices I'd heard earlier then. Kenny could be rather boisterous when he wanted. 'Roll your tongue in, Mrs M!' he said on a giggle as he poked Mum in the ribs, making her jump and then flush with embarrassment as she turned back to Nathan and I.

'Mum, this is Nathan. Nathan, this is my mum, Susan.'

The look on Mum's face was still highly amusing, but after a few more seconds she managed to re-engage her brain, set her features again, and smile. The only clue that she was still flustered was when she spoke and the rest of her greetings came out all in one long, excitable, and slightly repetitive sentence. 'Merry Christmas! You must call me Sue. Gosh, what a nice surprise! Nathan, it's lovely to meet you. Merry Christmas! Come on in out of the cold!' Rolling my lips together to prevent me from openly laughing, I looked up to see the bewildered look on Nathan's face as he stood there stiff and uncertain. He did at least have a small smile on his face, which was one good thing.

Once we were inside and my mum had gotten herself together a bit she ushered us into the lounge. The tree looked fabulous as always, stockings hung from the fireplace, and I immediately felt myself relax and smile at the fond familiarity of the scene. Kenny immediately took the best seat by the fire and started to chomp on a bowl of salted peanuts while watching us all with glee. It was like he was at the bloody cinema waiting for the dramatic bit of the film to happen.

'Martin, this is Nathan. Stella's *friend*. Come and say hello,' Mum told my dad before flashing a very unsubtle look at Nathan and I and wiggling her eyebrows. God, she was like the mother out of bloody *Bridget Jones*. The way she said 'friend' was hilarious, but luckily, Dad was his usual calm self, shaking hands with Nathan before indicating out of the window with his thumb.

'Nice car, Nathan. Good drive over?'

Nathan engaged in some brief talk with my dad about his Audi whilst Mum fussed about taking my coat and grinning at me before leaning in and whispering, 'He's a very nice-looking young man, Stella.'

Rolling my eyes at her excitement I couldn't help but return her smile and nod. She knew I was seeing someone, I'd said as much on the phone, but as far as Mum knew it was all quite a recent thing. Given the irregular nature of my initial relationship with Nathan I'd decided to keep

172

fairly quiet about him at first, but now things seemed to be smoothing out and the 'real' couple thing was going well, I'd dropped his name into conversation a few times during our recent chats.

With regards to Christmas though, I'd said I was probably bringing a friend with me, but being concerned that Nathan might change his mind and back out of the family gathering at the last minute I hadn't wanted to get her hopes up, so I'd stayed vague about exactly who my guest might be.

'Santa Baby' suddenly burst from Kenny's phone and after letting out a whoop of joy he shot from the room with a blush that I took to mean it was someone important calling. Probably a new fella. Mum took Nathan's coat and handed them both to my dad to hang up before heading into the kitchen. Now it was just Nathan and I in the lounge along with the soft sound of Christmas carols coming from the radio and the crackling of the fire. Even though it was calm the next few seconds were an exceptionally entertaining experience as I watched Nathan's behaviour in the unfamiliar surroundings of my parents' house. Bless him. He really didn't seem to know what to do with himself as he shifted restlessly on the spot and constantly tugged at the cuffs of his shirt.

To be honest he hadn't exactly helped himself. Instead of dressing casually like I'd told him to, he'd insisted on fully doing himself out in a suit. Not just any suit either, but one of his full-on-knock-em-dead-good-enough-to-eat grey three piece suits complete with done-up buttons and a navy blue silk tie. Now that his coat was gone I was admittedly struggling to tear my eyes away from him.

The rest of us were slightly more casual; Dad had smart trousers paired with a polo shirt, Mum was in a skirt and nice top, and I had a shirt dress over some leggings, but we were nowhere near as smart as Nathan, so he stood out just a tiny little bit as he loitered slightly awkwardly by the

173

fireplace in my parents' living room watching the flames flicker.

'Well, what a lovely start to Christmas!' my mum said as she re-entered the room, her eyes twinkling as she only just held in her obvious excitement at seeing me with a man. 'Would you like some bubbly?' she asked, before frowning and glancing at her watch, 'Actually, it might be a bit early for that ... how about a cup of tea, love?' This question was directed toward Nathan and I immediately saw the brief look of horror that crossed his face as he flashed me a desperate glance that once again almost had me doubling over with laughter. Nathan didn't drink tea, *ever*, only coffee, and only then if it was proper coffee, but it was clear from his face that he was desperately trying to be polite and avoid upsetting my mum. My poor man, he was so out of his depth in an everyday, normal family situation. The fact that he found this all so odd briefly made my chest compress with hurt for him as our conversation in the car rushed back to my mind, but knowing there was nothing I could do to change this past, I instead focused on making this day as pleasant an experience as possible for him.

'Actually, Nathan doesn't drink tea, Mum, just coffee.' But then imagining the look of revulsion that would grace his perfect face if mum presented him with a cup of instant coffee – God forbid – I smirked and quickly added, 'Can I put the cafetière on?'

'Well, why not, it is Christmas after all! There's some Harrods chocolate biscuits in the tin if you want one,' my mum said as she continued to grin broadly at my dad and then flash really unsubtle looks at Nathan. God, could she be any more obvious?

'I'll give you a hand,' Nathan blurted in a panic as I stood to go into the kitchen. Supressing my own smile I rolled my lips tightly between my teeth and nodded as I wandered into the kitchen with my tense man close on my heels. I could just imagine my mum leaping into excited discussions about Nathan as soon as the door closed behind us, and just hoped that she would at least manage to whisper so we didn't have to overhear.

A lengthy sigh of relief left Nathan's lips as we entered the turkey-scented kitchen and I once again found myself having to hold in my laughter – which at least was better than crying like I'd wanted to in the car, I suppose. Carrying the kettle to the sink I began to fill it with water as I turned to see Nathan examining my mum's collection of fridge magnets with odd fascination. 'It's just Christmas, Nathan, relax.'

Huffing out a breath he fingered a Florida magnet and continued to avoid eye contact. 'I know. But like I said, I haven't done a family Christmas for years, not since …' But the rest of his sentence faded out and once again made me bite my lip to stop myself blurting out something sympathetic which he would hate. If there was one thing I'd learnt about the Jackson boys in my time with Nathan, it was that both Nathan and Nicholas hated any form of pity to be bestowed upon them. Turning away from the fridge he squared his shoulders and then met my eyes with a frown. 'Anyway, I am relaxed,' he said in a soft, low tone that was completely incongruent to his stiff body language.

Spluttering a half laugh I couldn't help but smile. 'Really? You don't look it.'

Narrowing his eyes Nathan slowly lifted his right hand and made a deliberate show of undoing the buttons on the front of his suit jacket. My eyes were immediately fixated on his slow movement, something I'm sure he was well aware of. 'I've undone my buttons, look,' he said, pointing to a slither of silver waistcoat now exposed between the panels of his open suit jacket. He didn't need to tell me to look – I was already staring at it, licking my lips and thinking a hundred naughty things that shouldn't even be crossing my mind in my mother's kitchen. 'That means relaxed,' he informed me, a near smile twitching his bottom lip.

Swallowing loudly I went back to my job of putting the kettle on and then dug around in the cupboard to locate the cafetière. *Perhaps he would be less distracting to me if he just took the damn jacket off altogether*, I thought stroppily as I hid my head in the fridge and pulled out the milk. 'Can't you take your jacket off or something? You look like you're attending a board meeting,' I muttered sullenly, annoyed at my own lack of self-control where it came to this man and unfairly taking it out on him by being stroppy.

But what a stupid mistake that request was. Pulling myself together I turned from the fridge to find Nathan now jacketless, stood with his legs splayed and his hands in his trouser pockets. *Oh my God.* I think my heart actually stopped for a few seconds as I stared at him. *He. Was. Stunning.* My mouth hung open as I registered his jacket neatly folded over the back of a chair as I'd requested, giving me a full view of him in all his waistcoated gorgeousness. If I'd struggled to concentrate before, now it was damn near impossible, because Nathan was simply adorned in a fitted silk waistcoat that pulled tight over his muscles in all the right places and showed off his broad shoulders to utter perfection. He looked like some silk-clad Adonis, powerful and sexy to the extreme, and boy did he look out of place in my mum's homely little kitchen!

Keeping his hands in his pockets Nathan started a slow stalk across the kitchen, his gaze never leaving mine once. A smirk that I recognised well formed on his lips and I saw his eyes darken as he got closer to me. Apparently my flustered state was calming him somewhat, or perhaps he just enjoyed seeing me squirm. Pausing right in front of me, so close that I could smell his delicious scent and see

176

the pulse beating steadily in his neck, Nathan leant forwards until our cheeks were touching, causing me to let out a soft sigh as his stubble grazed my skin. I was frozen to the spot in anticipation of his next move.

Seeing as we were in the kitchen of my parents' house I assumed he was just going to whisper something in my ear, but instead, to my complete shock he ducked down and licked a hot trail up the column of my neck. Gasping loudly I promptly dropped the milk carton, which Nathan somehow managed to catch and place on the counter before leaning in to me again with a smirk on his face. Our breaths were mingling now, my lips tingling in expectation of the kiss that was surely coming next.

'How the tables have turned, eh, Stella?' he mused smugly as he finally brushed his lips across mine. Sighing happily I leant against him, thoughts of coffee now long forgotten, and let my man relax me the way only he could. Our mouths were unhurried, tongues moving slowly against each other in a soft appreciation as our hands joined in an exploration that while not overtly desperate or sexual, was still managing to ramp up my arousal.

The noise of the kitchen door crashing open caused me to try and jump back in surprise, but Nathan's hands held me firmly to his chest, apparently uncaring of who might see us so intimately entwined. Thankfully it was Kenny, who upon seeing us pressed together grinned naughtily before rolling his eyes, 'Get a room, you two!' he smirked, before dropping into one of the chairs at the kitchen table and running a hand dramatically through his long hair.

'Guess who's got a date tonight?' he asked, still observing Nathan and I with amusement. Marginally recovering from the shock of being disturbed 'mid-make out' I calmed my breathing and managed to turn slightly in Nathan's arms to tuck myself at his side instead of being plastered to his front like a desperate limpet.

Instead of letting us answer Kenny continued

regardless, 'It's me! I've got a date tonight!' he beamed proudly. 'I'm so glad I didn't get my hair cut yesterday, it looks so much better long like this, don't you think? Much more like Johnny Depp.'

'It looks wondrous, Kenny,' I agreed, grinning at another mention of his obsession with looking like Johnny Depp. 'Who's the lucky guy?'

'David,' Kenny replied dreamily, 'We met last month in a club. I've seen him out for drinks a few times, but I think him asking me to meet up on Christmas Day is a pretty good sign.' *Either that, or David knew that Kenny was a sure thing and fancied a festive frolic*, I thought a touch sceptically, feeling slightly sorry for my friend. Kenny might be a bit of a tart, but deep down he was desperate for a proper relationship. The problem was, he enjoyed sex too much to take things slow and always ended up putting out on the first date, with increasingly fickle men who never seemed to call him back once they had got what they wanted from him.

Shaking my head at the way he was now grinning goofily I tensed up slightly as my mum breezed into the kitchen and came up short when she saw Nathan firmly holding me to his side with my hand resting on his chest. 'Oh!' she gasped, delight evident on her features. 'Don't mind me, I just need to check the turkey.'

Leaning back on his chair Kenny was grinning from ear to ear now. 'If you'd come in a minute ago, Mrs M, you'd have caught them at it. All over each other they were.' My eyes flew open, Nathan smirked rather proudly and Kenny cackled wickedly.

'Oh, Kenny, you are a tease.' My mum said, thankfully dismissing his remark as a joke. Glaring at Kenny he winked at me, but I couldn't help but smile when he visibly wobbled on his chair and nearly tipped over backwards. Serves him right.

Things were noticeably more relaxed after that. Kenny

was on cloud nine, no doubt because of his upcoming date, Nathan was a bit like my shadow, following me everywhere but seemed calmer and relatively content, and mum was in her element playing hostess. By the time dinner was ready and Simon had arrived – thankfully without any flirtatious friends in tow – Nathan was even managing the occasional genuine smile and I decided I'd succeeded in my task of making this an enjoyable Christmas for him.

'Right everyone, dinner's ready, let's get you all settled around the table!' Mum said happily as she steered us through to the attached dining room, 'Nathan if you sit here next to Stella,' my mum said guiding him to a seat and ushering him down. 'Dad, you go at the head of the table, Simon here next to Kenny, and I'll sit nearest the door so I can go in and out of the kitchen.' I watched in amusement as Kenny blushed at his position next to my brother and rolled my eyes as I saw Simon tease him with a suggestive eyebrow wiggle.

'I'll just get the starter.' Smiling at Mum I suddenly became aware of Nathan twitching beside me and shifting uncomfortably in his chair. Looking across at him in concern I had no idea what the matter was until I watched him gather his hands in his lap and start to rub them together in agitation. *Oh shit*. With all the festivities going on I'd forgotten his obsessive need to wash his hands before eating. Why he hadn't just excused himself to the bathroom I had no idea, although my mum had basically herded him into his seat, I suppose, so perhaps he was just trying to be polite again.

Standing up I did the only thing I could think of to ease his agitation without being too obvious, which was to rub my own fingers together and make a face, 'Ugh, my fingers are sticky from those biscuits earlier, I think I'll just wash up before we eat.'

'OK, love,' Mum beamed as she placed a platter of

smoked salmon, pate, and cured meats with posh brown bread on the table. Wow, she really had gone to town this year.

'Yes, me too,' Nathan blurted, jumping up so fast that he knocked the table and had to steady his wineglass to stop it toppling. Thankfully no-one commented on the fact that Nathan hadn't even eaten a biscuit earlier, and let me lead him in the direction of the stairs. When we got to the family bathroom upstairs I stood back and waved in the direction of the sink but Nathan paused right next to me and looked down at me intently. 'How did you know what I needed?' he asked quietly, his eyes intently watching me.

Shrugging lightly I smiled sweetly up at him and leant forwards to place a kiss over his heart. 'I just did.' I didn't embarrass him by mentioning the fact that his few obsessive tendencies were screamingly obvious when you spent as much time with him as I did.

Taking me by surprise Nathan raised his hands and gently cupped my face before tilting it upwards and laying a kiss so soft and beautiful on my lips that I couldn't help but let out a low, needy moan.

'You know me better than anyone ever has, or ever will, Stella, and I'm grateful for that fact every single day.' A lump of emotion formed in my throat as I gazed into his sincere blue pools, his face just centimetres from mine as our accelerated breaths mingled, and then suddenly Nathan was pulling me against him in a hug so fierce that I almost couldn't breathe.

Returning his embrace with just as much passion I buried my face in his neck as he nuzzled by my ear. 'I … I … lov… fuck!' he growled in apparent aggravation at not being able to complete his words. 'You mean so fucking much to me, Stella,' he whispered hoarsely into my hair.

He'd nearly said the 'L' word, I couldn't believe it, and suddenly the lump in my throat felt so big I thought it might choke me. Finally swallowing I pulled my head back a fraction and looked into Nathan's glimmering eyes. He might not have been able to complete his declaration, but his attempt still meant so much to me. Talk about the best Christmas present ever. Well, nearly. But I'd take an 'I lov ...' from Nathan any day.

After Nathan and I had washed our hands we headed back towards the dining room. As he walked down the stairs I noticed that Nathan was humming happily to himself before he turned in the hallway and held out the crook of his arm for me with a shy smile. My eyebrows rose at the man before me; this was possibly the most contented I'd ever seen him, so I happily slipped my hand through his elbow and allowed him to lead me back to the jovial conversation of my family.

As usual Mum had surpassed herself with the cooking, even Kenny the master chef commented on how amazing everything was, and boy was he right. Crispy roast potatoes, pigs in blankets, Yorkshire puds, vegetables, and of course not forgetting the mountain of turkey and homemade gravy.

The wine was flowing, although as the designated driver I was still sober, and as I looked across to see how Nathan was doing I noticed that his cheeks were now quite pink, and rather uncharacteristically his shirt sleeves were rolled up haphazardly and his tie hanging loose and wonky. I'd never seen him looking anything but impeccable in his suits, even on the occasions that he rolled his sleeves up they were usually done with the upmost precision, but now he looked almost scruffy, but totally relaxed, and I loved it.

As the afternoon turned into evening and we rested our full bellies in the lounge Kenny checked his watch and then jumped up. 'Right! I've gotta go. Mrs M; that was delicious, thank you,' he said as he planted a kiss on Mum's cheek before shaking hands with Dad. After embracing me and giving an embarrassed handshake to

Simon and Nathan – I suspected his man crush now extended beyond Simon to include Nathan now too – he dashed from the house, leaving us all gathered in the hallway.

'You two are welcome to stay if you want. The spare room is all made up,' Mum offered, before blushing furiously and then giggling nervously, 'Both guest rooms are made up … you know … if you wanted separate rooms …' Mum stuttered, obviously trying to work out just how new our relationship was and getting herself in a right old state. Now as red as a tomato Mum turned away towards the kitchen, 'I'll make a start on the clearing up! Martin, you can help,' she called to my dad in a high pitched yelp.

Laughing at my mum's blunder I shook my head before daring to look at Nathan, who surprisingly was also a little flushed with embarrassment. 'Separate rooms?' he said, raising an eyebrow as if the idea was totally abhorrent to him.

I gave a lame shrug. 'She doesn't know how long we've been together.'

'We can stay if you'd like?' Nathan asked next. 'But not in separate rooms.' He placed his warm hands on my shoulders and ducked down to look in my eyes. Shaking my head I licked my lips slowly, and hopefully provocatively, 'No, I'd rather you took me home to your bed.'

Nathan's eyes darkened as he nodded his approval and began to unroll his shirtsleeves before re-buttoning the cuffs. 'Once you move in with me permanently you can call it *our* bed,' he reminded me softly, but then just as I was expecting him to initiate yet another debate about why I hadn't moved in yet he instead stepped back. Raising my eyes I was fully expecting to see his determined gaze, but instead I got his little boy expression of wide blue eyes as he reached out and dragged me against his chest. 'Thank you for inviting me today, Stella. I had a really good time.'

Partly amazed that he had dropped the moving in subject so quickly, and also stunned by his soft words of appreciation, I found myself not knowing how to respond, so I simply allowed him to fold me into his arms for an especially long Nathan-style squeeze.

FIFTEEN - REBECCA

The sky was clear and blue and despite the chill in the frosty air it was still a beautiful day. Even the usual chaos of London seemed to have dulled to a peculiar sense of calm this morning, although that was probably because everyone was sleeping off their New Years' Eve excesses from last night. Standing tall I leant over to the right to stretch down my side in preparation for my run. The first run of the New Year and it was a perfect day, which somehow seemed to bode well for the future. This was the year that I would be getting married, I thought with a huge grin. How exciting was that!

Glancing at my watch I frowned. Stella was obviously running late today which wasn't ideal because it was bloody freezing. Shrugging I carried on with my warm up, not wanting my muscles to stiffen up in the cold temperature. Planting my right leg before me I stepped back into a lunge and stretched out my rear Achilles. As I stretched I let my gaze wander over the sights of Green Park before me as the low winter sun cast its rays across the park, forming beautiful glimmering jewels in the frosty grass. I was getting quite into these runs now, they were part of my 'lose weight to fit into my wedding dress' fitness regime, but a month or so ago Stella had decided to join in to keep me company and so I now enjoyed them even more

'I'm here!' I heard Stella's voice behind me and came out of my stretch to see her jogging towards me smiling. 'Sorry I'm late!

'Morning!' Selecting our route on my phone's running app I clicked 'start' and pocketed it before Stella and I started off on an easy jog down the long path that ran around the edge of Green Park. 'Did you and Nathan go out to celebrate New Year then?' I asked, wondering if her evening had been half as eventful as mine with Nicholas had been. A blush heated my cheeks as I remembered back to last night; after cooking a lovely dinner Nicholas had produced a set of challenge cards, a bottle of single malt whisky, and a bottle of amaretto before announcing that we were going to pass the remaining time until midnight playing drinking games.

Needless to say, the challenges in Nicholas' version of the game weren't your usual singing or dancing ones, no, most of the cards Nicholas had made involved something sexual, or intimate, and had certainly been a *very* pleasant way to bring in the New Year.

'No, we stayed in. I just overslept,' she explained with a rueful smile as a slight flush reddened her cheeks. Hmm ... that blush looked very similar to the one I could feel heating my cheeks, and I'd almost place money on the fact that Nathaniel Jackson had also created a rather eventful way to spend their New Years' Eve last night.

We jogged on in silence for a few minutes until we came to the edge of the park and had to cross The Mall so we could enter St James's Park. Glancing up the road to check for any traffic I saw Stella leaning forwards on her knees with a decidedly peaky complexion now on her face. 'Crikey, Stella, you look a bit pale. Are you all right?' I asked, frowning as she stood upright and staggered slightly.

Scrunching up her face Stella shook her head. 'I feel a bit sick, actually. Think I might have had a glass of wine too many last night. Do you mind if we just walk for a bit?'

Nodding my head I linked my arm through hers as we

crossed the road, 'Of course.' I was easily at my target weight at the moment, so I didn't really have any issues with skipping one day of my running. Besides, my wedding dress was a lace-up, so it was pretty flexible in its fit.

After taking a few steady breaths, presumably to try and ease her hangover, Stella then looked across at me. 'So, come on then, while we walk tell me more about your trip to Iceland, we've hardly spoken properly since you got back last week. I want details, woman.'

My heart fluttered in my chest and a grin instantly popped to my lips as I thought back to my Christmas holiday with Nicholas. It had been such a magical trip, and so romantic that I could still hardly believe that Nicholas had planned the whole thing himself. As surprise Christmas presents go I think it would take something pretty monumental to ever surpass it.

'Well, I told you the basics on the phone really,' I said as I considered how to condense our fabulous holiday into a few select highlights. My breath was fogging the air in front of me, but even though it was cold today the temperature was nowhere near as low as it had been during our week in Iceland. 'We flew direct to Reykjavik and stayed there for the first night.' I missed out the fact that Nicholas had got me naked on the balcony, teased my body with cold snowy fingers, and then proceeded to make love to me whilst I wore nothing but a woolly hat ... but those were details I'd need to share with Stella while under the influence of alcohol.

'The next morning we headed off to see a few sights. The country is just *amazing*, Stella, like a cross between some rugged alien landscape and a David Attenborough nature documentary.' My enthusiasm was obvious, and I actually had to forcibly calm myself down before I continued. 'We saw thermal springs at Geyser, sunrise on a black volcanic beach, a frozen waterfall, and the Northern

Lights, which were just incredible. Honestly, I've never seen anything quite like it.'

'It sounds amazing, Becks. What were the hotels like?'

Smiling I thought back to the three places we had stayed during our trip. 'Incredible. We were only at the first hotel for the first and last nights, but it was lovely, very plush and had a great view over a town square.' Sidestepping a lady running with a fitness pram I continued, 'The second hotel was in the wilderness, we could actually see a volcano from our room, the one that caused all those flight disruptions a few years back.' Giving her a glance as we power walked over the bridge that crossed the lake I saw Stella's eyebrows rise in interest. Remembering back to where Nicholas and I spent Christmas night I couldn't help but let out a little sigh of happiness, 'For Christmas night Nicholas had booked us an igloo in its own private forest clearing.' Stella stopped walking and grabbed my arm whilst staring at me with wide eyes.

'You're kidding me?' she exclaimed, looking almost as shocked as I had when I'd first seen the igloo.

'Nope. Well, it wasn't made of actual snow, it was glass and had central heating, but it was still phenomenal! The view of the stars that night was just out of this world.' OK, so were the things that Nicholas had done to me in the gigantic circular bed, but once again that was a conversation that required some liquid courage to bring up.

'God, I'm so jealous!' Stella said as we reached the run up to the Churchill Museum and paused to let some horse riders pass us by. 'It's been ages since I went on a proper holiday,' she mused. 'The last time I went abroad was on a conference with work to Brussels. Don't get me wrong, it had some stunning architecture, but it was all a bit stuffy and boring. Mind you, that was probably just the other colleagues I was with!' she joked. I was glad to hear her sounding more like herself. Hopefully she was feeling a bit better now, maybe the fresh air had worked some magic on her hangover.

Stella indicated that she was OK to continue with our walk, so we set off in the direction of Horse Guards Parade at a slightly brisker pace than before. 'Why don't you ask Nathan if he wants to go away somewhere together? I'm sure he'd like to.'

Nodding, Stella smiled. 'Maybe I'll book something as a surprise for him. It's his birthday in a few months and I have no idea what else to get him. He has every modern gadget and convenience known to man. Besides, he was away on a conference last year so we didn't really get to celebrate it, so I could make this year extra special.' Fiddling with the sleeve of her running jacket Stella blushed and looked at me with a twinkle in her eye. 'Actually he wanted to take me away for Christmas, he suggested New York, but I'd already promised my mum that I'd spend it with her so we went there instead.'

'You might not have been abroad, but I bet that having Nathan with you on Christmas Day made it pretty special too, though? I still can't quite believe that Nathan actually went with you to your parents' house.' And I really couldn't, I mean Nathan? Mr Intimidation, meeting parents? It really had never seemed like a likelihood at all.

'It was good. He was really nervous beforehand, but I think he actually really enjoyed it.' Stella might be keeping fairly quiet about the details, but I could see from the fond smile on her face and the crinkle at the corners of her eyes just how much it had meant to her, and just how much she must have enjoyed it.

Well I never, quite apparently since asking for my advice on how to 'mainstream' with Stella over a year and a half ago Nathaniel Jackson had developed and grown more than I would ever have imagined or hoped.

SIXTEEN - NATHAN

It was lucky I was up and about, otherwise the slamming of my front door would have pissed me right off. It was the weekend, which meant my cleaner Miranda wasn't due, and seeing as Stella had only left a short while ago for her now weekly run with Rebecca I knew it could only be Nicholas – the only other person with a key – letting himself into my apartment so bloody loudly.

Pulling on a polo shirt I paused briefly by the mirror to flatten my hair again, which for some reason was choosing to go springy since my shower this morning.

Wandering towards the hallway I leant on the wall as I watched Nicholas by the front door pulling a navy blue hoodie off over his head. My brother, the impeccable dresser, in a hooded jumper was *not* a common sight and I narrowed my eyes as I observed him further. 'Morning, Nicholas. It's a little early isn't it?' I asked with a cocked eyebrow, but in return Nicholas simply made a dismissive noise in the back of his throat and threw me an unconcerned look.

'Good morning. Considering how many times you have turned up on my doorstep at ungodly hours I think that eight thirty in the morning is actually rather a respectable time.' To be fair, he had a point.

'Noted,' I agreed with a smirk. 'So, to what do I owe the pleasure, brother?' I asked in amusement as he folded the jumper and placed it on the table by my coat stand. Gazing at him standing there in sports shorts, a plain black

T-shirt, and trainers I frowned. What was going on? I literally hadn't seen Nicholas in sports gear since college.

'Well, I just dropped Rebecca off to meet Stella for their weekly run in Green Park. Apparently last week during their run on New Years' Day they decided that Stella would drive them back here afterwards for breakfast today. I had the morning free so I thought instead of going to my usual gym I'd make use of yours and then we can all breakfast together.'

'Invite yourself to eat my food, why don't you,' I murmured dryly, but I was only joking. I actually rather enjoyed the fact that I saw more of my brother nowadays since Stella and Rebecca had become so close. It was … nice.

'Yeah, yeah, whatever, Nathan,' he said, rolling his eyes. 'I brought croissants and a bag of those amazing coffee beans from my local deli.' Passing me a re-useable linen shopping bag I glanced inside and smiled. God, I loved this coffee – Panama Esmeralda, a bit of a rarity, but fuck me, it was good, like liquid gold in a mug.

Bringing the paper bag of coffee beans to my nose I inhaled and then rolled my eyes back in pleasure at the beautiful aroma, 'I shall accept your bribery and allow you to use my gym,' I conceded with a grin.

'Cheers, bro. I thought seeing as Rebecca is making such an effort to tone up for the wedding I probably should too.' This time it was my turn to make a dismissive noise. I was the fitness freak, but even though my brother might be slightly slimmer than me build-wise, he was just as muscular and I knew for a fact he used the gym at least four times a week. 'Because you really need to tone up, Nicholas,' I murmured sarcastically, giving him a backhanded punch on his rock solid abs.

Giving me a small shrug he blushed slightly and rubbed his stomach, 'Every little helps. You fancy a run? Even with a few excesses over Christmas and New Year I've gotten my mile pace down pretty low now, think you can beat me, old man?'

Raising an eyebrow I felt my heart rate accelerate slightly. He might be my little brother who I would usually do anything to protect, but boy did I like a challenge, something Nicholas was fully aware of, and with my fierce competitive streak there was no way I was going down lightly.

'You're on. Just let me change before I run you into the ground, little brother,' I said with a smirk.

After a quick change of clothes I found my brother in the gym leaning against the wall and stretching out his quads in preparation for our run. Glancing up as I entered he gave me a nod of greeting as I joined him on the mats. Even though Nicholas and I had both made fairly radical changes to our lives since meeting Stella and Rebecca neither of us had developed into huge conversationalists, but as we stood there stretching in silence I felt a need to fill the gap. As much as I had tried to avoid discussing the upcoming wedding with Stella in case it gave her ideas, it seemed to be the most logical topic with Nicholas. 'So now you're back from your fancy holiday are the wedding preparations back on track?'

Nodding, Nicholas swapped legs and repeated his stretch. 'They are actually, the venue is booked and guest list sorted. Rebecca's ordered the flowers, found her dress, and has nearly finished the table plan too. She's an efficient little thing,' he commented fondly with a smile.

'Sounds pretty good going to me,' I murmured, not entirely comfortable with the dreamy quality to his voice, or the topic at hand, and feeling a little unsure what else I could constructively comment on.

'I need to get my arse in gear and book some cars though,' Nicholas said as he shook out his legs and glanced at the running machines. 'Ready for me to run you into the ground?' he quipped.

Relieved at the change in topic I nodded sharply and then barked out a laugh at his cocky confidence. I ran five times a week so Nicholas 'running me into the ground' wasn't at all a concern for me. Looking at my brother I could see the competitive gleam in his eye though, and couldn't help but grin. We were so similar in that trait; both of us stubborn as mules and unwilling to go down without a substantial fight – so this could be quite interesting, not to mention fun.

Stepping across to the iPod dock I selected a folder of running tracks and pressed 'play', causing the heavy, fast beat of The Prodigy's 'Invaders Must Die' to fill the gym's silence. This music player was a new addition since Stella's arrival in my life because apparently she simply 'couldn't run' without music, and seeing as I insisted on fitness being part of our lives the dock arrived shortly after she did.

Crossing the room to the running machine next to Nicholas I peeled off my T-shirt, as I always did when I ran, and then glanced across at him to see my brother smirking at me. 'Showing off, Nathan?' he quipped, tipping his chin in the direction of my flat stomach. Grinning, I shrugged. I knew I had a good body; I worked hard to keep it that way, so why the hell shouldn't I be proud of it?

Rolling his eyes at me I was stunned the next second when Nicholas followed my movements and removed his own T-shirt to reveal a well-formed set of abs. Christ, my brother had a real, actual six pack. Well I never. He'd always been trim, but it seemed Nicholas really had been upping his exercise in the run up to the wedding.

'Come on then, Mr Muscle, show me what you've got,' I bantered as I leant across and set his machine for ten kilometres. 'Loser makes the breakfast.'

REBECCA

'Oh my God,' I murmured, my voice sounding a little high and breathy.

'Mmm-hmm,' Stella agreed next to me, apparently too enraptured to form actual words.

As my eyes took in the vision of Nicholas and Nathan sprinting on the running machines I lifted my hands up and placed them on the glass of the window so I could lean in closer. The Jackson brothers made quite a stunning pair running there together, but my eyes were predominantly drawn to Nicholas. A little moan of appreciation slipped past my lips as I watched him without blinking. Back muscles slick with sweat and rippling with each pump of his powerful arms, that gorgeous bum of his hidden inside some snug shorts, and his dark hair flopping on his head and wet with perspiration. He looked so good that I wanted to lick him. All over.

'It's like a living incarnation of a wet dream.' Realising that it might sound like I was after her man I quickly qualified my point to Stella, 'Don't get me wrong, I don't fancy Nathan or anything, but you gotta agree that those two running like that is a pretty hot sight.' From their speed it looked like they were racing. Both brothers were topless, their backs to us, wet with sweat and utterly focused on their task as their feet pounded relentlessly on the fast moving tracks. 'I'm *sooo* glad you suggested breakfast here last week.' It was a glorious sight of taut flesh and heaving muscles, crikey, I could almost smell the testosterone seeping from the room.

Obviously I knew Nicholas had a great body, but wow, both the Jackson boys were clearly in good shape, and I mean *really* frigging good shape. What a sight. Much better then Stella and me, who were red from our run and looking a bit dishevelled from the cold, breezy day outside.

'Yeah, I'll stick with Nathan, but I totally agree. They look hot. And I'm not talking temperature,' Stella agreed as she stepped away from window, fanned her face with her hand, and giggled, 'I feel a bit flustered now!'

Taking one last look at the muscle-fest in Nathan's home gym I let out a contented sigh before forcing myself to turn away. 'Let's set the breakfast out, I suspect those two are going to need to re-fuel after their contest.'

SEVENTEEN – STELLA

Valentine's decorations still adorned card shop windows as I set on my way to meeting Rebecca at the bridal boutique for our final dress fitting. I could hardly believe how quickly time was flying. Christmas seemed like just yesterday, but now Rebecca and Nicholas' wedding was just a month away. Four tiny weeks, crikey, it would be here in no time.

As well as getting the final measurements for our bridesmaids' dresses Louise and I were also going to be getting a crash course in how to lace up Rebecca's wedding dress. The gown she'd picked was stunning, simple yet elegant, just perfect for her, but the bodice back looked pretty daunting so I was relieved when the assistant had offered us some lessons.

As Louise was getting measured up I killed some time by absently perusing some of the dress racks outside the fitting room at the back of the shop. Pushing one gown to the side I found myself looking at a wedding dress that very nearly made my eyes pop out of my head. If in fact this 'thing' could even be classed as a wedding dress. Grinning from ear to ear I pulled it down. It was light to hold, which wasn't surprising as there was barely anything to it, and made my way inside the changing rooms.

'Oh, Rebecca, you're going to be so disappointed you didn't spot this beauty!' I teased as I held up the hanger. Rebecca, Louise, and the assistant all turned simultaneously in my direction and I watched as their faces all took on similar expressions of shock. The 'dress' in my hand was made of black leather straps, a few buckles, and not much else. Judging from the placement of the straps they would just about cover the essentials, still leaving plenty of skin exposed. To add to the obvious bondage design there were metal rings attached in several places, presumably for wedding night fun. *Nothing says romance quite like some attached bondage straps, does it?* I thought with a giggle.

'Ah yes, we have a few like that for our more, uh, *specialist* clientele,' the assistant said with a knowing smile. 'There are matching knee high boots too.'

'Well, given his history I think Nicholas would have loved it! I know Nathan would!' I said, trying to imagine Nathan's face if I walked into the bedroom wearing this get up. He'd probably blow a gasket. Shortly before taking full advantage of the various clips and buckles to pin me down while he did incredibly naughty things to me.

Louise's eyes opened wide at my words, just at the same time as Rebecca flashed me a warning glance and gave a minute shake of her head. Judging from the curiosity on Louise's face I quickly realised that Rebecca hadn't shared any details of the Jackson brothers' penchant for control in the bedroom with her. Oops.

'I mean, what man wouldn't like to see a woman wearing this …' I said quickly, trying to cover my steps, but thankfully, at that very moment the assistant stood up and gave Louise a pat on the shoulder. 'All done. Right, Stella, your turn.' Phew. *Talk about saved by the bell* I thought, as I began to strip off my jeans and jumper, all the while deliberately avoiding eyes contact with Louise.

Mid-way through pulling up the zip on the side of my dress the assistant stopped and frowned. 'Hmmm,' she said, bringing a hand up and rubbing her chin. 'I don't think we need to take it in anymore, it's actually a bit snugger than last time already.'

Frowning, I ran my hands down over my stomach and bum. Everything was still pretty flat, but I suppose I had basically deserted my diet during the Christmas holidays and gone a bit wild on the mince pies. It was quite disappointing though, because even though I might not have been counting my calories I had still maintained my running routine with Rebecca in the month or so since Christmas, which I'd thought would have balanced everything out. How depressing, perhaps this was early middle age starting to kick in, and fat would suddenly become harder to burn off now I was in my late twenties.

'We'll leave it as it is, there's still a little room,' the assistant said with a smile, completely unaware of my slight upset. I'd run my bloody arse off in the last month, I think I had the right to be slightly perturbed. 'Feel free to pop in the week before the wedding if you think your weight has changed at all.'

My low mood didn't last for long though, because as the assistant bent to check the hem of the dress I saw Louise and Rebecca bobbing about and teasing me by puffing out their cheeks and curling their arms into rounded humps at their sides to make it look like they were really fat, which instantly made me smile. I knew what they were trying to do – bring me back down to earth. I was hardly obese, was I? So really I shouldn't be getting myself upset by a few extra pounds here and there.

'On the plus side, we now have more time to practice lacing the wedding dress,' the assistant said as she stood up again. 'Let's make a start, shall we?' she chirped, topping up our champagne.

EIGHTEEN – NICHOLAS

'*Please* tell me you haven't organised anything big for today, Nathan,' I queried apprehensively as I eyed my brother and his impeccable suit while he stood on my doorstep with his legs splayed and a cocky expression on his face. Why was he wearing a three-piece suit at this time of the day anyway? It was barely nine in the morning on a Saturday for God's sake.

Raising an eyebrow Nathan gave me a level stare and crossed his arms over his chest. 'Have a little faith please, Nicholas,' he said tersely. Picking up a small holdall he pushed his way past me, through the front door and headed into my kitchen with me trailing behind sullenly. Placing his bag down Nathan then propped himself on a counter and crossed one ankle over the other before tugging on his shirt cuffs, smoothing down his jacket, and running a hand carefully over his already immaculate hair. He looked like he was auditioning for a *GQ* photo shoot, and I couldn't help but roll my eyes.

'I have faith in you, brother, but I said I didn't want a stag do and yet here you are.' Turning to him I heaved out a sigh and waited for him to expand on what the heck he had planned for me today. 'I recall perfectly; you said no night clubs, no strippers, no groups of fake friends. So basically no stag do. I have adhered to all these points, Nicholas. Think of today as two brothers simply having a day out together, nothing more.'

My eyebrows rose. 'It's just the two of us?'

Nathan nodded his head slowly. 'It is.' Realistically it had always just been Nathan and I. Our parents might have brought us into the world, but their treatment of us as kids had forced us into relying heavily on each other as we grew up. Nathan was my rock. He was literally the only reason I was still alive today, and although our lives were evolving now as we moved on with Rebecca and Stella, I genuinely valued the brotherly bond we had.

Thinking about it in those terms I nodded; spending the day with Nathan would be great. I'd banned a stag do months ago, because quite frankly I couldn't think of anything worse than being surrounded by vague acquaintances and so-called friends all drinking to my health and happy marriage – when realistically I didn't actively socialise with any of them on a regular basis. But today would just be Nathan and I, just like old times. Nodding my head my shoulders felt looser already.

Taking out a bag of coffee beans I began to set up the grinder when Nathan walked over and unplugged it. 'You won't need that, we'll be having coffee soon enough. Go and change, Nicholas, you need to be smart this morning, but pack a bag with some casual clothes,' he said, plucking the bag of coffee from my hand and eyeing it appreciatively. 'And I mean really casual, like a T-shirt, jumper, tracksuit bottoms. Gym gear, that type of thing.' Gym gear? What the hell were we going to be doing? Working out?

Just as that moment Rebecca breezed into the kitchen with a small day bag in her hand. 'Don't worry about packing the bag, Nicholas. I've done it for you,' she said with a sweet smile that I couldn't help but return. A moment later however, I realised that the bag in her hand meant Rebecca obviously knew about the plans for the day, and I quickly dropped the smile and narrowed my eyes at her instead. 'You were in on this?'

Her sweet smile morphed into a megawatt grin, 'I was.'

Rolling onto tiptoes she landed a firm kiss on my lips, stepping back before I could take hold of her. 'You're going to have a great day,' she added confidently before walking over to Nathan and whipping the coffee from his hand.

Trying not to be such a miser I rolled off my shoulders, pulled my face into some semblance of a smile, and then with a nod of acceptance turned and headed for the stairs to change.

Strolling down the stairs I made my way along the hall but froze as I saw Nathan and Rebecca still in the kitchen chatting amiably. My eyes narrowed for just the briefest of seconds as I watched them together, before I rolled my eyes at myself and allowed a small self-derisive smile to twist the corner of my lips. It was Rebecca and Nathan for God's sake – my trusted brother and the woman I loved – I had no reason to be jealous or concerned. Slipping my hands in the trouser pockets of my suit I loosened off my neck and wandered along the hall to meet them. The way I'd so easily brushed off that spike of jealousy made me realise just how far I'd come in the last year or so and as I reached the kitchen I allowed myself a smile.

Rebecca's eyes turned to me as soon as my shoes made contact with the marble of the kitchen floor.

Blowing out a low wolf whistle she licked her lips and grinned. I watched with pleasure as my girl's eyes lit up as she took in my appearance. It was *me* making her look like that, and that thought was like liquid euphoria flowing through my veins and making my chest puff out.

'You look *good*, Nicholas. *Really good*,' Rebecca murmured in a low, husky tone. I was wearing one of my favourite navy blue three-piece suits, paired with a white shirt and a pale blue tie, but from the look Rebecca was giving me it was clearly one of her favourites too. Or at least it was now. In fact, her obvious appreciation almost seemed to verge on outright arousal, which while pleasing me immensely, was also quite surprising, because although Rebecca had no issues with displays of affection in public, she usually kept her lusty side more carefully hidden. It had to be said after Rebecca's wolf whistle, throaty words, and intense stare, my ego was feeling pretty damn good at the moment.

'You two look way too handsome,' Rebecca said with a fake frown as she lifted a hand to her chin and inspected Nathan and myself intently. 'Take him away, Nathan, before I change my mind about letting you both loose on the world.'

Grinning like a kid I couldn't help but close the gap to my girl and pull her in for a heated kiss which quickly caused her to soften against me and loop her hands around my neck. God, I loved this woman so fucking much.

'Christ, Nicholas, cool it off, brother,' Nathan muttered as he gave me a shove in the shoulder that was hard enough to make me stagger sideways as I clutched a giggling Rebecca to my chest to stop her slipping.

'OK, OK! Let's go.' Placing one final quick kiss on Rebecca's lips I flashed her a wink and stepped towards my brother as he led me from the kitchen.

'You're not getting in my car if you've got a fucking stiffy, Nicholas,' Nathan complained grumpily, but from the small chuckle I heard, I suspect his comment was far more light-hearted than he was making out. Picking up my bag I followed Nathan to the car unable to wipe the smirk from my face.

Eight minutes later Nathan's company car pulled to a halt in the heart of Marylebone and I glanced out of the window before raising my eyebrows. 'Are you serious?' I asked, turning to my brother in surprise.

'I am indeed, Nicholas,' Nathan said as the driver opened the door for us and he slid from the car without waiting for me to continue the conversation.

Following my brother out of the car I nodded my thanks to the driver, straightened off my suit, smoothed down my tie, and then looked up at the impressive façade of the old fire station building in front of me. As innocuous as this frontage might seem, I knew that this building had been converted to house one of the hottest restaurants in London; the Chiltern Firehouse. This place was infamous for its fabulous – and expensive – food, not to mention sightings of the rich and famous.

'Is this not a little pretentious for breakfast?' I asked as we crossed the pavement towards the doors.

Smirking at me, Nathan shrugged carelessly. 'Perhaps. But the food is fantastic, and surely I'm allowed to push the boat out to celebrate my little brother getting married?' When he put it like that I couldn't really disagree, so I joined Nathan in his smile and followed him inside.

As its name suggests, the Chiltern Firehouse is exactly what it says. The exterior is still that of a fire station, but even inside they have managed to maintain the original features in combination with a funky dining room setting.

We were seated promptly by an incredibly smart waiter who served us a complimentary glass of chilled mango juice to drink whilst we perused the breakfast menu. The rather expensive menu. I might have money, but I didn't tend to splash out to this extreme that often, and I had to say I was still a little cynical about how the chef would make a few eggs be worth the prices listed on the menu.

After my initial scepticism I had to say the food really was amazing; I had a crab omelette and the most delicious coffee, while Nathan opted for lobster medallions with scrambled egg, an espresso, and small water. Perhaps this wasn't the type of place you'd frequent every Saturday morning, but seeing as this was my stag do, of sorts, it certainly made a special start to the day.

Once we were back in the cool interior of the car I fully expected Nathan to produce a bottle of champagne from the fridge between the seats to really get our day started in style, but when I enquired about the possibility of a Buck's Fizz he merely gave me a cryptic look and shook his head. 'Later, brother,' he said, handing me a chilled bottle of orange juice instead.

The reason behind Nathan's reluctance to give me an alcoholic drink began to become apparent an hour and a half later as the car pulled off the M40 at the sign for Silverstone Circuit. Winding through country roads for a few minutes the car slowed as we turned into the car park of the world famous race track itself. Immediately my heart rate rose as my mind leapt to various different conclusions about why we might be here. All of them included cars and speed and made a huge childlike grin stretch my face.

'I'm sure you can guess why we're here, Nicholas,' Nathan said with a matching grin. 'You said no strippers, dancing, or nightclubs, so I thought I'd opt for something else which might get your pulse racing.'

I was so eager to see what we would be driving that I completely lost my usual poise and control as I practically threw myself out of the car as soon as the driver had pulled to a stop. 'This is perfect, Nathan, you know how much I love a good, fast car.'

Patting me on the back Nathan handed me my bag, grabbed one of his own, and then led me towards the reception area. After changing into our casual clothes we were quickly checked in and given a very thorough safety briefing before being led to the track side, where the mere smell of petrol and burnt rubber had me fidgeting with excitement.

Four hours later my heart was still hammering in my chest from the adrenaline and excitement of the experience. It had been absolutely *unbelievable*. We'd started in a Ferrari F430 Coupe, a beautiful car whose 4.3 V8 engine was capable of nought to sixty in four seconds flat. The thrill from the screaming roar of the engine as I paddled up through the six gears and tore around the corners of the circuit was unlike anything I had ever experienced in my life before.

I'm lucky enough to have had the opportunity to drive fabulous cars before, and I've driven them fast. Really fast. But being on the circuit at Silverstone in the Ferrari had just been awe-inspiring. As our professional driver and guide for the day, Joe, had led us across to the pit lane and stopped beside a Formula 1 style car my jaw literally fell open. I'd never driven one of these beauties before, but bloody hell, I had *always* wanted to.

As soon as my foot had dabbed at the accelerator of the racing car I had been able to feel the difference to every single vehicle I have driven in the past. The near perfect aerodynamics, lightweight frame, and high power engine blew me away as it clung to the corners and leapt along the straights like a stallion. The driving position was so low to the ground that I could feel every single pulse-raising vibration run through my entire skeleton and soon enough I lost myself to the moment, much like I did when I played piano. There was nothing but me, the car, and the track. It truly was one of the most astonishing experiences of my entire life.

Changing back into my suit after such an incredible afternoon was actually rather difficult. All I wanted to do was stay on the track until the sun went down and the floodlights came on and then drive until I ran out of fuel. But eventually our time was up and Nathan and I made our way back to the car with grins on our faces like two little kids.

As the car pulled out of the car park and I gazed wistfully at the disappearing stadium complex, Nathan popped the cork from a bottle of champagne, making me jump. The loud noise seemed to ricochet round the small space and I chuckled, my attention now well and truly back inside the car.

'*Now* you can have a drink, brother,' Nathan said, handing me a cool glass which I chinked with his and then immediately took a large sip from.

Considering I hadn't wanted a stag do, or even a fuss to be made, I had to say today had been out of this world. I'd been treated to great food, experienced thrills on the race track beyond my belief, and was now sipping champagne in the back of a plush car with my beloved brother. After all my previous reservations about what the day would hold Nathan had certainly succeeded in making me enjoy myself, and I had to say he'd done the job rather well.

NINETEEN – STELLA

I couldn't believe it was March already. Shaking my head I blew out a breath and wondered where the weeks had gone. It seemed like just yesterday I was pulling crackers with Nathan at my parents' house. Nathan and I were doing better than ever, but the last two months had seemed to pass in a blur of flowers, cakes, dresses, and jogs as I'd helped Rebecca with all her wedding plans. Nicholas was doing his part too, but was taking a bit of a back seat with the girly stuff, hence my willing assistance.

I'd had to skip this morning's run again because I'd not felt too great. I hadn't even made it to the park to *walk* with Rebecca today, because I'd had my head stuck down the toilet. Truth be told, I hadn't felt good all week, and now here I was sat in my bathroom with sweat breaking out on my forehead, my hands trembling and heart pounding.

No, no, no, no, *no*. This could not be happening. Practically ripping hair from my scalp I ran a trembling hand over my head as I stared again at the pale pink lines appearing on the stick in front of me. Instead of disappearing as I was desperately hoping, they were growing darker by the frigging second. *Shit*. Looking back at the box clutched in my other hand I skimmed the writing to the important part: one pink line in the display window equals not pregnant. Two pink lines in the display window equals pregnant. *Fuuuuck*. Whichever way I held this damn stick there was no getting away from the fact that there were two very clear pink lines staring me in the face.

I was on the goddamn contraceptive injection, how the hell could I be pregnant?

Shock crawled its way over my skin, replacing sweat with goose-bumps. My vision started to blur as my limbs went numb and I only just managed to grab the side of the bathtub as I slid from the toilet seat and sunk to the cold tiled floor in a heap. Trying to concentrate on taking deep breaths I thought through the situation rationally. I wasn't in shock at being pregnant so much, in fact that didn't really worry me at all. What was currently forefront in my mind was Nathan. Or rather the fact that Nathan was going to go absolutely berserk.

Oh God. There was no way Nathan was going to want a child. Regardless of how far he'd come in his emotional development in the past year, he didn't want kids, of that much I was sure. He'd not said as much, but he hadn't needed to, horrible flashbacks of the day we'd bumped into his ex, Melissa, flashed in my mind. He'd briefly thought her baby might be his and he'd looked utterly horrified by the idea, completely repelled really.

Christ, what a mess. No doubt this would be a huge shitstorm for Nathan and I, one I wasn't sure we'd survive. He'd probably finish with me and I'd be left broken-hearted and pregnant. What an utterly depressing thought. A dry sob escaped my throat as I tried to stand up. I grimaced as I realised it was probably just as well I hadn't moved in with him then, that would have been a bit pointless really – move in just to move out again a few months later. I ran a shaky hand over my face and pushed some hair from my eyes. God, a glass of wine would go a long way right now, but I suppose that would be out of the question for a fair few months to come.

What to do next was the question. Realistically, there was only one thing I should be doing next, so on shaky legs I made my way to the kitchen, picked up my mobile, and dialled a number. Not Nathan, not yet; first I needed a trip to the doctors to get this properly confirmed.

Why do doctors and hospitals ask you to provide a urine sample and then proceed to cheerily give you the smallest plastic cup known to mankind? I mean for God's sake, as if it isn't bad enough trying to semi-squat over a toilet and pee into a cup in the first place, making it the size of a goddamn thimble really doesn't help matters. Blowing my hair out of my face I screwed on the cap and placed the now full cup on the sink and sorted myself out. After washing my hands I attempted to minimise my embarrassment by concealing the cup in my clenched fist while walking back through a packed waiting room of curious glances and into the doctor's room.

The arduous task and mortifying walk of shame were over, and now I was sat in Dr Rayner's small office on an uncomfortable plastic chair, twirling the ring on my thumb so frantically that the skin below it was getting sore. In my peripheral vision Dr Rayner was typing something on her computer, but my eyes were glued intently on the freshly deposited pot of pee that was sat on her desk with a dip stick in it.

'Staring at it won't make the three minutes go any quicker,' Dr Rayner said with a kind smile, making me look across at her and bite my lip in embarrassment.

'I know, sorry, I'm just a bit nervous,' I mumbled shifting uncomfortably on my seat.

Pushing her small circular glasses up her nose she nodded, 'That's perfectly natural. While we wait why don't you give me a few details? When was your last period?'

Good question. When *was* my last period? Pulling my phone from my bag I scrolled through the calendar and frowned then looked up at Dr Rayner, 'It's difficult to tell,

I've been on the injection for a while now and it's messed up my cycle quite a bit.'

Nodding again, Dr Rayner smiled reassuringly, 'That's perfectly normal, Stella, some women stop their periods completely on the injection, others have light periods or irregular bleeds, it's very individual.'

'OK, well,' I glanced at my phone again, 'I was having very light periods most months, the last one was just over...' pausing I used my finger to count up the weeks, '... *God*, just over eleven weeks ago.' Shaking my head, my eyes widened at my carelessness. I'd missed several months, how the hell had I not noticed that? I'd been so busy helping Rebecca with the wedding preparations I guess I just hadn't realised. My eye twitched guiltily; it had probably also slipped my mind because in every free minute not spent with Rebecca I'd been preoccupied shagging Nathan to make up for not seeing him as often. Damn it.

'Actually thinking about it, I've been nauseous quite a few mornings too ...' My words faded away, I'd been sick, or felt sick, most mornings last week, not to mention on and off since Christmas, but I'd blamed it on all the extra early morning runs I was doing with Rebecca. Closing my eyes I ran my hands over my face. I felt like such an idiot. How had I not put all these signs together?

Glancing at her watch Dr Rayner nodded and then leant forwards to pick up the stick, causing me to tense in anticipation and hold my breath. Tilting the stick under the light from the desk lamp she briefly inspected it and then smiled up at me, 'Well, Stella, it seems your suspicions were correct; you are pregnant.'

I'm going to have a baby.

I breathed in deeply through my nose and then let it out through my mouth. *I'm going to have a baby.* The words rung in my brain over and over again until Dr Rayner's concerned tone broke into my spiralling thoughts, 'You look a little pale, dear – would you like a glass of water?'

I shook my head and smiled limply across at her, 'No, I'm fine thanks, it was just a bit of a shock, that's all.' And wasn't that just the understatement of the year. *I'm going to have a baby.*

Oh dear God, I really was pregnant, and Nathan really was going to freak out.

'Hey, Stella!' Kenny chorused cheerfully as I walked into the flat later that evening. 'Want a glass of wine? It is the start of the weekend after all!' He had a cheeky grin on his face, a bottle of Merlot in one hand, and a full glass in the other and all I could think was yes, yes, yes, I'd love some wine.

A whispered sigh escaped my lips. 'No thanks,' I said instead, dropping my bag down on the counter and sliding onto one of the kitchen stools.

Coming round the counter Kenny made a show of checking my forehead, presumably testing for a fever, and then stood back as he examined me with narrowed eyes, 'You always have a glass of wine with me on a Friday night before going to Nathan's. What's wrong, are you sick?' Looking up at Kenny, my flatmate and probably my closest friend in the world, I drew in a deep breath and decided to just get it out there.

'Not sick, no.' I shook my head and pursed my lips, preparing to drop my bombshell, 'Pregnant.'

If I hadn't been so desperately worried about Nathan's reaction to all this I would probably have found Kenny's response hilarious. First he put the wine down with a shaking hand, then behind his trendy little glasses his eyes expanded to almost comical proportions, and finally his mouth bobbed open and closed like a goldfish as he repeatedly tried and failed to speak, which made his beard

213

twitch visibly. The vast range of expressions that accompanied his gasping was also rather impressive; shock, happiness, confusion … but finally he settled on concern as he stepped closer to me and reached out to take my hand.

'I can't help noticing that you don't look thrilled, Stella,' he said softly, 'I'm assuming this wasn't planned?'

A desperate and slightly manic laugh escaped my throat at his words as I tipped my head back and let it out as a humourless cackle. 'Not planned. No.' I shook my head vigorously and chewed on my lower lip until I tasted the copper of blood on my tongue, 'I just found out a few hours ago,' I told him, picking up an apple from the fruit bowl to fiddle with.

Wandering to the sink Kenny filled me a glass of water and placed it in front of me. 'Wow … so you haven't told Nathan yet?' he asked carefully pulling up another stool to join me. Tossing the apple back on the counter with a little too much force I watched with a grimace as it missed the bowl and bounced skittishly across the surface before rolling off the edge onto the floor. 'Nope, and I don't plan to either. Not yet anyway.'

Kenny's silence told me all I needed to know and after it stretched on for an age I finally looked across at him to see him frowning at me. 'He has a right to know, Stella,' he said softly, stating the exact words my conscience had been yelling at me for the last fifty-five minutes since I'd left Dr Rayner's office.

'I know. But he won't want it, Kenny, so what's the point?' I huffed impatiently. The thought of Nathan rejecting me, not to mention our baby, was enough to make me decidedly snappy. 'Dr Rayner has booked me in for a scan next week to try and see exactly how far along I am, so I'm going to wait until after that, then I'll tell him.' This was what I'd convinced myself anyway, but seeing as I'd already decided that I was keeping the baby regardless of

Nathan's wishes or behaviour, I suspected that actually saying the words to him might be quite a different matter.

TWENTY – STELLA

I had just thrown up the majority of my breakfast when I heard my phone ringing in my bedroom. Ugh, morning sickness really was the pits. It was like my stomach became allergic to anything being within a five-mile radius of it, and annoyingly I found it affecting me at completely random times of the day. Yes, I frequently had it in the mornings, but for the past week I'd also been getting it near lunch time and around four in the afternoon too. *It should be called 'all-day sickness'*, I thought with a grimace as I grabbed a towel and wiped my mouth before hurrying to my ringing phone.

Looking at the display I saw Nathan's number and frowned. Usually getting a call or message from him was the highlight of my day, but in the two weeks that had passed since I'd found out that I was pregnant I had come to dread his calls. The now familiar mixture of guilt and fear gnawed at me as I held the phone. I knew I should tell him about the baby, but I was utterly terrified of him leaving me, a feeling of dread so overwhelming that it had repeatedly stopped me confessing to him on every occasion where I had tried.

Grimacing I realised it'd be out of my hands soon enough when I started to show a bump. I was already a little plumper out front, but thankfully he hadn't noticed yet, or if he had, he'd been too polite to say anything. Unable to ignore him I pressed "answer" and held the phone to my ear. 'Hi, Nathan,' I murmured softly, hating the feeling of my hand trembling.

'Morning, sweetheart,' he replied, his tone so soft, loving, and heated that it made my legs weak and my heart tighten in my chest. Closing my eyes I swallowed down a lump that rose in my throat. I loved him so much, if I lost him I really didn't know how I could go on. 'Nicholas and Rebecca want to meet up with us this weekend and treat us to dinner for all the extra help you've been giving them these last few months. Which night would you prefer, Friday or Saturday?' Even in my glum state I couldn't help a small smile lifting my lips at his question. The Nathan of old wouldn't have bothered asking my opinion at all, he'd just have arranged it and then assumed I'd go along. He really had made such drastic leaps in his emotional development. Squeezing my eyes shut I scowled; he might have made drastic leaps, but expecting him to accept a baby was surely like asking him to jump across the Grand Canyon – impossible.

Pushing that miserable thought away I sighed softly. 'Either is fine by me.' My voice came out a little hoarse as I felt the start of another roiling wave of sickness creep into my stomach. Oh God, not now, not whilst I was on the phone to Nathan.

Oblivious to my panic Nathan continued, 'Saturday then,' he said, and a sad smile crept to my lips as I imagined him nodding efficiently and writing it in his diary as he spoke. 'OK then, sorry to disturb you at work, sweetheart.'

At work? My sickness temporarily forgotten I glanced at the clock and saw it was half past nine, shit! How had that happened? I was so late for work! Then, without meaning to, a dry wretch escaped my throat and had me dashing to the bathroom and lunging for the toilet. I could hear Nathan's panicked voice ringing out down from the phone that was still clutched in my hand, but I couldn't reply; the second half of my breakfast was making a rapid reappearance and there was nothing I could do about it.

Within ten minutes I felt marginally better, my sickness had reduced and I had phoned the office to explain that I was working from home this morning – a blessed bonus to being the office manager. I'd tried calling Nathan back, but there had been no response, so instead I'd sent a brief message explaining that I was fine, just a little under the weather, and then sat down to boot up my laptop.

I'd barely checked a single email before I felt my stomach lurch again. Rolling my eyes I blew out a long breath trying to calm the roiling sensation in my gut, this really was the worst it had ever been. The doctor said it was usually worst in the first three months, so hopefully it wouldn't last too much longer. The deep breathing wasn't helping so depositing my laptop swiftly onto the sofa I stumbled towards the bathroom, making it just in time. I was mid vomit when I heard the apartment door slam shut followed by thumping footsteps and a loud voice calling, 'Stella?'

There was no way I could ever not recognise that voice. *Nathan.* Panic encased me and I desperately tried to flush away the evidence of my morning sickness as I heard him stomping his way around the flat. 'I'm in the bathroom ...' I gurgled. 'Don't come in, I'll be out in a minute.'

But obviously being head-strong Nathan he was inside the bathroom and crouched by my side in less than thirty seconds. Bloody stubborn man. Soothing damp tendrils of hair away from my face he stared intently at me, his blue eyes roaming over me in concern. 'Christ, you look dreadful ... how long have you been throwing up?' Deliberately ignoring his question I moaned and leant over the toilet again, my stomach churning with both my morning sickness and the guilty turmoil of Nathan possibly finding out about my pregnancy. *Our pregnancy.*

'I'm taking you to the doctors,' he continued, as I stood up on wobbly legs and flushed the toilet. Shaking my head I brushed my teeth and then pushed past him towards the kitchen, 'I don't need the doctor, Nathan, I'll be fine, back to normal in no time.' Which ironically was about as far from the truth as possible; I'd be fine, yes, physically, but back to normal? I'd have a baby in just over six months ... life would never be 'normal' again, especially if Nathan found out and freaked out like I suspected he would.

Taking a glass from the cupboard I filled it with water and took a long and much needed drink of the cool liquid. What I really wanted was some ginger tea, but seeing as the box said 'Maternity Aid' on the side I wasn't going to pull it out in front of Nathan.

'Stella,' Nathan growled, as he came up behind me and stroked my shoulder possessively, 'I'm taking you to the fucking doctor *right now*.' He might be more amenable these days, but Nathan's Dominant side was never too far from the surface and as I turned to face him I saw from the taut expression on his face that he wasn't going to be otherwise persuaded. Ironically, in different circumstances I would have been thrilled by how much he obviously cared about me. Sighing, I realised I had a big decision to make, – did I tell him myself, or chicken out, play dumb, and then let my doctor break the news to him?

Just then Kenny sauntered into the kitchen, took one look at my pale face, one look at Nathan's imposing and tense stance, and swallowed loudly. 'Uhhh, what's going on?' Kenny asked hesitantly. He was always a little hesitant around Nathan, uneasy and fidgety, but I still had no idea if that was because of Nathan's domineering presence, or because Kenny still had a little bit of a crush on my man. From the way Kenny's eyes always skimmed up and down Nathan's appearance I suspected the latter.

'Stella's been throwing up almost constantly for the last hour and she won't let me take her to the doctor,' Nathan hissed between clenched teeth. 'Get your coat, Stella, I'm taking you now.'

Tutting, Kenny dismissed Nathan's remarks and to my utter horror walked straight over to the cupboard, pulled out my ginger tea bags, and waggled the box. 'Ooh, feels like we're running low, best stock up tomorrow.' Then turning and clicking on the kettle he smiled at Nathan, 'She doesn't need a doctor for morning sickness, ginger tea has be working brilliantly, hasn't it, Stel?' Kenny said cheerfully before freezing and turning to face us as he realised his error.

Oh my God. It felt like time had paused for a short moment as my breathing froze in my lungs. He didn't just say that, did he? Suddenly morning sickness was the last of my worries as breathing in a new breath became rapidly more difficult. *Fuck.* Nathan was glaring at Kenny like he'd just grown an extra head, and in turn Kenny looked like he was considering whether to try and cover up his massive blunder or run for the hills. Dumping the box of teabags on the counter he flashed me an apologetic wince before silently dashing from the kitchen. Great support mechanism my best friend turned out to be. *Thanks a lot, Kenny*, I thought.

Snatching up the box Nathan inspected the label, his face getting redder and redder every second, to the point where I thought he might actually combust, before he finally turned his icy stare on me. 'Morning sickness?' he demanded holding the box up.

Fight or flight? Lie or confess? Bugger it, thanks to Kenny there really was no way to get out of it now, so with a rise of my shoulders I bit down on my lower lip and nodded. Seeing how much he hated it when I nodded this was a risky strategy, but right now I was all out of words.

Placing the box of tea down I watched as Nathan's fists clenched by his sides until the knuckles turned snowy white. 'You're pregnant?' His voice had dropped to a deadly whisper, a tone I actually found more terrifying than his raised voice, so once again I nodded at him, before remembering his hatred of my silent communication and confirming it vocally. 'Yes … about twelve weeks. Ginger seems to help a lot with my symptoms.' When I'd had my scan a few days ago the nurse – unaware of my situation with Nathan – had smirked at me and said that I must have had a great run-up to Christmas because the baby was probably conceived at some point in early December. Seeing as we'd had a lovely festive season together I would have found that all quite romantic if Nathan hadn't been currently looking quite so furious.

The next few minutes stretched on in torturous silence. First Nathan simply stared at me while blinking rapidly, far too rapidly – I could practically hear the cogs in his head grinding as he studied me with his head tilted and his jaw sawing relentlessly at his lip. He body remained tensed and furled, his anger obvious, then he let out a long, low breath through his teeth, turned away from me, and ran his hands repeatedly over his face as if trying to wash the last few moments of his life away.

My heart sank. Whichever way I looked at it, his response showed he clearly wasn't thrilled by the news. I'd suspected he didn't want children, with his abusive upbringing and peculiar lifestyle until he'd met me I don't think he'd ever even considered it, but a small shred of me had clung to the hope that maybe, just maybe, he'd be thrilled by the news and scoop me into his arms with a delirious laugh.

'You don't look pregnant,' he stated in a low tone, which was true enough, my stomach was still quite flat if you just gave it a quick glance, but since I'd found out about the baby and looked carefully in the mirror I'd realised that I was starting to get a bit more of a pronounced tummy – which now made sense of my tight fitting bridesmaid dress.

Suddenly Nathan's hands shot to his hair and ran

through it almost violently, making me wince. 'Three fucking months and you didn't tell me?' He growled the words and I grimaced at his gritty tone, biting my lip and trying to bravely hold his stare. In my defence I'd only just found out the dates myself really, plus I hadn't told him because I thought he'd freak out, and boy was he proving me right – not that he gave me a chance to say any of these thing before he spoke again.

'How?' he questioned suddenly, and even though I knew what he meant – how was I pregnant when I was on the contraceptive injection – I couldn't help but let my disappointment escape in the form of sarcastic anger. 'In the usual way, Nathan, you fucked me, repeatedly and frequently, and hey presto!' I made a dramatic sweeping motion with my arm towards my stomach, 'Just like magic, I'm pregnant.' That was a bit unfair really – yes we shagged like randy bunnies, but I'd instigated just as many of our liaisons as Nathan had, in fact, in that area of our lives we were equally as insatiable, something that hadn't reduced at all in our time together, but right now I didn't care about any of that, I selfishly wanted him to hurt, just as I was.

Nathan's eyes narrowed at my tone and he took a step towards me, but it didn't bother me, I was so upset at his obvious rejection that all I wanted to do was get him out of here and go to bed to cry. '… and I didn't forget my bloody injection, if that's what you're wondering. I had it done on time, but it's only ninety-eight percent effective.'

'A baby,' he repeated in a low tone, apparently speaking to himself, before turning and punching his hand down into the marble work surface so hard that I physically jumped on the spot and yelped in surprise. Crikey, he'd hit it so hard we'd be lucky if that surface wasn't cracked, and goodness only knows what damage he'd just done to his hand.

I suddenly felt immensely drained, both physically and

emotionally, and decided my morning of working from home could turn into a day off. 'I don't feel great, Nathan, I'm going to bed,' I said on a sad sigh, wanting him to pull me into his arms for comfort, but knowing that it would never happen.

'Fine, I'll leave.' Spinning on his heel he didn't say another word and then walked out, slamming the door behind him and leaving me speechless and numb in the kitchen. He hadn't even looked at me as he'd left, not even a tiny glance. So that was it? No *'Let's talk about this, Stella,'* or *'Let me tuck you in and make you some tea'.* Nope, just *'Fine, I'll leave'.*

Well, shit. If possible that had gone even worse than I'd predicted.

TWENTY-ONE – NICHOLAS

I'd spent the last hour looking at possible cars for the wedding day. Rebecca was planning on spending the night before the big day at her parents' house, which was only a few miles from the hotel, so we only needed the cars to take her down the road on the morning of the wedding. To be honest I'd been tempted to just use my Aston Martin DB9 to pick her up – it was an absolute beauty but seeing as it was only two door it might cause issues for Rebecca getting in and out in her dress. Besides, I knew she wanted to take the drive from her parents' house to the hotel with her mum, sister, and all the bridesmaids, so I needed to be looking for something a little larger. Sitting back from my computer with a smirk I assessed the car currently on my screen and wondered how Rebecca would feel arriving in a fleet of gleaming Ferraris. We'd need one per person though, which might be a tad costly. Perhaps I could just hire one for me to take Rebecca for a spin in afterwards … now that *was* a tempting thought …

Clicking back to a page of more suitable cars I saved the website of the company that had confirmed earlier that they had a 1951 Rolls-Royce Silver Wraith available. Even as a lover of modern fast cars I could appreciate the beauty of this classic. It seated six within its leather and walnut cabin and was a beautiful beige and black on the outside. Basically, it was perfect, and I was pretty sure Rebecca would love it.

At that very second my mobile started to ring on the

table beside me, flashing Rebecca's name. Giving a small chuckle I picked it up. It was almost like she somehow knew I was thinking about her. Much to my irritation she'd left for a conference in Scotland early this morning, something about marketing for small businesses, and I assumed this was her calling to tell me she'd arrived. Smiling I flicked the screen and raised it to my ear. 'Hi, Becky, you made it safely then?' On the other end of the line I heard heavy breathing and immediately frowned. 'Rebecca, are you OK?' My tone was far harsher this time and I found myself standing up in agitation.

'Hi, Nicholas! Yes, yes, I'm fine,' Rebecca answered, still sounding breathless. What the fuck was she doing?

'Why the hell are you out of breath? What are you doing?' I demanded. Images of Rebecca making those exact breathy sounds in bed with me flashed into my mind and I felt my composure cracking as I lifted a hand and tugged at my hair.

'Sorry! I've been jogging. There's absolutely no phone signal in the hotel or grounds so I had to nab a lift into the village with the cook, but when I got here the postman told me the only place for good phone signal was the top of the high street.' I listened as she sucked in a few breaths before continuing. 'The cook is on a bit of a tight schedule, she's only picking up a few things from the shop and needs to get back so I jogged up the high street to call you. I miss you already,' she finished softly, and just like that my agitation vaporised to be replaced by a warm feeling spreading in my chest.

'I miss you too,' I admitted. I'd grown so used to her being around that the next three days alone in the house would feel distinctively strange. 'Your flight was OK?' I wasn't keen on her going away for so long, which I knew was irrational but was just how I felt. Actually, we'd had a bit of a disagreement about it last night; she'd called me overprotective and I'd called her stubborn before we both refused to apologise. Luckily, I'd woken Rebecca up extra early this morning to make it up to her with some lazy lovemaking so that things weren't left on a sour note between us. To make it up to her I'd also insisted on driving her to Gatwick this morning for her flight to Inverness. It was the least I could do really.

'The flight was great, smooth and quick. We just had the two hour drive to the hotel. It's stunning up here, Nicholas, so beautiful. Just a shame there's no phone or internet signal at the hotel so I'm afraid I won't be able to call you again until I'm back at the airport.'

My teeth clenched at the idea of Rebecca being away from me and unable to contact me, but I calmed myself down by thinking through one of the strategies that Dr Phillips, my anger management counsellor, had taught me. Rebecca was a grown-up. I might feel protective of her, but she was an individual and I needed to allow her the space to do her own thing every now and then, it was the only way I'd ever manage to hold on to her.

'Look, I'm sorry I can't talk for longer, Nicholas, I just wanted to call so you knew I was all right,' I heard the phone shuffling about in Rebecca's hand, 'Coming!' she yelled, making me move the phone away from my ear with a wince. 'Sorry. The cook's just come out of the shop and she's waving at me desperately, she's can't be late back because she needs to get on preparing the dinners. I better go. I think I'll lose signal again as soon as I walk down this hill though.'

Smiling sadly I held the receiver tight as if it were Rebecca's hand, 'OK, well, enjoy the conference, baby. I love you,' I murmured.

'I love you too, Nicholas. And thanks, I think I will enjoy it, there's some great speakers lined up for tomorrow. I'll miss you though. Better go. Bye then.' I could tell from her quickening breaths that Rebecca was already on the move again.

'Bye.' I waited until I heard the call finish from her end and then hung up, feeling a little bit sorry for myself.

Almost as soon as I'd put my phone down on the desk it began to ring again and I chuckled thinking she was calling me back. Picking up the phone with a grin I placed it by my ear without even bothering to check the screen, 'I thought you said you'd have no more signal,' I said with a smile. But the voice I heard on the other end of the line wasn't Rebecca. It was a man.

'Mr Nicholas Jackson? I'm calling about your brother, Nathaniel.' *Oh God*, I thought with a roll of my eyes, *what's the daft, quick-tempered bugger done this time?*

TWENTY-TWO – STELLA

'Stella?' My name was being called loudly and in a distinctly desperate tone. I turned on the spot to see Nathan, haloed by the sun from the window behind him and standing with his arms wide open looking repentant, and hopeful, as he gestured for me to go to him.

'Stella? Stella? Where the fuck are you?' Blinking awake at the confusing sound of Kenny's voice calling my name somewhere in the apartment – not Nathan. I rolled onto my back as reality began to permeate my sleep – I had been dreaming. Even in my sleepy state disappointment surged through me as I realised that Nathan wasn't really here, he wasn't apologising, and he certainly wasn't calling me into his waiting arms. My eyes squeezed shut in distress as my hands flew to my face and almost clawed at my eye sockets to try and stop the flood of on-coming tears. As soon as those depressing facts settled in my brain a wave of nausea swept through my body, causing me to sit upright far too fast and clutch at my mouth to try and keep it in. Swallowing loudly I cleared my throat and reached for the packet of ginger snap biscuits which had taken up residence on my bedside table over the past few days. It might be an old wives' tale, but these babies worked a treat on my morning sickness and quelled the nausea brilliantly.

'I'm in bed,' I called to Kenny whilst shoving a biscuit in my mouth. Chomping on the sweet gingery goodness – no doubt the first of many – my bedroom door flew open to reveal Kenny looking almost unrecognisable – his hair was a mess, he was panting hard, and his face was deathly pale. First off, Kenny *never* did exercise, unless it was bedroom gymnastics with some hot young thing, so the panting struck me as decidedly odd, and secondly, my flatmate wouldn't even leave the building unless his hair and face radiated perfection, so the fact that he looked pretty damn awful made my stomach tighten with apprehension.

'Thank God you're here … Get dressed.' His sharp tone didn't help my unease one little bit, but something in it sparked me into action and I popped the last bite of biscuit in my mouth before turning myself in the bed and hanging my legs over the side while giving him a curious glance.

'You look awful, Kenny, what is it?' I asked, pushing myself to my feet and wondering what on earth could have upset my flatmate so much. Another dating disaster perhaps? But surely that wouldn't rate this type of theatrical reaction, not even from drama queen Kenny.

'You've obviously heard nothing on Nathan, then?' he asked, causing me to instantly sag back onto the bed irritated that he should bring Nathan up again when he knew how sensitive I was feeling at the moment. Talk about an emotional bomb ready to explode. Even with all the tears I'd cried lately my eyes suddenly started to sting a little, which I blamed on my rampant pregnancy hormones.

'No. Why should I be the one to call? He could have damn well contacted me if he gave a fuck.' It had been three full days since my argument with Nathan and there had been nothing, not even a text for God's sake. I'd started to hate my mobile phone, all I did was repeatedly check it only to see no new calls or messages.

'Christ, Stella … I didn't mean that. I … I don't know how to say this,' Kenny paused, a grimace furrowing his usually smooth brow as he dragged a hand through his long hair.

Come to think of it, he sounded unrecognisable too ... Kenny was a constant joker, he was never this serious, even when the shit hit the fan he'd manage to make light of it and keep everyone else upbeat. His odd disposition made me pause halfway through pulling on my jeans to frown at him. 'Kenny, you're kinda scaring me. What the hell is the matter?' I yanked up my jeans and decided my sleep T-shirt could stay for now. I was wearing a bra underneath anyway, so it wasn't too revealing.

Running an agitated hand through his hair again Kenny picked up my everyday handbag and shoved my phone into it before clutching it to his chest and looking back at me again, 'Look, don't kill me all right?' he started, which I met with a fractious look.

'Just spit it out Kenny!' I hissed in exasperation, snatching my bag from him.

'OK, OK.' He let out a long breath and fidgeted on the spot before looking back at me with lowered brows. 'After seeing you so miserable the last few days I decided to pay a visit to Nathan.' Seeing my face turn thunderous Kenny raised his hands in desperation. 'He's the father to your child, Stella, he needs to take responsibility, not run away.'

I closed my eyes and drew in a long breath through my nose as one hand instinctively moved to cup my stomach protectively. I was too mad to even look at him at the moment, how dare he go and see Nathan behind my back? *How dare he?* This was my mess, I needed to be the one to sort it out. Or more precisely Nathan needed to be the one to sort it out, if he ever got off his arse and had the decency to call me. A wave of panic rushed through me, chilling my skin as it passed, what if Nathan had walked away for good and *never* called me? Surely even with all his issues he wouldn't do that to me, would he? But I was distracted from dwelling on this by Kenny's next words.

'The thing is, Nathan wasn't there.' Kenny's tone had gone decidedly odd again so I pushed my tumbling thoughts aside, opened my eyes, and looked up at him, 'You might want to sit down, Stella,' Kenny hedged, indicating towards my rumpled bed. I huffed out an increasingly impatient breath, propped my hands on my hips defiantly, and watched as Kenny gave in with a grimace, 'He'd not been in work for three days, Stella. There was an accident … Nathan's in hospital.'

For several seconds I felt as if my world had stopped spinning as I stood there blinking at him slowly and repeatedly running his words through my mind. No matter how many times I repeated them, Kenny's words just didn't make sense. Surely he couldn't mean what I thought he did. *There was an accident ... Nathan's in hospital ... Nathan's in hospital ... Nathan's in hospital.* My vision blurred as my legs went wobbly beneath me, and then my sickness returned with a vengeance, forcing me to break from my trance and dash to the bathroom where I proceeded to throw up the entire contents of my stomach, ginger snap included, and more, by the look of it. This bout of nausea was so violent that I was pretty sure it was from shock, not my usual morning sickness, and the whole time I was bent over the toilet retching the only words rolling round my brain were *'Nathan'*, *'accident'*, and *'hospital.'*

I don't know how long I threw up for, it seemed to go on forever, but eventually my stomach settled enough for me to become aware of the bathroom around me again. Kenny's hand was rubbing soothing patterns on my back and as I focused on his reassuring touch I gradually began to come back to reality.

'How is he?' I asked, my voice scratchy and barely audible as I continued to stare into the toilet bowl.

'He's unconscious, Stella; that was all the receptionist

232

at his office could tell me.' Unconscious. *Fuck*. All the spiteful things I'd been thinking about doing to him for running out on me suddenly reared up into my mind, making me feel like an utter cow. Over the past few days there had been many occasions where I'd wanted him to hurt like I was. But not like this ... and now I was left wondering that if perhaps this was all my fault, was Karma giving me a great big bitch slap for thinking such horrible thoughts?

Finally flushing the toilet I wiped my mouth on some toilet paper and silently accepted the glass of water and toothbrush that Kenny was offering me, briefly brushing my teeth on autopilot before staring at him for any further insights.

'That's all I can tell you, Stella, I don't know anything else.' Kenny was looking more anxious by the second, my usually laid back friend had seemingly turned into a mass of uncomfortable, nervous energy. 'Come on, he's at the Princess Grace Hospital, I'll drive you over.'

Unconscious. I felt numb and simply stared blindly forwards as Kenny led me through the flat towards the front door, feeling like my brain was detached from the rest of my body as my feet moved on autopilot, stepping one in front of the other. Nathan, the only man I'd ever loved and the father of the baby inside my belly was unconscious and in hospital.

We didn't speak a word on the journey through London. Not one single syllable. Kenny seemed to understand my need for silence and merely helped me into the car and after giving my leg an encouraging squeeze set about getting us there as quickly as he could. Given the boundaries of the speed limits and the numerous bloody speed cameras lining the wet London streets he did a pretty amazing job. As soon as we were parked he guided my dazed body into the main entrance with a firm hand on my lower back and after a heated discussion with a woman on reception he turned to me and indicted for me to move closer, which I just about managed on my unfeeling legs. 'Only direct family are allowed up,' he informed me in a low voice before turning back to the receptionist, 'This is his girlfriend, she's having his child for God's sake, can't you make an exception?'

The girl looked at me. She couldn't have been older than twenty at a guess, and as she took in my no doubt dreadful appearance – deep in shock, un-showered, no make-up on, and still in my sleep shirt which was quite possibly covered in vomit – I saw her eyes soften as she bit her lip and relented. 'Let me make a call to the ward and see what I can do. Take a seat.'

Emotionlessly nodding my gratitude I turned to the rows of plastic chairs in the waiting room and slumped into the nearest one, watching as Kenny took up a furious pacing across the vinyl floor of the waiting area. Bless him, he was usually so laid back about everything that I'd never seen him this agitated.

This floor was hideous. Although the one advantage to the mosaic of green, purple, and orange squares was that it had a vaguely numbing effect if you stared at it for long enough. I lost track of time, my eyes roaming almost sightlessly over the jumble of coloured tiles as if in a trance, when suddenly I felt a hand touch my shoulder causing me to jerk in surprise. Looking up I expected to see Kenny, but instead I found, Nicholas towering over me, his once handsome face now looking haggard, pale, and exhausted.

'Stella, thank fuck you're here,' he murmured in way of greeting as I pushed myself to standing on wobbly legs. He hesitated, briefly swaying towards me and looking like he desperately wanted to hug me, as if he needed the reassurance of contact as much as I did, but then gathered his cool composure and took a step back. 'I don't know why they didn't let you up, I left yours and Rebecca's names with the reception as permitted visitors just in case you turned up. Come on, I'll take you up to him.'

Turning to Kenny he nodded at me.

'I'll pop home and grab you a change of clothes, Stella, call me if you need anything babe, I mean it, *anything*,' Kenny muttered thickly as he pulled me into his arms for a strong hug. I suspected Kenny was close to tears, as was I, but somehow I felt so detached from everything at the moment that the tears just wouldn't come.

Extracting myself stiffly from Kenny's embrace I nodded and then turned to Nicholas, who silently guided me towards a block of lifts. Jabbing the button for the fifth floor the doors closed and Nicholas let out a long breath before running his hands roughly over his face. My chest tightened because his gesture was achingly similar to the move Nathan had done when he'd found out about the baby. Swallowing my pointless sentimentality I folded my arms around my body and asked the question at the forefront of my mind, 'How is he, Nicholas?' I whispered, my voice reedy and thin as I held my breath, utterly terrified of what his answer might be.

His dark blue eyes met mine and my stomach churned with distress at the look of raw pain and fear that I saw. 'Unconscious. He's got swelling on his brain, but it's going down every day and the doctors are pleased with his progress. Initially they had him sedated to keep him unconscious whilst the swelling lessened, but they've stopped the drugs now. The consultant expected him to wake up yesterday, but he didn't.' There really was no way to sugar coat news like that, was there? Turning away from me Nicholas ground his jaw together and stared up at the display in the lift which seemed to be taking forever as I tried to absorb his news. *The consultant expected him to wake up yesterday, but he didn't …* That really didn't sound good at all and regardless of how much I knew Nathan would hate it, I started to chew mercilessly on my lower lip.

Nicholas gazed down at the floor, giving me a chance to look over him. His dark blue eyes were dull and bloodshot, his hair greasy and dishevelled, and his usually handsome face was pale and drawn. At a guess I'd say Nicholas hadn't slept much recently, if at all, which made me question exactly when all this had occurred.

'What happened?' I croaked as the lift finally came to a stop and the doors slid open to reveal the orangey lighting of a fancy looking hospital corridor, empty except for the impersonal chairs lining its sides, a water machine, and the horrible low buzz of the lights.

Nicholas walked out first, pausing to let me catch up with him. 'Nathan was in his car, pulling out of a shopping centre, when a lorry smashed into the side of him.' His voice was low and gravelly and barely loud enough to hear, but as the words sunk in I felt a new wave of nausea threatening to creep up on me again. 'The driver of the lorry had a heart attack at the wheel, it wasn't his fault. Nathan was just unlucky enough to be in the wrong place at the wrong time.'

Now it was my turn to rub my hands over my face as the awful reality hit me, Nathan's car had been hit by a lorry. His small sports car … it stood no chance against a truck. Gulping in air I struggled to swallow as gruesome images of Nathan trapped inside a twisted ball of metal flooded my mind. 'When did it happen?'

'Friday morning, around about eleven o'clock.' Nicholas said, not elaborating any further as he had paused at a door labelled 'Private Suite 10a'. 'He looks pretty bad, Stella,' he explained awkwardly in preparation, before he opened the door and ushered me inside.

As I entered the room I lost myself in a strange, lonely bubble for a few seconds. Subconsciously I must have needed something to ground me, because my brain latched on to the steady beep, beep, beep of Nathan's heart monitor as my glazed eyes tried to take in the alien scene before me. Nathan, the man I loved, the man whose baby was nestled in my stomach, was lying in a hospital bed surround by machines and hooked up to so many tubes and pipes that I could barely comprehend it, let alone stand it. A full body shudder shook through me, leaving me covered in prickling goose pimples as every hair on my body seemed to stand up at once. I wanted to run into the corridor and demand a doctor come and wake him up, or rip the tubes from his body myself and kiss him awake, but as the cold reality settled around me again I realised that neither of these options were a possibility, this scene here and now was my new reality, I was awake, and Nathan was very seriously ill.

Staggering forwards I grabbed the rail at the base of the bed to stop myself falling over. The top of Nathan's head was heavily bandaged, I could see cuts on his pale cheeks and his right arm was in a plaster cast and supported in a sling. God only knows what other injuries lurked below the blankets. A choked sob caught in my throat and made the most ridiculous bubbly noise, and if I hadn't been so distraught I would probably have laughed at how silly it had sounded. But I *was* distraught, almost to the point of hyperventilating, and as the entire situation finally hit home I felt my legs give way beneath me like rubber.

Thank goodness Nicholas had quick reactions, because he caught me under the arms and stopped me just seconds before I hit the floor, then helped me over to a chair. As my mind caught up with the massive extent of the situation something occurred to me. Eleven o'clock on Friday morning was about two hours after Nathan had left my house … two hours after our horrible argument where he'd found out about the baby and walked out. Lowering my head into my hands I rubbed at my face and my stinging eyes with the heels of my hands until the skin hurt. All this time I'd been cursing him for not calling me or answering

237

his phone, while the whole time he'd been here, bandaged up and unconscious. If possible I suddenly felt even worse about the whole situation as guilt settled into my stomach alongside the fear and dread which had taken residence since Kenny had told me about the accident.

'Why didn't you call me, Nicholas?' I muttered, too distressed to voice the anger that I felt in my tone. To my astonishment Nicholas laughed, a dry humourless bark, but a laugh nonetheless. 'Believe me I tried. Nathan's phone was crushed in the accident, I don't have your number, and Rebecca's away at some book conference in Scotland with no fucking phone signal so I couldn't get it from her either.' Running a hand through his hair Nicholas grimaced and shook his head, 'Do you have any idea how many Stella Marsdens there are in the greater London area?' I thought his question was probably rhetorical so remained silent, my eyes slipping back to the bed and Nathan's unmoving figure. 'Fucking dozens. I called directory enquiries and explained the situation and they sent me a list, but I gave up after phoning the twenty-second one and getting yelled at.'

Twenty-second? My eyes flicked back to Nicholas and seeing the grim set of his jaw I realised he was being serious, he really *had* been phoning all the Stella Marsdens trying to find me. 'They only knew to call me because my name is registered to Nathan's driving licence as his next of kin,' Nicholas explained in a low tone.

'You know where I work, Nicholas, you could have called me at the office,' I mumbled. Even though I knew it was pointless saying it now that the time had passed, I couldn't help myself. If I'd known earlier I could have been here for Nathan, and right now that was all I could focus on.

Nicholas looked at me, his face suddenly so distressed that I thought he was going to cry. 'I didn't think.' Shaking his head his eyes darted around the room, 'I couldn't think of anything except my brother being alone here in this awful place.'

Wow, so if Kenny hadn't gone to Nathan's office today it could have been days or even weeks until I found out about Nathan's accident. The thought was so horrifically shattering that finally my tears broke through and began to silently slide down my cheeks and drip from my chin onto the covers by Nathan's feet. I had never felt so wretched or utterly useless in my life.

Just then the door opened and a medic walked in, followed closely by a frantic-looking Rebecca. She dumped down the suitcase she was carrying and her eyes flickered over me, Nathan's still form, and then landed on Nicholas before she dashed across the room and pulled him into an embrace so hard that I heard the air rush from his lungs. 'I'm so sorry I didn't call you back, we had no signal, your emails and voicemails only came through when I got to Gatwick an hour ago and turned my phone on.'

The medic left the room, closing the door behind him, and as I watched Nicholas and Rebecca hug I felt a lead weight settle in my stomach. That closeness was what I'd had with Nathan before I'd gotten pregnant, and now I was all alone because he was unconscious and injured and had made it clear he didn't want me, or our baby. As soon as I thought it, I felt horrendously guilty – even if Nathan didn't want to be with me any more I wouldn't ever wish this upon him, not in a million years. I wanted, *needed*, to know that he was alive and well and living his life somewhere, not stuck unconscious in some hospital bed.

'Christ, these last few days have been atrocious … I'm so fucking glad you're here, Rebecca,' Nicholas murmured into her hair. Finally untwisting himself from his fiancée he looked over to me again as Rebecca came to my side and pulled me into a wordless, but supportive hug, 'This all feels more positive now you're both here,' Nicholas said with a firm nod, 'I'm hoping that you being here might make a difference to him, Stella,' Nicholas murmured stepping up to the bedside and gazing down at his brother.

I'm not sure if it was Nicholas' hopeful words or the sympathetic nature of Rebecca's hug, but suddenly the final straw in my composure broke and I clung to Rebecca, sobbing desperately hard. My entire body was shaking from the huge sobs and my tears soaked the shoulder of her shirt in just seconds. After a few minutes I managed to get myself marginally more under control. 'I ... I doubt it will make a difference ...' I managed between choked breaths, 'We ... we had an argument ... I don't think Nathan wants to be with me any more ...'

And then, around a series of strangled sobs the whole story came out; the pregnancy, my horrendous morning sickness and craving for ginger that had let the secret out, Nathan's shock at my news, my memories of how horrified he'd been when we'd met Melissa, his old submissive and he'd thought her child might have been his ... everything, even stupid insignificant details that now seemed so precious and dear to me. Finally depleted of energy and tears I stopped speaking and after sucking in some much needed air I accepted a wad of tissues from Rebecca and retook my seat on the sofa before my legs gave way.

Sitting forward I rested my elbows on my knees and tried to clean my wet face as I finished my story, 'So when he left my house on Friday, not long before his accident I suppose, I wasn't really sure where we stood ... but I'm pretty certain Nathan didn't want to be with me anymore.' If only we hadn't argued, then he might have stayed at my house and not been anywhere near the shopping centre or the truck. Closing my eyes I struggled to breathe. If he didn't recover and the last words we ever said to each other were our spiteful argumentative comments I would never get over it. I'd forever blame myself.

Looking up I saw Nicholas' frown give way slightly and he turned to the chair in the corner to pick up two plastic bags. 'This makes more sense now.' He put the bags on the table at the end of Nathan's bed and indicted for Rebecca and I to join him. 'This is what they retrieved from his car,' Nicholas explained as he tipped the first bag out to reveal Nathan's keys, wallet, watch, and his crushed mobile phone. Picking up his watch in one hand I weighed the familiar item in my hand as a jerky sob escaped my throat, quickly followed by several more. Putting my free hand over my mouth to stop my lips from wobbling with more tears I clung to his watch with a bunched fist. Suddenly though, as if it had jabbed me with an electric shock I dumped the watch almost violently onto the table as I realised the metal was cold and lifeless, not warm from his skin like usual, and offered me no support whatsoever. God, this was fucking horrendous.

Moving the second carrier bag Nicholas held it up. 'And these things made no sense to me, but apparently it was in the car with Nathan too, the receipts show that he'd just bought it all.' Nicholas tipped the contents of the second bag on to the table, 'After your story I think I understand now, and if I'm right then I'm pretty sure Nathan does want you, Stella, and your baby,' he murmured, giving my shoulder an encouraging squeeze.

My eyes were too watery to see properly, so I rubbed at them with the soggy tissue and looked at the objects on the table, blinking quickly to fight back more tears as I registered what they were; a giant packet of ginger nut biscuits, six stalks of fresh ginger, a bottle of ginger cordial, and a packet of ginger teabags. My brow puckered into a frown as I ran my fingertips gently over the items which had become rather familiar to me recently to cure my morning sickness – it was almost too much to hope that Nathan had been buying these things for me.

'There were these too, they mean anything to you?' Nicholas enquired curiously, handing me a small stack of pamphlets. Confused, I looked at them and belatedly realised they were estate agents brochures. Flicking through the first couple I saw they were houses in London, big houses if the floor plans were anything to go by, but I didn't recognise any of them at all. Just then some pen marks caught my eye and I paused. Opening the page properly I saw red biro marks on the paper in several places, a red ring had been drawn around the word 'nursery', and the word 'conservatory' had been underlined three times.

Oh my God. Goose pimples flooded my skin and the hairs on the back of my neck stood up until I shivered. My eyes widened as I stared at the brochure and realised what this meant. Nathan had looked at houses with nurseries. A nursery for *our* baby. A new house for us that would be *ours*, not his flat with its lingering memories of the other women he'd entertained. Even with all his messed-up issues he'd listened to my concerns about his apartment and acted, he'd even remembered my joke about wanting a conservatory, and judging from all the ginger products he'd absorbed my comment about it helping my morning sickness.

A hiccupy sob broke from my lips as I continued to stare at the papers in my hands. From this evidence it would seem that after our argument Nathan had immediately gone shopping for new houses and ginger biscuits. That seemed pretty good evidence to support Nicholas' theory that Nathan did indeed want both me and our baby in his life. Just three days ago this knowledge would have made me jubilantly happy, but with just a few moments of horror that had all changed now. Nathan might very well die before we'd ever get a chance to live that new life together, a possibility that seemed too cruel for me to even consider.

The urge to cry crept up on me again, but instead of allowing it to rule me I swallowed down the tears, straightened my spine, and rushed my way around the bed towards Nathan's sleeping form. I needed to be positive and strong. *He* needed me to be positive and strong for both of us. Reaching out a hand I realised I was trembling, my fingers shaking so much I could barely control the limb, but I persevered and gently stroked my fingers across his cheek. His skin was cold to touch, nothing like the usual heat that seemed to almost radiate from him and I frowned, hating seeing him like this and wishing there was something, anything, that I could do.

As my gaze swept over him again I noticed that as well as his arm being in plaster, his right hand was also bandaged. I realised with a twist of guilt that the gauze was most likely covering cuts from when he'd found out about the baby and punched my kitchen counter.

Hearing a click of the door opening I glanced over to see Nicholas and Rebecca leaving the room, obviously wanting to give me some privacy with Nathan, which I appreciated immensely. Taking his undamaged hand in mine I stroked my thumb over his palm before clutching it to my lips and kissing each knuckle in turn. The sound of Nathan's air being regulated by a ventilator combined with the constant beep of his heart monitor was both reassuring and sickening to me. I was glad he was in such good hands, but in the quiet of the room the sounds just acted as a reminder to me of just how sick Nathan really was. 'Nathan? It's me, Stella. I'm here now, sweetheart.' Calling Nathan, such a dominant and proud man 'sweetheart', seemed a little strange, but it slipped from my tongue effortlessly and after considering it, I decided I quite liked the way it sounded.

TWENTY-THREE – NATHAN

Whatever it was that was beeping was driving me insane. For fuck's sake. *Beep, beep, woosh, beep, beep, fucking woosh.* It seemed a vaguely familiar noise, but for some reason my mind was too foggy to place it. As well as a cotton wool head my mouth felt like sandpaper and my throat was burning like I'd scraped it repeatedly with my best frigging cheese grater.

Beep, beep, woosh. Christ that noise was really getting on my nerves now and certainly made me forget my discomfort. I tried to open my eyes to see the cause of the irritating sound so I could stop it, preferably with a swift but effective punch, but my eyes felt sticky and sealed shut. Everything was so hazy. Maybe I had a hangover? Although feeling as bad as I currently did, it would have had to be one hell of a drinking session. I certainly couldn't remember drinking last night, but then again, I couldn't really focus well enough to remember much of anything. What the fuck was going on? Maybe I was asleep and having a really trippy dream. That would explain why I couldn't seem to move.

Just then I felt a lovely warmth enclose around my fingers, and my useless, leaden arm was lifted into the air. A beautifully familiar scent floated to my nostrils shortly before I felt a softness brush my knuckles and a breath tickle my hand. I wanted to smile from the sensation, but I couldn't. 'Nathan? It's me, Stella. I'm here now, sweetheart.' Stella? Stella was here? My spirits soared. But where exactly was "here"? My brain struggled to picture her for a second, but my senses were suddenly engulfed as Stella's image flooded my mind in all its heart stopping glory. I loved her, there was no doubt in my mind. And those eyes of hers, jeez, she'd had me at the first glance, they were like frigging windows to her soul.

If I could have frowned I would have, because Stella's voice sounded as if it was trembling, like she was crying, or at least had been. No doubt I'd upset her somehow by being the insensitive prick that I usually am. Fuck, I loved this woman so much. Desperate to finally tell her out loud I tried again to open my eyes, every muscle straining with the effort, but all I managed was a minuscule flinch of my fingers. For a strong gym user like me that was well and truly fucking embarrassing. Maybe I'd had a stroke? It seemed the only logical explanation at the moment. The exertion of trying to move caused a spinning darkness to fog my already tired brain, and as much as I wanted to see Stella, I decided that perhaps I should just sleep for a little bit longer …

TWENTY-FOUR – STELLA

Tick, tock, tick, tock. The bloody clock seemed to be so loud tonight as I once again sat a vigil beside Nathan's bed. Talk about time dragging. Minutes, hours, and days had never passed so frigging slowly. I sat by Nathan's bedside twenty-four hours a day, only leaving his side to use the toilet, take a brief snooze on the sofa, or have a shower to try and wash away the feeling of dread that the small hospital room was starting to give me. I hadn't breathed fresh air for days and the only daylight was filtered through the tinted windows, not that I really looked outside. Talk about claustrophobic. I had the four walls pretty much memorised, from the noisy clock which always told the correct time but whose second hand bounced repeatedly back and forth between fourteen and fifteen seconds, to the vinyl floor which squeaked under my shoes, and smelt of disinfectant, which although clean, made me think of nothing but illness.

The positive news was that Nathan remained in a stable condition and the doctors were very pleased with the reduction of the swelling to his brain, but I found it hard to focus on these optimistic elements because he still just lay there unconscious and unresponsive, which was soul destroying for me. I tried to stay upbeat for him, constantly speaking to him softly and holding his hand while I reassured him that I was there and that everything was going to be all right, but inside I just felt numb.

Initially Nicholas had been convinced that my presence

would be like a magical balm to his brother and wake him from his unconscious slumber like some sort of fairy-tale. But he'd been sadly mistaken, and as the days passed I'd watched as Nicholas' hope faded and he'd withdrawn into himself, barely speaking to Rebecca or I until he was almost as quiet as Nathan.

No, there had been no miraculous recovery from my presence. In fact it was almost two full days after my arrival before Nathan showed any signs of life at all. My heart nearly exploded in my chest on Sunday afternoon when his fingers gave a tiny flick as I'd held his hand and whispered soothing things next to his ear, but to my near devastation the doctor checked the rest of his vitals and then put it down to a muscle reflex and nothing more. I knew the doctors were growing increasingly concerned about Nathan's inability to wake up, and as each day passed Nicholas and I seemed to go a little crazier too.

Just after eleven o'clock on Wednesday night I slipped into the en-suite toilet and was sat with my head in my hands having a good old-fashioned cry when I heard Nicholas laugh. My head snapped up at the sound of the happy noise, seeming so utterly bizarre after days of moping around in desolate silence and I instantly frowned in confusion. The television wasn't on so it couldn't be that, and wondering what on earth Nicholas was doing, I quickly finished up, zipped my jeans, and washed my hands thinking that perhaps Nicholas really was starting to lose the plot.

As I returned to the softly lit main room I found Nicholas standing by Nathan's bedside looking like an ominous shadow in the dimly lit room. Flashing a glance at me he grinned, causing my concern to deepen, but then his next words totally threw me. 'Here she is, brother,' he said, and to my astonishment I saw Nathan's head turn slowly in my direction. My heart nearly jumped from my chest in excitement at his movement. His eyes were narrow and sticky but open nonetheless, and the sweet smile that curved on his lips when he saw me nearly broke my heart in two.

I squealed like a little girl, I couldn't help it, and with tears of happiness flooding down my cheeks I dashed to the bedside where Nathan was reaching out for me with his good hand. Only the sight of his bandages and vast array of tubes stopped me from the temptation of flinging myself fully onto him. 'He's not become any easier, Stella,' Nicholas joked dryly, 'As soon as he opened his eyes he demanded to know where you were. I didn't even get a hello.'

'Hello, Nicholas,' Nathan croaked with a smile towards his brother before turning his head back to me, 'Hey baby …' he said grittily, reaching up to wipe a tear from my eye, but it was a pointless task because they were surely falling faster than his sleepy, uncoordinated hand could ever clear them. Seeming to come to the same conclusion, Nathan gave up and simply cupped my cheek, rubbing his thumb in circles across my skin which caused me to make the most ridiculous moaning noise in relief. 'I love you, Stella. So fucking much,' Nathan murmured, apparently unable to help himself and at that point my heart really did try and hammer its way through my ribs. Did he really just say that? Nathaniel Jackson saying the 'L' word? Wow, the bump on his head must have really scrambled his brain.

'Oh God, I love you too, Nathan. I've been so scared,' I sobbed, a watery smile spreading on my lips regardless of the tears that were still soaking my cheeks.

'I'll get a doctor,' Nicholas said with a roll of his eyes as he stepped away towards the door.

'What the hell happened?' Nathan's voice was dry and scratchy as he eyed the cast on his arm curiously and then titled his head back at me. 'Did I piss you off or something?' he joked hoarsely. The relief from hearing his attempt at humour made me laugh almost hysterically and I sunk forwards and scattered gentle kisses all over his battered but beautiful face.

'I've been going out of my mind,' I murmured, 'I love you so much.' Even though I'd only said them seconds ago the words just fell from my lips again. For the past few days as Nathan had remained unconscious I'd been so terrified that I'd never get the chance to say them to him again that I couldn't hold back any longer. I would probably say them a thousand times in the next hour and it still wouldn't seem like enough. He opened his mouth to speak, but I put my finger to his dry lips. He clearly needed a drink before he spoke again but I didn't want to give him one without the doctors permission, so instead I set about trying to explain what had happened.

'After you left my house on Friday you must have gone shopping. As you were driving out of the shopping centre a truck smashed into you.' I ran a hand across his brow and down over his cheek with light fluttering touches of my fingers to reassure myself that this wasn't all some sick dream and that he was really here and awake. My contact made him hum happily and turn his face into my palm and a long overdue sigh of relief slipped from my lips, making my shoulders sag.

Nodding slowly as he processed this Nathan blinked slowly several times as if his mind was working in half speed, and then frowned, 'Everything's pretty hazy. What day is it?'

'Wednesday.' Once again his big blues fluttered with those long, lazy blinks. Following his gaze to the clock on the wall I glanced at the time and after seeing that it was now gone midnight I corrected myself, 'Actually, it's Thursday morning. *Very* early Thursday morning. You've been in here nearly a week.' Clenching my teeth I rushed to say the next words that expressed some of the fears that had been spiralling in my head all week. 'I'm so sorry,

Nathan, if we hadn't argued that day you would have stayed at my house and this would never have happened.' Tears started leaking down my cheeks again, but as Nathan seemed to run my words through his mind I watched as his eyes lit up as if recalling something. Shifting his palm from my face he wiped a couple of tears away with his thumb before lowering his hand and placing it gently on my stomach and rubbing soft circles.

'I remember the argument ...' His eyes were clearer and more focused as he found and held my gaze, 'I was in shock, I acted like a complete idiot,' he rasped, 'I'm sorry, I love you so much, Stella ...' he said again, his repetition of earlier making my heart skip several beats in my chest. I'd wanted to hear those words from his lips so desperately for so long that I didn't think I would ever get sick of hearing them.

Looking down at my stomach he very nearly grinned. 'You're getting a little baby pooch,' he murmured fondly, rubbing the slight bump of my tummy, but then flinched as the muscle movement crinkled some of the cuts on his cheeks. Pushing his pain aside he continued to stare at my stomach and rub gently with his hand. 'Christ, a baby ... *our* baby,' he murmured, sounding in awe. Before he could say any more a doctor strode into the room, followed by Nicholas and a sleepy-looking Rebecca who had been napping in the empty room next door.

Amazingly, even though it was the middle of the night, a team of specialist doctors and nurses appeared from nowhere over the next ten minutes. That's obviously what hideously expensive private healthcare gets you, I suppose. The gathered medical team proceeded to spend the next hour running test after test, before finally looking content and announcing that Nathan was firmly on the road to recovery – news that obviously caused a simultaneous sigh of relief to escape from me, Nicholas, and Rebecca. The majority of Nathan's tubes were removed before the doctors left us to our thankful celebrations, promising to come back again at nine o'clock in the morning to check on Nathan again.

The relief in the room was palpable, but so was the fatigue. Nicholas, Rebecca, and I had barely slept a wink in recent days and after a few more minutes talking with Nathan, Nicholas and Rebecca bid their goodbyes and headed for the door and a much needed rest.

Nathan gingerly removed himself from the bed before stretching out his muscles and lifting his eyebrows in surprise. 'Actually, I feel surprisingly good,' he stated before flashing me a wink and limping towards the bathroom.

Rolling off my shoulders in relief I drew in a long breath and walked towards the door to close the blinds. My eye was caught by the sight of Nicholas, who was still in the corridor outside speaking to an older lady with greyish blonde hair swept back in a loose chignon. Even from a distance the tension in his body was clear; his hands were clenched into fists at his side and his face taut, pale, and scowling. What on earth was the matter? Surely it couldn't be any bad news about Nathan? But then as I watched them further I realised the woman was just wearing everyday clothes, admittedly rather tatty clothes, but she certainly didn't appear to be a doctor.

Scanning the corridor I saw Rebecca was at the nurse's station a few feet away flashing a concerned glance at him too, before nodding to the nurse and then hurrying to Nicholas' side. I was just about to open the door to find out what was going on when Nicholas leant over the woman and growled something before pointing towards the stairs. The woman's face briefly crumpled, before she seemed to gather herself, and after looking up and seeing me watching her she gave one final glance to Nicholas, turned, and pushed open the door to the stairwell.

Nicholas tipped his head back and stared at the ceiling

for a moment before grabbing Rebecca's hand and disappearing into a waiting lift carriage.

How very bizarre. I suppose after the tension of the last few days Nicholas might have bumped into her by accident and lost his temper? It was the only logical explanation I could come up with.

Just then the noise of Nathan coming back in from the en-suite made me turn, and the sight of him up and about and moving – albeit cautiously – had me smiling with relief and immediately forgetting the woman as I went to help him get back into bed.

It was like the news of Nathan's good health had pulled the plug on my energy levels. I'd kept myself going for him over the last few days, but now I knew he was OK I suddenly felt the very conflicting emotions of complete jubilation counterbalanced with utter bone draining exhaustion.

'You should go too, Stella, you must be so tired, it won't be good for you, or our baby'. *Our baby.* Regardless of my need for sleep I couldn't help but grin at his words. Gosh, the way Nathan said it made my insides positively blossom with warmth. 'No, I'm staying here,' I told him firmly, 'I've been sleeping on the pull out bed,' I said, jerking my head in the direction of the couch which I turned into a bed at night – not that I'd really slept a great deal. 'Tossed and turned while frantically worrying' would have been more accurate. 'I've not left this room for three days, Nathan, I'm certainly not leaving it now.'

The smile Nathan gave me was incredible, almost bright enough to light up the room and certainly powerful enough to make my legs weaken. 'Come here,' he said, grabbing my hand and pulling me towards the bed. With some difficulty he then somehow shifted himself across and patted the empty half with an irresistibly beseeching look on his face.

'No, I shouldn't, you need to rest, and besides, I might

hurt you.' Although by God I was tempted, I'd been so terrified I was going to lose him that I couldn't think of anything I'd rather do than climb in and snuggle up to him.

'You'll hurt me more if you don't get in,' he murmured, placing his good hand over his heart in an exaggerated fashion, but there was a hint of warning in his tone, a hint of the old Dominant Nathan seeping back in that I just couldn't help but welcome. The return of Dominant Nathan meant he *really* was feeling better. 'Besides, I don't pay through the nose for private healthcare for nothing. Look at the size of this bed, there's plenty of space.' He did have a point, the bed was frigging huge, probably bigger than the double in my flat.

Seeing my continued hesitation Nathan raised his eyebrows, 'Please?' he added in an alluring tone, which was so sweet that it finally wore me down.

'OK, but just until you fall asleep, then I'll move,' I said, trying for a firm tone but just ending up sounding really frigging excited. Grinning at my acquiescence he lifted the blanket to allow me to crawl in beside him, letting a small giggle of happiness escape my lips as I snuggled in closer to his warm, solid chest. After dreading the worst for the last few days I finally felt the tension and stress leave my body in a long, low breath as I relaxed into Nathan's familiar one-armed embrace. I felt like I'd arrived home after an arduous journey, and it was an utterly amazing place to be.

'Ugh, too many layers separating us,' Nathan grumbled in mock irritation as he fingered the sleeve of my T-shirt. I felt like pointing out that he was dressed too, but then I felt a flutter of sickness as I belatedly realised that he hadn't really had a choice, had he? He'd been unconscious and I'd had to helplessly look on as the nurses changed his thin hospital pyjamas every day.

Breaking me from my unpleasant reverie Nathan smirked down at me. 'Hang on, isn't this that ratty old T-shirt you sometimes sleep in at your house?' he asked, craning his neck to inspect it further, making me blush.

'Yes. It was what I was wearing when I found out you were in here,' I explained quietly, 'It was also the last thing I was wearing when you were at my house before the accident ... it seemed sentimental somehow, so I've not taken it off.'

'I thought you smelt a bit,' Nathan joked, giving me a squeeze on a ticklish spot by my hip and making me relax and giggle again.

'I have showered, Nathan!' I replied with mock indignation, 'I've just put it back on afterwards.' I knew I didn't smell, the nurses had even washed the T-shirt for me at one point, lending me a less than flattering nightie to wear in the meantime, but thinking about it, it was pretty disgusting to wear the same clothing for nearly three days straight.

Nathan might have made some jokes about too many layers between us, but clearly exhaustion was affecting him too, because he left me dressed and simply pulled me against him with a happy sigh. We laid together in companionable silence for several minutes, each lost in our own thoughts until Nathan shifted slightly so he could look me in the eye. The suddenly serious expression on his face made my stomach plummet and instantly woke me up. 'Stella ... I want to talk about that day, about our argument.'

Shaking my head vigorously I frowned. I didn't want to think about that day ever again; the bone deep, gut wrenching sense of rejection I'd felt, then finding out about the accident ... it was all to raw, too much to go through again. 'No, it's in the past, Nathan, let's work from here, shall we?' It was childish of me to try and ignore it, but the thought of hearing Nathan voice any uncertainty about the baby, me, or our relationship, terrified me.

'No, Stella, I need to say this. I acted like an idiot and probably gave you completely the wrong impression. I'm so excited that you're having our baby,' he paused to smile down at me, and to my delight the truth was obvious in his features, he *really* meant it, '... and I was that day too ... although I'll admit it was a bit of a shock at the time. But then when you said you were twelve weeks pregnant and hadn't told me ...' He shook his head, his eyes drifting away as a frown puckered his brows, 'I couldn't think of any reason that you would have kept it from me, apart from if you didn't think I'd be a good father ...' Before I could interrupt to correct him Nathan continued, his face twisting with the memories, 'The idea that you kept it secret really hurt me, so instead of showing you that you were wrong, I acted like an idiot and stormed off. I'll do it differently this time, Stella, I'll prove myself to you.'

He ran his good hand up and down my arm in agitation and my heart just about broke for how little credit he gave himself. I'd have told him there and then how much I believed in him, but my throat was too constricted with new tears and he continued before I got a chance. 'I'd gone to the shops to get you some more ginger teabags and things that might be useful and I was planning on coming straight back to your house and apologising ...' His voice trialled off and finally I had the chance to swallow back my tears and correct him on his mistakes.

Pushing myself up to sitting I crossed my legs and grabbed his hand tightly in mine. 'I didn't think you'd be a bad father!' I exclaimed desperately, 'I'd only just found out a few days before, I was in shock too.' It had actually been more like a week, so that was a little white lie, but the part about being in a state of shock was one hundred per cent true. 'The reason I didn't tell you is that I was getting used to it myself, I ... I was scared you would be annoyed. I didn't think you wanted kids – in fact, I got the feeling that you were totally against it.'

'What gave you that idea?' he asked, looking genuinely confused.

Biting my lip I decided that honesty was needed from here on out. 'Well, after your childhood it would be totally understandable. Plus, when we saw Melissa and you briefly thought the baby was yours, you looked utterly horrified at the idea.'

Pausing, Nathan frowned before nodding thoughtfully, 'I *was* horrified, because it was Melissa, not *you*. Melissa was just a casual acquaintance really, as awful as it sounds she was pretty much just a plaything, although that's how she wanted it too. I wouldn't dream of having a child in a situation like that.' Tugging my hand up he placed a gentle kiss on my knuckles. 'What I have with you is different from anything I've ever experienced in my life. Entirely different. God, I love you so much.' He groaned, kissing my hand again, but this time followed up by tugging me back to lay beside him and landing a kiss on my lips that had far more intent. The sound of him saying the 'L' word was so magical I decided to start a tally – so far that was three in less than an hour.

Lifting his head so his eyes were just centimetres from mine Nathan reached down under the covers and gently stroked over my belly again, his eyes never left mine once as his hand then pushed under my T-shirt until it settled on my bare skin. Rubbing the tip of his nose around mine in a sweetly affectionate gesture Nathan smiled. 'I can't believe our child is in there,' he whispered in awe.

What I couldn't believe however, was the growing erection that I suddenly felt pressing against my upper leg. Raising an eyebrow I looked at him disapprovingly, but in response he just grinned his full watt 'knock-'em-dead-Jackson' smile which just made my heart melt. 'What? I find the idea of you pregnant with my baby, *our baby*, incredibly arousing. I'm not going to apologise for it,

Stella.'

The horrific stress of the last few days seemed to finally be dissipating from my body as I shook my head in amusement and couldn't help but join in his good mood. 'You certainly have made a quick recovery!' I joked dryly, before straightening my face and biting my lower lip. 'For the record, I think you'll be an amazing dad, Nathan. We might have to work on your over protectiveness a bit though ... and your swearing.' I was expecting Nathan to make a joke of my remark, or perhaps tickle me for being cheeky, but he didn't, instead his face opened up and softened with emotion, possibly more than I'd even seen it in all the time we'd been together.

'Really?' he whispered, uncertainty clear in his tone, 'You really think I'll be a good dad?' And from just those hesitantly spoken words I could tell he was both excited about the prospect of bringing a child into the world with me, and also utterly terrified that he might let the baby down if he turned out to be like his father.

His hand unconsciously gripped me tighter as he waited for my reply. 'I do, Nathan,' I agreed with a sage nod, and I really genuinely did, deep down to my core. Yes, he was sometimes irrational, domineering, and fiercely protective of me, but when I really thought about it I saw these as intrinsically good traits that showed that he truly cared.

Leaning forwards Nathan placed a gentle, loving kiss on my lips and made a contented humming noise in the back of his throat as I accidentally deepened the kiss and pushed my tongue against the seam of his lips before slipping it into his mouth. I say accidentally, but really I just couldn't help myself around him, even bandaged up in a hospital bed I found Nathan irresistible, and after days of thinking I might never get the chance to kiss him again I was fully intent on making up for lost time.

'So, how does this work then? If I'm going to be a good dad to our baby, do I have to become all boring and domesticated, or can I still be kinky and an outrageously good lover?' he murmured against my lips, causing me to immediately laugh into his open-mouthed kiss. There it was. There was the arrogant, jokey remark I had expected earlier. Although to be honest he *was* an outrageously good lover, so it wasn't really that much of a joke.

'Oh yes, kinky can stay, as long as it's done in private,' I replied, sliding a hand down his chest towards the waistband of his pyjama bottoms. 'In fact I think I might make that one of the stipulations of our relationship.'

'I agree, we're going to need stipulations, but we can discuss them later.' He breathed hotly against my cheek. A small frown tweaked my brows, I'd been joking, but his tone actually sounded rather serious. Deciding it was my lusty state making me hear things I moaned as Nathan's tongue circled on my neck before he kissed along my jaw with small nibbling motions that quickly began to drive me wild.

I was almost beyond speech but it vaguely occurred to me that I really needed to stop this – he was in recovery and we were in a hospital bed for goodness sakes. Even knowing that I couldn't seem to find the effort to pull away, 'Yes, stipulations are important ... daddy duties include changing your fair share of nappies and being tolerant of me when I'm atrociously hormonal and fat ...' Nathan's good hand slid from my belly up my stomach towards my chest, making me arch my bra-clad breast into his hand and gasp as he gently kneaded its weight, 'Oh! That's good!' I gasped, 'Your other duties include providing me with frequent sex, kinky or otherwise, and generally indulging my every whim and desire.' That was it, I was done with talking, my body now flooded with arousal and desperate for Nathan. If I had any sense I'd be climbing out of this bed and putting some distance between the two of us, but quite apparently my common sense had flown right out of the window tonight.

'Indulging your every whim and desire?' he enquired smoothly as he slipped his fingers inside my bra and began to play with my already erect and needy nipple. 'And would one of those whims be to have sex in a hospital bed, I wonder?' he murmured.

It really shouldn't be, but, oh God I wanted him. Clenching my jaw so hard that my teeth hurt, I used my very last shred of control and pulled back to smile sheepishly at him. 'Nathan … we need to stop,' I gasped breathlessly, '… you've only just woken up after almost five days of unconsciousness. I don't want to get you over-excited.'

Nathan wiggled his eyebrows cheekily at my words. 'I think it's too late for that,' he murmured, thrusting his hips and eyeing the impressive bulge in the sheet that his erection was making. Giggling, I gave him an apologetic look. 'I was actually referring to your head,' I said, gently stroking the bandage with my fingertips as a frown puckered my brows. 'You had pressure on your brain from the accident, I know the doctor said it's basically back to normal, but I don't want to take any chances. As much as I'd love to jump you right now, let's just snuggle for tonight and then when you have a full bill of health we can pick up from here.'

Nathan turned his head so he could kiss my palm and made a groaned noise of protest, then with a rueful grin he nodded, pulled me back down against his chest, and for once in his life, followed my orders and fell asleep.

TWENTY-FIVE – REBECCA

Talk about a shocking few days. I don't think I ever want to go without mobile signal again, not after the horrific dread that had settled over me when I'd arrived back at Gatwick and switched on my phone to hear the numerous beeps as my phone updated a stack of missed calls and text messages. The inbox of my phone had been completely filled until it couldn't accept any more messages. Seeing my mobile go loopy with flashing message alerts had made me instinctively wary, and then seeing that all the calls were from Nicholas my stomach had dropped with apprehension before I'd even listened to his first message. I have to admit, I'd immediately assumed the worst, thinking that perhaps something had happened to one of my parents, or perhaps even to Nicholas himself. *Ugh.* A shudder ran through me as I thought about it, but I tried to shake it off – we were home now, and thankfully Nathan was going to be OK.

Nicholas had been incredibly quiet in the car on the way home, but then, so had I. Both of us were exhausted after the virtually sleepless nights at the hospital, so I'd put his silence down to tiredness, although I had yet to ask him about the strange encounter with the woman at the hospital. I'd been too far away to hear what they were saying, but the meeting had certainly seemed to shake him up.

It was only as we reached the door to his house and I watched him struggle to get the key in the lock that I

261

realised just how fraught he was. Stepping closer I frowned as I saw his hand visibly shaking at the lock. Not entirely sure what the problem was I decided to get him inside before broaching the subject, so I simply took his trembling hand in mine, gently removed the key from his fingers, and unlocked the front door.

Stepping into the hallway I switched on the lamp and guided Nicholas inside. It was still practically the middle of the night so Mr Burrett wouldn't be around for another few hours yet, which seeing Nicholas' current state, was probably a good thing. 'Nicholas? Are you OK?' I asked softly, placing myself in front of him and tentatively taking both his hands into mine. God, he was shaking so much that I could feel his whole body trembling.

Closing his eyes I watched as Nicholas tensed his jaw and drew in several deep breaths through his nose, his nostrils flaring with the effort of each one. 'Your brother is going to be OK, Nicholas,' I reassured him, assuming that concern for Nathan was the cause of his distress. His eyes stayed shut, but Nicholas shook his head slowly. 'I know. It's not that.' Now I really was at a loss for what to do or say. If it wasn't his brother's accident upsetting him then I had no clue what the matter was.

Just then Nicholas' blue eyes opened and focused on mine, his face disturbingly pale in the dim lamplight. 'I am so fucking glad to get out of that place,' he said suddenly. 'That's the first time I've been back in a hospital since …' An even bigger shudder ran through his body and in response he pulled me into his arms and held me against his chest as his muscles continued to twitch and convulse around me. It was like he was in shock or something. '… Since my suicide attempt,' he finished in a low tone. My body softened against his in sympathy at his words and I winced as I remembered his recount of that awful night; his whole horrific childhood. My poor, troubled man. I loved him so much that it hurt.

'Even the smell of the antiseptic and disinfectant took me right back to that night,' he said grittily. 'And the noises of the machines ...' This time the jerk than ran through him shook me as well, but all I could do was bury my face in his chest and hope that my touch was reassuring for him.

'Apparently I was unconscious for a while from the loss of blood,' he explained, 'But I was aware of everything around me for quite some time before I could actually move or communicate. It was so surreal. I could hear the machines beeping and feel people touching me but I couldn't respond ... one of the nurses even commented that my heart rate had changed slightly, but I was totally able to communicate with her.' Shifting me in his arms he let out a huge long breath and lowered his head so his face was buried in my hair. 'The last few days were horrendous enough, but then as we were leaving the hospital it got worse ...' Wondering what he meant I leant back and saw that Nicholas' eyes were closed, an agonising expression on his face.

'That woman,' he said quietly. 'The one outside Nathan's room before we left?' I nodded, even though his eyes were shut and he wouldn't be able to see me. 'That was my mother.'

The spacious hallway suddenly felt claustrophobic as the air stilled in my lungs. His mother? I felt Nicholas shudder as his grip tightened on me, and in return my own fingers curled around his waist and pulled him more firmly against me.

'Your mother?' I whispered, too horrified to vocalise anything remotely useful or supportive.

'Indeed.' Nicholas' eyes opened, and the coldness there made me shiver, although his expression definitely warmed when he finally focused on me again.

'Seeing as all the memories of my suicide attempt had been crashing down on me for the last few days it was particularly spectacular timing on her behalf,' he commented dryly. But I suspect his weak humour was merely a way of deflecting the pain he was feeling. 'Apparently she's been keeping tabs on Nathan and me for all these years.' His voice was almost devoid of emotion now. 'When she got news of Nathan's accident she got on a flight from the States to see him.'

It seemed bizarre to me that his mother would care about the wellbeing of her sons now, as she clearly hadn't given a toss about them when she'd knowingly allowed their father to beat them as children, but I stayed quiet, allowing Nicholas to recount this evenings meeting to me.

'She said she'd never wanted us to get hurt …' Nicholas swallowed loudly, 'Blamed it all on Dad for being too overbearing, and said she had been too scared to do anything to stop him.' I watched as his lower lip took a battering between his teeth until the flesh had visibly reddened. 'Every word was bullshit. She never really cared for us, Nathan was the only one to show me any affection or care as a kid.' Running a hand through his hair Nicholas then rubbed at his stubbly chin. Wow. This had to be so incredibly hard for him, and yet I seemed to have nothing useful to say at all.

'Did she want to get back in contact with you for good?' I asked quietly.

Nicholas rolled off his neck, and I winced at the audible click. 'She did, tried to give me her phone number, but I refused it. To be honest, I think she's only sought us out now because she wants some of our money. She claimed she spent her last cash on the flight over, and did you see her clothes? They were a mess. But that was probably all a staged lie too.' Looking down at me his gaze connected with mine, his eyes fierce with a mixture of pain, but also a renewed strength. 'I told her to fuck off,' he muttered. 'She had her chance when we were kids. Dad was formidable, but he never forced her to stay. She could have

264

done something to get us all away if she'd really wanted.'

Shifting me in his arms Nicholas sighed and then placed a kiss on the top of my head. 'You are my family now, Rebecca. You, Nathan, and Stella. That's all I need.'

Nodding I snuggled into his chest. Seeing his mother again must have been incredibly upsetting, but I couldn't help but agree that he was better off without her in his life.

'Let's put this behind us now, OK?' he asked quietly, to which I nodded, although one thing did pop into my mind.

'Will you tell Nathan?' I enquired.

Nicholas winced. 'I don't know. Perhaps in the future, but not yet, he needs to concentrate on his recovery. Besides, I know he would react the same way as me. He wants nothing to do with either of our parents now.'

'I'm sorry about all this,' he suddenly mumbled into my hair causing my eyebrows to rise, I couldn't believe he was apologising. 'You don't need to apologise, Nicholas,' I murmured softly, wondering what I could do that would help him stow away thoughts of his dreadful past again and ease his tension. 'Come on, let's go upstairs. Let me bathe you. Clean away the memories and the hospital smell.' I stepped from his embrace and started leading him towards the stairs.

Following me obediently he gave my hand a squeeze. 'That's a nice offer, but I'll be OK, it's late, Rebecca, you're tired, we both are. I'll be fine now we're home,' he murmured, and while he might have been calming a little I could still feel his grip tensing around mine with an occasional spasm.

Stepping into the master bedroom I let go of his hand and quickly switched on the bedside lamps, feeling intent on looking after him even after his attempted dismissal of the idea. He was usually the strong one and cared for me, so it was only fair that I repaid the favour when he clearly needed it so badly. 'Nicholas, we've had so little sleep in the past few days that half an hour longer won't make a difference. Let me make you feel better, baby. Please?'

Walking back towards him I raised my eyebrows hopefully and saw the dimple in his cheek appear as he smiled his cute, shy smile – the smile he reserved just for me. 'OK. Thank you, Rebecca.'

Practically skipping into the bathroom before he could change his mind I turned on the bath taps, popped in the plug, added a decent glug of bath foam, and then turned to find him leaning on the doorframe watching me with amusement. His hands were in the pockets of his crumpled suit trousers and his shirt was a crease-ridden mess, making him look scruffy and tired, but still so handsome to me. 'A bath? I assumed you meant a quick shower,' he commented as I crossed the space and reached up to undo his top button.

'A bath will be more relaxing, which is just what you need right now. Besides, with the amazing taps you have it will be full enough in no time.'

As the bathroom began to fill will the sweet smell of orange blossom – still my favourite scent – I finished undoing his buttons and slipped the shirt from his broad shoulders. He was being very compliant, which made me smile, but I didn't pass comment, merely made the most of it and quickly dispatched his trousers so he was stood in just a pair of rather fine black boxer shorts. Hmm. My eyes narrowed and I licked my lips; Nicholas in boxer shorts was one of my favourite sights in the entire world.

Checking the temperature of the water I nodded with satisfaction and quickly peeled away my own clothes before chucking them straight in the wash basket, turning around, and holding out a hand to him.

Taking my invitation Nicholas pushed off from the door frame and with his gaze fixed on mine he casually slipped his boxers down his legs and stepped out of them. As much as I tried to keep my eyes on his, I couldn't help just the tiniest peek at the taut body parts that he was exposing and I felt my heart quicken in my chest. Apparently he wasn't *that* upset or tired then. It took quite a forceful thought to remind myself that this was about making him feel better, not about sex. So when he reached my outstretched hand and placed his palm in mine, I was super self-controlled and led him straight into the bath water without so much as a second glance at his glorious tackle.

Leaving the taps running I lowered myself into the water first, which was a bit of a mistake because it put his groin right at my eye level. The temptation to lean forwards and lick him was almost overwhelming, but instead I leant back against the curved bath end and opened my legs underneath the rising bubbles. 'Sit,' I instructed, indicating that he should sit between my legs. Once again following my instructions Nicholas folded his long legs down into the water and then with a gentle encouragement from me leaned himself back so he was reclining with his back on my chest.

Almost immediately he tried to lean forwards, but I wrapped my legs around his waist to halt him. 'But I'll squash you,' he protested.

'No you won't. Just relax.'

He didn't entirely relax, but Nicholas did at least lie back again, which caused me to hum happily in his ear and tuck my hands underneath his arms so they were laying on his chest.

After a few moments I felt the remaining tension in Nicholas' body completely dissipate on top of me, and smiled. OK, so he was squashing me a little bit, but after how distraught he'd looked earlier it was worth it. The tub was full enough now so I turned off the taps and allowed the quiet of the bathroom to surround us. The only sounds over the next fifteen minutes or so were the gentle popping of the bubbles and our slow, relaxed breathing as I felt my eyes closing, tiredness creeping up on me again now that my body was warm and happy.

'This is really good,' Nicholas murmured sleepily, turning his head to kiss my upper arm. 'You're amazing, Becky, thank you.' His soft endearment made me smile and even in my drowsy state I managed to sum up enough energy to pick up the sponge and shower gel and start to wash him.

Once we were both scrubbed clean of any remaining traces of the hospital we quietly dried ourselves on two huge bath sheets before Nicholas scooped me into his arms and carried me to the bed.

A sigh of pleasure escaped my lips as he lay me down under the soft sheets and I grinned – after catnapping on spare hospital beds for the last few days I can honestly say that his bed had never felt so bloody good. As Nicholas climbed in behind me he pulled me against his body and slipped his arm around my waist until we were as close as we could possibly be. Interlocking my fingers with his I felt my eyelids closing almost immediately. As sensual as the bath together had been I knew we were both too tired for any sex, besides, after the run-in with his mother it hardly seemed an appropriate time either. But we were together, safe and happy, and so it really didn't seem necessary. We could always make up for it tomorrow once we were more refreshed. Besides, I knew from first-hand experience that morning sex was when Nicholas was at his most inventive, so I didn't mind delaying for a few hours one little bit.

TWENTY-SIX – STELLA

Even after my firm promises that I would only stay in Nathan's bed until he fell asleep I found myself waking up the following day with my nose full of his delicious scent, which gave me a fairly good indication that I was still snuggled up to him. I'm not talking about the smell of his aftershave either, because clearly after five days of being in hospital he wasn't wearing any. No, the scent I loved most in the world was just him; his body, or perhaps whatever weird oils his skin produced. Whatever it was, it was amazing and I wished I could bottle it.

Keeping my eyes closed and body relaxed I ran a quick system check and decided that I actually felt pretty good. After days of intense worry with barely any sleep I must have crashed out on him and slept like a log. From the deep, even movements of his chest below my ear I guessed that Nathan was also still asleep, so rather than wake him I maintained my position and took a moment to relish just how amazingly refreshed I felt after my first proper rest of sleep in over a week. Grinning to myself I couldn't resist the temptation to run my hand over his chest. Mmm, warm, solid muscle, I bet if I continued my exploration lower I'd soon find another warm solid muscle … but my fun was brought to a sudden halt by a firm cough from somewhere in the room.

A cough that definitely didn't belong to either Nathan or I.

Practically jumping out of my skin I sat up so fast that I

got head rush. Lights flashed before my eyes as I blinked several times and raised a hand to steady my spinning skull before my vision began to refocus. Once my sight had cleared enough I managed to see a stern-looking nurse who was stood at the end of Nathan's bed, holding his chart and giving me a rather disapproving look.

'Morning, sleepyhead,' she said with a raise of one eyebrow, but her voice was only just audible over the hammering of my poor shocked heart.

My cheeks flooded with mortification – not only had I been caught sleeping in Nathan's bed which surely wasn't allowed, but I had also been midway through a proper good fondle of his chest when I was interrupted, something that the nurse surely must have seen. 'I, er, good morning.' Stumbling for words I decided not to attempt to justify my actions. I'd clearly been caught red-handed feeling up my boyfriend, so staying quiet now seemed the only way to marginally lessen my embarrassment.

'Or perhaps I should say afternoon,' the nurse added. This time I could have sworn she was attempting to suppress a smirk. Clambering from the bed in a very inelegant manner I straightened my creased clothes as best I could and blew the hair from my face before glancing at the clock to see that it was almost four in the afternoon. My eyes shot open, good God, we'd slept for nearly fourteen hours!

Seeing Nathan shift amongst the sheets I glanced across to the bed to find him looking incredibly wide awake, perky, and grinning at me, all the while chuckling softly under his breath. One look at the amused expression on his face told me that he'd been awake the whole time, and was loving seeing my embarrassment. Bastard, I would make him pay for this later when we were alone.

'So, as I was saying before Miss Marsden, err … *woke up*, you'll be allowed home in the morning, Mr Jackson,

270

your consultant Dr Powter just wants you to finish the course of IV fluids we've been giving you for your dehydration.' Had they been speaking before I woke up then? It certainly sounded like it, crap, that just made my 'morning fondle' even more embarrassing. I suppose it could have been worse, my stroking could have been on a lower part of his anatomy like I'd been imagining. Now that would have been *really* embarrassing. Chewing on my lip I averted my gaze from the smug nurse and instead looked at Nathan, who was gingerly adjusting himself into a sitting position in the bed and giving a reluctant nod, 'Fine, one more day. But apart from that I'm OK now?'

'Apart from your arm and bruises, which you'll need to be a little careful with, yes.' The nurse said with a smile.

Flashing a glance at me, Nathan winked and I felt my heart flutter with happiness. He really was going to be OK. After the hellish days we'd gone through waiting for news I almost couldn't take it all in. The next words from his mouth however, had me spluttering with embarrassment and wishing the floor would open up and swallow me. 'So can you tell my girlfriend I'm allowed to have sex with her then please, she's treating me like I'm going to break in half.'

Oh. My. God. My cheeks returned to full blush mode as mortification swept through me for the second time in two minutes. My mouth fell open in shock as I stared at Nathan in complete horror – he didn't really just say that, did he? Turning my wide eyes from him I flashed a glance at the nurse and saw her desperately trying to suppress a smile by biting down hard on her lower lip.

Lip biting? Now that was a habit she really didn't want to be doing in front of the finicky Mr Jackson. *Although it was probably just my lip biting that my demanding man had issues with,* I thought with an eye roll. At Nathan's comment the nurse gave up her earlier pretence of sternness and turned to me grinning broadly. 'Been trying

271

his luck, has he?' she asked with a gentle chuckle, which was so close to the truth that I only just managed cover up my splutter of embarrassment with a cough and give a limp smile and a nod.

'Well, you really must be feeling better then,' she said, glancing at Nathan. 'Sex is completely fine, but please have some compassion and save it until you're home, Mr Jackson, remember that I have to change the sheets once you leave,' she said with another smirk. 'Watch that arm of yours though, no acrobatics just yet.' Shaking her head with another smile she placed his chart back and began to pick up the tray stacked with Nathan's lunch plates as she turned to leave. 'As much as I've enjoyed looking after you, the sooner you go home the better. Maybe then my nurses can stop faffing with their hair and make-up every five minutes and get back to work,' she said with another grin before closing the door behind her.

Staring at the door my mouth opened and closed several times, but I was at a complete loss for what to say. I think I was in a state of shock from Nathan's unbelievably blunt comments about sex – the man clearly had no shame whatsoever. But then again, that shouldn't really have been a surprise to me – in our time together he'd done all sorts of naughty things to me in public places without ever so much as blushing.

Slowly I turned back to him with raised brows. My brain had restarted after my shock and I was now fully intent on giving him an earful about embarrassing me in public, but I was abruptly stopped from saying anything by the arrival of Nicholas poking his head in the door. 'Hi, brother, come on in,' Nathan said, shifting to sit himself upright. Glancing at me he caught my look and flashed me a wink and grin so glorious that they made me forgive him almost immediately. God it was so good to have him back and healthy.

Nicholas was whistling under his breath as he breezed

into the room with a tray of food in one hand, a large cup of coffee in the other, and a copy of the *Financial Times* under his arm and I had to say that Nathan's brother looked, and sounded, a whole lot better after a good night's sleep.

'Ah, Stella, you're finally awake,' Nicholas said pleasantly with a small smile. 'I got you some food, you must be starving by now.' If possible my embarrassment grew further – had *everyone* been awake and collected in the room around me while I slept on obliviously for the day? Apparently they had. I suppose all I could do now was try to move on and hope I hadn't been snoring.

'You could have woken me up earlier, Nathan,' I muttered a little grumpily, which he apparently found amusing because I saw him try and fail to smother a laugh.

'Don't worry about it, you obviously needed the sleep, sweetheart,' Nathan said reassuringly as he patted the edge of the bed to indicate I sit down. Sighing, I knew I couldn't refuse him, so I moved forwards and perched next to him. Besides, he was right, I *had* needed the sleep. I felt so much better now, I really shouldn't be moody about it.

Once I was settled, Nicholas placed the tray of food on a wheeled trolley and pushed it towards me, filling my nose with the delicious smell of warm cheese sauce. 'Eat up,' Nathan murmured, rubbing my back gently as I examined the food before me.

'So you woke up earlier?' I asked him as my stomach protested loudly at my slow start to the meal.

'Yep, a couple of hours ago. We've had the specialist in here and everything.' I wasn't sure if he was teasing me with this last remark, but by now I'd given up on being embarrassed. Sod it, my man was conscious and healthy, and at the end of the day, that was all I really cared about.

My stomach rumbled again, so with a grateful smile towards Nicholas I picked up the fork and tucked in to the plate of macaroni and cheese with gusto whilst Nathan chatted casually with his brother. As I chewed the warm pasta I couldn't help but moan my appreciation – it was really delicious and way better than I had expected from hospital food. 'This is so tasty. I can't believe the canteen here made this!' I remarked, going back for a second forkful. Snorting a laugh at my comment Nicholas raised an eyebrow.

'It's not from the canteen. Nathan mentioned that you like Italian food so I went to Buono to get it for you. It's one of the best Italian restaurants in London,' he informed me airily. Oh. Well, that certainly told me then.

The pasta was so amazing that it didn't take me long to hoover the whole lot up. In fact, the food had been so good that I only just held myself back from licking the plate. 'God, it's so good to eat again.' Seeing Nathan's frown and curious look I shrugged. 'My appetite sort of vanished this week. I couldn't eat whilst you were just lying there,' I explained in a tiny voice as memories of the long, terrifying hours of his unconsciousness came back to me and made me shudder.

Using his good hand, Nathan pushed himself fully upright and turned a fierce glare on Nicholas. As I watched Nathan's sudden change I immediately spotted how his body suddenly bristled with annoyance, the muscles across his back hardening and a flick appearing at the corner of his jaw as his eyes fired a stare so menacing that even I cringed a little. 'Why didn't you make her eat?' he demanded in a near-deadly tone, but Nicholas met his scorn with a raised eyebrow and small smile, apparently well used to Nathan's temper.

'Tell me this, Nathan, have you ever succeeded in forcing Stella to do something she didn't want to?' At this remark I smiled too, but the question was obviously rhetorical because he continued almost immediately, 'I tried to make her eat, believe me, but she wouldn't.' Turning his eyes towards me, Nicholas smiled fondly,

'You have one dedicated, but bloody stubborn, girlfriend.'

Grinning, I turned to Nathan and shrugged as he held my gaze for several seconds before shaking his head in defeat, 'Tell me about it.'

Happy at my minute victory I picked up a spoon and the bowl of pudding on the tray, tiramisu, and popped a spoonful into my mouth. *Oh. My. God.* It was like heaven on a frigging spoon. Starring at the bowl I hummed my approval before looking at Nicholas. 'Where is this restaurant?' I asked with my mouth half full, 'Because this is seriously the best tiramisu I've ever eaten.'

Giving my bowl a look of disapproval Nathan clicked his tongue. 'When we get out of here I'll take you to Buono for a full meal, but first I'm going to make sure you eat properly, Stella, not just desserts all the time, whatever it is that you and the baby need.'

'Right now I need more tiramisu,' I said hopefully around a delicious mouthful of coffee-flavoured cream, but one look from Nathan told me I wouldn't be getting seconds, not that I really needed it, but he was such fun to tease.

It had been so late when I woke up that the rest of the afternoon passed relatively quickly, Nicholas stayed for several more hours entertaining us with updates of his weddings plans, then once he had departed Nathan had his dinner and spent the entire time moaning that it didn't look anywhere near as appetizing as my takeaway from Buono had. I didn't say it out loud, but I had to say I agreed with him.

Once he'd finished his meal and the nurse had been in to check on Nathan for the night I popped into the en-suite to brush my teeth and freshen up for bed. Again. To be honest after all the sleep I'd had I wasn't sure I needed to sleep again, but Nathan was still recovering and would need rest, so I'd do my best to join him even if it was just to keep him company until he fell asleep. I had my Kindle in my handbag, so I could always settle down with a good book if I needed to.

Instead of finding Nathan lying down for sleep when I emerged from the bathroom, I was instead met by him sitting upright with a look on his face that I remembered very well. It was his '*I'd like to ravage you*' look, and was so hot that it really should be illegal. Just meeting his heated gaze was enough to increase my heartbeat and have me licking my suddenly dry lips.

'In all seriousness, we do need to discuss how your pregnancy will affect our sex life, Stella. But if we stick to vanilla for today, I'll jot some points down once we're home and we can discuss them.' Well, he was certainly feeling sure of himself, wasn't he? A frown formed on my brow and I pursed my lips cautiously, a little alarmed about his talk of 'jotting down points,' because that sounded an awful lot like the contract we'd signed at the start of our agreement. Even though we still lived a small percentage of our lives as Dom and sub, and did the occasional scene with safe words and toys, I had to say I thought we'd gone way beyond a paperwork relationship by now.

'Nathan, I'm not sure I like what you're suggesting,' I said quietly, not wanting to upset him, but feeling the need to voice my concerns.

Cocking his bandaged head to the side he watched me intently for a second or two. 'It's nothing major, just a few things I want to put in place to keep you and the baby safe. We'll talk properly when we're home, I promise.' Hmmm. I still wasn't entirely convinced, but if it was just to keep the baby safe then I suppose it would be OK, so I nodded my agreement.

'Good. So, now that's sorted ... you heard the nurse earlier, apart from my arm I'm firing on all cylinders, and when Dr Powter was here earlier I asked about sex during pregnancy and he said it's fine, so we're good to go.' My eyebrows rose at his presumption, and thank God I'd been asleep for the conversation with Dr Powter! I'd assumed Nathan would have known that you could have sex during pregnancy, but it was rather endearingly sweet that he'd bother to check I suppose. 'And I believe you said the other day that one of your whims and desires was sex in a hospital bed ... now I've got my full bill of health I think we should take care of it before I'm released tomorrow, don't you?'

'I also remember the nurse asking you to take pity on her because she changes the sheets,' I reminded him whilst crossing my arms and raising an eyebrow at him. This gave me a moment to think – I mean sex with Nathan was always tempting, but in a hospital bed, where we could be caught at any second? 'There's a full box of tissues right here, we'll clean up,' he said helpfully, still staring at me intently. I began absently twirling my thumb ring as I considered it, but then Nathan lowered his brows, 'Now, Stella. Come here,' he murmured in a low, commanding tone that was so magnetic I found myself helpless to ignore him. Within just a split second I was unbelievably horny, and found my nerves evaporating and being replaced by a grin as I immediately began walking towards the bed.

Even looking as he did I couldn't resist him, his head was bandaged to help the large cut on his scalp heal, and his broken arm was in plaster, but apart from that he'd made quite a miraculous recovery, no other major injuries at all to mar Nathan's usual physical perfection. Even though I knew I shouldn't be considering sex in a hospital bed, I couldn't help but wonder if we could do it and get away with it ... it hadn't really occurred to me before, but I had to admit that there was something quite thrilling about the possibility of getting caught.

'Seeing as I'm in plaster and technically in recovery I think perhaps you should lead the action tonight, Stella,'

Nathan suggested with a wiggle of his eyebrows. Nodding, I headed to the door to lock it, but stopped as Nathan spoke. 'Leave it.' he said, but it wasn't a request, it was an order, his tone leaving no room for discussion and I immediately realised that he'd had the same thought about the thrill of being caught as I had.

Raising an eyebrow I looked at him and saw the lusty look he gave me which sent desire pooling to my belly. 'It's practically the middle of the night, Stella, the chances of a nurse coming in are slim to none,' he murmured, his eyes dropping down to look at my body. Slim, yes, but still possible. Ah, what the hell, why not? Leaving the door unlocked I advanced on the bed in my most seductive walk, swaying my hips I took my time to peel my T-shirt up over my head as I walked.

'Christ, Stella …' Nathan gurgled, 'It's been nearly two weeks, woman, there's no way I'm going to last if you carry on like that.' Smiling at the effect I had on him I paused at the side of the bed and unzipped my jeans, deliberately facing away from him to show him a good view of my behind as I bent down to remove them and my knickers. Once again I heard a strangled noise escape from Nathan's throat and my smile grew – the power thing was immensely satisfying.

When I finally turned to him I was completely naked, my bra quickly discarded, but to my surprise Nathan was sat up on the bed, not lying back as I had expected. He'd also somehow removed the loose hospital pyjama top and now had his glorious chest on full display. 'You're so beautiful, Stella. I can't believe our baby is in there,' he murmured, eying my stomach. 'If you are uncomfortable at any time, or you want to stop, or shift positions just say, sweetheart, OK?'

His concern was incredibly sweet, but at this precise moment I didn't need sweet, I was horny and I needed Nathan in all his glory deep inside of me. Nodding to acknowledge his comment I raised my hands and briefly toyed with my breasts, just out of his reach, before taking one step closer.

Reaching for me with his good arm Nathan dragged me onto the bed with a growl, 'Enough teasing, Stella, you better fuck me right now or I swear to God, bandages or no bandages, I will punish you when we get home tomorrow. Within the boundaries of my new conditions of course,' he added. I was tempted to push him, just to see what he'd do to me tomorrow, but he was right, it had been nearly two weeks since we'd made love and my body was literally thrumming with the prospect.

Climbing onto the bed I straddled him, placed a hand in the centre of his chest, and gently pushed him back into a lying position. Shifting the bed sheets out of the way I proceeded to free his manhood from the constraints of his pyjama bottoms, a task that made me realise that sleeping naked like we usually did really did have its benefits. Once his raging erection was free I positioned myself over him and leant forwards for a kiss while rubbing my moist centre back and forth along the head of his cock in a teasing series of swipes. There really was no need for foreplay, I could tell I was wet and way past ready, but I just loved kissing Nathan, and seeing as he enjoyed it too I indulged us both for several minutes.

'Stella,' Nathan groaned against my lips in what I took as a plea, so before he had even finished saying my name I sunk myself down onto him, inch by delicious inch. Once I was fully seated on him I paused to control myself, concerned that with my huge arousal even a small movement would be enough to set me straight off into a climax. Breathing hotly against his cheek I chuckled softly, 'Sorry, I just need a minute or else I'm gonna come straight away ...'

Nathan's good hand was roving across my back and came to rest on my buttocks as I felt his head nod. 'I know what you mean, sweetheart.' Thinking that he was agreeing with me, his next move took me completely by surprise. Gripping my buttock he used his hold to swivel himself inside of me with a very thorough roll of his hips which rubbed perfectly against all the right places inside, and outside, of me. As much as I tried to hold back I was immediately cascaded into a mind-blowing orgasm, my channel pulsing around him as he remained unmoving and deep within me, and I almost wept form the power of it as I collapsed forward onto his chest, gasping for breath and clutching at him as my body continued to spasm around him.

When I came back to reality Nathan was laughing softly below me and after a second of recovery I looked up to see his flushed face grinning up at me. 'That was for teasing me earlier,' he stated calmly. 'Now that's out the way, let's continue, shall we?' Even though he had one arm in plaster, Nathan still managed to mostly control our lovemaking by using his other hand on my hip to guide our pace, but to be honest, after the amazing orgasm I'd just had I was feeling floaty and relaxed and happy to just go with the flow. Even with one orgasm under my belt, however, our weeks of chastity meant it didn't take long for both of us to build to another quick climax, as our bodies moved together and drew out simultaneous climaxes, our cries of satisfaction muffled in a deep kiss as we clung to each other in the darkened hospital room.

TWENTY-SEVEN – NATHAN

'Thank fuck we're home,' I huffed irritably as Stella and I made our way into my apartment after a morning of seemingly endless tests at the hospital. My goddamn arm felt like a pin cushion from the amount of blood samples and injections I'd had, but none of that mattered now – I'd finally been discharged and we were home. My eyes narrowed at this thought as I scanned my living room. *I* was home, but seeing as Stella had told me she essentially hated my living space I suppose she just felt like she was accompanying me to *my* apartment. My bottom lip took a battering as I chewed on it momentarily. I hated the thought of Stella's discomfort here, but then nodded decisively, knowing it was something that I could, and would, be rectifying in the very near future.

I noticed that Stella stayed quiet about my 'home' statement, but instead she came towards me, carefully manoeuvred around my sling, wrapped her arms around my waist and snuggled in close to my chest, which was all the welcome home I needed. 'God, Nathan, I'm so glad you're OK.' Her voice sounded thick, and not just because her face was muffled in my shirt. No, I suspected Stella might be on the verge of tears and hearing her genuine emotion for me almost made my own eyes well up. Christ, I might be softening up these days, but crying I *did not* do. Mind you, I never thought I'd say the 'L' word to a woman either, but I must have said it ten times in the last two days if not more. The *really* crazy thing was that I'd completely and utterly meant it too.

Glancing down at the top of Stella's blonde head as she clung to me I felt a small smile slip to my lips. She'd held it together so well in the hospital, but perhaps the stress of it all was finally catching up with her. Sliding my good arm further around her I pulled her as close as I could without squashing her. The way this woman made me feel was just incredible. Not to mention totally unprecedented. If someone had told me a few years ago that I'd be cutting back on my working hours and moving out of my beloved apartment to be with a woman, I'd have laughed scornfully in their face. Nuzzling my lips into Stella's sweet smelling hair I grinned – I guess the joke was on me then.

We hadn't even moved from our embrace on the threshold of the lounge when there was a knock at the front door. Stella stepped back and the glassy appearance of her wide eyes spoke volumes about just how terrified she'd been when I was in hospital. I couldn't help myself, ignoring the knocking at the door I yanked her back against me again, 'It's OK, sweetheart, I'm OK.' I pressed a firm kiss to the top of her head as I clutched her tightly to my chest. 'More importantly, *we* are going to be OK. You, me, and our baby.' Jesus, now *my* voice cracked as I spoke. Suppressing another grin I shook my head as I released Stella, I really was firmly on the route to being well and truly under the thumb, and I truly couldn't be happier about it.

'Are you expecting someone?' Stella asked as she discretely wiped at her eyes and then smiled at me to show she was OK. My chest expanded as I watched her pull herself together, there was no doubt about it; Stella was a brave one.

Stella knew no-one would have gotten past security without my prior go ahead, but I nodded anyway, '*We* are expecting someone,' I corrected her as I flashed her a secretive wink and opened the front door. 'Marcus, right on time, come in.'

Standing back I greeted my good friend Marcus Price as his huge six foot five frame stooped to enter the apartment, his arms full with a large box. Stella's shocked expression as she took in my man mountain of a friend was hilarious, and if possible her jaw dropped even further when a procession of three further men followed him with loaded carrier bags.

The delivery guys dropped off their bags in the kitchen area and left, leaving myself and a confused Stella to watch as Marcus placed his box on the kitchen surface and turned to us with a broad grin. 'Nathan, glad you're recovering, mate. It was a hell of a shock when I heard about your accident.' We did an awkward left-handed shake and half hug, which made me wish this bloody cast was already off my arm, before stepping apart to a good distance. 'It's good to see you again. It's been too long, my friend.' And wasn't that just the truth – I didn't exactly have many people I could call close friends, but Marcus was certainly one. Until very recently his job as a head chef had had him in America, but now he was based back in London I'd have to make more effort.

Turning his all-seeing green eyes towards Stella, Marcus smiled warmly and extended a hand which completely dwarfed Stella's tiny fingers, 'And you must be Stella, it's a pleasure to finally meet the woman who has successfully brought this irritable bastard to his knees.' I couldn't help but laugh at exactly how accurate his words were – until I'd met Stella I *had* been an irritable bastard, and even Stella joined in with a chuckle beside me.

'Uhh … nice to meet you,' she stuttered as she looked to me for clarification of the situation.

'Stella, this is Marcus Price, a very good friend of mine, and an even better chef,' I said with a knowing smile, quite enjoying watching her trying to work out what was going on.

'Right ...' Still sounding confused Stella blinked several times, 'Nice to meet you, Marcus.'

I could see Marcus weighing up Stella with an extended look, his inquisitive eyes ran head to toe and back again before he raised an eyebrow and pursed his lips appreciatively. My inner temperature began to rise and I felt that deep, hidden monster begin to rise to the surface again. If I'd had spines on my back they would definitely have risen defensively by this point, 'Back the fuck off, Marcus,' I growled, stepping in front of Stella with a bunched fist and shooting him a killer look. Bandage on my arm or not, I'd still take him on if needed. But instead of backing down and looking sheepish as I'd imagined, Marcus bent double laughing and slapped one palm on his thigh.

He was still laughing when he stood upright again and wiped a tear from his eye. 'Chill out, mate, I was just testing to see if the old Nathan was still in there somewhere.' Clapping me on the back hard enough to make me stagger forward a step he then turned and started to unpack his box, a grin still plastered on his face, 'Good to see you're not totally whipped yet, mate.'

Ignoring my male posturing Stella rolled her eyes and moved to the breakfast bar, watching what Marcus was doing with interest. Pulling out a set of professional knives, a hand mixer, and a roasting dish Marcus looked up at her and cocked his head. 'I hear congratulations are in order.' His eyes flicked between Stella, her stomach and then me, and I could see the genuine pleasure in his eyes. 'I'm chuffed for you both, I really am.' Nodding my acceptance of his words I felt myself relax again – this was Marcus, my long-time friend, not a threat. Turning to the sink Marcus washed his hands then addressed Stella again, 'OK, I'm going to need a full list of your favourite foods, but for tonight how does oven baked salmon with potato gratin, broccoli, and asparagus sound?'

Stella's eyebrows almost rose out of her forehead, 'It sounds incredible ...' Brushing her hair behind her ears Stella leant closer to examine the contents of the boxes and shopping bags as she realised they were all full with food. 'I don't mean to sound ungrateful, but why are you cooking for us?'

Wiggling his eyebrows Marcus shrugged, 'Because your wonderful man dragged me from my new restaurant kicking and screaming and promised to pay me a bucket load of cash to be here.' Chuckling, Marcus turned to continue with dinner preparation, and I suspect give me some time alone with Stella, who currently looked like she was about to explode as she turned to me with a horrified look on her face.

'He's kidding, Stella!' I laughed, taking her hand and helping her up onto one of the tall bar stools by the counter. 'Marcus is just back from the States and has a new restaurant open, he's trained up a head chef, but now he needs to see how he gets on without him for a few weeks. This just fits in well, he offered to do it, didn't you, Marcus?'

Turning back from the fridge I saw Marcus with a cheeky glint in his eye. 'I did. I did.' He held up his hands in apology, 'Sorry, Stella, I was just winding you up.' Marcus added with a wicked chuckle before turning back to the cooker.

'But I can cook, you can cook –' I cut off Stella's sentence by taking one of her hands in mine and rubbing my thumb across the soft skin on the back of her hand.

'I know we can, but after the accident and you not eating properly ...' I shook my head, my teeth clenching at the thought of her starving herself with worry because of me. 'Having Marcus here for a few weeks will just make sure you eat right, sweetheart. After all, it's not just you I have to worry about any more,' I murmured, before leaning in to place a quick kiss on her lips.

'I saw that,' Marcus said, and from his amused tone I just knew he was smirking at me for being so soft.

'Fuck off, Marcus,' I replied, sounding equally as jovial.

Casting my attention firmly back onto Stella I put on my most persuasive look. 'It's only temporary until I get this cast off,' I explained. I didn't mention that I planned on spoiling her rotten for the next six months too, but that was certainly on the agenda. Stella still looked like she might be about to argue further, so I opted for my back-up plan and grabbed the folder that was sat on top of my hospital bag. 'Plus if he's cooking every night it will give us more time after work to go and look around some of these.' Fanning out the estate agents' brochures that were in the folder I gave her a hopeful glance, not quite willing to accept how desperate I was for her to agree to move in with me. Watching her reaction carefully I saw her face soften as Stella looked at the brochures and then back at me with what my ego wanted to believe were adoring eyes.

We hadn't mentioned the brochures in the hospital, but I knew Stella had seen them because my brother had told me so. Nicholas had also taken great pleasure in telling me that I was 'under the thumb', the bastard, but he was totally right. I wanted to live with Stella more than anything else, and if she couldn't be happy here in my apartment then neither could I. We would have to move, it was as simple as that.

Taking Stella's hand I helped her down from the stool and led her towards the sofas and a little more privacy away from Marcus. Sitting ourselves down I tucked a leg under myself so I could fully face Stella before I spoke. I wanted, no, *needed*, her to see how seriously I was taking this. 'I want to do this properly, Stella, you and me together. If you need us to move to a new place that is just ours that's fine by me, take your pick, or go online and look for different houses, I don't care.'

Taking hold of her hand I brought it to my lips and kissed each knuckle, delaying my next question in case I didn't get the answer I wanted. Finally I let out a long breath and met her eyes with a serious gaze, 'Please live with me, Stella.' The pleading tone was not one I was used to using, and I was glad Marcus was out of earshot, but where this woman was concerned it seemed I was getting pretty good at compromising my usual behaviours.

After what felt like an eternity of waiting for her reply she smiled at me almost shyly. 'Yes,' she breathed with a nod, her fingers tightening around mine.

I almost couldn't believe my ears, and before I thought about it I found myself repeating her answer in a tone of disbelief. 'Yes?'

The shy smile on her lips broke into a full grin as she nodded enthusiastically and climbed into my lap. 'Yes, yes, yes. I'll live with you, Nathan.' Then she sealed the deal by lowering her lips to mine and kissing me softly and sweetly until I moaned and tugged her more firmly against my hardening groin.

'Oi! If I'm going to be around for a few weeks there needs to be a "no nookie outside of the bedroom" rule,' Marcus called from the kitchen, but this time I couldn't tell him to fuck off because he was making a valid point. Besides, no-one got to see Stella when she was aroused and lusty, only me, so reluctantly I shifted her off my lap and instead tucked her next to me on the sofa.

Stella was flushed and breathing a little quicker than usual as she leant forward and picked up the estate agents brochures. 'How exciting,' she murmured, beginning to flick through them. 'I'm contributing to the mortgage though, Nathan, otherwise the deal's off,' she stated in her no-nonsense voice. I could have told her that with a little shuffling of my finances I could quickly have enough in my bank account to buy at least two of these houses without even needing a mortgage, but I knew how independent Stella was, it was one of the qualities I loved about her, so instead I simply nodded my agreement. 'Fine, we can work out details at a later date. The London market is insane though, so be prepared to make a quick decision. Houses in good neighbourhoods can literally be sold within hours of going on the market. Luckily I have contacts within several of the estate agents through work, so I've asked them to give me a heads up about suitable properties before they advertise them, which might at least give us a few days' advantage over the rest of the buyers.'

Now that she had finally agreed to live with me there was one final idea I wanted to run past her, and it was a pretty monumental one for me too. 'I was hoping that you might agree to me designing a house for us, Stella.' Her eyes widened, from excitement, I think, and her lips parted, but I wanted to finish explaining first. 'We'd pick a normal house now, move in as soon as possible, and live there for a few years, but during that time I'd really love to design a longer-term home for us and get it built. What do you think?'

Her mouth bobbed open and closed a few times and she blinked rapidly for a minute or so, before her head suddenly started to nod up and down almost frantically. 'I think it sounds amazing, Nathan. I think *you're* amazing.'

Score three for me. I was home from hospital, Stella had agreed to live with me, and best of all, she thought I was amazing. Life really couldn't get any better.

TWENTY-EIGHT – STELLA

It was a few days after our return from the hospital and Nathan had been growing noticeably more and more distant around me. I'd thought that perhaps he was just coming to terms with his near-death experience, but he also hadn't touched me sexually since our liaison in his hospital bed, a fact which was intensifying my worry to almost insanely high levels. I'd tried my best to leave him alone, assuming that he was still recuperating and catching up on work after missing a full week, but it was only five days until we would be heading off for Nicholas and Rebecca's wedding, and I was getting worried that the tension was going to carry on until we left.

This morning however, I decided I couldn't bear to let the strain go on any longer, so I finally gave in and wandered along to his study to see if he wanted to talk. To my surprise, and concern, he wasn't behind his desk as I'd expected and I immediately started to panic. Searching the apartment I finally found Nathan in his bedroom, standing and staring out of the picture window, with his back to me and one hand dug deep into his trouser pocket.

Pausing inside the doorway unnoticed, I admired the beautiful view of his broad shoulders through the form fitting shirt and the lovely outline of his bum in his work trousers, before noticing his side profile and the frown that had been on his brows for days. 'Hey you,' I murmured softly, and even though he immediately turned at the sound of my voice it seemed to take Nathan several seconds to break from his thoughts as he stood there silently blinking at me, his face almost completely blank of any discernible emotion.

His peculiar behaviour made me feel decidedly on edge, and I crossed my arms over my chest as I began to fidget on the spot. 'You've been quiet the last few days. Everything OK?' I asked hesitantly.

Seeming to wake from whatever trance he'd been stuck in Nathan's eyes narrowed and focused on my mouth, which I now realised was partaking in some illegal lip chewing, then stepping around the bed he began prowling towards me smoothly like a panther. Even with the tension of the last few days I found that just these simple but overtly dominant movements had my heartbeat rocketing with arousal. Coming to stand directly before me Nathan immediately raised his good hand and used his thumb and forefinger to ease my lip from between my teeth, quietly clicking his tongue in disapproval as he did so. *I must have subconsciously started chewing on it without even realising*, I thought, as a flush of guilt coloured my cheeks. Even with Nathan's attempts to break the habit which he so hated, it seemed I still resorted to it in times of nervousness.

Fully expecting a chastisement, or perhaps even a punishment, for my breach of his rules, I was rather surprised when he instead just rubbed the pad of his thumb thoughtfully over my lip and leant forward to place a swift kiss on my mouth.

Letting out an almost inaudible sigh he stepped back and rested himself on the edge of a set of drawers, folding his sling across his chest and tucking his free hand back into his trouser pocket, continuing to stare at me with that penetrating blue gaze of his.

'I'll admit that I've been feeling a little off kilter, Stella.' He paused and raised a hand to rub at the stubble of his jaw thoughtfully, but sensing he wasn't finished yet,

I stayed quiet, observing him with growing apprehension. 'This situation has somewhat thrown me,' he said, indicating between himself and my barely rounded, but pregnant, stomach, with a flick of his wrist.

A tingle of fear slithered up my spine. He was still concerned about the baby? I thought we'd cleared all of this up in the hospital. Not to mention all the huge decisions we'd made to live together recently – he'd said he wanted to build us a house for God's sake, surely he wasn't changing his mind about that, was he? Swallowing loudly I felt a ball of nerves erupt in my stomach that must have reflected on my face because Nathan was instantly at my side again, placing his strapped arm on my lower back to steady me, and the other protectively on my belly as he gazed down at me in concern.

'Are you looking forward to the wedding next week, Stella?' he asked in a low tone, his apparent change in topic totally confusing me. He looked like he was about to impart some hideously awful news and then he asks me if I'm excited about the wedding? Did I miss something? Uncertain where he was going with this all I nodded slightly, 'Uh, well, yes, your brother is getting married to one of my closest friends, of course I'm excited.'

Nodding, Nathan began chewing on his lip again to the point where he must surely have broken the skin, then running a hand through his hair he glanced distractedly at his watch, before gazing at me apprehensively. 'Look, I know you need to get to work, so this isn't ideal timing, but there's a couple of things I need to discuss with you, Stella.'

I was working from home today, but I didn't get around to mentioning that because he was scaring the crap out of me with his mysterious comments – talk about keeping me in suspense! My stomach had basically bottomed out about five minutes ago and now all I could do was stand there like an idiot and try not to fall over from the tension that surrounded us.

'Please try and relax, Stella, I'm sorry, I'm not wording this very well ...' Letting out a frustrated breath he licked his lips, and then tried his explanation again, 'You've probably already gathered this, but I need to confess that I'm not really a fan of the marriage thing ...' Shaking his head he dropped his gaze, 'Nicholas obviously wants it, which is fine, but personally I don't see why people make such a big fuss of it, and to be honest, after witnessing my parents' joke of a marriage I just see it all as a bit farcical.'

Pausing to draw in a long deep breath Nathan stepped closer to me and met my gaze. 'The thing is, I'm concerned that it's something you might want ... especially with the baby coming ...' Running a hand through his hair again Nathan grimaced and let out a hissed breath, before taking my hand and practically dragging me to his office where he gently settled me on the sofa.

Instead of speaking straight away Nathan took a moment to pace up and down his office, his bandaged arm hanging loosely in its sling, but his good arm raised to his mouth as he chewed nervously on the nail. '*Fuck!*' he cursed, and then swung to stare at me. 'Look, if I'm honest then I'm scared shitless that you're going to leave me if I don't want to get married, Stella,' he stated in a frustrated, quivering voice. I was about to try to calm his fears with some soothing words – after all, I'd suspected this about him for some while and it didn't bother me, but he stopped me with a small shake of his head as he withdrew an envelope from his briefcase.

'In my old life as a Dominant it would have been assumed I would make you go through an official ceremony with a collar to show that you were my submissive,' he paused, joining me on the sofa as he reached across to touch the necklace that he'd given me in place of a collar. I loved it and hadn't removed since the

292

day he'd given it to me – apart from when *he* had removed it, but that was a misunderstanding that was well and truly behind us now. 'You're helping me move on from that lifestyle, but I want this,' he said, flapping the envelope in his hand. 'I want *you,* Stella.'

While I had no idea what the papers were, his words about wanting me at least helped to relax my tense shoulders, as did his next move, when he took my hand and looked me straight in the eye. 'I'm was wondering if we might be able to compromise … again,' he added dryly.

Compromise? I was completely lost now, so trying to keep up with his train of thought I gazed at the envelope in his hand. Clearing his throat Nathan removed several sheets of paper. 'The fact that I don't want to marry you doesn't lessen my commitment to you, Stella, please don't think that …' Once again he moved in an agitated fashion on the sofa, almost seeming like he didn't know what to do with himself, a complete contrast to his usual control.

After gnawing on his bottom lip Nathan finally dropped his gaze from mine, but his body remained tense, which didn't ease my nerves at all. Clearing his throat Nathan finally looked up at me. 'Fuck … I'm really bad as vocalising this stuff. Just read this,' he said, opening the envelope and removing a single sheet of paper.

Confused, I let my eyes drift down to the paper in my hands, an official looking document with the heading 'Voguel and Brand Solicitors' across the top in elegant gold font and I immediately frowned. Above the start of the typed section was a gap with a handwritten message that I immediately recognised as Nathan's writing, so taking a breath I tried to steady my trembling hand and read.

Stella,
    I struggle to describe the way I feel about you out loud, but you need to know this – you are my friend, partner,

lover, soulmate, saviour, mother of my unborn child … you are all of these to me, and yet so, so much more. You are it for me, my one, and my only. My present and my future until the day I die. Never have I been surer of anything in my life. You own my heart, body, and soul.

I love you, and so much more.

Yours always, Nathan

A lump the size of a tennis ball rose in my throat and as my eyes misted with tears I looked up to find Nathan staring at me, awaiting my response, his face at once both excited and apprehensive. 'Read on, Stella, then we'll talk,' he whispered. Nodding jerkily I was immensely glad that I hadn't done my make-up yet as I tried to blink away the tears that were threatening to spill down my cheeks. Drawing in a long breath I turned my eyes back to the paper.

In italics was a sub heading that stated 'Contractual agreement between Mr Nathaniel Peter Jackson and Miss Stella Louise Marsden'. The words that followed were full of legal terminology and jargon, but the more I read it, the clearer it became that this was an exclusivity contract. Crikey. Reading on it stated that Nathan and I would be an exclusive as a couple, just without a marriage certificate. His one stipulation was that my necklace would be upgraded, again, to one with a lock on the back that only he had a key for. At first this sounded a bit bizarre to me, but as I thought about it I knew it was fairly common practice at Club Twist for Doms to lock a collar around the neck of their long-term subs. Mulling it over I realised just what a huge statement something like this was for Nathan, a bit like his version of a wedding ring. He wanted to lock himself to me, and I smiled, deciding that I rather liked his version of compromise.

As well as stating that we would for all intents and purposes live together as man and wife, it then went on to say that I was granted full access to Nathan's money, and should we spilt for any reason I would receive half of his net worth. Holy heck. To be honest it was all quite overwhelming.

Seeing me frown as I read one particular clause Nathan moved to my side to read over my shoulder. 'Ah,' he murmured, his mood seeming to lift slightly as he placed a hand on my waist and pulled me closer to him possessively, 'I might not want to tie you to me with a formal marriage, but I'm also a hypocrite … I want our baby to have my surname, and you as well if you'll agree. I would very much like you to change your name to Jackson, Stella … People need to know you're mine.'

Blinking, I found myself speechless, something of a rarity for me. 'I understand it's not a marriage certificate, but what do you say? Will you sign it? Make us official?'

I was silent, still trying to deal with just how much of a big deal this was for someone like Nathan and feeling a little lost for words.

Apparently taking my silence as hesitation Nathan took my hand and held my gaze, 'I'm not the marrying kind, Stella, I would never want you trapped with me if things don't work out, but that doesn't mean I'm not fully committed to you.' My heart clenched at his self-doubt, the fact that he thought he'd be trapping me to him was an obvious sign that he worried that one day he might turn out to be like his father. It seemed I had more faith in him than he did himself.

'Actually, before you sign …' He dug around in the envelope again, awkwardly shifting things with his one hand, and then removed a second piece of paper which he clutched tightly. 'This is part two. Perhaps you should read it before you make your decision.'

Part two? There was *more*? I was completely gobsmacked, he'd just laid his heart on the line and basically done his own version of a proposal, and now he expected me to be able to read another piece of frigging paper? I wanted to jump up and down and scream my delight, not bloody read an essay! Clearing his throat, Nathan seemed to pause as he considered how to begin. 'Before you read, let me explain … I'm a very sexual man …' Describing himself as 'very sexual' was such an understatement that I nearly laughed out loud, but curiosity about what he might say next kept me quiet. 'As long as you are willing and in the mood, I intend for us to continue to have sex during your pregnancy, but …'

This time his pause lasted far longer than I was expecting, what the heck was the 'but' for? B*ut only if you're not too fat? But only if I still find you attractive?* But, but, but … So many thoughts were flying through my brain that my eyebrows rose so high they probably touched my hairline. 'But?' I finally questioned weakly, almost dreading his reply.

'*But*, I need to know you will be safe at all times.' Almost reluctantly Nathan moved his hand from my stomach and ran it across my hair, pushing some loose strands back behind my ears as he did so. 'I've never felt like this about anyone before, Stella, I won't risk harming you, or our baby.'

Blinking in surprise at his miniature outpouring of emotions I relaxed further now that I could see the direction of his thoughts and realised this was what he'd been talking about in the hospital when he said we'd need stipulations. 'The nurse told us sex was fine, Nathan, there's nothing to worry about,' I said, soothing a hand across his toned forearm.

Nodding slowly Nathan picked up the second piece of paper that he had retrieved from his briefcase earlier. 'I know, but let's face it, Stella, we might not have a written contract anymore, but some of the things we do together go way beyond normal sex.' Pausing, he drew in a deep breath, 'I'm more excited about your pregnancy than I even know how to vocalise,' he admitted as he gently stroked my stomach with a small smile flickering at the corners of his lips. 'It's just that I've always lived by a code. Control is a big thing to me, as you know, my rules have always featured in my life and I'm just having a little trouble adapting.'

Flushing bright red with embarrassment I was almost tempted to bite my lip again. He was right, although we did it less now, the scenes we did that involved toys, restraints, spankings, and paddles were definitely outside the lines of what might constitute 'normal' sex, and now that I thought about it, were often a fair bit rougher too. It's funny how Nathan's particular brand of sex had just become my norm now, to the point where I'd almost forgotten what plain ol' vanilla could be like. Smiling at this thought I nodded, 'OK, point taken …' I conceded, 'So what do you have in mind? I might not be showing much yet, but my pregnancy hormones are already making me horny as hell, so there's no way I'm going six months without you giving me some sexy time. The nurse said you should always give me what I want, remember?' I reminded him haughtily.

'There will be plenty of "sexy time", don't worry, Stella,' he assured me with a wicked grin before his face straightened out. 'You might recall in the hospital I mentioned adding some stipulations to our relationship, this is what I was referring to.' With that Nathan handed me the second piece of paper and gave me a chance to read it.

Placing the paper on my lap, which after a brief read I summarised was basically another contract of sorts, this time covering all sexual aspects of our relationship with a huge list of do's and don'ts. This type of contract I *didn't* need. Shaking my head I looked him directly in the eye. 'Nathan, we don't need this.' Turning to him fully I cupped his face and stared directly into his worried blue eyes. 'I trust you, *implicitly*, I know you'd never hurt me or the baby.'

Sighing, Nathan rolled off his neck. 'I know you do, and you're right, I would never hurt you intentionally, but I know that I can sometimes be rough with you.' He paused, almost looking guilty as he shifted in his seat. I liked it rough as much as Nathan did, a fact he was well aware of so he really didn't need to be plagued with any guilt at all. 'But on top of that, what we sometimes do together involves greater risks than vanilla sex and with my … *issues* with control … this whole situation is throwing me. It's way beyond the realms of my control. But this contract will set in stone the boundaries for me. As excited as I am about you carrying our baby, I *need* this,' he implored, wafting the piece of paper again with a strange, pleading expression in his eyes. Crikey, Nathaniel Jackson begging, I never thought I'd see the day.

As much as I was happy – *thrilled* – to sign the first paper, this one I wholeheartedly did not want. We might still take part in scenes where we reverted to our roles of Dominant and submissive, but as our relationship had grown so had our boundaries. Our old contract had long been ripped up in favour of a more mainstream lifestyle with the occasional kink mixed in and I liked it that way. It suited both of us perfectly, meeting the needs we had and giving our life balance, but to put our sexual limits on paper again? To me that felt like a huge step backwards.

Looking down my eyes skimmed the points he'd made on the contract; safe words to be used freely and without hesitation at any sign of discomfort. No bondage, no impact play, no rough sex, and no use of penetrative toys. The list went on, and on, *and on*. Nathan had clearly thought long and hard about this, even including things in the contract that we never even attempted, like 'no scenes involving suspension' and 'no breath play'.

Blowing my hair out of my eyes I looked at Nathan and

rolled my lips between my teeth until they formed a tight line. 'This includes things we've never even done together, Nathan. Does that mean you've always wanted to do this *stuff* to me and need it on here to remind you not to?' I asked cautiously, feeling a rumble of concern in my stomach, 'I mean – breath play? Does the idea of affecting my breathing turn you on?'

'What?' he frowned, snatching the paper from me and trailing down the list with his finger. 'Fuck. No, of course not. I must have left that on the list by mistake.' Turning to me he shrugged apologetically, 'I was feeling uneasy this morning so I emailed an acquaintance of mine, Frazer, for some advice. I met him through Club Twist, but he lives up in Scotland now. He lives a Dom/sub lifestyle with his wife that is pretty similar in setup to ours. They've got two kids and one on the way so he sent me a list of do's and don'ts that I might find useful.'

Picking up a pen from the side table he crossed out the line involving breath play, 'I was a bit rushed and obviously didn't edit it properly. I'll blame the fact that I was typing left-handed,' he murmured, shifting his bandaged arm again as he began re-scanning the rest of the list. His pen paused above the line about 'suspension' and my eyebrows rose. 'This isn't something we've done, but I'd like to try it in the future at some point if you're willing. After the pregnancy, of course.' Turning to me with a wicked glint in his eye Nathan smirked, 'You'd like it too, Stella, I'm sure of it.' Just his lower, breathy tone made my stomach clench with excitement. 'Trussed up and hanging helplessly while I tease you and pleasure you in all manner of ways ...' He left the rest of his sentence hanging and I found myself shuffling on the sofa as I became aware of moisture gathering between my thighs. Laughing at my shift Nathan similarly adjusted his groin before turning back to me with a serious expression on his face as he held the papers towards me.

'Please sign? For me? Both parts?' he asked in a softer, almost desperate voice. 'I need to know you're mine, almost as much as I need to know that I'm in control, Stella, it's really important to me. This contract will give me both of those things. Don't let the second page bother you, it just enforces the ways I can keep you safe whilst also satisfying my dominant side. It'll help keep me grounded. *I need it.*'

Watching his eyes you would never know that Nathan was laying it all on the line to me. They were fixed with determination as they flickered across my face and returned to my eyes. But I'd heard the insecurity in his declarations, and after being with Nathan for this long I knew just how big of a deal this must be for him if he was willing to open himself up to me this much.

Before I could vocalise my agreement Nathan reached up and using his one good hand preceded to pry off my precious necklace with some considerable difficulty. Then he silently reached into his pocket and removed a long black box. Clicking it open I gasped as he took out another necklace, still beautiful, but with a noticeably chunky clasp at the back. 'Think of this as my version of a wedding ring?' he asked huskily as he held the box out for me to inspect. It was gorgeous, similar in design to my old one but with the addition of some tiny light pink stones. 'Please say you'll wear this and sign the papers?' he urged me again, his tone touched with a hint of desperation now.

Raising my head I locked my stare with his. Blue pools swimming with hope and love reflected back at me and it was all I could do not to cry with happiness. 'Yes, Nathan, I'll sign. I love you.'

Before I even registered him moving I heard the box snap shut as he circled my waist with his good arm and tugged me sideways to crush me against his warm chest, 'Thank God for that, I thought you were going to say no for a second there,' he muttered into my hair, dropping a series of hot open mouthed kisses along my neck.

Finally levering myself away I gazed at the box again and smiled a huge goofy grin as I took it from his hand and opened it up again. OK, so it wasn't a huge sparkly engagement ring, but to someone like Nathan this was just as significant, if not more so, and for that reason it was utterly perfect to me. 'I love it, Nathan, thank you.'

'I'm glad.' He held my hand and gently rubbed his thumb over my knuckles. 'I wish I wasn't one handed at the moment,' he grumbled. 'Can you put it on while I lock it?' Smiling shyly I felt my heart accelerate in my chest as I took the beautiful necklace from the box and held it around my neck, securing the clasp. I felt Nathan fumbling one handed at my nape, and then heard a tiny click followed by a satisfied hum from Nathan. 'Mine,' he murmured, dropping a kiss on my neck. 'I love you, Stella.' Lowering his tone he leaned around and this time dropped a kiss by my ear, 'and so much more ...' I loved the way he repeated the words he'd written in his heartfelt note to me.

Leaning back from him I picked up the paperwork again, 'Do you have a pen?' Grinning like a little kid Nathan strolled over to the desk and retrieved a very fancy-looking fountain pen, which he handed to me. Skimming the contract again my hand hovered over the dotted line as I frowned, 'I don't want your money, Nathan,' I said, indicating to the clause that stated that I had full access to his bank accounts and would receive half of his net worth if we split.

'The clause stays,' Nathan responded in a gritty tone. 'You are carrying my child, Stella, I need to know that if something happens to me you'll both be OK financially.' Rolling his shoulders awkwardly he continued, 'And the second part about us splitting up stays too, if we did ever split up it would no doubt be down to some fuck-up I've made, and again, I'd want to know you were provided for.'

'It seems I have more faith in you than you do yourself,' I whispered as he slid an arm around my waist, but frowned. 'I'm with you, Nathan, and I love you. *All of you*, your past, your dominance … everything. You're not going to fuck up.' I stated defiantly against his lips before scrawling my name on the contract.

'There you go, hot shot, all signed. Just make sure you stick to your end of the bargain and keep me regularly serviced. Just because I'm pregnant doesn't mean I'm going to snap in two,' I joked sarcastically.

'Mockery, Stella?' he murmured ominously. Sitting up a little straighter Nathan narrowed his eyes at my sardonic comment and observed me heatedly for several seconds in a way that very quickly made my knickers even wetter than before. How he could arouse me so much without even touching me still never failed to amaze me. Taking his time, no doubt to build the anticipation, Nathan carefully folded our new contract in half, aligning the corners, and creasing the paper with the utmost precision before he placed it on the arm of the sofa and gave it one simple tap with his index finger. 'There's nothing on this new contract that says I can't keep you in line and demand pay back for these outbursts of your cheeky mouth.'

I was utterly stunned into silence by his sudden change. Not to mention *ser-i-ous-ly* turned on. When Nathan did his full domination thing it was literally one of the sexiest things I'd ever experienced, and I was thrilled that it was making an appearance now. Quite apparently signing that contract had been all he'd needed to get his Dominant mo-jo back.

'If you do a good job at this apology task, then I'll make sure you get *very* well pleasured afterwards, Stella,' he said, emphasising the word 'very' in a dark, velvety tone full of wicked promise. I was about to ask what my task would be, but then Nathan lifted his hips slightly, unzipped his trousers, and shuffled them down with his

302

good hand to free his solid erection. Then tipping his chin in the direction of the floor he smirked at me, 'On your knees, Stella.'

Even with the pretence that he was 'ordering' me to go down on him, Nathan seemed intent on looking after me even more than usual and took my hand to help me into place. Once I was knelt between his legs he nodded in satisfaction, but then before I'd even had a chance to start he frowned and set about shifting me so he could place a cushion below my knees. I nearly laughed, he'd never outwardly considered my comfort to this degree before, and besides, the study had thick, plush carpet so the pillow was quite unnecessary. I felt like reminding him that I was just in the early stages of pregnancy, not rheumatism, but I didn't complain – his little fussing motions just acted to show how much he cared.

Once he seemed content with my positioning he gave an almost imperceptible nod to signal that I could begin. Licking my lips in anticipation I wrapped a hand around his pulsing cock and began a slow lazy up and down with my fist, watching with satisfaction as his head fell back in pleasure and his usually controlled hair flopped messily across his brow. Smiling to myself at how well recovered he looked, I decided that after last week's fear of losing him I'd try to make this the best blow job of his entire life.

I desperately attempted to call to memory every woman's magazine and advice column I'd ever read about oral sex, and then set about applying what I could remember. Leaning forwards I maintained the slow pace with my hand, but gently grazed my lips against his erection, fluttering light kisses along the underside and making sure to lick at the little bundle of nerves where the head of his cock met the shaft. This move was particularly successful and had Nathan groaning and thrusting his hips upwards, seeking my mouth. After teasing him for a few more seconds by licking his tip like it was my favourite ice-cream I finally gave him what he wanted and took him into my mouth, exploring with my tongue and sucking gently.

Truthfully I wasn't great at taking him too deep into my mouth – Nathan was pretty big and I had a sensitive gag reflex, but I simulated a deeper penetration by firmly gripping the base of his shaft and wrapping my lips around the head so they nearly met the top of my hand. Moving my hand and mouth simultaneously caused Nathan to swear and start shifting restlessly below me. Although he was getting rather fidgety from excitement I noticed that Nathan was still treating me like I might break at any moment. He usually liked to sink his hands into my hair and guide the rhythm, but today he wedged his good hand below his thigh, presumably to avoid the urge of grabbing me and thrusting into my mouth with abandon.

With the cushioned knees, gentle treatment, and his obvious attempts to reign in his urge to thrust, I had to say that Nathan's self-control was rather admirable, and made me feel so loved and protected that my heart swelled in my chest and I upped my game in an attempt to make up for everything Nathan was holding back. I carefully got my teeth in on the action, gently gliding them down his shaft and following it up with soothing licks of my tongue. 'Christ, Stella! Fuck!'

I grinned at his desperate tone and hummed my appreciation around his cock, which only seemed to further fuel his arousal as I felt him swelling even more. My eyebrows rose at his response to such a simple act and I mentally added 'humming with him in my mouth' to my checklist for next time.

From the groans resonating from Nathan's throat and his barely contained movement I could tell he was fast approaching his climax and so I began to move my mouth at just the speed he liked, hollowing out my cheeks as I added in the harder sucks he loved, and got my fingers into

304

the mix by fondling his balls and perineum which made him moan loudly in appreciation and give the tiniest upward thrust in response.

Any concerns I had that Nathan might not be enjoying this 'vanilla' version of a blow job were erased the second he came; exploding into my mouth violently with a barked curse, his hips finally jutting upwards and his hand coming up to stroke my hair as he groaned my name repeatedly and gradually began to come down from his high.

Dragging me up his body he snuggled me against him and we must have stayed there for at least ten minutes in contented silence, half sitting and half lying on the sofa. 'Well, I have to say, you exceeded all expectations with that one, sweetheart,' Nathan growled, 'Now you've made my day, *my fucking year,* by signing the contract I think it's only right that I fuck you to seal the deal ...' he stated in a low tone that was saturated with lust. Considering he'd come just a few minutes ago I was still pretty amazed when he shifted below me and I felt his rock solid erection rub against my bum. Swallowing loudly at this sensation, not to mention his heated words, I felt my insides heat with the promise of things to come. Who knew that writing my name on a piece of paper could have such an impact on him?

The fire in his eyes told me that this wasn't going to be a drawn out lovemaking session, plus we'd be dangerously close to being disturbed by Marcus who was planning on coming round today whilst we were both at work to spend the day in the kitchen.

'Get naked, Stella.' There was no hesitation in my mind, my dress and underwear were gone in a flash and then Nathan was standing, grabbing my hand, and dragging me towards him and kissing me like he wanted to crawl inside me. Sliding a hand around his neck I pulled his mouth down to meet mine in a hard kiss which he returned with gusto, his hot tongue seeming to be everywhere all at once. All of a sudden the signed contract wasn't on the desk any more, and neither were his pen, briefcase, or stationary pad. All had been brushed to the side with a wild sweep of his arm. Nathan, still fully dressed just with his zip undone and cock standing out proudly, propelled himself backwards onto the desk and dragged me to him with a groan that sounded like a roar.

Nathan helped me up onto his desk so I was straddling him and then kissed me once more for good measure, 'I'd like to be the one in control, but this bloody plaster gets in the way,' he grumbled, but then his eyes flashed and he grinned up at me, 'Actually, given the circumstances of our new contract this is perfect. Give yourself to me, Stella, make love to me. I'm yours now, just as much as you are mine.'

His words were just perfect, so nodding slowly I lifted my hips and used a hand to guide him to my entrance before sinking down on him inch by inch. Even though he was underneath me there wasn't much doubt about who was in control; Nathan used a tight grip on my hip to lead our movements as our hips ground against each other, the fabric of his trousers deliciously soft against my thighs. 'I'm going to stain your trousers,' I gasped in between breaths, realising that because he was still basically dressed my excessive moisture would be rubbing all over the expensive suit.

'I don't care. Don't fucking stop, Stella,' he demanded through gritted teeth as he thrust upwards into me. With a grin I decided to be the perfect sub for a change and obediently followed his instructions.

TWENTY-NINE – NICHOLAS

'That *surely* must be everything?' Scratching my head I looked at the stack of decorations, name cards, table plans, and boxes of gifts scattered on the dining room table. Shaking my head in disbelief I blew out a breath and looked across at Rebecca, who was also eyeing the pile while nervously chewing on her finger nail with a very cute frown creasing her eyebrows.

'Umm … I think so.' Seeing her wince as she caught a bit of skin in her chewing, I rounded the table and gently eased her hand away from her nibbling teeth before pulling her into my arms. 'Hey, stop chewing, you'll ruin your nails.' I wasn't exactly up on the latest manicure trends, but I was fairly sure that chewing on them just a day after they'd been done probably wasn't ideal. Not that I cared what her nails looked like, I was marrying *my* Rebecca, the woman that had made her way inside my messed up heart and head, and after a good look around at all the crap stowed away in there, had miraculously decided to stick around.

I didn't need her all primped and prettied, as far I was concerned Rebecca was perfect as she was. Stella and Louise, however, had had other plans and had surprised Rebecca with a spa trip yesterday in preparation for the big day tomorrow. They'd been gone for most of the afternoon and when she had finally walked back in the front door Rebecca had looked so utterly relaxed from her facial, massage, and manicure that it was almost enough to tempt

307

me to try it. Only the massage part, obviously – the girly facial and manicures I'd leave for Becky.

Holding her close to my chest I rested my chin on top of her head and felt a grin stretch my lips as I surveyed the bombsite of my dining room. All the mess was worth it, because tomorrow I was marrying Rebecca. I couldn't believe it had come round so quickly, but I couldn't be bloody happier. She would finally be mine for good, and I couldn't wait. 'Stella's got the list of things we need,' she murmured into my chest, 'Let me go and tick things off then we can start packing the car.' Placing a kiss above my heart Rebecca hurried off in search of Stella just as Nathan appeared in the doorway.

'If it's OK, I really need to leave now, Nicholas, I just had a call about that house I mentioned to you earlier. It seems like the vendor might consider a slightly earlier sale if I view it today and give an answer by tonight.'

'Is this the one in Belgravia?' I enquired as I started to box up everything on the table ready for our drive up to the lakes.

'No, even if you and I had combined our money that one would have taken us to near bankruptcy!' Nathan laughed, and I smiled affectionately at his easy laughter. The difference in my brother since he'd made things more serious and 'vanilla' with Stella really was astounding; smiles, humour, he had even eased up on some of his obsessive ways. Possibly for the first time in our lives I was seeing him genuinely happy. After all he'd done for me I sincerely believed that he deserved it more than anyone.

'Do you have any idea how much a six-bedroomed house in Belgravia costs these days? Tens of millions! Fuck me, I thought I was up on the property market given my job, but I nearly died when the estate agent told me the cost of the first place I'd enquired about! Sixty-nine million pounds!' Shaking his head Nathan blew out an amused breath, 'I mean I know I'm well off, but not *that* well off!' he said with another laugh. 'My plan had been to buy a place as an investment and then rent it out when Stella and I move into the house I'll build, but I'm reconsidering now. I might speed up the schedule for our own build and just rent one in the meantime.'

'Sounds sensible.' I loved my townhouse, but I have to say I had actually been a little jealous when Nathan had told me his plans for designing and building a house for him and Stella somewhere outside of London. I liked London, and I knew Becky loved it, but sometimes all the crowds and bustle were too much for me. Although seeing as Nathan was my only family I could easily see Rebecca and I moving out somewhere close by them once they were settled, or at least buying a second smaller property so we could visit frequently.

'This house is much cheaper and technically not on the market until tomorrow. It's the one I mentioned in South Hampstead, so not far from here, really. Three bedrooms, nice road. The house has a garden, but there's also a private park for residents running along the centre of the street. The vendor will consider sale or rental, so we can choose.'

'Sounds perfect, you should get over there now and seal the deal.' We were pretty much ready to set off now anyway. Besides, the morning rush hour was over, so this was the perfect time to be driving out of central London. As far as I was concerned, the quicker we got on the road, the sooner we would be arriving at the hotel and then it would just be a matter of one night before I'd be marrying my girl. Thinking of the word 'marrying', something I'd noticed earlier sprung back to my ever curious mind.

'By the way, bro, that's a nice necklace Stella has on today.' Stella had her hair up when they arrived early in the morning to help us get organised, and the clasp on the back of her necklace had immediately caught my eye. To your

309

average person on the street it would probably just a look a bit chunky, but I'd seen enough collared subs around Club Twist to recognise that clasp design anywhere – it was the work of Diango, a jeweller used by many of the clubs patrons.

The look on Nathan's face was a picture; his eyes darted to mine then away again and his cheeks actually flushed. 'Hmm. Yes, it's new,' was all the reply I got, which only hastened my curiosity. I had kept my tone casual for my first questions, but I was prepared to dig a little deeper to see if my suspicions were correct. It seemed Nathan was intent on being cagy with me about it, so fine, I'd simply push for more information.

'Did you buy it for her?' Again I used a mild tone, but I watched as Nathan scratched almost viciously at the back of his neck in his discomfort.

'*Fuck*. I wasn't trying to beat you to it, or compete with you, brother,' he explained sheepishly as my eyebrows rose. I'm not sure I'd ever seen Nathan demonstrate real actual guilt on his face, but that realisation was pushed aside by the more important thought at the forefront of my mind – *I'd been right*. 'You collared Stella? Like officially?' I asked in astonishment, almost in disbelief at this gigantic step for my brother.

Once again Nathan's eyes darted around the room until finally he expelled a gigantic breath and looked me straight in the eye. 'Yes. I'm not keen on the whole marrying thing … I think after Mum and Dad … and then the way I've lived my life, I don't know, I guess it put me off.' Pulling out a dining room chair Nathan sat down, looking very much like he was about to fall down, so following suit I did the same, my eyes riveted to my big brother. 'But Stella … *fuck*.' He shook his head in wonder, and I knew just what he was experiencing, because it was the way I felt every time I thought about Rebecca.

'I can't be without her, Nicholas, and I couldn't risk

losing her if she knew I didn't want to get married, so I did the only thing I'm capable of and offered her this link with me.' I nodded my head in understanding, seeing as Nathan had told me that their relationship was mostly vanilla but with some aspects of Dom/sub living thrown in, it made perfect sense, really. 'It's another compromise to add to the many that have come before,' he said with a dry laugh. 'Anyway, after finding out about the baby I didn't want to wait any longer to ask her, so I did it last week and she said yes.'

I felt my chest puff with pride at the huge step that Nathan was taking and I reached across and gave him a hearty slap on his shoulder – his uninjured one – before smiling. 'Congratulations, Nathan. I think you two are perfectly suited.'

Nathan looked a little bashful, staring at the table in embarrassment, but I didn't miss the smile that tugged at the corner of his mouth. 'Thanks, brother, I think so too. She's amazing. I'm sorry it's just before your wedding, believe me, that wasn't intentional. After I got out of hospital it hit me how close I'd come to ... well ... let's just say it made me realise what was important and I knew I just had to make her mine.'

Nathan's accident had put things into perspective for me too, all those days sat in the hospital thinking I was going to lose him, the man that had saved me all those years ago, had been unbearable. I didn't care when, how, or where he'd sorted out things with Stella, I was just pleased that he'd done it. Trying to ease his concerns I gave a firm shake of my head. 'Don't be daft, I think it's excellent news. Did you have the full collaring ceremony at Club Twist?' I asked, marginally hurt that if he did, he hadn't invited me.

'God no. We hardly go there anymore now. It was just the two of us. I kind of caught Stella unaware actually, sprang it on her, but luckily it all turned out all right in the end.' Just then we heard the mumble of voices signalling the return of Rebecca and Stella to the dining room so after giving my brother one more reassuring wink we stood up to meet them.

'Well, super organiser Stella says we have everything we need now,' Rebecca said with a grin, indicating to the huge handwritten list that had spent the last two months stuck to our fridge and being amended and updated daily – probably hourly, actually.

'You sure there's nothing else we can help with?' Nathan questioned shrugging his jacket on.

'I think we're good, brother. Thank you both for coming round so early to help us out.' With our wedding being up in the Lake District it wasn't exactly like we could 'pop home' if we forgot something, so I knew that having Stella check over the list of things would help put Becky's mind at ease. 'Just don't forget the rings, will you?' I said in a solemn tone. My brother was so controlled over everything in his life that losing the rings was *not* something I had any worries about, but Nathan was so easy to wind up that a little joke never went amiss.

'Give me some credit, Nicholas, do you seriously think I would fuck this up for you?' he muttered as he straightened his cuffs. Despite the slightly stressful start to the day I was in a seriously good mood and very tempted to tease him further, but at the reproachful look Rebecca flashed me I relented and grinned at him instead. 'I know they're in safe hands, Nathan, I was kidding. So, you'll be driving up to the hotel this afternoon after viewing this house?' I confirmed.

Sliding an arm around Stella's waist Nathan nodded. 'Yes, we shouldn't be on the road much after you, actually. Once we arrive I'll drop Stella off at Rebecca's parents' house then drive over to the hotel and we can relax with a few drinks in the bar.'

'And we can settle in for some bubbly with your mum

and sister!' Stella said enthusiastically, but then almost immediately sighed as Nathan gave her a disapproving look. 'Well, you can all have the bubbles. I'll stick to grape juice,' she joked with a roll of her eyes as she rested a hand on her tummy and smiled up at Nathan. I still couldn't quite believe that my brother was going to be a father, but as I watched the way his eyes drifted to Stella's stomach and a tiny smile curve his lips I just instinctively knew that he would be great at it.

THIRTY – REBECCA

I couldn't believe it was finally here. The big day. The day I would vow to love and honour Nicholas until death did us in. *Our wedding day.* And to top it all off it was an absolutely beautiful day – the sun was shining and there wasn't a cloud in the sky, which for late March was pretty lucky. Someone somewhere was obviously looking out for us today.

Shaking my head in disbelief at my sheer luck I smiled. Wow. It felt quite surreal actually, all of us girls crowded into Mum's living room – we were down here because it was bigger than the bedrooms – and I gazed around at my closest family, Mum and Joanne, and my best friends in the world Stella and Louise and just tried to soak up the excited atmosphere and commit it all to memory.

Smiling affectionately I watched Mum and Louise as they fussed over Joanne's hair, pinning and clipping it in various different trial runs as they tried to decide what style would best suit her for the day. It had taken a little persuasion, but after several long visits to Joanne in the residential centre where she lived, my sister had decided that she *would* like to be involved in my big day after all and so was being my third bridesmaid. Considering her condition this was a pretty big deal to not only her, but me and Mum too. Obviously with her fear of crowds and strangers Jo couldn't travel on public transport, there were far too many possible triggers for her, and squeezing her in the car with Nicholas, me, and all the garb we'd needed to bring up for the wedding yesterday had been impossible, so my parents had driven down earlier in the week to get her. To be honest, I knew my mum would love it if Joanne lived up with them, or in a care home near them, but for now my sister was content to be near me.

I heard a muffled banging in the hallway outside the door to the living room and then it swung open as Stella waltzed in carrying a tray containing a bottle of fizz, a small jug of orange juice, and five glasses. 'I might not be able to drink, but I decided we may as well start the day off as we may to go on!' Placing the tray down she looked over to us with the champagne bottle hovering above the glasses. 'What's it to be, ladies? Champagne, Buck's Fizz, or boring old orange juice like me?'

'Champagne, please!' I chorused at the same time as Mum and Louise. I was feeling a little nervy so a glass or two of fizz might help to relax me. Only one or two though, I didn't want to be tipsy and falling down the stairs at the hotel as I made my grand entrance. Stella poured and disturbed the bubbling glasses before filling an orange juice for herself and turning to Joanne who was looking a bit unsure. Walking over to my sister I sat down and slid my arm around her waist. 'Glass of fizz?' I asked softly, 'You can have one or two without affecting your meds, I checked with Nurse Claudine yesterday.' I felt her relax against me before she looked to Stella with a shy smile and accepted a glass of champagne.

My mum suddenly cleared her throat and raised her glass. 'To my two wonderful daughters!' she managed, before choking back a sob and dashing towards Jo and me for a three-way hug. Clutching at them both I suddenly felt an immense wave of emotion sweep over me; partly from the excitement of the day, but also because a rush of memories about my sister's attempted suicide flooded my brain. Even though she had a few issues now and would probably always be on the medication to keep her calm, I was so very grateful that she had survived.

316

'You two are squashing me!' Jo squeaked from somewhere in between me and Mum, and as I released my grip and saw the tears rolling down Mum's face I suspected she was experiencing a similar set of feelings to me right now.

'Enough of the tears! This is a happy day!' Louise said, picking up her make-up bag and straighteners. Louise was one of those women who was just instinctively good at doing hair and make-up, unlike me, who was the complete opposite. As a wedding gift she'd offered to do me, Mum and all the bridesmaids today, which was not only very kind, but also saved the stress of having another stranger here with Joanne too. 'Mum's already done, although you might need a bit of a touch up with waterproof mascara now you've been crying, Leanne! Who's ready to go next?' she asked, wiggling the make-up in the air.

'Oh! Me!' Jo squawked, plonking her glass down and jumping from her chair. 'I'm already showered and I loved the way you had my hair, can you make it look like that again?' Jo asked, just as I heard Mum mumbling to Louise that she didn't need clumpy waterproof mascara and that she just had something in her eye. Louise held back her laughter and instead flashed me a wink as she headed over to my sister and set down her bag. 'Waterproof, Leanne, it's the way forward,' she announced to my mother, before looking back to Joanne. 'Of course I can re-do that hair style, it looked beautiful, and I'll do your make-up if you like?'

As I sipped on the deliciously cool champagne and allowed the chaos around me to continue I saw Stella wave the bottle at me before heading my way to give me a top up. The champers was relaxing me nicely, but I wouldn't have too much more; as well as worrying about falling over I also wanted to remember every detail of today. Giggling, she nudged me playfully in the ribs, 'So Miss Langley, soon to be Mrs Jackson, how are you feeling?'

At the thought of being Mrs Jackson and being married to Nicholas I couldn't help but grin broadly, because as sappy as it sounds, he really was the love of my life. 'Pretty amazing, really.' There was one thing niggling at the back of my mind, but I'd been repeatedly telling myself I was being stupid so pushed it down yet again and decided not to mention it.

'What's the matter?' Stella asked suddenly, causing me to turn to her swiftly. How did she know what I was thinking? Seeing my look of shock she rolled her eyes at me and then reached up to tug my hand away from my hair where it had been frantically twirling and tucking a strand behind my ear. 'You're one of my closest friends, do you think I hadn't noticed that you do this when you get anxious?'

God, could everyone read me that easily? Nicholas had spotted my 'little tell' within hours of meeting me, although sometimes I felt completely transparent to him so it wasn't surprising, but now with Stella's words it became quite apparent that my traits were obvious to others beyond him. Well wasn't that just frigging marvellous?

Jerking my head to indicate that we move out of earshot of the others we took a few steps back for more privacy. 'I'm fine, no last minute nerves. I promise,' I told Stella honestly. 'The thing is, I am a little worried about Nicholas backing out.'

Frowning, Stella immediately shook her head, 'There's no way he'd do that. He's completely head over heels with you, Becks.'

Nodding I chewed on my lip. 'I know, but … our men aren't exactly relationship experts, are they? I keep panicking that I'm pushing this all on him and that he's going to freak out today.' This had been my fear for a few months now, for a guy like Nicholas with basically no relationship experience this must all seem completely mental to him.

It had turned out to be really convenient that Nicholas and Nathan's relationship pasts had certain similarities, because it was so good to be able to talk completely frankly with Stella about Nicholas and his issues without fear of judgement. Almost as soon as I'd said it I felt a relief just from having shared my concern and was immediately thankful for just how close Stella and I had grown since meeting.

Stella's right hand rose up and began to fiddle with her necklace as a wistful look crossed her face before she nodded, 'True. But he's the one who proposed to you, he wants to be with you, Becky. And besides, you've kept the wedding pretty small to lessen the stress for him. He might be totally smitten with you, but he's a tough enough guy to stand up for himself if he had really disagreed with any of the plans.'

I ran this through my head a few times and decided that Stella was probably right. I was no doubt panicking about nothing. 'Would you put my mind at rest by giving Nathan a call for me to check that everything's going smoothly over at the hotel?'

'Of course. I'll call him now. You need to go and get your hair and make-up on, it's only two hours until we need to leave.'

Glancing around the chaos of Mum's bombsite of a living room I could at least see some semblance of readiness beginning to emerge from the piles of breakfast plates, clothes, hangers, and make-up; Stella was dressed and looking gorgeous – Nathan was going to blow a gasket when he saw her – Mum was almost done, she was dressed and her hair was styled but she still needed her make-up re-touching. And there in the centre was Joanne, looking a little timid but beautiful in her navy silk bridesmaid dress, her hair all clipped up like a model and the final touches to her make-up being done.

Sipping my champagne I heard Stella giggle on the

phone and felt my shoulders instantaneously relax; if she was laughing everything must be fine over with the brothers. Phew. As she ended the call I watched her make her way around the discarded shoes and champagne bottles towards me, still smiling. 'I told you there was no need to panic. Nathan says everything's fine.'

In my relief I took a large gulp of my champagne, choked slightly, and very nearly sprayed it all over Stella. 'Nathan said there is not a cold foot in sight. In fact, Nicholas is so excited about marrying you that apparently he tried to call the registrar to bring everything forward by an hour.' This time I really did spray some champagne, but thankfully it just sort of escaped my mouth and dribbled down my chin rather than spraying Stella's gorgeous outfit. Nicholas tried to bring the whole thing forwards? Was he insane? Seeing my panic Stella grinned, 'Don't worry, it was just a moment of madness. Apparently they're nearly ready now and are planning on heading down to the bar to greet everyone soon.'

My eyebrows rose at this news – Nicholas and Nathan, both a little awkward in company and prone to being rather blunt, would be greeting my nearest and dearest … God, it almost didn't bear to think about!

An hour and ten minutes later and I was more primped than I had ever been in my entire life. Getting ready for a night out never took me longer than half an hour, but today I'd been subjected to curling tongs, a bronzer brush, eyelash curling … you name it, I'd had it! My stipulation had been to keep it simple, and although I'd been fussed over for over an hour, I had to say I was thrilled with the outcome. Light, natural make-up which emphasised my eyes, a classic up-do for my hair with several expertly curled strands hanging loose, and a light touch of gloss on my lips. I looked stylish, but down to earth, which was very me. In other words – perfect.

'OK. Now for the gown!' Mum cooed happily, sweeping in with the huge white bag hung over her arm. Luckily I could step into the dress, so my hair and make-up could remain un-harmed. This hadn't been a deliberate factor when choosing, but it was working out rather well now.

After Stella and Louise had finished pulling me about as they faffed with tightening the multitude of laces on the rear of the bodice – those lessons in the bridal shop had obviously paid off – I felt utterly snug as they finally released me as Mum dragged in the floor length mirror from the hall. Turning around I got the first look at myself done up to the nines, and upon hearing Mum's sob next to me I almost started crying myself. Thankfully I managed to hold myself together and get a proper look, deciding that after the numerous options I'd had, this dress really was 'the one'.

It was a strapless gown with an A-line cut and a sweetheart neckline. The bodice was pulled in tight thanks to Louise and Stella's torture, and then the waist dropped down to pool the fabric at my feet. There wasn't a train as such, I was far too clumsy to wear one without coming a cropper, but it kinked out enough to at least give the illusion of a small train.

The sound of a car crunching up my parents gravel driveway drew my attention away from the mirror towards the window and my eyes instantly widened. 'Oh my gosh! I thought we were going in Dad's car? Did you know about this, Mum?' I asked as I watched a beautiful vintage car come to a stop outside.

'Nicholas phoned up a few weeks ago to say that he'd ordered a car to take us to the wedding, but he didn't mention that it was a vintage Rolls-Royce!' my mum shrieked.

Grinning in delight I looked back out of the window at the stunning car. It had white and pale pink ribbons tied across the front, and even a few smaller navy ones to match the bridesmaid dresses. It was perfect, what an amazing gesture from Nicholas.

After some photographs with my bridesmaids and a good few with the car, and the lovely driver called George, we all climbed in and got ourselves settled. Joanne sat beside me and took a tight hold of my hand while Mum sorted out yet another tissue from her handbag to dab at her eyes. 'See, Leanne, this is why I used the waterproof mascara the second time round,' Louise said haughtily before grinning at me.

'Ooh! Wait!' Mum cried, causing the driver to pause and turn to us all. 'How does the rhyme go? "Something old, something new, something borrowed, something blue, and a sixpence in your shoe." Have we got all that sorted?' Mum demanded. 'It's unlucky if you haven't,' she informed me in a serious tone. I just loved the way she chose now to say this, sat in the bloody car ready to leave, and then deems it to be unlucky if I don't have them. Where the hell was I going to magic a sixpence from?

'I've got the garter that Louise has lent me, that's borrowed, and the cornflowers in my bouquet are blue,' I said, mulling over what my something new and old could be.

'The clips I've used in your hair are Victorian,' Louise said helpfully, 'Now you just need something new … and a sixpence, but I think we might have to forego that. I've a got a five pence if that helps?'

'Ta-da!' Stella announced from across the car, pulling a small silver coin from within her handbag. 'I'd nearly forgotten about it!' she said, handing me the coin. Sure enough, looking at the writing it stated that it was a sixpence. Looking at her in utter bewilderment, she simply shrugged and grinned, 'You can get pretty much anything on eBay these days.'

Slipping one of my white silk shoes off, I popped the

small coin under the inner sole and replaced it on my foot. 'Wow, thanks, Stella. Your super organisation knows no bounds!' I joked. I wasn't particularly superstitious, but where this wedding was concerned I'd do everything in my power to get it running smoothly.

'Just "something new" now then. My dress is new. So are my knickers. Will they do?' I asked with a lift of my shoulders as I saw my mum flush at the mention of my wedding pants. Technically I had two pairs, one I had on now and then a second 'special' pair for later. They were fabulous, Nicholas was going to love them.

Fishing around in her handbag I assumed Mum was avoiding eye contact because she was a bit embarrassed, but she suddenly produced a small, black velvet box. 'Your dress and, uh hum ... underwear are new, but Nicholas asked me to give you this as a special something new.' A gift? Now? Taking the box I opened it to reveal a beautiful pair of earrings. Silver drop studs, or perhaps platinum knowing Nicholas' fondness for extravagance, finished with a small diamond on the end of each. Simple yet elegant and just stunning.

'Wow,' Louise breathed from beside me. 'They are gorgeous. I don't suppose Nicholas has any rich brothers, does he?' she enquired, only to be met by an imperious look from Stella and a giggle from me. 'I mean *other* rich brothers, obviously.' Louise huffed in embarrassment, before holding out her hand for the simple studs I had been wearing so I could replace them with the new ones.

'Ready now?' Stella enquired with a smile. Drawing in a deep breath I nodded, touched the earrings with a smile, and then broke out into an excited grin. Oddly enough, I wasn't nervous at all. Nicholas was the man for me, I had no reservations whatsoever. In fact, I couldn't wait.

'Let's get this show on the road, George! Take my girl to get married!' Mum cried giddily.

NICHOLAS

Trying to get the white rose straight in my buttonhole I glanced across at Nathan and smirked when I saw him having the exact same trouble – the only difference was that he was attempting to do it one handed, so was also cursing colourfully under his breath, and being so violent with the flower that it was a wonder it hadn't snapped in two. As I watched my brother I noticed his adapted jacket; the tailor I'd hired last week to adjust Nathan's suit to fit his sling really had done a brilliant job. 'I forgot to ask, who was that on the phone earlier? Nothing important about today?'

Pulling the flower out and dumping it on the counter, he gave me a fierce look. 'You're the one getting married, why do I need a fucking flower?' But nothing could upset my good mood today, not even Nathan's false irritation so I merely chuckled in response. 'It was Stella on the phone,' he replied, before picking up the rose again and having another reluctant attempt.

'Why was Stella calling? Is Rebecca OK?' I sounded a bit breathless as a sudden burst of irrational nerves hit me square in the centre of my chest. In reply Nathan looked at me, rolled his eyes, and laughed, which just left me standing there blinking at him in confusion. 'You two are fucking perfect for each other,' he muttered as he finished his rose and gave it one final pat. 'Rebecca was worried about you as well. Stella was just checking all was good at this end so she could put the bride-to-be's mind at rest.' Thank God for that. A huge wheezing noise escaped my lungs as normal breathing resumed.

Walking over to the mini-bar in the room Nathan used his left hand to remove the glass stopper from a decanter half full of whisky and poured two glasses. Handing one to me he returned and picked the other one up for himself before swirling the amber liquid several times and turning to me with a small smile. 'You ready, brother?'

Truth be told, I couldn't be *more* ready. I was so excited that my stomach was churning and twisting itself into knots, but this wasn't the slightly sickening nerves I often got before I played a concert, this was an eager, excited type of anxiousness and I was relishing every single second of it. 'I am,' was the only reply I could really say without getting overly emotional with Nathan, who would probably want to avoid such sentimentality.

It seemed my fears about Nathan not wanting me to get overly expressive weren't warranted though, because the next second he swigged down half of his whisky, cleared his throat, and then looked up at me with a rather serious expression on his face. 'Nicholas, before we go down, I just wanted to say …' pausing he cleared his throat again and shifted his bandaged arm in its sling before resuming eye contact, 'I … I'm really fucking proud of you.' Shaking his head he gave me an ironic twitch of his eyebrows, as if he too knew just how out of character it was for him to be this demonstrative. 'After all the shit you went through,' he hesitated again and I couldn't help but jump in. '*We* went through, Nathan. You were there too.'

Shrugging he shook his head again, 'Yeah, but you had it far worse than me. Anyway, I'm not trying to put a downer on the day, I just wanted to say I'll always have your back Nicholas, you know that, but you and Rebecca, it just seems meant to be. I'm so pleased to see you so settled and happy.'

Unable to stop myself I stepped forwards and gave my

brother an attempt at a man hug. With his arm in a cast it was a bit awkward, but I at least managed to half hug him and pat him on the back. 'It goes both ways, Nathan. I'm proud of you too, brother.'

Once I had stepped away we stood there speechless for a few seconds until it was apparent that our little emotional outpour was over.

Trying to lighten the mood a bit I stepped back and grinned, 'You're not going to give me a talk on the birds and bees as well, are you?'

Smirking, Nathan doubled checked that he had the box with the rings in it by patting his inside pocket, then gave me a thoroughly smutty look. 'Nah, if the conversations I've overheard between Stella and Rebecca are anything to go on I think you got that stuff down, bro.' Blinking as I digested his words my mouth opened to speak, but I didn't have a clue what to say. How did you respond to information like that?

'Fucking hell, Nicholas, I'm joking, man! Close your mouth. I've never overheard them talking about us. Although I'm sure they do, that's what women do, apparently.' Shaking his head in amusement Nathan then winced, but still had a slightly cocky smile on his face, 'God only knows what Stella says about me. Christ, I dread to think.' He glanced at the clock on the mantelpiece and jerked his head towards the door. 'Enough girly chit-chat. Let's go and get you married.'

Sucking in a large breath I felt the back of my neck prickle with apprehension as the little hairs stood on end. I didn't want to turn around. I knew that if I did I would see a room full of people staring at me, most of whom I'd never met before in my life. I'd heard the shuffle of feet and quiet conversation as the guests had been filing into the elegant wood panelled room and taking their seats over the past twenty minutes, but I hadn't turned around once. I hated people watching me, it was quite ironic really, seeing as my trade of concert pianist meant I had to deal with crowds regularly, but there you go, it was just one of my odd quirks. Thank God Nathan was stood by my side keeping me calm or I might very well have sought out Rebecca and forced her to forget about the wedding and elope with me instead.

Nathan had told me that deep breaths would help, so that's exactly what I did as I stood staring fixedly at the top of the stairs, waiting for Rebecca to emerge. *In through my nose, out through my mouth. In through my nose, out through my mouth.* The set-up of our ceremony was slightly different to the usual; instead of coming in the back of the room and walking down the aisle to me, Rebecca would descend the ornate carved staircase in front of me until she was by my side. This way everyone had the pleasure of the view over the lake out of the windows. Of course it also had the added bonus of meaning that I could keep my back to the crowd the entire time, which was just fine by me.

As predicted, the ceremony only involved fifty people. Most of the gathered revellers were Rebecca's family and friends with the exception of one row for my chosen few guests. Not that I minded, to be honest this was all for her benefit anyway, all I wanted was for Becky to be my wife.

I wanted the world to know that she was mine and that I intended to have her for the rest of her life. Now it was just a matter of her arriving …

THIRTY-ONE – REBECCA

'We're going to be late,' I groaned as Louise faffed with my hair for the hundredth time and insisted on re-pinning the bit behind my left ear.

We had arrived at the hotel in plenty of time and had been in the specially allocated preparation room for nearly an hour now. I'd spent at least twenty minutes chatting to the registrar who ran through the order of events again and put my mind at ease, and now Louise was puffing, tweaking, and beautifying us all again.

'You're the bride, it's traditional to be a little late.'

Frowning, I fidgeted before gently batting her hand away. 'Well I don't want to be late. Stuff tradition, let's go.' The real reason for my urgency was that I knew Nicholas would be going crazy if I were even a minute or two late. To a stranger Nicholas must appear calm, demanding, dominant, and together, but after all the time we'd been together I knew the layer below that façade now. He *was* dominant and demanding, but Nicholas could also be incredibly insecure, especially where it came to me. I was probably one of the only people who saw that side to him. Apparently I was his weakness. Mind you, he was mine as well.

'OK, everyone in order!' Stella instructed. 'Louise, you're going first, then me and Jo and then you and your dad.' We shuffled ourselves into a little procession as Louise pulled open the door to our suite. Seeing as I didn't have a train on my dress that needed lifting I'd decided to be slightly mean and make my bridesmaids go first into the room. That way the attention wouldn't be immediately on me. Claudine, my sister's nurse, was also with us at the moment, just in case Jo changed her mind and wanted to return to the balcony area to just watch.

My heart was pounding. Not from nerves about marrying Nicholas, I was actually more concerned about falling down the sodding stairs. Entering via the beautifully carved staircase was going to make a great entrance to the ceremony – only if I could avoid my usual clumsiness and not tumble down them. A nervous giggle rose in my throat as I tried to imagine the look on Nicholas' face if I bowled down the steps and landed in a shrieking heap of silk and lace by his feet. Taking in a deep breath to reduce my near hysteria I stepped up to Dad, who held out the crook of his arm to me and gave me a wink. 'You look beautiful, Rebecca. I'm so proud of you,' he murmured, his eyes glazing up as he rapidly blinked to clear them.

'Thanks, Dad.' My voice was thick with emotion, but I was determined not to cry again. I wanted to look my best for Nicholas now, not tear-stained and puffy; besides, Louise was like the make-up mafia and would probably demand we delay our departure so she could re-do me if she saw so much as a single tear stain on my cheek.

It felt quite surreal as we stepped out on the walkway that ran around the perimeter of the room below. I didn't dare look down yet, but there was a static buzz in the air that told me that even though it was quiet, there were lots of people packed into the space. Seeing us emerge onto the balcony, the harpist began to play to announce our arrival. Picking my entrance song hadn't been too tricky, Nicholas and I had both agreed on Pachelbel's 'Canon' as a beautiful choice, but selecting the musician had been an absolute nightmare. Nicholas was such a musical snob. He didn't want a pianist because he said he'd be able to pick up any mistakes they made and it would ruin the day for him. Violins were out too, because his father used to play one. So that left us a little limited, I mean you can hardly walk down the aisle to a trumpet fanfare, can you? Now that I was preparing to descend the stairs and the soothing tones of the harp were surrounding me I was glad we'd opted for it; the floaty, gentle nature was perfect for calming me.

The staircase curved around two walls as it descended into the room below, so it was split into two flights, the top being the longest, before it curved with just seven steps taking me to the ground floor. As I placed my foot on the top step the bridesmaids in front of me suddenly drew to a halt and I saw Stella briefly lean her head into Joanne before flashing me a concerned glance. Jo was turning, coming back up the stairs, her face stricken and eyes wide. 'I'm sorry. I'm ruining everything. Everything. I can't do it. Can't.' Her rambling told me that Joanne was having a little moment and instead of speaking straight away I pulled my sister in for a tight hug and simply held her to me. 'Just having you here has made this day perfect, Jo-Jo.' I murmured softly into her ear. 'It's totally fine, nothing is ruined. Go and enjoy the ceremony from the balcony with Claudine and I'll see you after, OK?' I heard Jo snuffle and then she leant back and nodded, a small smile on her face.

'OK, love you, Becks,' she murmured, and despite all my good intentions not to cry I felt myself welling up.

'Love you too.'

Claudine flashed me a reassuring nod and smile before helping Joanne back up the stairs and around to a seated area overlooking the main room. Taking a deep breath I heard the harpist continuing her loop of the song and nodded to Louise and Stella, who were now side by side, that we were good to continue.

It was only once I was down the main staircase that I

allowed myself my first proper glance around. First my eyes swept the room and I saw that it was decorated like a fairy tale with lit candles on every available surface filling the air with my favourite scent of orange blossom. Tasteful ribbons and flower arrangements were scattered about, containing the white of my dress and the blue of the bridesmaids. Next I took in the smiling faces of my family and friends, coming to rest briefly on my mum, who was smiling, but patting the corners of her eyes at the same time, still looking relatively composed – looked like the waterproof mascara had come to the rescue again.

Finally as Dad guided me onto the last seven steps I allowed myself to look at Nicholas. My heart either stopped, or was suddenly beating so fast that I couldn't feel it, one or the other, I wasn't sure, because he looked utterly stunning. The wedding suit he wore consisted of dark grey tailored trousers, almost black, a lighter grey jacket with tails, crisp white shirt, navy blue silk waistcoat, and matching blue tie. Wow. He looked even better than he did in his concert suit, and that was a pretty big statement. His posture was perfect too, as always, confident and upright and his dark hair was actually behaving today, pushed neatly off his forehead.

As soon as my eyes met his blue ones my world pretty much stopped turning. The love, desire, devotion, and intensity in Nicholas' gaze was truly breath-taking. Our eyes remained locked as Dad delivered me to his side. Leaning in to place a kiss on my cheek Dad then took my hand and placed it in Nicholas' outstretched palm. 'Look after my little girl,' Dad murmured, his voice sounding all odd and squeaky. 'As if my life depends upon it, sir,' Nicholas replied, before my dad gave Nicholas a pat on the shoulder and took his place beside Mum in the front row.

I know everyone tells you to try and stay in the moment so you can remember all the details of the ceremony later, but I just didn't manage it. As soon as my eyes met

Nicholas' my entire focus had been on him. I hardly remember speaking when prompted, but I must have, because the next thing I knew there was a round of applause from the chairs behind me and Nicholas was leaning in to place a heated kiss on my lips. 'That makes you mine now, *Mrs Jackson*,' Nicholas hummed against my lips before deepening our contact until my head was spinning and I heard wolf-whistles from the crowd.

Mrs Jackson. I was married. To Nicholas! A huge grin split my lips and I flung my arms around his neck, giggling happily as he spun me around several times. Placing me down he ducked his head by my ear. 'You look absolutely stunningly beautiful, Rebecca. You've made me the happiest man alive.'

Leaning back I could see the same depth of feelings in his eyes as must surely be reflected in mine. But right now I was too overcome to speak so I bit down on my lower lip to stop me crying and simply nodded instead.

My eyes were drawn to the wedding band on Nicholas' finger as it caught the light from the large windows, and I couldn't help but smile. That was such a sexy sight. Our wedding ring on his finger, showing the world he was mine. Letting out a contented sigh I glanced down at my own beautiful rings; to match my engagement ring the wedding ring was a simple platinum band, but it had a central line of tiny diamonds encrusted within it. It was absolutely beautiful, and picked by Nicholas, which made it even more special to me.

'Let me lead you out, *wife*,' Nicholas said with a smirk, an expression I couldn't help but reflect.

'Please do, *husband*.' It was cheesy, but I was pretty sure we'd be using those terms quite a bit in the weeks and months to come.

Oh God, it was *that* time in the proceedings. The speeches by both the Jackson brothers. The day had been completely unbeatable so far, quite simply the best I could ever have hoped for. But to say I was nervous about this part was an understatement. My dad had gone first, and his speech had been quite funny and light-hearted, perfect really, but now it was time for Nicholas and Nathan's moment in the spotlight. Two of the most emotionally scarred, blunt, and forthright men I'd ever met were about to give speeches in front of my entire family and all my friends. I literally felt like I might throw up at any moment.

We'd had a brief break in proceedings while waiters went around with top-ups of champagne and small canapés, but the time was almost up now and I watched anxiously as Nathan took several deep breaths, straightened his tie, and rolled off his shoulders. Oh God, he was already frowning, which wasn't exactly a great start, was it? My stomach tumbled with nervous energy, I desperately wanted to save Nathan and Nicholas from this ordeal, but both men had been adamant that they would follow tradition and do it. My eyes followed Nathan as he stood up, flashed an intense, thin smile at Stella, and then knocked his fork against the side of his champagne flute to silence the room.

Here we go then.

I'm not sure if a fork being banged against a glass is always this effective, or if the gathered guests just took one look at Nathan's imposing figure and decided to shut the heck up quickly, but the room went silent almost immediately, as Nathan bent to carefully lay his fork down on the table and then rose to his full height.

'Good evening, everyone.' Nathan's eyes briefly flitted across the gathered guests and a tiny smile quirked the corner of his mouth. 'I run large business meetings every week, but I think it's fair to say that this is the first time I've ever addressed a room where everyone is actually listening and not bored senseless praying for the coffee break.' It was a mild joke, but Nathan's intro actually got a flutter of laughter from the room and I felt myself marginally relax.

'For those of you who don't know who I am, I'm Nathaniel, Nicholas's older brother and apparently the best man today. I'm afraid I'm not much of a joker, so instead of stomach clutching laughter, what I will promise is that I'll keep it short and sweet so you can get your dinner and free drinks.

'Before I say anything else, I'd better do the formal part first.' Raising his glass slightly, Nathan turned towards my mum and dad with a small smile, 'Please let's all take a moment to appreciate and raise our glasses to Rebecca's wonderful parents, Leanne and John, for what has been thus far a wonderful celebration on such a special day. Seeing as Nicholas and I have no family left to speak of, they have been especially considerate with all the help and support with the organising of this special occasion. Please raise your glasses to Leanne and John.'

The room replied in surround sound chorus and my mum flushed as red as the wine in my dad's glass.

'I can truthfully say that I never saw myself or my brother settling down. Without wanting to dampen the evening I shall merely say that life was difficult for us growing up and left us both a little emotionally closed off.' Nathan paused, before looking straight at me with his bright blue stare. 'But then Nicholas met Rebecca.' Nathan paused again, and I have no idea why, but the skin on my arms rose with goose pimples as he stared at Nicholas intensely and blinked several times. 'My brother has always been quite withdrawn, but suddenly there was a dimension of happiness to him that I'd never witnessed before. Not to mention the fact that he wouldn't stop going on about this amazing woman he'd met.' Nathan's amused tone for this last statement made the crowd laugh along with him and I saw an affectionate flush warm Nicholas' cheeks as he reached for my hand and gave it a firm squeeze.

'I think it took Rebecca a while to warm to me, but now that I've gotten to know her and her family I have to say I can completely understand where Nicholas' happiness comes from. These two are a perfect match for each other.' My chest compressed until I was almost struggling to breathe from the happiness. Lifting up his drink Nathan cast another furtive glance in my direction, 'I believe part of the formality also requires me to tell you all how gorgeous the bride and bridesmaids look, so at the risk of upsetting my rather possessive brother I must compliment his new wife on how beautiful she looks today. Rebecca, you are simply stunning,' he said with a curt nod of his head, 'and the same goes for the bridesmaids, all three of you look beautiful.' I loved how he included Joanne in his toast even though she was hidden away with Claudine at the rear of the room. Flashing a grin at Stella Nathan briefly licked his lips, 'Luckily I've already bagged one to take home tonight.' Choking on my champagne my eyes flew open – did he just say that? But as I began to panic that some of my more elderly relatives might not understand that he was dating Stella a burst of laughter rang around the room – they thought he was joking. Phew.

'So, with all of that said I'm not going to linger any further, what I'd like to do is hand over to the real best man here today, my brother Nicholas; one of the strongest, bravest, and most resilient men I've ever known.' Again my entire body tingled with goose pimples at the volume of emotion in Nathan's tone and I felt tears prick at the backs of my eyes. 'But first I'd like to ask you all to raise a toast to our happy couple, Nicholas and Rebecca, the new Mr and Mrs Jackson. Cheers!'

I felt really ashamed of myself for ever doubting Nathan's speech; although not the most comical of best men's speeches, it had been beautiful, sincere, and packed with heartfelt emotions and I found tears were still flowing down my cheeks as Nicholas gave my hand a firm squeeze and stood up.

Almost ignoring the crowded room Nicholas stepped behind me and pulled Nathan into a hug, slapping him on the back and murmuring some quiet words that I couldn't hear. Stepping away Nicholas seemed to need a moment to gather himself and took a sip of his water before looking up at the room and clearing his throat nervously.

'Like my brother, I'm not the most talkative of men, but *unlike* my brother I don't regularly talk in front of large crowds of people at work, and I have to say I'm already starting to sweat a bit with all your eyes on me and I've only been stood up for ...' Nicholas glanced at his watch and gave a nervous chuckle, '... thirty-seven seconds.' Looking down at the table for a second Nicholas reached out for me. As I linked my fingers through his he looked across at me in surprise as if he had reached for me subconsciously, but then smiling at our linked hands he nodded as if he could continue now he knew I was here with him.

'My brother was right when he said I have always been quite withdrawn, it's just how I am. Well, it's how I *was* until I met Becky. She swept into my life looking like this sweet, unassuming young woman, but then almost immediately knocked me sideways with her spark. There's just something about her. I can be intimidating, but Rebecca pretty much just brushed that aside and persevered with breaking down my barriers.' Pausing, Nicholas cleared his throat and it was at this point I realised he was adlibbing, the speech paper in his hand forgotten and replaced by him simply staring at me and spilling the contents of his heart. 'Most of you sat here are friends or family of Rebecca, so you'll know what I mean by her spark, and you'll also know just how special she is. It's like she lights up a room when she enters it. Well, she has certainly brought light to my life.'

Taking another sip of water Nicholas shifted nervously on the spot. 'As you can probably tell, I'm really not at my most expressive talking in front of a crowd like this, I do however, manage to successfully play my piano before very large gatherings with no problems. It's a very different sensation, I can lose myself in the music. It's a way I can express myself, so to save you all having to listen to me failing to be humorous or heartfelt for the next five minutes, I'd like to simply express how much I feel for Rebecca in the way that I know best.'

Dropping a kiss on my lips Nicholas walked to the side of the room as a light came on above a grand piano in the corner. 'Before I start I'd like to say thank you all for coming and sharing our special day with us. This is a piece I wrote in the first few months of knowing Rebecca – we weren't even officially together when I wrote this, but just by entering my life she had already changed it immeasurably. I hope you can hear through this piece just how much purpose she gave me, how important she is to me, and how very deeply I love her.' Blushing at his open emotions Nicholas then took his seat on the stool, bowed his head to the piano, and closed his eyes.

I held my breath as I waited for him to play, and judging by the complete silence in the room around me, I think most of the guests did too. You could have heard a pin drop. When his fingers finally began to grace the keys it was in a series of soft, gentle notes. Rocking and swaying, Nicholas looked completely lost in his music as the pace began to build. It was incredible, there were obviously no accompanying words, but they weren't necessary; the piece itself was enough, beautiful and emotive and rising to a crescendo that somehow seemed to almost fill the room with how much he felt for me.

By the time he brought the piece to a close, tears of happiness were streaming down my face. Through my blurry eyes I watched as Nicholas stood and strode back over to me. Taking his champagne in one hand he dragged me up to stand with his other as he raised his champagne flute. 'To Rebecca, my amazing wife.' His voice was thick and gravelly too, and although I'd only ever seen him cry once before, I suspected he was pretty close now. As the room around us erupted in applause Nicholas held me against him and rocked us gently as I clung to my wonderful husband.

THIRTY-TWO – NICHOLAS

It wasn't hard to find Rebecca amongst the crowds of revellers at the evening do of our wedding. There was the obvious fact that her gorgeous wedding dress stood out from the crowd, but it was more than that that drew my eyes to her; she was by far the most beautiful woman in the room, almost seeming to radiate pure happiness. Her eyes were twinkling, head thrown back in laughter at something Louise had just said to her, and she had a carefree relaxation in all her movements. I might not be a hugely open man, but I'd like to think that tonight even I might be exhibiting a little of the same happiness as Rebecca. I was certainly feeling it.

Glancing around the room it was clear the guests were gradually starting to retire after a long night of celebrating. There was smiling faces everywhere I looked, so it seemed that everyone had had a good time. The credit for that had to go to Rebecca, she really had pulled together a fabulous day.

My main input had been to keep the press away. Ever since my engagement to Rebecca had become public knowledge, journalists, newspapers, and magazines had all been clamouring to find out the venue so they could gatecrash our big day. But Rebecca was too special to me to put her through something like that, so everything had been kept extremely quiet. To my astonishment our secrecy had paid off; there were no paparazzi loitering outside the hotel this morning at all, but I'd still taken the precaution of hiring some security staff to man the gates for the duration of the weekend.

I might not have wanted our wedding to be flooded with press, but I *did* want the world to know that Rebecca was now officially mine, so I'd given an exclusive to one magazine only, one of the biggest celebrity gossip magazines there was. The deal had been that the journalist and photographer got to spend ten minutes with us after the wedding photographs, not a minute more. I'd stuck to it too, timing the interview on my watch and standing up as soon as the allotted time was over. The journalist had been mid-question at that point, looking a little stunned by my abrupt departure, but I didn't care; it was my wedding day and I could do what I damn well liked. He'd gotten an exclusive out it, so I'm sure he wouldn't be complaining too much either.

Checking my watch I decided that perhaps it was time to hand over the reins to Nathan so I could take my new wife to bed. I couldn't help but smirk and roll my eyes when I saw Nathan and Stella's position in the corner. Nathan had the shoulder of his right arm resting on the wall so that his sling hung in front of him, allowing his good arm to protectively rest across Stella's stomach as he leaned down to speak to her, practically caging her in the corner. She didn't look pregnant yet, not to my inexpert eye anyway, but it was in his body language just how thrilled my brother was by the baby. Stella was smiling up at him, one hand resting loosely around his waist and apparently more than happy to be the focus of his undivided attention.

Seeing my approach Nathan smiled at me, but I noticed with amusement that his good hand stayed firmly attached at Stella's tummy. I thought I was bad with Rebecca, but my brother really was a living, breathing example of 'possessive'.

'For a miserable bugger you have certainly put together a fabulous party, Nicholas.' Nathan said dryly.

'Thank you. It certainly seems to have gone quite well,' I agreed, ignoring his jokey dig. 'I was hoping to retire for the night, could you deal with any last minute issues if anything comes up? It should just be a case of making sure everyone finds their room or manages to get a taxi.'

'Of course, brother.' I had been expecting a dirty comment, or some sort of sly reference to wedding night sex, but to my surprise he didn't say anything like that, just nodded instead. Perhaps he was being polite because Stella was there.

'Great, thanks. We'll see you both at breakfast tomorrow then. Remember that family members are meeting in the conservatory for a private breakfast so that Joanne can join us,' I reminded him.

Turning to walk away Nathan reached out and gave my shoulder a light punch. 'Have a good night. Don't do anything I wouldn't do ...' There was the sarcastic comment I'd been expecting. Don't do anything he wouldn't? Seeing as my brother had pretty much done everything sexual there was to do, that didn't really set me any limits, did it? Rolling my eyes I nearly scoffed and made a comment about his extensive experience, but seeing as Stella was with him I refrained.

As I walked away from my brother I couldn't help but shake my head in disbelief; me a husband, and Nathan soon to be a father, who'd have ever thought it after the shitty start we'd had in life? Certainly not me, that was for sure, and yet here I was approaching my beautiful new wife and feeling more settled and happy than I ever had in my life.

It was late and after the length of today I was feeling quite tired, but I was still fully intending on worshipping Rebecca and consummating our marriage. Sneaking up behind her I leant down without touching her so she would feel nothing but the tickle of my breath on her ear. 'These people have had your attention for far too long. Are you ready to retire for our wedding night, wife?' I couldn't help the smile that spread on my lips as I spoke, I don't think I would ever tire of calling Becky my wife.

It took barely a second before she had swung on the spot and flung her arms around my neck, covering my jaw in feather light pecks of her lips. 'There you are! I was wondering where you'd got to. One more dance and then we'll go,' she said, starting to sway in my arms and rub her hips against mine. The two of us dancing closely caused a round of clapping and whistling, just like it had earlier when we'd had our first dance, but this time everyone was little drunker, me included, and I let my inhibitions down more and took hold of Rebecca's hips as I started to move to the music, causing even more excited calling and laughter in the dancers around us.

As the music died down and the next song started Rebecca turned her flushed face to mine, 'OK husband, take me to bed.' She blushed even further, almost as if she were embarrassed by the obvious knowledge that we would be having sex tonight. I wasn't embarrassed at all, in fact, after that close pelvis to pelvis dancing I was more than ready, willing, and able.

Unfortunately being the bride and groom at a wedding did have one drawback, we were popular with *everyone*, which meant it took us a further thirty minutes to actually escape all the well-wishers and break out into the cool of the night air to head down the front steps towards the lake house.

As we reached the door to the lake house I unlocked it, pushed it open, and swung around to scoop Rebecca up into my arms, causing her to shriek and wrap her arms around my neck as she laughed and squirmed in my arms. 'Shhh … you'll wake your sister!' I whispered as I carried her over the threshold and straight up the stairs to the suite of rooms we reserved exclusively. As originally planned, her parents and sister were in the rooms downstairs, but I'd organised it carefully and ensured that they were situated in the rooms to the right as far away from us as possible, which meant the rooms directly below our suite were empty. Oh yes, I planned on making my girl beg and scream tonight.

The door to our actual room was propped open and I felt a fizzle of excitement at what we might see when we entered. It had taken some persuasion, but Stella and Louise had eventually worn me down and made me agree to let them decorate our room for tonight, I had no idea what they'd done, I just hoped that Rebecca would like it. With her still in my arms we entered the room and I immediately drew to a stop and grinned like a kid when I heard Rebecca gasp loudly as she saw the room. 'Oh my God, Nicholas!'

Placing her down I spun Rebecca in my arms so she was facing the room with her back pressed against my front. It was all a bit girly for me, but even I could appreciate that the room looked very romantic. The four poster bed had been draped with tiny white fairy-lights, candles lined every available surface in the room – orange blossom, from the smell of it, a bottle of champagne sat in a bucket of ice by the side of the bed, and on the actual duvet itself they had arranged several dozen red roses into the shape of a heart.

'This is incredible,' Rebecca breathed as she turned her wide eyes on me. 'Did you do this?'

As much as I'd love to have been responsible for the pure delight on Rebecca's face I couldn't lie, so I shook my head slowly. 'You have your bridesmaids to thank for this.' Stepping fully inside the room I closed and locked the door and then turned back to Rebecca.

Lust, desire, and an almost primal need to claim Rebecca and make her my wife in every way possible was creeping up on me thick and fast, but it had been a long day, and as much as I wanted to pounce on her and have my wicked way I wanted to check she was up for it too.

'How are you feeling? Tired after today?' I asked as I stepped up and slid my hands around the silky material at her waist.

'I'm good. Today has just been amazing, Nicholas. I couldn't be happier. I love you.' Her small hands slid up the front of my suit until they were buried in my hair and tugging me down for a kiss. Rebecca was initiating it, was she? Perfect. That was just fine by me.

'I love you too, Rebecca.'

For a few moments we both just seemed content to lose ourselves in the kiss, exploring already familiar mouths as if they were new unchartered territory.

Finally breaking our kiss Rebecca sucked in some air and then smiled at me shyly, 'Will you free me from this dress? I love it, but the bodice is so tight I can barely breathe!' Those intricately tied ribbons had been catching my attention all day until my fingers had been itching to untie them, so I wasted no time in stepping behind her.

'It would be my pleasure,' I murmured as I found the neatly tucked ends and began unlacing her. With each new row undone Rebecca let out a happy little sigh that I couldn't help mirroring. Fairly soon it became clear that Rebecca wasn't wearing a bra underneath her wedding dress, and as well as speeding up my unlacing, this revelation also had my cock hardening at the thought of her breasts escaping at any second.

As the last few laces slipped free, the dress – which was actually remarkably heavy – slid down Rebecca's frame until it pooled around her feet like a large snowdrift. Rebecca was now stood before me dressed in nothing but a little pair of white lacy knickers. I took a moment to savour the sight of her back and its beautifully soft, flawless skin and ran my fingers in a trail from the centre of her neck all the way down her spine, eliciting a small shiver as I passed over her ticklish spots.

346

Quickly sweeping the roses from the bed I then scooped her up into my arms again, stepped past the discarded dress, and lay her down on the quilt before standing back to look at my beautiful new wife. A glimpse of something pink caught my eye as Rebecca quickly pulled her legs together and I frowned, an almost impossible vision springing to my mind. 'Rebecca, open your legs again,' I commanded softly, curious to see what had caught my eye – it surely couldn't be what I thought it was, could it?

With an embarrassed wiggle Rebecca shifted on the bed, raised one knee, and slightly parted her thighs. 'Happy wedding day,' she murmured softly, as my breathing accelerated and I blinked rapidly while openly staring at her groin. Then I think I may have stopped breathing all together. Holy fuck – it was *exactly* what I'd thought I'd seen. Rebecca, my sweet, unassuming, innocent girl, was wearing crotchless panties. Admittedly they were an incredibly upmarket pair, but they were crotchless nonetheless. I'm not entirely sure that I didn't black out for a second or two, but the next thing I knew I was on the bed pressing her thighs apart like a mad man and running a swift swipe of my tongue right up the exposed pink flesh between her legs.

'Ahhhh! Nicholas!' she cried, squirming in apparent shock at my sudden frenzy, but the sexy sight of her clad in nothing but a pair of exceptionally tasteful, lace, crotchless panties had been like a trigger and there was no way I could stop now. Over the next few minutes my tongue made a full exploration of her exposed flesh; licking, nibbling, and sucking at her clitoris until she suddenly bucked below me and came undone, her soft flesh throbbing against my tongue in climax and her hands sinking into my hair and tugging.

'Have you been wearing these all day?' I asked between breaths, the idea almost driving me insane with lust.

'Not quite, I changed in to these after the meal,' she murmured, her cheeks red and eyes large after her orgasm. Shifting my weight to my knees I continued to lick at her to ease her down from her climax as I tucked both hands into the delicate lace waistband. 'Lift your hips, Rebecca, otherwise I'll be ripping these things off you,' I murmured. It wasn't a false threat either; the only reason the knickers were still intact was because it was our wedding night and they might be something she deemed special. That, plus the fact that I wanted to see her wearing them again in the future.

Obediently, Rebecca lifted her hips and I dragged the thin material down her long legs and dropped them to the floor before kneeling up between her relaxed legs. 'OK, sweetheart?' I asked, trailing my fingers up and down the soft skin of her inner thighs. Nodding, Becky smiled up at me. 'Mmm-hmm. I'm more than OK. Except for the fact that I'm naked and my new husband is very, very overdressed.' Pushing herself upright Rebecca slid her hands inside my jacket and ran them across my chest until she came to my shoulders and began to slide it off down my arms. The tie that had taken me so long to perfect was next, and then her nimble fingers began to work on the buttons of my waistcoat and shirt.

As she finally released me from my shirt and it joined my other clothes on the floor I reached out and cupped her breasts in both of my palms, but to my surprise Rebecca gasped and grabbed my wrists to stop me. 'Oh! They're super sensitive after being trapped in that dress all day. Just give them a minute or two to recover.' Not a chance in hell, I would make her feel better, it was *my* job as her husband after all. Twisting my wrists within her grasp I pulled a simple but effective self-defence move that circled my hands over hers and swapped her grip to mine. Then, once I was gently circling both of her wrists I pressed

348

forwards with my body so she had no choice but to lie back on the bed below me. With her hands still trapped by her sides I lowered my head and licked gently at one nipple, flicking my tongue as softly as I could over the reddened tip. 'Good? Or too much?' I asked as I shifted my attention to her other breast.

'Oh!' she gasped breathily, 'Good, Nicholas, so good ...'

Smiling smugly I continued with my gentle ministrations until both of her nipples were hardened peaks and she was arching her back, trying to force harder contact from me.

Rearing up I practically leapt from the bed in my sudden desperation to rid myself of my trousers. Kicking off my wedding shoes I pulled down my trousers and boxers in one go and after shedding my socks I was back on the bed, practically smothering Becky in hot kisses on every part of her flesh that I could reach.

Rebecca's hands were roaming all over my back, leaving a tingling trail in their wake as her nails gently teased my skin. One hand began to skate around my hip and as she made contact with my throbbing cock I couldn't help but gasp loudly and thrust into her warm palm. Christ, I was so close to losing it. The mixture of desire and lust in my system combined violently with my previous excitement from the day, not to mention my recent discovery of her crotchless knickers, and was driving me to a point of arousal so close to climax that I almost couldn't cope with the touch of her fingers as she cupped me.

Taking both her wrists in one of my palms I removed her touch from my pulsing erection and shifted myself up slightly so I could pin them above her head. Rebecca looked slightly confused by my move so I gave her a shy smile, 'I'm so close, baby; one squeeze from you would have sent me over the edge.' I watched as she returned my smile, lust igniting in those beautiful green eyes as her wrists went loose and pliant in my grip and she raised her head and claimed my lips in a deep, passionate kiss.

Breaking our lips a few minutes later I felt marginally more in control and manoeuvred the tip of my erection to her warm opening. I released her wrists and her hands immediately went to my shoulders, and then making sure we had full eye contact I began to press my length into her until I was buried to the hilt. Her body felt like a hot velvet glove around my cock and I had to pause while I allowed my simmering arousal to dim slightly. Attached like this, so very intimately and gazing into each other's eyes, it seemed the perfect moment to tell her just how much she meant to me. 'I love you Rebecca,' I murmured softly, '*Mrs Jackson*.' I added with a grin.

'I love you too, Nicholas. I'm so happy.'

'You're incredible. I'm going to cherish you every day for the rest of our lives,' I vowed as I pulled out to the tip and thrust back in smoothly and firmly. Enough talking. Now it was time to express my love in a wholly different way. As hard as I tried to prolong things, I was just too aroused, too in love, to make this last for long and my careful, rhythmic thrusts soon evaporated into harder, more demanding movements as Becky clawed at my back and met every one of my thrusts with an upward movement of her own.

The room was soon filled with the scent of sweat and sex, and the air reverberated with the sounds of our heavy breathing as our naked flash slapped together repeatedly. 'Nicholas … I'm close … together, please …' Rebecca gasped, and I wasted no time in obliging my new wife as I thrust home hard and deep three more times, sparking her climax which in turn triggered my own as we both moaned and repeated each other's names into the night.

Rolling over I cradled Rebecca's replete body to my side and heard her sigh contentedly against my chest.

'You've made me the happiest man alive today. I love you, Becky,' I murmured again, before she had a chance to fall asleep.

'Not as much as I love you,' she said, saying the jokey little reply we used with each other. I knew she loved me, and I knew she always said she loved me more than I did her, but my heart was so full with feelings for this woman that it felt like it could burst, and I just couldn't fathom how she could possibly feel more emotion than I did.

She was my everything. She always would be.

As I cradled Rebecca in my arms and felt her gradually fall asleep on me I couldn't help but smile. I think she had a pretty good idea that I had been serious when I said that I would cherish her forever, but I intended to keep to that promise every single day, starting right now. What an utterly amazing day this had been. I literally couldn't wait for morning so we could start the rest of our lives together.

EPILOGUE – STELLA

'Just one more push should do it!' the midwife said from the bottom of the bed. One more frigging push and I was fairly convinced that I would split in half. 'Come on, Stella, you can do it! One more!' she said ridiculously cheerfully. I'd spent the best part of the last seven hours with this woman intermittently in between my legs, and I had to say, I now pretty much hated her cheery persona. I knew it was just an emotional response to the discomfort and pain I felt at the moment, but still, she'd clearly never given birth if she could refer to the ripping, heaving, heavy sensations in my lower half as 'just one more push …'

When preparing for the birth I'd read an article that said most new borns are in a state of 'quiet alertness' in the first hour after birth and that it is the best time to start the bonding process. Mostly due to this advice we'd opted for a relatively drug-free birth, a decision I was starting to seriously question, but I was determined for my first ever interactions with my baby to be lucid. Gritting my teeth I forged on and followed my orders by clinging to Nathan's sweat-soaked hand and screaming down half the hospital as I gave the biggest push I was capable of.

Two high-pitched cries rang out in the room, Nathan swore next to me, and then seconds later I saw the midwife holding a reddish-blue lump in her hands, covered in blood and what looked like cream cheese. *Ugh*. Well, that certainly wasn't as glamourous as the Hollywood movies portrayed it, was it? 'Mr and Mrs Jackson, you have beautiful baby boy,' the midwife said with a flourish, 'Let us just check him over and I'll get him straight to you,' she said as I craned my neck to try and see my son. *My son.* Glancing at Nathan I saw him looking equally as shocked as me with his eyes fixed on our son. *Our son.* We were parents now. Holy shit. This was all going to take some getting used to.

There then followed a flurry of activity as I was sorted and cleaned off a bit and then before I knew it, a swaddled baby was being placed in my exhausted arms. 'Completely healthy little fella. We'll give you a few minutes alone as a family and be back shortly to finish off the cleaning up and check-ups,' she said with a smile before the doctors left the room, leaving us alone.

Looking down I saw huge, blue eyes gazing up at me and I immediately felt my throat close up with emotion. Yes, he was still covered in a bit of blood and gunk, but oh God, he was beautiful. 'Would you like to hold your son?' I whispered, rocking him gently in my arms. When Nathan didn't reply I looked up to see him still stood staring down at us both, sweat rolling down his temples and his eyes wide with a slightly unfocused look to them.

Taking a step back from the bed I saw his chest heave with several jerky breaths, then he started backing towards the door before spinning round and grabbing the handle. 'I need to … I … um … just let me have a second … I just need to … go …' Yanking open the door I felt panic engulf me at the thought of him leaving me. Leaving *us*.

'You are nothing like your father, Nathan. Don't you dare walk away from us,' I blurted, hazarding a wild guess at the cause for his panic. Considering I'd just given birth and was in mid-panic my voice was amazingly firm and controlled, but as the door slammed shut I did allow myself a wince.

The noise of the blinds clanking on the back of the door filled the space as they swished back and forth from the force of the slam and I sat there still cradling my sleeping son.

I stayed silent for several seconds, trying to make my thoughts slow down to something resembling normal speed. The main thought dominating my mind currently was that Nathan hadn't left the room. He'd looked right on the verge of it, but then after my words he'd closed the door instead and was now stood with his back pressed against the wall, staring at me as he panted far too quickly to be healthy.

'I wasn't leaving you … I would never leave you … but I think I'm having a fucking panic attack …' He wheezed as I watched his white-knuckled fists open out to flatten on the wall. 'I need to do my breathing …'

The love and relief that filled me was so immense I almost laughed out loud in reaction to it, but instead drew in a breath to calm my own near panic attack and then looked him steadily in the eye. 'Do your breathing in here, Nathan, it's OK, sweetheart, I get it. I'm pretty freaked out myself.'

Nodding his head Nathan closed his eyes and tilted his neck back and began drawing in long, slow breaths through his nose and releasing them through his mouth. He was probably counting down too, but must have been doing so in his head, because I couldn't hear it. All I knew was he must be doing an extended version of his relaxation technique, because he carried on for much longer than his usual five seconds before finally opening his eyes.

Running trembling hands across his face he pushed back his crazy mop of hair and came to the bedside where he immediately lowered himself down to drop a long, hard kiss on my lips before placing a gentle hand around the little bundle in my arms. 'This is just so much to take in. I never thought I could feel love like I do for you Stella, and now …' He glanced down at our son and swallowed loudly, '… now it's happened twice. I don't even know

355

him yet, but I love him so much already.' Running a shaky hand through his hair Nathan looked up at me with a hesitant smile, 'Christ, I can't believe I got this lucky.'

Tears of happiness slid down my cheeks as I nodded my agreement. 'I love him so much my chest hurts,' I said with a hiccup. 'And I love you. It's crazy, isn't it?' I murmured, feeling so happy and content at that moment that surely nothing could improve it. Smiling shyly Nathan turned his wide eyes on me and licked his bottom lip, 'Can I hold him?' he asked in such a small voice that I genuinely think he believed I might say no. Wordlessly I handed over my son to his father and immediately withdrew my last remark – the sight of Nathan holding our son and looking so excited upped my contentment and happiness to near obscene levels.

'Have you thought of any names yet?' he murmured, gently rocking his arms back and forth. We'd discussed names, of course we had, but not knowing the sex we'd kept it fairly general and decided to see if inspiration hit us after the birth.

'Not really, you?' I asked.

Looking up to meet my eyes Nathan gave a small shrug, 'I was thought maybe William. What do you think?'

William Jackson. Smiling, I nodded, 'I like it.'

Nathan's face split into a huge grin. 'That way he can be Will when he's younger, or more formal as William if he chooses to. What do you say to that, Will?' Nathan said, stooping his head down to lay a gentle kiss on William's forehead. I wish I had a camera, because seeing Nathan like this was just the most amazing scene. 'He smells nice,' Nathan commented as his eyes continued to absorb the features of his son. It was a really simple thing to say, but it made my heart clench with love. If our little boy grew up to be even a quarter as handsome or charming as his daddy then we were in for some interesting teenage years, that was for sure.

A few minutes later there was a tentative knock on the door as Nicholas' head poked into the room. 'Up for a quick visit?' Nodding, I waved them in and was thrilled to see Kenny with Nicholas and Rebecca. I couldn't help the tears that fell as I watched in happiness as Nathan proudly introduced them all to William.

'Your mum and dad just called, they're on their way, Stella. You mum said to give you and the baby a huge hug,' Becky said after the initial excitement had died down a little. 'Any chance Aunty Rebecca can have a quick cuddle with the newbie?'

'Of course!' I replied immediately. Nathan gave a small frown, obviously reluctant to give up his time with William so soon, which made me smile – his possessive qualities were kicking in already – but he did eventually hand Will across to Rebecca's outstretched arms.

I smiled as I saw Nicholas watching Rebecca affectionately for a few seconds before he, Kenny and Nathan became engrossed in a conversation about the birth as Nathan recounted all the gory details in their fullest. At least his panic attack seemed forgotten now. Stepping closer to the bed so she was out of earshot of the brothers Rebecca lowered herself onto the bed, careful to support William's head. 'He's so gorgeous, Stella,' she cooed, rocking him gently.

'He is, isn't he?' I replied, although I was obviously a little biased. 'I hope he keeps the blue eyes, they're just the same colour as Nathan's.' Watching her blissfully smiling face for a few seconds I grinned, 'Something tells me you'll want one pretty soon,' I remarked playfully.

Rebecca's head popped up and after she flashed a quick glance towards the boys to make sure they weren't listening she licked her lips and leaned in close. 'After the wedding we decided to start trying,' she confided in me, causing me to gasp in delight. 'Actually, between you and me, I have a bit of a funny feeling this month. My period's late by nearly six days now. I haven't told Nicholas yet, but I think I might surprise the hell out of him by asking him to stop off and buy a pregnancy test on the way home. Watch this space!' she whispered with a wink.

Watch this space indeed! Nathan, Kenny, and Nicholas finished their conversation and came to join us at the bedside. The way that Nicholas slid an arm around Rebecca and affectionately leaned down to touch William's hand told me that he'd be pretty ecstatic if Rebecca really did turn out to be pregnant. Kenny took his turn at cuddle time and turned out to be a born natural at calming William when he had a little screaming session.

After stroking Will's head until he completely calmed, Nathan came to my side and took my hand in his, giving it a squeeze as we both gazed lovingly at our new-born son. What a random roomful of people we made, but so perfectly suited at the same time. If I cast my mind back to nearly three years ago when I'd first met Nathan in Club Twist I never would have believed that this would ever be the outcome of our contracted relationship. From everything I knew about their past it seemed almost impossible that both Nathan and Nicholas had overcome their abusive pasts and were settling into normal relationships. But here we were, all four of us and now William too. Not forgetting Kenny of course; he'd always be part of my life.

The journey both Nicholas and Nathan had taken to get to this point might have had some pretty severe bumps, jolts, and ups and downs, but they'd survived them all and pulled Rebecca and I along for the ride too. I was so very grateful that they had, because as I sat here gazing around at the people I loved most in the world I realised to my surprise that I wouldn't change a single thing. We were all about to start new chapters in our lives – Nicholas and Rebecca as husband and wife, and Nathan and I as parents – but as my hand absently sought out the collar at my neck and fiddled with it, I smiled, knowing that our old chapter wasn't quite finished yet either.

Thank you for reading and joining me on this amazing journey with the Jackson Brothers. If you'd like to get in contact or find out about future books please check out my website www.aliceraineauthor.com

Alice Raine

Untwisted Series

The Darkness Within Him
Out of the Darkness
Into the Light
Enlightened

CARIAD

For more information about **Alice Raine**

and other **Accent Press** titles

please visit

www.accentpress.co.uk

Made in the USA
Lexington, KY
30 May 2015